I0599481

Matilda Betham-Edwards

**The White House by the Sea**

A love story

Matilda Betham-Edwards

**The White House by the Sea**
*A love story*

ISBN/EAN: 9783337412241

Printed in Europe, USA, Canada, Australia, Japan

Cover: Foto ©Andreas Hilbeck / pixelio.de

More available books at **www.hansebooks.com**

THE

# WHITE HOUSE BY THE SEA.

*A Love Story,*

BY

MISS BETHAM EDWARDS,

AUTHOR OF " WILD FLOWER OF RAVENSWORTH," " LISABEE'S LOVE
STORY," "JOHN AND I," ETC.

*NEW EDITION.*

LONDON:

WARD, LOCK, & CO., WARWICK HOUSE,

SALISBURY SQUARE, E.C.

# WHITE HOUSE BY THE SEA.

## CHAPTER I.

"Den neue Gedanken und Gefühle wir schieszende Sterne durch
die Seele fliegen, und einen blaugoldenen Pfad hinter sich machen."
—TIECK.

IT was dismal enough; dreary within, dusky without—with
the gathering shadows of autumn twilight—and the gloom
and the silence weighed upon my spirits. There was too
much appearance of day to have candles, and though cold
and cheerless too early in the season for economical people
to have fires; so there was nothing for me to do but to look
out of the window and listen to the eternal surging of the
sea. I never grew tired of that, but I wearied of being
alone. My father dozed uncomfortably in his chair, and
only spoke now and then, to ask what o'clock it was, or to
complain about something or other in the way that nervously
affected people always do, and I could hear Ellice's voice in
cheerful conversation to the cat in the kitchen. Oh, if my
father would but talk so cheerfully to me !

"Chatty ? "

"Yes, papa."

"Did you say it was a quarter to six, or a quarter past
six, when you looked at the clock just now ? "

" To six."

" Are you sure ? "

" Yes, quite, father dear."

He gave a muttered ejaculation of discontent, and said no more. I thought he had fallen asleep, but in less than five minutes he exclaimed querulously—

" You must have made a mistake, Chatty, or it would have struck six by now; go and look, there's a dear."

I lingered in the kitchen as long as I could, feeling loath to tell him that I was right, and when I returned he had dropped into a light but sound slumber. I took my old place by the window, and went on thinking. I ought rather to say imagining, for in the monotony of my daily life I had very little to think about, and if it had not been for the enthusiasm and extreme impetuosity of my temperament, I should have been dull indeed. As it was, I could not help wishing at times for some good fairy's wand to make real and living the bright pictures and dreams that my mind so revelled in. But to-day my thoughts were not entirely of a visionary nature. It was a very slight thing ; a gossamer thread—a spider's chain were stronger even, and yet it had bound down my fancy to a substantial and tangible existence. Pleasure parties in skiffs, painted boats and light flying yachts innumerable had passed and repassed all the summer long by our dark rock, and I, perhaps, just raised my eyes for one glance, and thought of them no more. Autumn has come now ; the south wind blew soft and warm still at mid-day, but there was a treacherous look in the sun's bright rising, and every evening came with an uneasy war of the waves and a falling of rain : therefore summer visitors and gay holiday makers deserted us, and I could no longer sit on the sandy heath and be idle.

But hardly four hours ago, in spite of the misty cloud and air, I had seen a boat dance by, swift and joyous as though on wings, and it had come near, very near to the little rugged stone on which I stood. So near that I could distinctly see the faces of those who were in it, and hear the gay echo and laugh of their merry voices.

And somehow they dwelt on my memory. I could not forget the sweet, happy face of the young girl, or the magnificence of the ladies; least of all could I forget the dark-haired, bright-eyed hero (for I made him a hero at once), with the cavalierly figure and the handsome mouth which smiled proudly. He was the embodiment of my fairy-tale Prince, of my chivalric knight, and the lifelike personification of all my girlish, unspeakable ideals. How beautiful he was! And I had watched for the return of the boat with a wondrous feeling of eager expectation and longing; but with the coming darkness all my chances seemed to have gone. Yet it must pass, some time or other, I felt sure of that. Before and beyond lay the ocean, and the only return to Ingham was past our dwelling, for the high, bleak rocks which were our sole neighbours, narrowed on the one side into insignificance and to the town, on the other to a vast plain of dry, short heaths and brown grasses. So it must return, I thought, and in the hope I had lingered beneath the rocks till the clouds began to descend in drizzling rain, and the chill air made me shiver. My disappointment was great; but even yet I watched at the window, if only to see the boat glide by. I should feel satisfied then, and I was very restless now. Perhaps it had been upset; I had heard of such things happening in uncertain weather, and the party had no boatman with them. Besides, it was getting dark, and there was no moon till half-past eleven.

My father still slept; and stealing on tip-toe, lest Ellice should overhear me, I went to the hall window, opened it, and peered out. I fancied that, mingled with the roar of the winds and waves, I could hear the sound of a voice. I did not stop to listen any more; but, trembling with excitement and eagerness, put a rushlight in the old hall lantern, and throwing on my waterproof cloak, jumped out of the window gently, and ran down the garden path.

The rain was slight, but the wind had risen high, and the night was very dark. I ran on in wild haste, through the garden gate, down the zigzag rock-cut path, and over the damp shingle to the edge of the beach. Then I jumped on the top of a square slippery stone, and held my lantern high above my head.

Surely I heard a voice!

I listened again breathlessly. I was right; I did hear a voice, and it hailed me. Still holding up my lantern, I went a few steps farther in the direction of the sound, and then stopped once more.

The voice was near me now, and its tones were distinct—at least, almost distinct; what I could not quite plainly hear I could very well guess at.

" Can we land here ? "

I held up my lantern and strained my voice to its highest pitch in answer, but it was of no avail. Instead of a response there was only a re-echo,

" Can we land here ? " in a still louder key than before.

Then I made a final desperate effort, throwing all my energy of strength and lungs into a shrill—

" Yes; higher up ! "

The effort was a success; and I drew a long breath of glad exultation.

" A hundred yards ? "

" More ; about a hundred and forty."

Thanks to my knowledge of every nook and corner, I could find the spot in the darkest night, and in a minute or two I had gained it, and stood on the flat, shelving stone, calling out triumphantly—" Here ! "

At last it was reached, and the boat shoved in. I set down my lantern, and simultaneously a tall figure sprang beside me. It was my hero. Though too dark to see anything save the outline form, I knew it was him, and drew back, irresolute and shy.

Then there was a clamour of many voices, and almost a dozen questions and exclamations burst forth at once.

" How glad I am to be safe on terra firma ! "

" I really thought we were upset ! "

" What a fearful night !"

" Isn't it jolly ! "

" Oh, if I could but find my bonnet: and it cost two guineas last week ! "

" Where's Lindsay ? "

" Is the bottom of the boat out ? "

" What a hurricane ! "

" Who is it with the lantern ? "

" Ah ! where is he ? "

And all at once the general attention and interest were directed to myself: for some minutes there was a great whispering and discussion, I meanwhile standing aloof, silent and motionless. At last it was ended by some one taking up the lantern and holding it right before my face : the scrutiny lasted many seconds, and might have lasted many more if I had not raised my eyes.

A dark handsome face was in close contact to my own, wearing a comical expression of perplexity and surprise, and then a manly and sweet-sounding voice rang merrily through the air.

" Where on earth did you come from ? "

Immediately the party surrounded me. I could not answer their questions, they were so numerous, and my heart beat high and my cheek glowed with pride and pleasure when they praised and thanked me. I hardly remember ever feeling so happy before. The ladies shook hands with me, and the youngest clung to me and kissed me over and over again. I loved her at once, and felt convinced she was the one whose pretty gentle face I had admired so much in the morning.

"But what's to be done now, Lindsay?" said the tallest lady. "I have not the least idea whereabouts we are?"

"Really, Mrs. Dunstan, neither have I. Suppose we rest on the sand here till the morning. It would be the least troublesome way of settling the matter."

"But something *must* be done," rejoined the lady, languidly; "don't be so provoking, Lindsay; of course you do know where we are."

"On my word, my dear Mrs. Dunstan, I was never more serious in my life; but my firm opinion is, that we are somewhere near the Lizard's Point!"

It was impossible to resist his humour and raillery, and even Mrs. Dunstan joined in the general laugh and said, good-temperedly—

"How ridiculous you are, when it is hundreds of miles off—must be."

Then the former speaker turned to me.

"Here is our refuge," he said. "Come now, brave little Grace Darling, tell us how we can get to Ingham-Holmsley to-night. In the first place, how far is it off?"

"Not far," I said, hurriedly; "but won't you come home —to papa's, I mean—it is quite near and ——"

"Oh do, mamma; do, dear Lindsay," said the young girl who still held me tight round the waist. "Do, dear Lindsay."

"Yes, do," I exclaimed, eagerly, "and then you can settle about getting back to Ingham, and we can dry your cloaks by the fire, and ——"

"Perhaps it's the best thing we can do," said the elder

lady in a half whisper. "I don't know who these people can be, but anyhow we are all right with Lindsay."

At this, Lindsay (for such was the name of my hero) gave a shrug of the shoulders, and a significant, scornful laugh, and turning to me started off with a—

"Who is for a warm fire, and for Ingham, follow us."

His frank yielding to my guidance charmed me, and, silent from very delight, I walked on by his side.

"What a dreary out-of-the-way place!" I heard Mrs. Dunstan say, as we reached the house; and the other lady answered, in a voice of caprice and affectation—

"Horrible! It seems, as you say, as if it didn't belong to the world at all. Descendants of brigands, perhaps."

"Ellice," I said, running into the kitchen a few steps in advance, "here's a party of ladies and a gentleman who are wet and dripping, and lost their way in a boat from the Mere Point to Ingham: do put on some coals, Ellice, there's a dear, and let them come quite close to the fire, they are so cold."

Then, leaving her in utter bewilderment, I rushed to papa. He looked positively frightened.

"Strangers! you went to the shore?—How can you tell who or what they are, Chatty? and there are fourteen pounds and ten shillings in the house, and I am as helpless as a child, and not a creature within a mile round—Do they look like swindlers?—but how should you know?— Bless me—and the silver spoons are lying about——"

He was working himself into quite an agitation.

"Dear papa," I said, smilingly and soothingly, "the fourteen pounds are quite safe, and the spoons, too; it's only a party of ladies with a gentleman from Ingham-Helmsley who went this afternoon in one of Ben's boats to the Mere Point, and took a fancy to see the Boar's Head Hill, which made them so late. They are so wet and cold;

you won't mind them sitting by the kitchen-fire, will you, father dear?"

But he was not easily to be convinced. How could I know who they were?—I, a girl of sixteen, totally unaccustomed to the ways of the world; and the spoons were all lying in the kitchen! But as they were in now, so they must be: he couldn't turn them out.

So I left him. Certainly the party in the kitchen looked very sociable, and as if silver spoons were far from uppermost in their thoughts. Mrs. Dunstan (I knew her by her matronly look and air) had installed herself gracefully in Ellice's arm-chair, and looked half asleep; a tall and fashionable young lady, with a dark, Indian-looking, but handsome face, sat by her, and gave stray glances into a little mirror that hung opposite; Lindsay stood leaning against the wall, his arms folded, a cigar in his mouth, and the very picture of *at home* ease and comfort; and the youngest of the party, a girl of about fifteen, sat on a low stool beside him, with her bright, sweet face turned to the door, as if watching for me.

She jumped up when I entered, and made me sit next to her.

"How I wish we hadn't to go home," she said, dismally. "It's so pleasant here."

"So do I," rejoined Lindsay: "this is better than a boat with the bottom out, eh, Angelica?"

"Mr. Jocelyn, don't tease," said the tall young lady, with a coquettish smile; "I am sure I never thought it was out, but I really have no inclination to turn out in the cold again."

"I wish you could all stay here," I said, very meekly, "but we have only one spare bed, and I don't think that's aired."

I really felt grieved and perplexed at my utter incapabi-

lity of being hospitable, but was somewhat relieved by Lindsay's good humoured and decided—

" But if you had forty aired beds, little Grace Darling, we
should have to turn out just the same ; why, our anxious
friends would think we were, as Mr. Stirling's gardener
says, ' drownded to the bottom.' "

" Ah ! " said Mrs. Dunstan, consolingly, and as if suddenly roused, " Mr. Stirling will send the carriage for us, of
course."

Lindsay laughed outright.

" Of course he would; but, my dear madam, in the first
place, since your arrival in this house have you sent some
' tricksy spirit' to put a girdle round Ingham-Helmsley in
forty seconds, or minutes ? "

" Why, of course, I forgot that he doesn't know we are
here ;" and Mrs. Dunstan sighed.

Lindsay went to the window and looked out.

" It's a very dark, stormy night," he said, shrugging his
shoulders, " and by no means inviting, after this cheerful
fire ; but the only thing to be done, I think, is for me to
find my way to Ingham, somehow, and send the carriage.
I do not promise you how long I may be, for I have not the
slightest idea of the way."

" Couldn't one of the servants go ?" Angelica said, rudely.

Mrs. Dunstan touched her arm reprovingly, with a look
as much as to say—" Remember, my dear, what uncivilized
people we are among."

And before I had time to answer, Lindsay turned to me.

" Will you kindly indicate the way to me," he said, in a
low, pleasing voice, " and I shall have double cause to be
grateful."

" I will do my best," I answered, " but it is rather difficult ; there are so many cross-roads below the heath, and
no guiding marks."

He had buttoned his coat up tight now, and wrapped a grey Scotch plaid around him.

"I think, if you would not mind pointing the direction to me from the door, that I shall be able to manage it; things in the abstract are easy to me."

I smiled, and putting on my cloak followed him to the door; but it was very dark, and we had to walk some steps before we could distinctly see anything. At the garden gate he stopped and drew my cloak closer round me. I thanked him, and we walked on.

"I hope you will not take cold from this evening's adventure," he said; "you have been so truly a heroine to-night. I cannot thank you enough, and shall always remember it."

He walked slower, and continued,—

"This is a lonely place for you to live in; have you no brothers or sisters?"

"No: no one but papa." I answered with difficulty, for there was a joy and agitation at my heart that almost took away the power of speech.

"How strange!" he added; "and indeed there is a hue of romance about this night's adventure which has taken a marvellous hold on my imagination; it is so unlike the everyday occurrences of a busy or gay life in the world. I am very glad that it has happened."

We had now reached the spot from whence could be faintly seen the glimmering lights of Ingham. I stopped and pointed to them.

"If you follow straight in that direction," I said in a strangely trembling voice, "I do not think you can go far out of the way, and when you reach the town I think the directest route to Mr. Stirling's is to turn off by the new church."

Lindsay dropped his voice to a lower key, and said:--

"I wish I could have my guide the whole way."

I shook my head, and turned homewards, without reply, for I knew not what to say.

"Forgive me, if my words displeased you."

"Oh no," I said, "oh no, but I hope you will be able——"

"Don't say a word; you have been most kind already. Oh, I shall get there somehow!"

Then he accompanied me back to the door.

"Good-by," he said, holding out his hand.

"Good-by."

My voice quavered, and my hand shook in his. He echoed the parting word once more, raised his hat to me, and bounded off.

Before an hour and a half from that time we were again alone, papa, Ellice and I. The doors and windows were barred; the fire was put out; the mat was laid down for Bailie, and we retired to rest.

But it was a long time before I could sleep that night; and when I did, it was to dream and start and wake again. I was still standing on the shore on a dark evening, and trying to make my voice heard; then the boat went down, and I, all the time, was vainly trying to save it. Again the dream changed; the fair face of my new friend smiled on me with looks of sister-love and gladness, and he was near me too. I trembled with joy to hear his voice, and woke up sobbing. Then I dreamed again, and the dear faces were gone; it was twilight, and I thought I was looking out of the window, wishing for the return of something—I knew not what. But it was all a dream; and when I awoke, the sea was smooth and shining, the sun sparkled on it, and I remembered that the dream and the reality were both passed away.

## CHAPTER II.

Mine was a very lonely life. From my childhood I had been without a playmate : as a girl I was entirely without a companion, and therefore I had acquired some sober habits and ways that were not suited to my years. Still my disposition was a happy one, and my spirits were naturally high, and easily excited ; but the joyousness and the eagerness had to be much and often checked. My poor father wished me to have a pleasant life, I am sure ; and the thoughts of my isolated and friendless youth troubled him greatly : but mental sufferers, I have always observed, in a considerable degree get entirely absorbed and wrapt up in their own individual misfortunes. He saw me full of life, health, and vigour ; and, as far as the ordinary requirements of life are concerned, I was pretty well off; whilst he was paralytic, nervous, debilitated, and desponding. No wonder that, looking as he did from his own existence to mine, he did not often pity me. But I was dear to him—oh! very dear— and all the irritableness, all the fretful moods, all the complaining and discontent, I could forgive and bear patiently, for the sake of that one dear love, the only love that was bestowed upon me. I did weary of the loneliness at times : I could not help it. I longed for some change in the monotonous life, some affection for the yearning heart, some object or gift to alter and brighten the daily course. Every Sunday afternoon I used to stay at home with papa, and let Ellice go to church, for she was a kind-hearted, willing girl, and I wanted to make her contented ; when I watched her coming home, over the heath or by the beach, with troops of merry gay-dressed friends, I drew back with a dreary feeling at heart almost like envy. I am

ashamed to confess it, but it is true. I so longed and
sickened for home-happiness, home-love, home-sisterhood.
Papa and Ellice were both most kind, but they could not
understand me and be my friends. How could I expect it?
And I tried to be thankful for their kindness, and be
content. It was a strange life for one so young to lead. I
had no education except what I gave myself from books,
and I was left to choose my occupations and pursuits at will.
For this I might have fared ill, but I had an insatiable
passion for reading and somewhat of a reflective turn of
mind. I read not merely for amusement, but from curiosity,
and possessed a good memory.

And I had ample choice of books. Twice a week, or
oftener, I ran down to the Ingham Town-Hall Library, and
came home laden with miscellaneous literature. The old
librarian was quite a friendly patron to me, and (though it
is a great secret) always gave me back half the subscription
fee, and let me carry all the second day's *Times* for papa to
read. Ah, dear kind-hearted Mr. Binnie! It's a great
shame to betray your confidence to the world, but let's hope
that none of the committee will ever be the wiser. If they
are, I have only to say that the ten shillings invariably went
for a turkey on Christmas Day, which was a great treat to
poor papa (and nervous people think so much of their
dinners !), which we never should have had if it hadn't
been for Mr. Binnie. He was a funny-looking old man, and
shuffled about in a threadbare grey coat, as if he had been
on skates. That poor everlasting grey coat! he did not
defraud the committee for himself, that was evident. Often
and often have I wished, as I saw him fumbling over dusty
books, and patting down the dogs' ears with paternal fondness, that Government would give him a pension. He was
so poor and so contented! and I felt sure he must be
getting tired of the dogs' ears and dustiness. Poor geniuses

2

and poor clever people get pensions sometimes, and though
Mr. Binnie was neither, is he the less deserving?

But I must also mention another friend of mine, Mr. Bean
the Ingham surgeon : I will try and draw him skilfully, dear
reader, for there are not many Mr. Beans in the world, and
I would fain implant in your hearts the leaven of the pride,
the reverence, the love, and the heartiness which all Ingham-
Helmsley felt for its little, good, clever doctor.  I do not
think I shall say a word about his outward man ; and yet
why not?  It is only in childhood that we love the letter
rather than the spirit—the setting rather than the diamond,
the gaudy binding rather than the matter of the book; but
in riper years it is not so.  Who, if the picture is a genuine
Raffaelle, will admire or value it less that it is put in a
worthless frame of poor gilt or rude carving?  Oh, it seems
to me a poor and childlike wisdom to love and treasure and
extol this mortal facing and carving of ours, over which
time, disease, and veriest chance rule supreme, beyond the
inestimable and eternal jewel which God hath placed within!
Therefore I will be brave and speak candidly of Mr. Bean's
littleness of stature and outward imperfections.  But though
he was small and plain, he was by no means insignificant-
looking ; his eyes were bright, sparkling, and expressive ;
his thoughtful mouth often smiled with much good nature
and enjoyment, and his high forehead betrayed plainly
enough uncommon mind and character.  Uncommon he
certainly was, in appearance as well as in talent and
benevolence ; he always wore a very long tail coat and a
very broad-brimmed hat, and both in winter and summer
carried a huge cotton umbrella, which he shouldered much
as a soldier would his gun.  Then his shoes were extremely
short and broad; it must have been a whim to wear them
so—no feet *could* fit such shoes.  Ellice used to say that if
ever Ingham were flooded, as it was reported it once had

been, she should wish for no better canoe than one of the doctor's shoes. But in spite of his shoes, his umbrella, and other oddities, there could not possibly be a more excellent man than Mr. Bean, and I am sure no one was ever more respected. He was very kind to both papa and myself; and though he used to say a good deal which I could not understand, I was always glad of a visit to the surgery. He had ever something to show me; a curious picture-book, a chemical experiment, or some stuffed birds. Sometimes he asked me to tea; and in those days of solitariness it was a great treat, although I stood somewhat in awe of tall, handsome Mrs. Bean, whose magnificence of look and dress inspired me with a far greater awe than all the doctor's learning and philosophy : which timidity in question incited me very carefully to scrape my shoes, and rub them on the hall-door mat, and to take great care lest I should spill my tea and scatter any crumbs on the bright red carpet. Nevertheless Mrs. Bean was motherly and hospitable, and tried to make me happy.

And such was my life in the lonely White House by the Sea. A heap of books, changed once or twice a week ; a nod and a friendly chat with old Mr. Binnie ; a sumptuous tea of sponge-cake and potted hare at the doctor's, two or three times a year; a row round the Mere Point, or a walk to the little hamlet of Ashford every Michaelmas to buy apples ; these were all the changes and varieties that I ever enjoyed : and yet I was happy—happy in my loneliness, happy in my privations, happy in my trials. I confess sometimes that I felt inclined to long and pine for the advantages of which I was deprived, but I resisted the rebellious feeling whenever it came, for I knew it was wrong. Nothing tempted me to give way to it so much as the sight of day-pupils issuing from the large pompous door of the fashionable French boarding-school at Ingham.

Sometimes, as I returned from the library, they were coming out in merry groups with hands entwined, and carrying bags of books. I envied both the books and the companionship, but the companionship the most.

Sometimes papa used to say—

"Poor little Chatty—poor little Chatty, you ought to go to school."

Then I would coax and caress him, and say that I could do very well without school at all, and that the doctor said I wrote a better hand than any one of my age he knew.

Then papa would continue:—

"If you could but learn music! I should so like to hear '*Non piu mesta!*'"

And I wished so too, and imagined the "*Non piu mesta*" to be the most delightful thing in the world; but I have since ceased to regret that I never learned music, and have discovered that people can be tolerably happy without it.

No wonder that leading such a quiet and uniform life as I did, the occurrence that I have narrated in the first chapter made so deep an impression on my mind. The face of the young girl who had hung so affectionately and spontaneously to me, haunted me by night and by day, but the face and voice of Lindsay haunted me most of all. I thought of them over and over again, and recalled all the words that had passed between us, drawing unceasingly the bright, bright picture. I paused over the half-closed volume of Shakespeare or Bulwer Lytton to dream the dear dream again, and never longed for candles to come in the twilight hour, but sat in quiet enjoyment of the memory which could not fade.

Should I ever see him again, or would it remain a memory, and nothing more?

## CHAPTER III.

" My goodness gracious me, Miss Chatty, I won't believe it ! "

" Believe what, Ellice ? "

" Why, dear, don't you know ?  Oh, I forgot ; of course you don't.  How surprised master will be ! "

News in any shape was welcome to poor nervous *ennuyé* papa ; so, without enlightening me, Ellice ran straight into the little parlour, and exclaimed—

" Mr. Stirling is married, as true as I'm living, sir ! "

So here was the wonderful surprising intelligence ; but I felt quite disappointed.  Except as Mr. Stirling's name had been linked in my memory with my unknown friends, it had no interest for me, but far otherwise with papa.  He let the paper fall to the ground, and regarded Ellice with wide-open, wondering mouth and eyes.

" Married ! "

" Yes, and I say it's a burning shame, sir, that a gentleman like him should so disgrace himself, and——"

" It's to Ellen White, then ? "

" Of course it is, sir, and I saw them going to church with my very own eyes ; if I hadn't I don't think anything would have made me believe it ; such a scandalous thing— and Mr. Stirling is the grandest gentleman in the place, too. It's a disgrace to the place, sir."

" And who did you see, Ellice ? " said my father, musingly.

" I saw only two in the carriage, you see, sir—as I was coming up the street, and they were going down—and those two were Mr. Stirling and the girl Ellen White.  I did not see her face very well, nor his either, but well enough to 'dentify them, sir."

" Poor man !" ejaculated my father.

" Indeed I don't think he deserves to be pitied," Ellice said, impatiently ; " why, sir, if he likes to get himself into such a scrape, whose fault is it but his own? I've no patience with it. A gentleman like him, too, and of a high family and everything, to go and marry a—a—a girl whose name I'm sure my mother wouldn't hear me mention for the world."

" But why not, Ellice ?" I asked innocently.

" It is not fit for young ladies like you to hear about, Miss Chatty, because Ellen White was a very improper behaved girl, and not fit to be servant to a gentleman like Mr. Stirling. Married, indeed! a pretty encouragement to all——"

" Hush!" said my father; " he has a right to do as he likes, you know, Ellice ; and whatever he does, he is a very good and a very clever man; and people all have fancies."

" Fancies !"

Ellice's voice and look were the very essence of annoyance and irritation, and I wish very much I could draw the look and give the tone of the voice—they were so expressive ; but she said no more. When she was gone, papa and I both fell into a reverie.

He was thinking about Mr. Stirling, and presently said, as if working out a conclusion of the argument in his own mind—

" Perhaps he is acting up to principle."

" What principle, papa ?" I said, gently.

" Of right, Chatty."

Papa said no more, and though somewhat puzzled, I did not like to ask him any other questions; he seemed for once forgetting all individual troubles in a contemplation.

Meantime November came  The wind blew high and

loud around our dwelling, and the dull dark days made my
father low spirited and desponding. It was a dreary time
for Ellice and for me. All our ingenuity, patience, and
stringent efforts were taxed to the utmost, and concentrated
on the one sole object of instilling into our invalid's mind
something of cheerfulness and hope. Mr. Bean in such
times was an angel of sunshine and goodness. The topic of
Mr. Stirling was revived over and over again ; and if ever I
left papa and the doctor together, when I returned, they
had invariably gone back to the old subject. Once as
I went in, Mr. Bean was standing before the fire, and
said with a very pointed summing up of all and every reasoning—

"Depend on it, my dear sir, that it is so. Mr. Stirling
is a very fine character; and a man who will brave and defy
the world for the sake of a principle of right as he has done
—why, sir, where will you find another like him ?"

I could not reconcile conflicting arguments at all, and I
so wanted to see my way clear, and decide for myself. My
independent and responsible way of life had given me a
habit of reflective seriousness that I believe few at such an
early age possess ; I had no one whose opinion I could
take, or whose commands I could obey, as other children
have ; but when I was in difficulty as to the right or wrong
of anything, I had to work out a decision myself. But here
I felt that I could not judge; Ellice's words, and the reports
of Ingham indignation and scandal, Mr. Bean's settled
approval and admiration—and so good and wise as he was—
how could I reconcile or account for it ? Then Mr. Stirling's
high position, his talent, his honourable reputation, and his
exalted character, was it possible that he could stoop at
once to what was really a moral degradation ?—as, if he
was truly doing right, and sacrificing his reputation merely
for the sake of his right thinking, oh, was it not very noble

and beautiful of him to do so, and heartless of the world to
sneer at him for it?   I felt as if I should respect, and love,
and honour him tenfold.

I touched the doctor's arm gently.

" If Mr. Stirling has done right, then why do people talk
so about him ? "

" So, how do you mean, Chatty ? "

The tears filled my eyes.   I quite loved and honoured
Mr. Stirling already.

" As Ellice does, and as everybody in Ingham does ; as if
they had a right to say anything they pleased about him ; so
unkindly and cruelly, Mr. Bean."

He smiled, and looked at me curiously.

" They ought to like him the better for it," I continued,
sedately.

" But every one does not think alike, Chatty, and what
one holds law another laughs at ; besides, the world doesn't
always like people the better for doing what is right, little
one."

" It ought," I replied, very gravely.

" Yes ; but ought does not always take place, you know.
Chatty, listen to me," said Mr. Bean, in a serious tone.
" You little think how cruel and unjust the world and the
world's opinion can be sometimes ; but you will find out—at
least I fear so.   There are some crimes it never censures ;
and some virtues it never forgives.   Some time ago—a few
years only—Mr. Stirling was little like the man he is now ;
intellectual and generous-minded he always was, but in his
youth he was not strong enough to resist entirely the tempta-
tions to which all young men of rank are exposed.   I suppose no one is.   He committed a great fault—a sin I should
call it—and Ellen White was the person whom he wronged ;
but she was of humble birth, and the world smiled on the
young, rich, handsome Mr. Stirling, and glossed over his

fault. It never pitied Ellen White. Mr. Stirling went abroad, as the fashion is when young men leave college, and the girl was left alone to her suffering and shame. I know well what her trials were. She was an only child, and the pride, and darling, and hope of her parents, who were very poor, but respectable and hard-working, and she was pretty—of course. Her father died of a broken heart, and the mother, goaded almost to insanity by her child's humiliation, set off on foot to some friends in Scotland, and died on the way, of weariness and want. How the poor girl repented and sorrowed I cannot by any words express. Her grief and wretchedness were beyond all imagination; I believe if it had not been for even the small assistance and benefit I was enabled to render her, that she would have died too; but she lived, and by the greatest industry and patience supported herself for some years by needlework. A short time back, Mr. Stirling took up his residence at Ingham: every one courted him, every one sought after him, and fawned on him; but he has scorned it all, and has made openly, in the sight of God and of the world, a brave atonement for his sin."

Mr. Bean wiped a tear from his eye.

"Now, Chatty, don't you confess that this man's soul is truly Roman?"

"Oh yes," I exclaimed eagerly; "how good of him, how noble!"

"It is indeed, but Mrs. Bean's toast is being made, I know. Good-by."

The dull foggy weather lasted a long time. It seemed to me as if the clear, frosty, cheerful winter would never come, and Ellice and I longed for it more than I can tell. Do all we could, neither my father's low spirits nor nervous irritableness would go.

Every morning we woke to the same task, every evening

we felt that our task must be begun again on the morrow—the disheartening, wearying task of constant cheering, and patient endurance of poor papa's fretful humours. There was no possibility of pleasing him. If we got any little extra dish or delicacy for his dinner, he would sigh over it, and bewail our kindness with tears; if we brought up the remains of the yesterday's dinner, he moaned at the insufficiency of his means to procure an enjoyable meal; he wished all day for the night to come, and when it was Sunday wished it was Monday, and *vice versâ*. Ellice's high spirits and good humour bore her through everything, but sometimes her patience gave way; still, she was too fond of me to complain, and the utmost of her irritation never went beyond an emphatic, " *Fancies!* "

One night when papa was gone to-bed, I put out the parlour candle and went into the kitchen. I was too wearied to read, and my heart was full of a sadness that needed sympathy.

Ellice was singing to herself as she worked—

" Oh where, and oh where, is my Highland laddie gone? "

" Why, my heart, Miss Chatty dear, how pale you look! " she said, breaking off, and taking hold of my two hands coaxingly.

" I'm very well, Ellice ; only tired. "

" And so you may well be, poor little dear : it's those blessed fancies; they're enough to tire any one. "

" Do you know, Ellice, " I said, " I have been thinking of something to-night. "

" And what is it, dear ? "

" I don't think you ought to stay here any longer ; you could get a much better place, and it's so miserable for you, now papa is worse. "

The affectionate girl burst into tears.

"Go? To another place? Do you think I would? Never, as long as I'm a servant!"

"I should be very sorry to lose you, Ellice," I said, tearfully, "but it seems a shame for you to be here, when you could be so much better off somewhere else, and live much better and have higher wages, too."

Ellice had dried her tears, and now spoke quite indignantly.

"Bless my heart, Miss Chatty, do you think I'm so unchristianlike as to care about nothing but eating and drinking? Not I: and, after all, why I'm sure we live well enough, and as to the fancies—lawk, Miss Chatty, I've known people with ten times worse fancies than master. I might get a trifle more wages in a smarter place, I dare say, but I should have to dress it wholly entirely away if I did, and I couldn't do so much as I like as I do here."

Ellice's vehemence and earnestness reassured me; I felt that she was sincere, and thanked her for her affection gratefully. We sat up by the little fire a long time, and talked about many things.

"Miss Chatty," she said, after some time, "wouldn't you like to see them again?"

"Whom do you mean?" I asked in bewilderment.

"Why, the ladies and gentleman from Mr. Stirling's."

"Perhaps we shall some day," I said hopefully.

"We might have done, but we shan't now, Miss Chatty, dear, you know; for none of Mr. Stirling's friends will come and see him after this—they can't be expected."

And must I give up that hope, then? Oh, no. The only possible future in my life was linked to it, and it had coloured my hitherto futureless, joyless, isolated life with beauty and radiance, as the morning sky is golden with the glory of a sun not yet arisen.

Only they who have known such a youth of loneliness as mine can comprehend and enter fully into this feeling. True, that I had seen Lindsay Jocelyn once only, and true that we had interchanged few words; but if my readers will consider for one moment the utter solitude of my home and heart—the dreary, dreary sameness of my daily life—it will not sound extravagant to say that I yearned to look once more upon his face, and to listen once more to his voice, with a passionate and deep yearning—the more deep that he was the first human being who had awakened an interest in me. There had been something, I know not what, in the sweetness of his voice and in the earnestness of his look and manner which had inspired me with a confidence, so to say, and an impression that he could understand all that untold want of my heart—all the thirsting for sympathy and for friendship—all that blank and bitterness which was sadder to bear since it had to be borne in silence.

Besides, the isolated and unnatural position, so to speak, in which I was placed had conspired to tinge my mind with a hue of romance. I stood, as it were, on the boundary line of two classes, the aristocratic and the middle; yet, in truth, I could be said to belong to neither. The blood that ran in my veins was of a proud and high race; my hands were small and white, bespeaking a good lineage; and my brow had the chiselling of a dozen, and yet a dozen, and a dozen more ancestors of the same lofty birth. Yet the vain daughters of the rich Ingham merchants would have thought it far beneath their dignity to incline their heads to me from their shining carriages; and as in my early childhood I had been without a playmate, now, when I was growing to be a woman, I was entirely without a companion. And I was somewhat of an imaginative and ardent temperament. Constant loneliness, and constant monotony of existence, though they had both tempered and subdued the enthusiasm, had served strongly to heighten and foster the imaginativeness; no wonder, therefore, that a circumstance like that I have related in my first chapter should have taken so vivid a hold on my memory, and that I should have so cherished the recollection and the hope which arose from it.

To say that I loved Lindsay Jocelyn would be going too far; it was impossible to love one of whom I had seen so little; yet I cannot think of a fitting term to express the feeling I entertained for him. For this, O reader, if thou art no longer young, go back to thy youth; remember that I was almost a child in years and in knowledge, and remember also that he was to me as "the chiefest among ten thousand—his stature was like to a palm-tree—he was fair, yea, pleasant, he had dove's eyes, and his lips were like a thread of scarlet." Beauty I had seldom seen; such beauty and manliness, such strength and gentleness combined I had never seen before. So I looked into the dim future, and said, earnestly, "Let me see thy countenance, let me hear thy voice, for comely is thy countenance, and thy voice sweet; would that I were in thy eyes as one that found favour."

## CHAPTER IV.

"What a dreary place it looks!"

When there was no cold wind I used to coax my father into a little stroll; it always did him good, and, supported on one side by my arm, and on the other by a stout stick, he could walk very well. Anything was better for him than a whole long day in-doors.

"What a dreary place it looks!"

Well might he say so. Oh, how bleak and desolate our little dwelling looked, standing alone as it did among brown rocks and barren sandy plans! In the summer these plains would be covered with short grasses and heaths; the skies were blue above; the sun glittered on the glorious sea, and my dearly-loved garden-flowers bloomed in gay profusion. But now there was no blue sky, no bright sunshine, no sweet-smelling flowers. All was cold, and hard, and barren.

"Dear papa," I exclaimed, cheerfully, "we shall soon have spring now, you know!"

"February—March—April. It's a long time."

"It won't seem long."

"Ay, dearie, you are young: you can look forward and hope, and see the bright side of everything; when you are as old as I am it will be different. It will be ten years in May since I came here, ten years on the eighteenth of May. Oh, it was such lovely weather when we came, Chatty, and yet the place looked drearier to me then than it does now. I ought to have considered you more; I never ought to have come here, for your sake, dearie."

"But, papa, dear, why regret it on my account? Am I not happy? Have I not you to love me? Oh, I don't mind the dreariness. Why should we, papa? It is not a place that makes happiness; we have much to be thankful for."

"So we have—so we have," rejoined my father, sadly. "God forgive my discontent! If I had been left all alone I should have had no right to murmur; but I cannot help looking back to the old times, and at night sometimes I dream that I am at Arrowmere, and everything is as it used to be, and——"

He burst into tears of passionate emotion and exclaimed—

"And to wake and find how all is changed! To think

that you who were born an heiress are poorer than were the poorest of my servants' children, and that we shall never, never see Arrowmere again."

Tears stopped his utterance, and we entered the house in melancholy silence. A new sadness filled my heart. I yearned for a man's strength and for a man's freedom. I forgot for a time my duty of submission to the Eternal Power, and scorned in powerless bitterness and agony my woman's weakness and woman's sphere. Oh, for courage, for ambition, for energy, to set up a high hope and eminence and then to reach it! to win back the fair heritage and sunshine of the past, which misfortune and circumstance had wrested from my father's hand; to enter the lists of the great Tournament boldly, and dare all, with my ancestral bravery in my heart, and my ancestral badge on my breast—

"PER ARDUA SURGAM."

Alas, alas! It was not till later that I attained a serene contentment from the consciousness of a higher ambition and loftier courage.

To uphold and strengthen that generous but broken spirit which had no other support; to make up for lost happiness, lost friends, and lost comfort, by a supreme love and never-failing tenderness; and to feel this: to know that I was all in all to him, the sunshine in his darkness, and the savour and salt of his daily life; to know how he watched for my form and listened for my step; was not this sweet duty and this sweeter reward enough?

The winter passed at length, and spring came. My father was better, cheerfuller and stronger; in the sunny afternoons he dozed for hours together on our garden seat; and, having him still in sight, I could take pleasant strolls by the beach, or sit on the ridge of the heath and read. This ridge was my favourite spot; so solitary and so quiet. Before me lay the sea, vast, illimitless, and shining silver-

bright in the sun; and around were rocks, heathers, and
sandy strips of land. It was somewhat dreary, and yet my
heart loved it.

With the spring had come renewed hope; a hope which
was cherished in secret, but which never flagged.

Shall I see him again, or would it remain a memory and
nothing more?

---

## CHAPTER V.

IT is a calm and pleasant day in early summer. The sky
is flecked with soft white clouds which

> "Sail as if onward to some other sphere."

The purple waves dance and gambol beneath the merry,
golden sunlight, and flights of gull soar and make wide
triumphant circles in the air; flocks of sheep and lambs
are browsing on the fresh-looking heath, tended by ragged
boys who sing and shout gleefully; and the hills are spotted
with white clover blossoms, and violet and pink heather-
flowers, which smell sweetly. Even around our home there
is a look of freshness and of summer beauty. The rose-
trees that I have trained so carefully to the walls reward my
watchfulness at last with clusters of red velvet buds, the
gooseberry and currant bushes are in full leaf, the apple-
tree heavy with a glory of green foliage and delicate shell-
like blooms, and the air that comes into the room is fragrant
with the breath of mignionette. Such a day as this even
works a beneficial influence on papa; he cannot possibly
find fault with it, and passes his time by walking from the
parlour to the garden, and from the garden to the parlour

back again.  Bailie barks in the sun, and Ellice sings, over
and over again—

"Oh where, and oh where, is my Highland laddie gone?"

as happy as a queen at her work.

I am a sad idler to-day.  I cannot stay at my books;
and close them like a released child, to rove over the soft
heath, or by the shore, to pick up shells and look on the
shining, magnificent sea.  But I cannot rest in any place:
a strange volatile humour is over me which I am unable to
resist.  I wander up and down the beach listlessly, dreamily;
then I climb the hill, and with no settled purpose roam
from hillock to hillock, and from the heights to the shore,
alternately.  A little way from the rocks, and within view
from our windows, is an old shapeless ruin, no one knows of
what; perhaps a castle, perhaps a cottage—who can say,
since time lays the same heavy hand on both?  I sit on a
heap of mould and bricks, and my heart is filled with the
loveliness and joy and freshness that I contemplate.  By-
and-by I hear a voice a few hundred yards off, calling—

"Miss Chatty, it's time to make the tea!"

The evening was wondrously beautiful.  Papa still walked
in the back garden, and I sit alone in the little parlour by
the open window.  I look upon the path which leads to the
beach, and fall into a day-dream.  My mind recalls—

"The tender grace of a day that is gone,"

and then I think of one, and of one only.

Suddenly a voice calls me by name.

It was not papa, nor Ellice; I look up hastily, and my
heart beats with a wild, extravagant joy.  I can hardly
believe that he stands before me; but I look again and see
that I do not dream.  Then I start up, and meet him with
sparkling, overjoyed eyes and burning cheeks.

"I am so glad!"

3

It is all I can say, and hardly take in the meaning of his words for the rapture that fills my breast.

" So," he said, with a bright smile, and with the same quiet ease of manner that I could well remember, "I have found our little Grace Darling again at last ! You do not know how often I have wished and tried to come, and have been prevented ; but at length I have been successful, and have found you like some Nereis among the rocks." |

He held my hand in his for some seconds, and looked earnestly on my face. I blushed and turned away.

" I have been disappointed so many times," he continued, changing the playfulness of his tone to a graver key; "but a professional man can seldom hope for a holiday in London."

" London ? " I exclaimed.

" Yes, I came from London to-day."

" All that way ?"

" All that way," he replied, smiling.

A warm colour rose to my cheeks.

" And the motive that brought me here to-night was to renew, on the part of Mrs. Dunstan and Jeannie, the acquaintance which was begun and ended so abruptly last year. On the part of Mrs. Dunstan and Jeannie and some one else."

I vaguely comprehended his meaning.

" You consent to it; you are not unwilling to renew——"

" Oh no !" I answered, half joyfully, half shyly; "I have wished to hear of them, often and often. Mrs. Dunstan, you said ?"

" Yes. Mrs. Dunstan is the elder lady, and the mother of the pretty little girl.

" And the other ?"

" The other lady," he continued, carelessly, "is a niece of Mrs. Dunstan's, a West Indian heiress. Mrs. Dunstan

is a rich widow lady ; and I, Lindsay Jocelyn, am a poor
barrister, and the son of one of her oldest friends. This is
the entire catalogue. You will love Jeannie very much.
She is a sweet child."

I looked up in surprise. "Love Jeannie ?"

"Ah! I forgot to tell you that Mrs. Dunstan is coming to
spend the autumn months here ; you will see them often."

I clapped my hands in the fulness and suddenness of my
joy, and a smile passed over my companion's face at my
gleefulness. Just then my father entered from the little
garden door, and stood still from utter amazement.

"Mr. Jocelyn, papa," I exclaimed, blushing at my own
agitation.

"How d'ye do, sir ?—I am very glad to see you."

There was something quite courtly in poor papa's bow, to
me it was a shadow of other days ; but Lindsay's visit, so
unexpected and uncommon an occurrence as it was, flurried
him out of all memory and etiquette for the rest of the
evening. He sat in a corner, hardly opening his lips, save
for monosyllables.

"I can hardly believe that I am here again," Lindsay
said, as he stood by me at the window. "I am so tired of
London and business, but I suppose they are inseparable
evils from life. How quiet this place is, and how refreshing! It is a reward for many hard days' work in a city, I
assure you."

I smiled.

"You will think me very foolish when I say that this very
quiet and solitariness tires me sometimes. I almost envy a
life of activity and excitement."

"Ah, that is because your nature is enthusiastic ; when
you are older, and have been in the world and felt its turbu-
lence and restless stir, like me, you will long for repose."

He had a quiet contemplative way of earnest speaking

which affected me irresistibly, and there was a music in his voice which made me far readier to listen than to speak. So I was silent, and he continued :—

"I daresay you will smile to hear me moralize in this way, but I have always felt a sort of oldness, if I may so express it,—a sort of wearied *ennuyé* sensation which I would fancy any one feeling who had lived twice as long as I had, and lets me hardly believe I am young. I am so tired of the world—so tired of the universal selfishness and universal sin. But one seems quite out of it here. Surely the peacefulness pleases you."

" Yes, but even here —— "

"Pray go on; you should speak to me as if I were an old friend."

"I was going to say," I replied, smiling from very pleasure at his words, "that even here it is not all tranquillity—there will be some stormy days. I suppose they come to every one."

He looked at me for a minute and then said in a subdued voice,—"I understand your meaning. But there are some sorrows that are not of the world's making."

There was a perfect sympathy between us. Already I felt that I could have opened my heartful of loneliness and troubles to him, and that he would understand me. Though my pulses beat quickly and rapturously, the first wild trembling and exultation of joy had worn off, and I could answer him with composure, and realize the fulness of my happiness.

" I am so much alone," I said, sadly.

" Ay, I should imagine there would be little society here; a country town is the worst place possible for that; there are so many cliques, and so little real sociability."

" Yes; and unless you are of a certain standing no one will receive you; there are so many lines of boundary drawn which are never passed, and it is the more astonish-

ing to me that this exclusive spirit is seen so much among
the educated classes.   I cannot understand it at all."

"I daresay not; but they do not consider themselves
exclusive, and would be offended to be called so.   You are
right nevertheless, and any right-minded person must see it
in the same light.   You will be glad when Jeannie is here."

"Oh, yes, very glad; I have no friends."

"And no one can help loving Jeannie—she is so natural,
and has so much vivacity without affectation or the least
self-esteem.   What a splendid evening!" continued Lindsay,
suddenly changing the subject; "or I should rather say,
what a lovely evening; splendid is not the appropriate name
for anything so quiet.   Do look at the red light on the sea,
Miss Warne."

"How beautiful!"

My father rose at my exclamation.

"I don't like a red sunset," he said, uneasily; "it be-
tokens rain.   Dear me, how those horrid gulls scream; I
should like to shoot them all."

We both smiled.

"I think if the birds had any idea of your murderous
intent, Mr. Warne, that they wouldn't trouble you long;
certainly, their music is anything but pleasant."

"There is nothing pleasant here," rejoined my father,
and seated himself in his corner again with a heavy sigh.

Lindsay still stood at the window, and with his arm
leaning on the framework looked out thoughtfully.

Though years have passed since then, and somewhat of
the first enthusiasm and eagerness of my nature is subdued,
I can still recall the intensity of my feelings as I stood by
Lindsay that summer night.   Everything—all the individual
existences which affected my life—my father, Jeannie, my
loneliness, and sorrows, and endeavours, were forgotten.   I
had no thought, no memory, no joy, but the blissful con-

sciousness of his presence. No wonder that I could hardly speak, and that my words were forced and unnatural. I can remember, too, looking on him and wondering why it was so. Ah! not even now have I been able to solve the riddle.

His features seemed very perfect to me, as I saw them in the partial soft light of the twilight, and with such a glow of ardent emotion at my heart. I never saw a face that I admired so much before, and never one that I have looked upon with the same feelings since. And it seemed to me as if every one else must admire him with the same unqualified fulness! which is a general mistake made by those who have fallen in love. We cannot help thinking that all the world will be of the same opinion, and that the object of our adoration must be universally acknowledged.

> " In sweetnesse of both looks and minde ;
> Th' eclypse and glorye of his kinde ! "

I do not think I can give the reader a good idea of Lindsay's face if I try ever so, for, however much we may know of the features, even to exactitude, we come at no nearer approach to an imagination-picture if we have to guess entirely at the expression ; so much has expression, and so little has regularity of feature alone to do with the charm of a face we love ! But I was particularly struck that evening by Lindsay's looks—to me so different to any one's I had ever seen. Not only by the intelligence and contemplativeness of the brow, but also by the brightness of the shining hair that hung over it; not only by the handsome curve of the mouth, but also with the playfulness of its expression ; and lastly but not least, by the power and gracefulness of his figure.

" I have looked forward to this evening so much, Chatty —I beg your pardon, but from hearing Jeannie speak of you so often by that name———"

"I do not mind; every one calls me so."

"And you will give me leave to do the same?"

"Oh yes, certainly."

"Thank you. I do so dislike formalities. I am very pleased to have seen you again, Chatty. Somehow after that evening's adventure it was difficult to me to fancy that Ingham was a really existing place; it was so much like a dream. It was quite a little romance to me, I assure you. I could not fancy any of our present-day young ladies being so truely heroic as you were."

"No—no!" I said timidly.

"But indeed I am right. Luckily you have had little experience of fashionable young ladies; I hope you never will, it makes people uncharitable. Well then, speaking from personal experience, shall I tell you what I have found them? Don't be shocked: I am not a hard judge."

I smiled at his humorousness, and he continued:—

"There is nothing to judge: the spirits are gone and there only remains—lace, ribbons, silk, velvet, and mantua-makers' dressings-up. Now, do you think I am severe? I assure you I am far otherwise. I will be so far malicious as to hope that one day you will be enabled to see how truly I have spoken."

In another half-hour he took his leave, promising me that he would call on me the next day; the day after, he was to return to London. We retired early to rest, but sleep was far from me; nor did I wish for it. I felt that sleep would bring me no dreams so unutterably joyful as the day-dreams of my own heart; and, opening the window that I might hear the song of the waves, and see the starlit beautiful heavens, I sat down by it till midnight. Even then I could not sleep, for the manifold pleasant thoughts that hovered around my pillow.

## CHAPTER VI.

HE was gone. I still stood on the threshold, where a few minutes ago we had stood together, my hand had been taken in his, and the parting word had been spoken. But even those short minutes were gone now; nothing could bring them back again. Perhaps even their semblance might not return. Who could tell? Perhaps Lindsay Jocelyn and I should never meet again. The chances on both sides were equally balanced, but a feather might turn them.

He was gone. I was unwilling to leave the hall door. I seemed nearer to him whilst I was where he had last been, and the track that his footsteps had taken was before my eyes. It seemed impossible that it was so—that he had really gone. His voice had so lately lingered on the air, that I still listened for it. Oh, it seemed impossible that he was gone! A very heavy sorrow fell over my heart. I felt as if I had not half appreciated the full extent of my happiness when it was yet with me; as if I would have given whole years of loneliness and sorrow for its return, if only for one hour.

The evening had been unusually fair and lovely. I was glad when clouds overshadowed it, for then it was more in unison with my own feelings. How long I should have stood at the hall-door I know not; I was so unwilling to break the charm that still was on me whilst I remained there—the charm of his presence and voice; but before long I heard a very impatient—

"It's time for me to have my arrowroot; make haste, Chatty."

And I hastened to make the arrowroot, quickly and carefully, resolving to hide the sadness of my spirit, and

not to permit my love for Lindsay to make me forgetful of a
daughter's duty. But the arrowroot was not so good to-
night. I stirred it round and round in the cup with a very
guilty conscience. My heart had not been in my work, I
could not help tacitly admitting; the mixture had not been
well adjusted; there was too much milk, and too little
arrowroot; it had not a jelly-looking consistency about it,
and had a watery poorness more like starch. I had a good
mind to make some more, but papa was impatient, and
the milk would not boil just as soon as I wanted ; besides,
there was only sufficient remaining for breakfast. There
was no help for it; so, with self-humiliation and much
abasement of spirit, I put in the nutmeg and sugar, and
carried it to my father.

"I am so glad, Chatty—he went just at the right time."
I looked up in amazement.

"How in the right time, papa ? "

"Mr. Jocelyn, I mean. Why, if he had stayed any
longer, you know, I shouldn't have had my arrowroot."

" Why not ? "

" Fifty reasons. Why, I couldn't ask you to go out and
make it; only servants ought to do such things, and I'm
sure Ellice would burn the milk ; and besides, I don't like
people knowing when I have my supper and what I eat, it's
so disagreeable ; not that I think Mr. Jocelyn would make
remarks, either, he seems so good-natured. I'm so glad he
tasted the port; he knew how good it was—of course he is
in the habit of drinking wine every day. I wish we had
a little more of it, Chatty; we should have had all, if it
hadn't been for those rascally ——"

He stopped short, as he always did when he saw how
sorry I was to hear him speak of what it was much happier
for us both to forget ; and then continued :—

" Up to their tricks again; these Ingham shopkeepers

will draw the farthest tooth out of your head. What on earth can they have put in this arrowroot?—arsenic perhaps. I won't take it, I know they spite me ; no, Chatty, I won't have any supper to-night. I couldn't touch the cheese, I'm so tired of it, and the bread is too new by half. Meat? I hate cold meat. I will try a little ; but I am sure I cannot eat a morsel: I could, perhaps, if I had some cucumber and cream." He tasted the meat, and then exclaimed :—

"It is not bad mutton; but he cuts off the fat, and sends poor weight, so we pay dear enough for it. Dear me, what cucumbers we used to have at Arrowmere !"

Then he ate a minute in silence, and finally finished by pushing away the plate, with a—

"Chatty, how on earth came that Mr. Jocelyn to call here ?"

I looked up in some surprise.

" Why should he come ; what does he know about us ?"

" I have seen him before, you know, father dear ?"

" Ah, so you have ; but then it was only for a few minutes."

" And then Mrs. Dunstan is coming, and Jeannie. I don't see anything strange that he should call."

" Well, I suppose it is not. He is a nice young man ; so fine-looking and agreeable. Such young men can always marry well, if they like. Do you think he is rich ?"

" Not very ; I should think he is not very rich," I said, musingly.

Papa then rose to go to bed. The words that had just passed between us oppressed my spirits heavily. I could not read even Tennyson to-night ; and closing the book, fell into a reverie. All the rapturous excitement that had raised my spirits since the last two days had passed away ; there was such a wide, wide gulf between Lindsay Jocelyn and myself: oh, why did I love him ? For the first time the thought flashed across my mind—What am I to him ?

And the dreary echo of common-sense and conscience was—Nothing. Oh, unkind common-sense! oh, most unwelcome conscience! Why did you not leave me a little longer to the full enjoyment of my romance and of my love? Why did you not pity me, and let me alone a space to dream and be happy? I did not want to awaken yet.

But it was of no avail to shut my eyes now, for I had removed the mote myself. True that he had sought to renew the intercourse between us; true that he had seemed pleased to do so—that his words of greeting had been cordial, his words of parting kind. He had expressed, and earnestly expressed, the pleasure with which he looked forward to meeting me again; he had seemed to listen earnestly to my words, and to find happiness at my presence; yet for all this I might be cherishing shadows—shadows only. And if it were not so; if . . . . I hardly dared dwell on the thought.

I sat a long time in the still room by myself. It was an inexpressible pleasure to me to be alone, and to think of him. Even though at times the thoughts were sad, I was very unwilling to surrender my superb air-castle! and I was unwilling to feel that irrationalism had built it, and visionary expectations guarded it; yet I would not be brave and let reason and conscience smash it down and demolish it, even though they whispered in my ears, over and over again, "Coward! Coward!"

## CHAPTER VII.

AFTER this my life brightened. There was always a happiness to look forward to, and a happiness to remember. Jeannie was coming ! I should see her often ; we should be as sisters. I should no longer be alone. I was very happy in these thoughts, and went through my daily duties with a cheerful heart.

The hopefulness and sunshine altered my nature. I had had no child's holiday-life of happiness, no childhood even ; childhood and girlhood were alike melancholy, recluse, and self-contained ; and this strange and saddened atmosphere hung round my spirits like a heavy shadow. But now I threw it off. I was in love with Life, Nature, and Humanity, and opened a wide heart to receive all the good gifts which God poured therein.

He came once more ; he came many times. I used to put on my prettiest dress, and arrange my hair with careful fingers, that I might look my best ; and the expectation of his coming gave unwonted brightness to my eyes and cheeks. At such times, papa would be waiting impatiently till my toilette was over ; and if the dress was light and tasteful, my hair smooth and eyes sparkling, he would fold me in his arms, and smile and weep alternately. "Ah !" he would say, sorrowfully, " my poor darling will never be the mistress of Arrowmere—never—never ! "

No one can tell what those visits of Lindsay Jocelyn were to me. Not only because his presence gave such entire happiness ; but because I was shut out from the whole world beside ; and he was, as it were, a revelation of it. He talked of London—of foreign travel, of books, and men, and manners ; and he talked not only with humour and spirit, but with depth of thought and feeling. At least, I thought so, as I used to sit in the shadow of the window listening in silent entrancement to the music of his voice; loving better to listen than to speak. And he discovered this; and, so that I did but smile at his playfulness and satire, was content. I never felt ashamed of my ignorance and of my childishness in the world's ways before him.

Indeed, this very simplicity and unsophisticated character of mine seemed to please him. He never tired of my questions, and never wearied of explanations. He brought me books too—books which had it not been for him I might never have heard of; wild stories of strange adventure, pictures of sea life, travels in far countries; Edgar Poe, Marryat, St. John, Mayne Reid, and many others. Such books were masculine, and unsuited to me; but they were new and exciting, and the charm of his voice and memory hung round them. I liked them, and frankly said so.

"I am delighted to hear you say so," he said, with a pleased smile; "and the more so because it bespeaks an originality in your taste and thinking. Most ladies wouldn't sleep after reading a ghost-story, and are frightened at the sound of a gun; but you have a strength and vigour of mind which is all the more pleasing to find, as it is so rare."

I shook my head.

"You would contradict me?"

"I think that you give me credit for more than I possess," I answered, hesitatingly.

"But indeed I do not, and you must retract your words. I never flatter, least of all should I flatter you——"

I interposed again, and blushed.

"That is not flattering. I only meant to say, that I respect you too much to entertain for one moment a thought of flattery. You are too hard upon me." And there was such an irresistible sweetness both in his voice and smile that I could not but believe what was so pleasant and grateful a belief.

And sometimes, in the summer twilight, we strolled through the little garden, and walked slowly on the beach ; the waves had receded, and the majestic sea was hushed and still as the sky above. How delightful it was to lean upon his strong arm, and listen to his voice, which would sink to a lower and softer key, as if to suit the holiness of the hour ! Our shadows would fall unbroken on the sands ; my eye measured the difference between them. And sometimes the thought would strike me—Alas! is there not as much difference between us in all things ? Why do I love him ?

With the autumn came a great disappointment. Mrs. Dunstan's plans were changed ; she had given up the idea of Ingham, after all, and perhaps I should never see Jeannie now. I told my fears to Lindsay, and he reassured me.

" Mrs. Dunstan is changeable and Jeannie has a great desire to come to Ingham ; she will not disappoint the poor child twice, and I greatly suspect——"

He broke off abruptly, and then added in a careless tone—

" Poor Mrs. Dunstan is rather undecided, you know, and that Indian niece of hers manages to rule her entirely ; and it is not likely—that is, it is improbable—that she should prefer a place so retired as Ingham to a gay trip abroad."

" They are going abroad, then ? "

" Mrs. Dunstan only mentioned it as a suggestion of her niece, and I am invited to join the party."

" And you will go ? "

" Nous verrons," he said, indifferently. " It will be our professional vacation then, and Mrs. Dunstan will never forgive me if I don't ; and, poor thing, as she is so old and kind a friend, I don't like to disoblige her. But I have no wish to go, and I hope I shall be enabled to get out of it in a creditable way. I am so very sorry that she gave up the idea of Ingham."

So for this year my hopes were again frustrated, and I heard no more of Mrs. Dunstan's trip, till one day Lindsay came to say that his efforts had been all unavailing, and to bid me good-by; and though I laughed at the whimsical account he gave of his manœuvres to escape the honour of chaperonship, and his despair at unsuccess, tears were in my eyes, and I felt very sad.

Then winter came, and I saw him again, but his visits were not what they had been in the summer. He came rarely, and for a shorter time. He spoke of law-courts, and cases, and sessions, and of midnight study after a hard day's work. But for himself he was unchanged, and the visits only became more dear and more looked-for that they were less frequent.

---

## CHAPTER VIII.

SUMMER came round again. Lindsay was gone to New-castle on professional business; I should not see him for some weeks. To-day was the first of July, and he talked of coming in August, Thirty-one days, perhaps five weeks, to wait! It was a long time. Yet the beautiful blue sky, and the summer freshness and gloriousness of all around, con-spired to make me sanguine; and perhaps this autumn would bring Jeannie to my heart. The question stood, as it had stood the year before; no definite arrangements had been made, and Lindsay invariably stopped my fears by a decided—

"Trust my word for it—Mrs. Dunstan will come; she will occasion an excitement with all her wealth, and what more delightful? In any other place the case is different. Le jeu n'en vaut pas la chandelle. She sinks into insignificance in the more splendid galaxy round her. And, as Milton says, 'Better to reign, &c.' Pray excuse my quotation; but, 'Aut Cæsar aut nullus,' you know. She will come."

And his impressive "She will come" encouraged me. One day my father took a fancy into his head that if Ellice and I could pickle some cherries as they used to be pickled at Arrowmere, he really should be able to enjoy a cold dinner. But the cherries must be of a particular kind, and he was sure I could not get them anywhere but at Wallis's Nursery Garden; so, as the place was at Helmsley-End, through the town of Ingham, I set off one morning early, whilst it was yet cool. Helmsley-End was the prettiest part of Ingham-Helmsley. White villas and gentlemen's houses, surrounded with shrubberies and tasteful grounds, were dotted here and there; and a picturesque descent led to the beach. Suddenly, as I walk along, I hear my own name called.

"Chatty, Chatty dear, it's I."

The warm, joyful colour mounts to my cheek, and I turn round.

An arm is clasped round my neck, and a bright, happy face is close to mine. Yes, I have found her at last; the same wild-rose cheeks, arch lips, and shining chestnut hair. The Jeannie of my remembrance and anticipation; a little altered, perhaps—less childlike, but almost a child still; with a child's frankness in her eyes, and a child's purity on her brow. I could not speak at first, for pleasure and bewilderment.

"It's I, Jeannie Dunstan; don't you know me, Chatty dear? oh, I'm so glad!"

She stood holding me by the hands whilst she kissed me over and over again. How fair and gentle she was! The friend and sister of whom I had dreamed; who could help loving her? But I could not utter my grateful thoughts; I could only say—

"Dear Jeannie! Dear, dear Jeannie!"

"Oh, I am so glad!" she ran on, gaily and eagerly, "so glad to be here at last. I was coming to find you out to-day. Did you know we were coming? No? Ah, Lindsay kept the secret; I wanted to surprise you. We only came yesterday, and we are going to stay till October; isn't that a long time? and you will come and see me often, won't you? We can have such nice walks by the beach, and I shall be so glad to get away from Angelica. I ought not to say so, but I cannot help it. That is the young lady who was with us that night; do you remember her?"

"Yes, perfectly."

"She is an orphan, and lives with us; she is very rich, but I don't like rich people; I mean not often. I like you, whatever you are."

"We are poor," I said, somewhat sadly, for I thought of poor papa's privations.

Jeannie glanced at my simple cotton dress, and straw-bonnet with its well-worn ribbon; and I think she understood the tone of my voice, for she kissed me warmly, and said—

"Never mind; rich people are not happier than any others. So mamma says."

"Have you no sisters?" I asked, jealously.

"No. Have you?"

"No."

"And who lives with you?"

"No one but papa and Ellice."

For a minute she paused in wondering silence, and

4

then, changing the subject, pointed to a large white gate near.

"That is where we live; I was walking in the shrubberies and saw you pass—but come in; you must come in and see mamma."

But in spite of her entreaties I would not go to her home that day. Reader, pardon the vanity, in consideration of the candour with which I confess it: I was unwilling to appear before the rich, fashionable Mrs. Dunstan and the Indian heiress in my humble cotton and faded ribbon. So with many kisses we parted, and I hastened home to recount the morning's adventure.

Thank God, oh, thank God for this; I have found her again!

---

## CHAPTER IX.

Mrs. Dunstan sat enthroned in the state of blue satin and bland condescension as I entered her showy and smart drawing-room; Angelica lounged on a sofa, bedecked and glittering with untasteful jewellery, and between both ladies sat the Reverend Decimus Dowley, round-faced, twinkling-eyed, gay little Mr. Decimus Dowley, the rector of St. Mary's-on-the-Mere.

"Ah, there's Miss—what's-her-name?—whom Jeannie has taken such a fancy to. How d'ye do, my love?"

She extended her hand to me with a languid air, as if it were a great deal too much trouble to her, and added, in an affected voice—

"Pray sit down, miss—excuse me, I can't remember your name—Jeannie, do tell me."

Jeannie coloured with vexation, and said hastily—

"I've told you so often, mamma dear, that to punish you I won't tell you again."

"Now how provoking!" said Mrs. Dunstan, in an aggrieved voice. "Really, Jeannie, you're too bad. And I am quite dying to know."

All this time Angelica had stared at me with an inexpressible degree of curiousness and assurance. Her only salutation was a slight bow, and an unpleasant—

"Good-morning."

Then she stared again, as much as to say, "Your bonnet cost about ten shillings, or, perhaps, eight-and-sixpence when new; the straw is middling, but the shape is last year's, and the ribbon was certainly never put on by a milliner; the dress is a tolerable quality, but do you know, young lady, that it's only muslins that are worn in the morning; *barèges* are by no means *à propos*; and your mantle is decidedly shabby. You must be very poor, and yet you don't look common, either. Poor and genteel, I suppose; how pitiable! You certainly never saw life or fashion, or you wouldn't wear your hair in that childish way. As to your look, I'm not yet decided, but I don't quite like you altogether."

Such was my reception by the two ladies; but, as to the Rev. Decimus Dowley, he did not honour me by a single word or nod of recognition. The fact was this—papa was by no means a favourite with the clergy at Ingham; he did not like them, and they knew it. But taken altogether they were not a pleasant or estimable class, and I do not wonder at poor papa's feelings with regard to them. The High Church preachers were pompous, bigoted, and uncharitable; the Low Church, vulgar, declamatory, and inordinately self-conceited; and both parties were somewhat unfriendly and jealous to each other. Now, papa did not agree with either he did not approve of fasting in Lent, and he read (if he were well enough to read at all) Sir Walter Scott on a Sunday, and did and said a good many things which, though really harmless, offended them greatly. So the Rev. Rector of St. Mary's-on-the-Mere visited the sins of the fathers upon the children ; never asked me to his annual child's festival, though all the other children in Ingham-Helmsley were there, and when he saw me enter, shy, blushing, and with downcast eyes, at rich Mrs. Dunstan's, gave me no smile or kindly look.

" Warne ; do you know anything of any Warnes here ? " said Mrs. Dunstan to the rector in an undertone of voice, but which was perfectly audible.

" Mr. Inglis Warne, the young lady's father ? oh yes."

Here Jeannie, with the quick intuition of a delicate mind, drew me to the farther end of the room, under pretext of showing me some fanciful shells of her own finding, but I could still hear something of the dialogue going on.

" Poor ? " asked Mrs. Dunstan, with intense curiosity.

" Very."

Here Mrs. Dunstan raised her hands and eyes, as some susceptible people do when particularly called on to exercise their tender feelings, and Mr. Dowley continued—

" Nice little property in Essex—married an heiress—highly extravagant—wife's guardian cheated—ruined in no time."

Mrs. Dunstan glanced at me, then wiped her eyes with a lace handkerchief, and said—

" The folly of some people is quite pitiable."

At which the Rev. Mr. Dowley looked as if he thought Mrs. Dunstan was very wise.

" I dare say you will wonder how she comes to be here to-day, but we know her only from a little adventure that happened two years ago to us when we were staying at—in this town I mean;" and then Mrs. Dunstan gave a little explanatory account of our first meeting, and concluded with—"I wish Jeannie had not taken such a fancy to her, as from her station and education she is so unfitted to be her companion; but it can't be helped, and Jeannie never imbibes bad habits or vulgarities, that's one comfort."

"What would Lindsay say if he heard you?" said Angelica, sarcastically; "he has taken quite a fancy to this child of nature, Mr. Dowley, and if I want to get him into a good humour, I always begin to sound her praises."

"It isn't so very often that Lindsay is out of temper with you," said Mrs. Dunstan, in a reproachful voice, which seemed to please Angelica very much. Soon the conversation turned on the topic of Mr. Stirling's marriage; Jeannie and I sat quietly at the open window at the other end of the room am using ourselves with pictures, and the conversation went on without restraint.

"To tell you the truth, Mr. Dowley," said Mrs. Dunstan, energetically, "when I first heard of it, I was quite humiliated; such an outrage on all dignity and on all high ranks of society. Sir, it's frightful!"

"Frightful!" echoed Angelica.

"Yes, so it is," answered Mr. Dowley; "so it is; and actually, madam—actually that very man has a brother a clergyman of the Church of England."

"What must his feelings have been, poor man!" ejaculeted Mrs. Dunstan, in a sort of sobbing manner.

"It would have been the death of me, I'm sure," said the rector, putting on somewhat of his pulpit solemnity. "The Lord be thanked that it was not."

"And to think—to think," added Mrs. Dunstan, with renewed vehemence, "that I was staying in the house of that very man, as a visitor—I, Mr. Jocelyn, who is nephew to a judge, and Angelica, my niece; to think that we should have been staying in his house only a few months before; the deceitful, heartless man!"

"The mystery to me is," said Angelica, "that people who do such horrid things can hold up their heads afterwards: I'm sure I should die at once."

Mr. Dowley said that he wished the world had only a particle of such fine feelings as Miss Laurison possessed; after which flattering speech he took his leave.

"A delightful man!" exclaimed Mrs. Dunstan.

"So funny, so amusing," joined in Angelica.

"And so beautifully pious," said the first.

"Not a bit like a clergyman," added the other.

After this both ladies went up-stairs to prepare for the morning drive; not before Mrs. Dunstan had told Jeannie, in a loud whisper, that she might ask me to dinner, if she liked, only not to get too intimate. We were very happy together; of all the frivolity, the worldliness, the vanity and pride I could see in Mrs. Dunstan and Angelica, there was not a trace in her. Though she was so superior to me in wealth, position, education and prospects, there was not a shade of arrogance or of that spirit of selfishness which spoiled children so often have. She was amiable, loving, and yielded to my wishes whenever I expressed any, however much they might differ from her own; and, in spite of the differences between us, we were sisters at once. Oh, how happy this new love made me! There was always something to look forward to, something to think of, something to hold in my own heart, and of which I felt none could rob me. My visits to Mrs. Dunstan were not all happiness; I confess they were not. I dreaded Angelica's inconsiderate and rude questions, and I shrank from Mrs. Dunstan's affected pity and sentimentality over my lonely lot; but once with Jeannie alone, and there was no cloud over our sky.

" I wish Angelica had never come from India," she said
to me one day, very earnestly.

" Why so; she is very kind to you ?"

" Oh yes! of course she would be kind to me, as she
lives with mamma, but I don't really think she likes me;
and I can't bear to hear her say such unfeeling things.
What business has she to question you as she does ? If
Lindsay were but here!—she wouldn't before him, I know;
and, Chatty, she used to get so angry last year when he
talked about you; and he used to talk all the more for
that."

The warm colour deepened on my cheek, and my heart
beat quickly, at Jeannie's word; not so much at the thought
of Angelica's unpleasantness as at the mention of Lindsay's
remembrance of me.

" She would do anything to please Lindsay," continued
Jeannie, indignantly, " she is so fond of him; but I
don't think he can like her, disagreeable, and proud, and
passionate as she is; he used to talk a great deal to her,
but teased her too, sometimes; and if he cared about her
much he wouldn't have done that. At least, I should
think not."

I smiled at Jeannie's logic, and she continued—

" Oh, how I hope he will come in September!"

" Do you expect him ?"

" Yes, mamma does, to stay with us; and some others
are coming, too. I long for the time, and yet I shall be
sorry."

" Sorry ?"

She put her arms around me lovingly, and kissed my
forehead.

" I don't wish the time to come for us to go away."

" Will you go, then ?" I exclaimed, aghast at the very
idea.

" Yes, I think we shall, in October ; at least, I am sure
we shall."

" And then I shall not see you again till another
summer ? "

" No," Jeannie answered, gravely.

We both sat in sad silence for some minutes. All the
long dreary winter months, the monotonous round of daily
life and daily trials came in perspective before my mind,
and the distant cloud took away, for the time, somewhat of
the present sunlight and joyfulness.

" I wish we were not going," Jeannie said, sorrowfully.
" I shall be shut up with a French governess all day long
in London, or sent to a school abroad, where I shall have
lessons to learn from morning till night, and no one I know
to speak to ; of course Angelica likes to be in London in
the winter ; for she and mamma go to parties, and theatres,
and operas every night, all the spring—the ' season' they
call it ; but I don't like my ' season' at all. It's all
German grammars, and French exercises, and sharps and
flats."

I thought Jeannie would like my " season " still less,
but said nothing. I had a sort of pride within me that
always made me reserved as to my own privations and the
res *angusta* at home. Less with Jeannie than any one was
I so constantly silent ; but Jeannie knew enough : she
knew how dear to me her sisterly love was, and the consciousness influenced her to be doubly tender and doubly
considerate.

" Never mind, Chatty, the winter will soon go," she said,
with a glowing tear-wet face ; " and I will love you all the
more when I am away."

My intercourse with the Dunstans was not without its
beneficial effects on poor papa. It was something to talk
about, to ask about. and to think of ; one visit of mine

sufficed for interesting matter of conversation for days.
There was, first of all, to hear how Mrs. Dunstan's dinner,
tea, or lunch was served, and all the dishes of which I
had to describe minutely; then there was to hear what
Mrs. Dunstan had said, what visitors I had seen, and her
opinions on the Ingham-Helmslionians, particularly the
clergymen—for papa was ever most curious to hear of those
for whom he felt a shade of unfriendliness.  So I always
felt that in going to see them, though I left him for a time,
I benefited him in the long run, and we were quite a lively
party at my return.   But the greatest liveliness I had ever
seen was one evening when I returned with the startling
intelligence that Mrs. Dunstan liked Mr. Decimus Dowley
better even than Mr. Vasey, who kept a carriage, and Mr.
Newton, who was nephew to a Bishop; and that Mrs.
Dunstan always went regularly to St. Mary's-on-the-Mere,
and had put her name first on his subscription list for
furnishing fifty ragged girls with a Bible, and fifty ragged
boys with whitey-brown shirts!

## CHAPTER X.

PAPA said—well, I don't think I ought to betray domestic
secrets, but Ellice thought master ought to know better,
and that he wasn't a bit religious.  Of course she only
whispered this to me in private with a smile; still, what
papa said isn't worth repeating: all I will say is, that he
was quite indignant with Mrs. Dunstan.

"What can she be thinking about!" he exclaimed,
vigorously, "to sit and hear a man like that, who rolls
his eyes, turns his mouth topsy-turvy, and lengthens his

words out like thunders in the distance. Chatty, I know that hearing him three Sundays running had a bad effect on me; it helped to bring on this nervousness."

Papa was continually finding different causes to which he attributed his maladies, but I do think in this case he was unjust; the sermons of the Rev. Rector of St. Mary's could not have hurt his nervous or susceptible organs much, for, as long as I can remember, whenever papa did go to church he invariably dozed when the prayers were over. He couldn't help it, I dare say, but I mildly suggested that I thought he would sleep more comfortably at home; and so, of late years, even before his paralytic attack, his attendance at church had been rare.

"Mr. Vasey is drony enough, to be sure, and Mr. Newton's broad Scotch affectation is insufferable, but Mr. Dowley—oh dear! if we had but a respectable preacher, it would be the making of me."

"I should not mind the preaching so much," my father continued, "if we had but a man whose character was within a little what it ought to be; but to be preached to by such men as Mr.—— pshaw! it makes me out of patience: and a good, sensible, humble man to talk to, I tell you, it would do me a world of good. I don't want any of the now-a-day clergymen, who will leave one of their trashy tracts, and be too proud to shake hands with you, but one who would really be friendly and sociable. I believe if I had a little society I should get better."

When papa was in a discontented strain it was best to let him go on and have all his grumble out; it refreshed him, so I said nothing.

"There is no one here to speak to," he added; "people with money won't look at us, because we are poor, and people without money make it up in pride. What a thing it is to be poor!—the world can forgive anything but that."

" It didn't forgive Mr. Stirling," I said, smilingly.

" Ah ! if every one else were but like him ! He wouldn't despise us because we are poor, Chatty ; I knew him some years ago. I wonder——"

" Knew Mr. Stirling, father ? I never heard you say so before."

A very grave, anxious look passed over papa's face, and when he spoke his voice was troubled ; it always was when he recalled the far-off time—the time of his happiness, and prosperity and youth.

"Yes, I saw him once or twice at——at, I forget where ; but it's a long time ago—a long time ago—he was not above twenty then ; I wonder whether he would know me now !"

" Would you like to see him, papa dear ? "

" If we were differently placed. But to ask any one like him to a place like this ! If we kept two servants, and had a new carpet in the parlour, it would not matter so much."

" I should not think Mr. Stirling would think less of us for that," I said, thoughtfully. "I wish that he knew you were here, papa ; I know you would like to see him."

Papa sighed deeply.

" If we were a little better off, Chatty, I should, but now ——"

I said no more at the time, but turned the subject over in my head, as I sat busily employed on my Saturday's household mending and darning. I wished so much that Mr. Stirling could come and see papa ; he sadly needed cheerful, intelligent society, and at present he had none. Ellice and I never left him for a moment, and did our best to cheer his mind and lighten his heart ; still, a change, such as Mr. Stirling's intercourse would be, I felt convinced would bring inestimable benefit. Mr. Bean often called in, and his visits for the time were of good effect ; but papa

looked upon them as professional. He knew that the kind
doctor tried his utmost to amuse, entertain, and soothe
him; but, except as his Ingham life was concerned, they
were total strangers. There was no link connecting Mr.
Bean to the past (for however sad the past may have been,
the heart will cling to it when little is left), and though he
amused him with stories, and gossip, and philosophical
discourse, a word—a recollection—a rumour of Essex, the
beloved Essex of youth, wealth, and love, would have been
to him worth them all. It was otherwise with Mr. Stirling;
papa had had little intercourse with him, but it had taken
place in the palmy days, the "olim" of fortune and friends.
Mr. Stirling would not address him and regard him as poor,
paralytic, nervous, bankrupt Mr. Warne, of out-of-the-way,
bleak, cheap-living Ingham, but as the Inglis Warne, Esq.,
of Arrowmere, and parks, and riches, and plenty, the owner
of estates, and the husband of a lord's daughter.

Going back to old memories like this, oppressed my heart
with a gloomy sadness; and I put the thoughts away, and
thanked Heaven, with glad and rejoicing spirits, for the
new blessing that had fallen in my path. Dear, dear
Jeannie; it always made me happy to think of you!

I felt a strange, yearning, wistful sensation the next time
I passed Mr. Stirling's house; I longed to enter and tell
him that his entertainer of former days was in poverty,
affliction, and despondency; to ask him to go to him for
the sake of those former days and remembrances. But it
was impossible, and so I lingered and passed on.

"Chatty," said Angelica to me one day, "will you be so
obliging as to favour me with your name in full length? It
is so excessively curious, and I always forget it."

I think it must have been the fiftieth time Angelica had
asked me my name; however, I answered patiently—
"Charlton Warne."

"Ah, Charlton Warne, that's it! I thought it was Warner, or Warren, or Warring, or something of the sort; and pray who gave you that absurd name, my dear?"

"Charlton was mamma's name," I replied, timidly.

Mrs. Dunstan looked astonished, and half rose from her easy chair.

"And was your mamma related to the Charltons of Haverwick, do you know?"

"Mamma was their cousin."

"Dear me, how very curious!"

Then she said, in a low voice, to Angelica—

"One of the first families in the county. How queer! I can't make it out."

They had a further discussion about it, when I chatted with Jeannie at the farther end of the room; and I heard Angelica exclaim—

"Of course it's something of that sort, or why don't the rest of the family notice them?"

And Mrs. Dunstan added—

"It would be satisfactory to know. I wish Jeannie had never been allowed to know her, some people are so queer."

"Mr. Dowley said something about a dishonest steward——"

"Ah, I forgot! but you know, my love, that Mr. Dowley is a clergyman, and that clergymen make the best of everything."

"And I dare say he goes by hearsay," Angelica replied, 'th a yawn; "how should people here know anything about Mr. Warne or Mr. Warne's doings?"

"After all," Mrs. Dunstan interrupted, consolingly, "it's a comfort to think they have been well off once; and Chatty isn't so much amiss."

All the pride of my nature—the renowned Charlton pride —rose within me as I listened, or rather as I heard the

conversation which was carried on in the front room. I felt
as if I could never come to the house again—as if it were
impossible for me ever to meet Mrs. Dunstan and Angelica
with kindness and unmeaning courtesy. The hot blood
rushed to my temples, the bitter, bitter tears filled my eyes,
and there was an angry, quick beating at my heart. But I
subdued it; for the love of Jeannie I subdued it. Thank
God I was enabled to do so!

One day Jeannie asked me very gravely to let her visit
my father and my home; she wished so much, she said, to see
the spot where she had first met Chatty, and to be enabled
to think of me as at the White House; she wished to asso-
ciate round her recollection of her friend all the atmosphere
of home, daily life, daily surroundings, and—for I loved
Jeannie too much to be proud with her—I consented. With
all the simplicity of her nature, there was a refinement of
feeling, and a delicacy of intuition, that I never saw in any
one before; and with this simplicity and refinement was a
naïve freshness and frankness that was perfectly bewitching
to me—poor, lonely, friendless as I was, and to whom no
one had ever appealed before in love, and trust, and un-
bounded candour of affection. What a happy afternoon we
spent together! Papa was somewhat upset, and half smiled
and half cried all the time to see my eyes and cheeks bright
with pleasure, but there was no other drawback. I quite
forgot the grand Helmsley-End Hall, Mrs. Dunstan, and
Angelica altogether, and led Jeannie all over the house.
And she did not seem surprised at the poverty and simplicity of everything. Then I told her for the first time (for
this visit of Jeannie's seemed a new bond of love and sister-
hood) the daily occupations, house-keeping duties, economical ways, and all the various *et cetera* of my humble at-
home life. For a while Jeannie listened with wondering
eyes, and interrupted me ever and anon by exclamations of

surprise, but as I went on, and she comprehended in full
the privations and trials to which I was subject, over her
bright face fell a shadow of deep thought and sorrow, and
she spoke no more.

When she was gone, I returned to the little parlour with
a heart full of quiet happiness, and, seating myself by papa,
said gaily—

"Have I not done the honours well, father dear?"

But papa did not speak, and when I looked up I saw that
he was weeping bitterly.

"Oh, papa, papa, don't cry, what is it?" I exclaimed,
kissing his forehead over and over again.

"Do tell me, papa dear?"

"Chatty," he broke forth, in passionate heart-breaking
tones, "oh, Chatty, my poor little girl, my darling, it
breaks my heart to think of the hard, hard lot to which
I have brought you. To think that my Chatty—my only
one, my Helen's baby—should come to this! to be poor and
pinched, and to waste her childhood, when labourers' children can play and be happy; to think that your young
health and hopefulness should be destroyed in waiting on
me, wretched, discontented, miserable that I am—oh! I
cannot bear it. What have I done, that my innocent child
should suffer? Heaven help me, if——"

I felt a thick, sobbing sensation at my throat, as if I could
not utter a word; and my eyes were blinded with burning
tears, but I must be firm; Mr. Bean told me I *must* be firm,
and I made a desperate effort, and said calmly—

"I am happy enough, papa; what have I to wish
for?"

"God bless you, my dear, dear child; my poor patient,
good little Chatty. Oh, my God, have pity!"

Again I felt as if I were choking, but strong fear and
stronger love controlled me. After much persuasion and

coaxing he was gradually pacified, and by leading him on to other topics, the agitation gradually subsided.

Father in Heaven, aid me, aid me to do my duty, to be patient, watchful and long-suffering, even as Thou, O Father, never growest weary of Thy care for us !

---

## CHAPTER XI.

"PERHAPS you remember Lindsay—Mr. Jocelyn—Miss Warne ?"

I started involuntarily at Mrs. Dunstan's question ; and blushed deeply.

" Oh yes, I have seen him——"

" Why, dear mamma," interposed Jeannie, smiling, " don't you remember Lindsay telling us last summer that he had been down to Ingham and had seen Chatty ?"

" Ah, very likely I did, but my memory is so bad about those things ; and what time of the year was it, my love ?"

This question was addressed to me ; but Angelica's eyes were flashing on me, and provoked me to composure. I therefore answered coolly—

" Mr. Jocelyn came many times."

Mrs. Dunstan looked puzzled, and turned to Angelica ; a mutual expression of "What does it mean ?" passed from one to the other, and then they both fixed their eyes on me ; Mrs. Dunstan's inquisitively, Angelica's with searching scrutiny. But I was determined they should read nothing, and said, carelessly :—

" I think Mr. Jocelyn likes Ingham in summer time."

After that day the subject was never resumed. I avoided

it studiously, and Mrs. Dunstan blushed and Angelica curled her lip when Lindsay's name was mentioned in conjunction with Ingham. But I felt that from this might be dated a rivalry between Angelica and myself; antipathy, there had always been on her part; now there was more—there was positive aversion.

And, strange to say, from that day there was no more surmising as to the period of Lindsay's visit at Helmsley-End Hall. What had formerly been such a topic of antici- pation and discussion was never now recurred to, and there was some talk of leaving Ingham in September. Why was this? It perplexed me deeply. Angelica ruled Mrs. Dunstan, and Angelica was jealous; perhaps so. Might not this account . . . . . Yet I will not be uncharitable.

But why had not Lindsay come? Oh, why had he not come? My heart grew sad for longing, and my cheek pale from thought and love of him. Lindsay, Lindsay, is all this hope, and love, and yearning for thee in vain?

At length the month of August drew to a close; and one day, whilst I was at Mrs. Dunstan's, a letter came from Lindsay; she read it hastily, and then said, with a peculiar emphasis—

"I thought so: Lindsay is not coming to Ingham this autumn, and has agreed to join a party to the lakes. He would be so pleased if we could go also."

She handed the letter to Angelica, whose brow contracted as she read.

"Eh bien; qu'en pensez vous, ma chère?"

Mrs. Dunstan and Angelica often had little private con- versations in French; they knew that I did not understand the language.

"Qu'en pensez-vous?" said the elder lady, repeating the question.

5

Angelica threw the letter on the table, and curled her lip.

" Je ne resterai pas ici, et je n'y vais pas," she said, in a voice of strong resolution.

" Mais où aller ?"

" Où vous voudrez."

" Ce m'est égal."

" Et à moi aussi."

Angelica moved away with impatience, and poor Mrs. Dunstan continued watching her uneasily. Just then Jeannie entered ; the letter was hastily put aside.

" A disappointment for you, my love ; Lindsay cannot come ; that is, you know, we are going away."

" Oh, not yet, mamma."

" Yes, my dear ; Angelica's—I mean my wishes must be considered."

" But, mamma dear, why cannot Lindsay come ?"

" Why, that is his own affair ; he has no shooting here, you know, and I think he is going to the lakes."

" But he won't have shooting there."

" Well, at any rate he doesn't have it here, and besides, my dear, we are going away."

" But I thought that if Lindsay came you were not going away yet."

Mrs. Dunstan looked slightly confused.

" It can't be helped, Jeannie," she said, petulantly ; " why make such a fuss about it ? It is very unamiable when I arrange a plan to be so discontented with it."

Tears came into Jeannie's eyes, and she said no more. I was sorely puzzled. Some underhand work had evidently been done. One thing was clear ; Lindsay's visit to the lakes was only a mere idea which Mrs. Dunstan had taken possession of, for her own purpose, and that Angelica was the mover of it all. Anything to keep Lindsay away from Ingham ; this was the one end and aim of the whole affair ;

and so far it had succeeded. Oh, when should I see him again !

" Then you won't forget me, Jeannie ?"

" Never ; if we are away twenty years instead of one, I promise you."

It was a mild, damp day in autumn ; Mrs. Dunstan and Angelica were paying farewell visits in Ingham ; Jeannie and I sat alone together, and with the confiding hope of children, as we were, looked into the future life, and drew a fair and perfect picture therein.

" The time will soon go, dear," she continued, hopefully, "and then, when we come here next year, I can teach you French, and German, and drawing; won't that be nice ? We can have the little breakfast-room to ourselves, and I know you will get on ten times faster at them than I. Oh, Chatty, how I long for the time !"

"And if Mrs. Dunstan will not come ?"

" Yes, she will—I know she will; because she has spoken for the house again. It will all be right; I know it will all be right, dear, if we have patience to wait."

And then she put her arms round me, and called me her sister—her own dear sister.

Slowly, very slowly, I returned from my farewell visit to Mrs. Dunstan's ; I could hardly realize that I had parted from Jeannie ; that so much of the brightness and sweetness was taken from my daily life ; that I was again solitary, again companionless ! But it was so ; many months, perhaps years, might elapse before I should see her once more, and meantime the changeless round of trials would return for me daily. My father's recovery was not to be reasonably expected now ; it was impossible. Mr. Bean had almost said so, and I felt that I must rather prepare myself for increasing infirmity, and increasing depression of spirits. And there was no prospect of a change in outward circumstances; no possible, or probable chance of an altered condition, or of even a partial return of fortune. Oh no, I must not hope for that now; but I had hoped for it once; as a little child I used to dream of it when sitting at my father's side; thoughtful, visionary as I was now at seventeen I had been at twelve, and I had pictured to myself papa, well, strong, and happy, re-installed in the antique, gorgeous mansion of Arrowmere, and surrounded by his old friends and tenantry, drinking his health and mine! Young as I was even yet, I felt now that the dream could never be true. A reality was before me far different, and for that I must nerve myself and be strong. I must look to the recurrence of old days, and nothing more, save as the thoughts of Jeannie, and the hope of meeting *him* again, cast an enchantment over the future. Plaints, desponding fretfulness, and utter prostration of mind and body, all these I must meet with patient endurance, un-wearied care, watchful love; and even such were a poor recompense for the depth of my father's sorrowful affection. Oh, I would try hard to soften the bitterness of his lot—I would try very hard to do the duty of a loving child, with Heaven's blessing.

I stole upstairs into my little bedroom with careful, noiseless steps; I did not wish my father to see the tears that streamed down my cheeks, so I shut the door softly, and sat down by the window. It was not yet five o'clock, and already thick mists and fogs were gathering round the low grass lands and heaths, and hiding the distant town. My poor little garden looked very dreary; the tall-leafed artichoke-plants stood up in the midst, straight, yellow and desolate—all else was bare, leafless, broken, and withered. Beyond lay the sea, dim, hazy, and deep purple in the partial light. How immense, how grand, how fearless it looked! I grew sadder as I gazed on it; its terrible vast-ness and chainless freedom were so contrasted to the poor-ness and humility of my lot, over which I had no control. As I contemplated it, a feeling of longing came over me—a longing for somewhat of its power, of its freedom, of its nobility. Then I thought of Lindsay, and grew calm.

When I entered the little parlour, papa was talking to our old cat, Bailie, who looked up into his face with a comical look of contemplative sympathy; the fire burned brightly in the grate, and the water in the kettle sang with a cheerful social sound; papa turned towards me with an expression of intense relief on his face.

" What a time you have been gone, dearie! I have been so dull; I believe it must be seven o'clock. Well, is Mrs. Dunstan gone ? "

" Not till to-morrow, papa."

" And has she decided where to go at last ? "

" Yes, to London, and on to Paris with Jeannie. She is going to remain in a school there for a year."

" And when will they come here again, then ? "

" Next autumn, perhaps; but I am afraid it won't be so soon. I think it all depends more upon Angelica than any one."

" That young lady from India ? Is Mrs. Dunstan so very fond of her ? "

" I don't think it's much affection, papa—at least Jeannie says so—but that is more because Angelica has a violent temper, and if she cannot have her own way in everything sulks and pouts the whole day long, and poor Mrs. Dunstan has no one to speak to, and go out with."

" Those Indian-born people are always fiery—did you not say that this Miss Laurison is very rich ? "

" Yes ; her father was a planter."

My father looked into the fire musingly.

" And did you not say that that young man—Mr.—— I mean the friend of Mrs. Dunstan's——"

"Jocelyn—Mr. Jocelyn."

" Yes; did you not say he was a barrister ? "

" Yes."

" No doubt he will marry this rich girl: it would be a good match," said papa, in the same reflective manner.

" Lindsay marry Angelica, father dear ! "

I was speaking quite in a voice of alarm, and broke off.

" Why not ? you say she is rich, and young, and—— What sort of looking girl did you say she was, Chatty ?"

It was rather difficult for me to define my idea of Angelica's face ; she was certainly good looking, that is, if good looks consist in regular features, dark hair, and clear complexion ; but, whether it was something in the expression of her eyes, or the outline of her mouth, I cannot say; I only know that I never saw any one's countenance that was less pleasing to me than hers.

"Jeannie says people call her handsome, papa, but I don't think so at all; perhaps it is because I don't like her."

" Ten to one if they don't make a match of it," rejoined my father, quite interested in his supposition; " I do not see any obstacle at all ; she would never refuse a handsome young man like that. How I should like a piece of toast."

" I'll soon make some," I said, starting up.

" No ; it's time for you to pour out the tea; I'm dreadfully thirsty."

" But Ellice can do it whilst I'm after the tea."

" No, never mind, I don't care about it, and servants never know how to toast properly. What blue-looking milk ! I believe it's half water—people always impose on such as us, poor and genteel; it's horrid to be poor and

genteel! every one despises you. To think that we cannot
get new milk even after paying for it! At one time I
couldn't touch tea without cream, and now if we could only
have what the servants used to give the cats at Arrowmore
I should be content."

But I did not let papa complain of the milk again; every
morning I put a small quantity into a flat dish, and skimmed
off the cream which had arisen by tea-time. So he said the
milk was really much better; he believed the dairyman must
have bought a cow of the Arrowmere breed; no others gave
such milk.

After a few days, Jeannie wrote to me. It was a short
letter, but it brought me immeasurable pleasure; she described the journey to London, the house in Belgrave
Square, the thick fogs and black mud. Mrs. Dunstan and
Angelica were going to take her to Paris, where she was to
remain a year, to finish her education. There was a post-
script, which, after the first reading, was engraved word for
word on my heart.

"Lindsay called on us yesterday; he asked me a hundred
questions about you. Mamma and Angelica seemed rather
cool to him; I cannot understand it at all. He seemed so
sorry that he was not coming to Ingham. He has been
very busy."

I read the letter over and over again, and then put it
carefully in my work-box; and even when the formation of
every letter was familiar to me, it was a pleasure to me ever
and anon to look at it. My mind was differently employed
to what it once had been, as I sat over my sewing, or busied
myself in my household occupations. I was not so constantly day-dreaming; picturing all sorts of impossible
happiness, all sorts of visionary existence and fanciful fairy-
land hopes. This was in my childhood; now I had something real to think of and hope for; and the contemplation

lent a new charm to my life and a new contentment to my heart.

He had not forgotten me, then; oh, how joyful Jeannie's letter made me! He was not changed. If he loved me once, he loved me still;—happy—happy thought!

But then, why this long absence? Was his love like mine? Even in my radiant Eden, must a serpent enter? I was sad and joyful alternately.

---

## CHAPTER XII.

My father still talked wistfully of Mr. Stirling. His name was an awakener of old memories—the sad, sweet music of joy and sunshine gone; and he spoke more frequently of those halcyon days now. When I sat by his side at the dusk hour, and all was silent save the booming noise of the waves, a subdued and more patient mood of grief seemed to steal over him. He spoke of my mother, of her tenderness and of her beauty; of Arrowmere; of jovial friends and happy hours. There was no bitterness in his regret, no vehemence in his sadness, at such times; but the tears that stole one by one down his wasted cheeks, appeared to relieve and soften the despondency of his spirit.

How I longed for Mr. Stirling! but whenever I mentioned the slightest chance of his coming, papa raised an infinity of objections. I tried to think of a plan by which I could contrive a visit from him which should be almost accidental, but could hit on none. I feared papa's vexation and Mr. Stirling's annoyance; still, the subject was constantly on my mind. It seemed to me that the intercourse with him

was to be a sort of angel visit—a panacea for papa's *ennui*
and restlessness; he spoke of him as of a being of a higher
sphere, with a reverential commenting on his virtues, as if
they removed him from all other men.  Surely the influence
of such a mind and character would be an evangelus of
peace and calmness to a heart like my father's, broken-
down, wearied, heavily-laden.

My love for Lindsay, and Jeannie's friendship, made me
ambitious.  I thirsted for a means of cultivating the talents
which God had given me, and without which cultivation I
felt unfit for the sphere in which they moved; and in this,
though there were many obstacles, I resolved to succeed.
I felt my need of more strict intellectual training than I
had received from the course of my miscellaneous and most
varied readings.  I had read enough to make me curious
and eager for knowledge, but not enough to form my taste
and correct my judgment.  Besides, the thought occurred
to me, I might one day have to earn my own living; knowledge was not only useful to me, it was essential.  The first
thing I did was to go to Mr. Binnie, who foraged up a heap
of grammar, history, and geography, which I carried home
to read, mark, and inwardly digest.

But these did not satisfy me.  One day, last year—how
well I remembered it!—we were sitting together by the
beach, Lindsay and I, and somehow our conversation turned
upon the superiority of the education of boys to that of girls.

" I wish you understood Latin, Chatty," he said.

" Why do you wish so?" I asked.

" Because there is a vigour and stern beauty in the
language, which you would comprehend and appreciate
better than many others."

And ever after that I longed to learn Latin; and, after
many cogitations in my own mind, set off one day to
Mr. Bean's.

" Ah ! how d'ye do ? " said the little doctor, rubbing his
hands, as if with a kind of mental glee; " it's very sensible
of you to take a run this fine day. Exercise is the key of
health, you know, eh ? What fine noble fellows the Greeks
and Romans were, eh ? and they didn't sit over the fire all
day, in arm-chairs and felt slippers, eh ? they knew better.
We're not half so clever, with all the steam, and daguerreo-
type, and telegraph, and science, to help us. We haven't
half such heads; but it is the natural consequence—don't
you see everything is made so easy for us that we are not
spurred on; everything astonishing and impossible has been
accomplished, and if you want to be great now you must
find a way to the moon; we won't look at any one who can't
do that. I say, if you want to be great you must find a
way to the moon—eh, Chatty ? "

I laughed; and then, in a hesitating voice, spoke my
errand. I had been thinking, I told him, that I ought to
be learning something useful, as I could not tell what might
happen; and I thought if he would lend me some Latin
books——

" Bravo ! " said the little excitable man, vigorously, and
with the speed of lightning mounted some wooden steps,
behind which were two or three cases of books. " Bravo !
there isn't a language that can hold a candle to it—a wax
candle in a silver stick—I say it's the cream, and pith, and
indestructible essence of all languages—the *succus subtil-
lissimus* of that wonderful thing called language. The tongue
of Cicero—of Virgil—what could you learn better ? What
is all the harmony of catgut and wires in the world to
eloquence like theirs ? Pshaw ! it's a mere nothing, a
mere sound and idle amusement. You are right, Chatty ;
go to the classics,—go to the fountain-head. Classics for
ever ! Well, to begin. Here's a grammar, somewhat yellow
and dusty, but, like me, not a bit the worse for the wear.

Learn it through; if you can't understand it at first, learn till you do. Then you come to translating. Here's ' C. Julii Cæsaris de Bello Gallico Commentariorum.' The very book; you couldn't have a better; and here's a dictionary, half as big as yourself. When you have transferred the contents of the grammar to your head, take to Julius Cæsar. Translate every minute you can. If you don't make sense, make nonsense; anyhow translate, and when you have got through one book come to me. I will then tell you how Latin ought to be read, and anything else you want to know. And when you quite understand it, I will teach you Greek. Set to work hard, you'll soon master all the ups and downs, and in a year or two—come, I'll be bound to say Ingham won't be able to produce another young lady like you. All right, I know you will persevere. Remember me to papa. Good-by."

"Thank you, sir," I said, holding out my hand.

"Don't thank me, you have nothing to thank me for; thank yourself for your good sense and perseverance : or, rather, thank God—and so go on, little Chatty, working, working, working, till you attain not only to the complementum of knowledge but of goodness also. Ha! I think we shall have a shower; but it won't be yet, not till you're home; that's right, run."

So I set to work over my Latin books and histories to lay the first foundation of my own intellectual culture ; I set to work to render myself worthy of friendship and of Lindsay. In solitude, in difficulty, in various disadvantages, was the work begun. Ah! how would it be finished ?

Much as I wished it, I could not secrete my occupations from papa. I had to be so constantly with him that most of my study hours, excepting those I stole from my night's rest, were taken as we sat together in the little parlour. One morning, after eyeing the books uneasily, he said—

"I don't see the use of your poring over those things so by yourself, poor little dear; you ought to have some one to teach you."

"But Mr. Bean helps me, papa," I said.

"What use will it ever be to you? What on earth put it into your head to try and learn?" continued my father, in an unsatisfied tone of voice.

"Knowledge is always useful, of any kind," I said, bending my face over the open page, for I did not wish to divulge either of the reasons which had induced me to begin seriously studying.

But I think poor papa guessed one, for he put his hand caressingly on my head, and said, in a mournful voice—

"Pray God you may never come to worse than this, dearie."

Every spare moment was devoted to this work of self-improvement. My desultory reading,—all the travels, and poems, and life stories, with which I had formerly amused myself in my leisure time, were put aside. To remedy the deficiencies of early instruction was now my sole aim; so I read, wrote, and learned with a good and earnest heart. Accomplishments—refinements, as Mrs. Dunstan called them—were far out of my reach; but so long as I was well-informed and intellectual, I thought that neither she nor Angelica would think me unfit to be Jeannie's companion. Still I sighed over the music sometimes, and thought of the pleasure a piano would give papa, but it was no use.

"Dear, dear Chatty," wrote my warm-hearted Jeannie, "how I wish you were here, and were to be one of this soft-speaking, flounced-out madame's pupils, till next holidays. I don't dislike being at this school so very much, after all. I like it ten times better than being in Belgrave Square, shut up with a French governess, and showed down every day after dinner to play 'La Violette' or 'The Wedding

March.'   We are very near the Tuilleries Gardens, and
walk in every day, where we see a good many people and
——but I forget what I was going to say, and will begin
something else.   We don't breakfast till twelve, or dine till
five, and have no tea or lunch—isn't it funny? but then we
eat all the more at breakfast, so it is the same in the end;
and all the little ones have their meals separate with the
governesses.   There are three governesses, one a Parisienne,
one a Swiss, and one an English lady.   The Parisienne is
the smartest and pleasantest, but gets dreadfully into debt,
and doesn't hear half the lessons when madame is out of
the class-room (there are four class-rooms), which some of
the girls like, but I don't think it's right, do you?   The
Swiss is very good-natured, but very stupid and sleepy, and
the girls make fun of her, and mimic her ways and manners,
the minute her back is turned;   and the English teacher is
starch, stiff, and prim, the pattern of good principles and
bad temper.   Her name is Vince; oh, she has such sharp
eyes! they are everywhere at the same time, and nothing
pleases her better than to find something wrong, and make
a fuss about it.   I know that people ought to be conscien-
tious, and that lessons should not be skipped over, or sums
rubbed out; but I don't think she has any business to go
spying about as she does; it only makes the girls more sly,
for you know, Chatty, that school-girls are generally rather
defective in moral principles, as mamma says.   If they can
get any one to do anything for them they won't mind passing
it over as theirs, and if they can get off anything they will.
But I don't like Miss Vince to tell tales; and I can't help
thinking she often does more harm than good.   You ask me
if I learn a good deal.   I don't know, I'm sure.   I practise
on the piano two hours and a half every day; have lessons
in drawing, music, dancing, and Italian twice a week; speak
German or French all school-hours: hear a French book

read to us all breakfast time, and a lecture on astronomy and general physics once a week by a M. Le Duc, a professor at college or institute or something; write out a verb every blessed morning before the clock strikes seven, and all the spare minutes read out of a little book called 'Boileau's Satires.' I like music very much, but all the rest, excepting dancing, I hate. As to the German, Chatty, it's positively abominable. I am afraid I shall never know enough to teach you, but you can have all my books; and, let me see, one—two—three, I think I have seven altogether. The French girls here (half the pupils are French and half English) are very quick at learning, but very lazy and dilatory, not half so persevering as the English ones. I believe if you were here you would learn quicker than any one. Some of the girls tell stories often! it's very wrong, isn't it? but they don't seem to think anything of it, and the French governess never corrects them. Madame often goes to the theatre on a Sunday evening, and nearly all the shops are open till noontime. I wonder it is allowed. I can't write any more as it's breakfast-time. Good-by. Write soon. Oh, how I long to see you!"

The spring was a long, and cold, and dreary one. There were no heavy falls of snow, such as make everything look strangely beautiful and unearthlike, but continuous dry, sharp, biting winds, with now and then showers of sleet that rattled against our rickety, unsound windows like near thunder. Situated as our lonely dwelling was on a high, bare hill, we got an unusual share of cold and wind; and, though we kept a bright fire in the little parlour, and shut the doors tight, and put up screens to keep out the draughts, within half a dozen yards of it the atmosphere was chill, and if I ran upstairs and only stayed a minute I came down with benumbed hands and shivering frame. My studies went on slowly. Papa was confined all day to the

fire, and his arm-chair; I did not like to sit by him in
silence long together, and a great part of the day was spent
over work, so that I could be more companionable. The
days passed with no variation except Jeannie's letters, but
summer was coming, and I was cheerful. How dreary the
White House looked! I could not help thinking so, as I
returned from my daily run with glowing cheeks and disordered hair. The dark rocks, sombre and gloomy, around
and beneath it, and a leaden sky over its white, ghost-like
shadow, for it looked like a shadow of some other world, so
solitary, so isolated, so far away from all other signs of
man's habitation and home.

"What a dismal place to live in!" said my father one
day, looking out of the window, "and yet I don't think
I should mind it, if it were not for you, Chatty; it's such a
dismal place for you, my poor little girl; and so young as
you are, too, you ought to be happy."

"I am happy, papa," I said, energetically; "don't think
about me; I don't mind being dull so long as I have you to
talk to, and Jeannie will soon be back again."

"I wish I could talk to you cheerfully, and be more like
a companion, Chatty; I wish I were more like what I used
to be: I didn't want my spirits and humour so much then.
But all went at once—health, spirits, fortune, and friends,
and only the wreck is left for you as a heritage; only a poor,
broken wreck. Heaven help me! I know I should not
complain, but it seems so hard upon my poor, helpless, innocent, patient Chatty."

"I won't be patient if you talk so, papa," I said, cheerfully and fondly. "I am sure if I had seen you before—
before your illness and troubles, I couldn't have loved you
better than I do now; but I won't have you talk so, papa, I
won't indeed."

Then I kissed him affectionately, and said, in a jesting

voice, that I wondered how he could bear with me at all, I was such a little headstrong self-willed thing, and actually poor papa smiled as he stroked my cheek, saying—

" You are so like your mother, dearie ! "

And often now he would liken me to the beloved one gone ; and, after watching me in silence, would murmur softly and sadly—

" Helen Charlton ! "

---

## CHAPTER XIII.

" Rue du Mont Parnasse,
" Faubourg St. Germain.

" It won't be long now, Chatty—it won't be long now. Oh, how glad I am that I shall soon be into the dear little town by the coast ! I am getting on better with the Ger-man, and so, perhaps, shall be able to help you a little, and——But I am forgetting the principal thing I have to tell you. Who do you think came to see me yesterday? None other but Lindsay ; I can't tell you how delighted I was to see him ; and he looked so handsome ! and when he walked in the Tuilleries Gardens with me, I could not but contrast him with all the other men we saw ; there was not one who was half so manly and strong and tall as he. Well, the Ingham stay will be managed all right this year, for he has promised to persuade mamma, and mamma, or any one else either, can't resist him, you know. He seemed so pleased that you and I corresponded, and said he should be delighted to see you again, and that he had been working dreadfully hard or he would have run down, many and many a time. He asked a hundred questions about you, and is

coming down to Ingham in October, as he laughed and said
that he had got in high favour of late with mamma and
Angelica. I think mamma will invite some other visitors
to Ingham as well, but nothing will hinder our enjoyment.
Oh, the long, long walks we shall have together on the
shore! If I can, I shall persuade mamma to remain at
Helmsley-End till March. She says Ingham is so cold in
winter—is it? I don't think I should mind the cold. Next
spring I shall 'come out;' I wish there was not such a
thing as coming out, or that we could take things quieter.
I dare say I shall like some part of the coming out very
well; but I have never looked forward to it as most girls do.
I hope the gaiety won't alter me. It never will alter my
affection for you, Chatty, but I mean that it will never
make me heartless, and selfish, and world-loving, like——
but I won't say whom I mean. I ought not to judge. I am
getting heartily tired of this school. At seventeen, one is
too old for school; although my school consists now only in
lessons from masters, readings, compositions, &c. Fancy,
in music, I have one master to teach taste, and another
execution! There is not one pupil here that I can make a
companion of: the French girls flatter and coax me over, as
if I were a baby, and then try to get something out of me;
and the English ones talk so much nonsense, and have so
many childish secrets, and ridiculous school-girls' ways,
that I am very wearied of them all. There is no one here
like you, dear, nor I suppose another Chatty in the whole
world. At least, I think so. Good-by. Write soon.

"P.S. Have you got still that white muslin dress, worked
with pink spots, which you used to wear? Some one said
you looked so pretty in it!"

Jeannie's letter made me very happy. I sat holding it
in my hands for some minutes, with a smile upon my lips,
drawing a bright picture of the meeting in October. Then,

actuated by some unaccountable impulse, I went upstairs, and put on the dress I had worn during Lindsay's visits. I was quite a child in my exuberance and hopefulness of spirits. I felt as if I trod on ambient air—as if I breathed a new atmosphere, and had discovered a new world, and like Columbus's it was fair, and rich in gold. For the first time in my life, I experienced somewhat of a woman's vanity—for the first time, I felt how delightful to be beautiful in the eyes of him I loved. I stood before the looking-glass, in irresolute contemplature. I wanted to draw a conclusion with respect to myself—to feel assured whether or no I could boast of aught graceful or lovely to please his eyes. I could not quite arrive at a decision. I had in my mind no standard of beauty save that which should be beauty to him; and no ideal of perfection, beyond a thing which he could love. Perhaps of all the female faces I had ever seen, Angelica's was the handsomest; yet I had never seen one which had charmed me less. Jeannie's arch smile, ingenuousness, and sweetness of expression, even without entire regularity of features, to me, was far more loveable and engaging, and I could hardly imagine any one who would not think as I did. But I was so totally different to both Angelica and Jeannie that this conclusion in no way helped me. There was a sparkle in my eyes of hope and present gladness—a brightness on my cheek of youthful freshness and healthfulness—a look of thoughtfulness, almost seriousness, about my mouth, at times mingled with eager joy—but that was all; I could go no farther, excepting as I matched my hair with the dark-brown colour of the rocks. I could not tell, or guess even, if my face was a tale-teller of my inner life and mind; if my emotions were shown in it—whether the depth and tenderness of my heart—whether my capability of loving, my power of endurance, my ardent and enthusiastic impulses, my impetuous seeking and loving

of goodness and beauty——Were all these shut tight down,
and locked up within ?—all that I considered most amiable
and worthy in my nature hidden always ?   I hoped not—I
believed not, but I was not assured.   Circumstance and
habit had so accustomed me to restraint and self-control-
ment, that I almost feared it might have grown to a constant
and dull quietness, ere I was aware.   And yet no . . . .
He had not said so.

So I put on the same light summer dress, the cheap,
pretty muslin, which had cost Ellice such a heap of pains
and pride in the doing up, and went to church; for it was a
Sunday morning: and henceforth I resolved to keep |it for
high-days and sunshine holidays; his words had hallowed it,
his memory endeared it.   Ah, what a little thing suffices to
make us happy !

Thus the days pass.   I have been reading nothing lately
but Fenimore Cooper's novels.   I should never have thought
of reading them myself, for I have little love for novels of
any sort, but he recommended them to me, and I am
anxious to be able to give my opinion of them.   Mr. Bean
comes in sometimes, and is as kind as ever.   I still go on
perseveringly with the Latin; but, somehow, I have now no
fears for the future; I do not look into the far, far time,
when the home of my youth, and the protector of that home
shall have passed away—when I might be left friendless,
fatherless, homeless—I might almost say homeless, for a
great part of the very small income which constitutes my
father's livelihood is only life-interest and dies with him.
Poor papa ! he has too many daily troubles and vexations
engrossing his mind to think or deprecate the future.   Sometimes he says—

"I would give anything in the world if we knew Mr.
Stirling—he would be so kind to you, Chatty."

I suppose he meant that he would be kind to me when I

was left alone, but I know not. Papa often talked about
dying, but only in that sort of way that afflicted people
always do ; as if it was a thing he wished for too much
ever to come to him. He talks often and often to me about
my dead mother, and old days. And I let him go on, for
he never seems so happy as when so engaged. I take my
walks as usual to the library and to Mr. Bean's, but he
never likes to have me away from him for an hour even, and
the consciousness of being so necessary to him, and so dear,
fills my heart with thankfulness. I cannot read or study
nearly so much as I used to do, for his sight fails him, and
I go through the *Times* every morning; and read him to
sleep after dinner.

So time flies. It is only three months now till the time
of meeting. That meeting is all the world to me. I have
no other hope—no other love—and when the house is silent
at night, the happiest part of my life comes. For I am
alone, and

> "Contemplation is a thing
> Which renders that I have not, mine."

---

## CHAPTER XIV.

I NEVER passed Mr. Stirling's house but with a lingering
step and wistful look. I felt sure, that in spite of papa's
many and stringent objections, he would have felt pleasure
in seeing again one who had shared the hospitality of his
sunny days—who had known him in his youth and prosperity—and who would understand, without questioning, the
sad, sad changes. And I had a very great desire to know
him. Of late, since the Dunstan interest had died off, my
father had continually reverted to the subject of their former

intercourse; and all he said was calculated to heighten my curiosity, and raise my admiration. His character had made a considerable impression on my mind; I had never heard of one resembling it before, and I knew of none to whom it could be compared. It was not only now—not only as the thoughtful, virtuous man, that I thought of him, but as the Mr. Stirling of years back—and it seemed so strange to me, that in spite of the world, of which he must have seen so much, nothing of the nobility and elevation of his character had been impaired. And from all I had learned from papa of a gay life I always likened it in my mind to Nebuchadnezzar's fiery furnace: so much selfishness—so much hypocrisy—so much uncharitableness, and such an infinity of ignoble and mean passions. Ah, he was brave indeed who escaped unscathed!

One summer evening, on my way home from a country ramble which led me by Mr. Stirling's house, the garden-gate stood wide open, and I crossed the road that I should get a better view of the house. I heard a voice speaking very gently and kindly, and when I passed the gateway, I saw the tall figure of a man leading a little child by the hand, and bending down to talk to it. It was a baby almost; apparently about a year and some months old, and just able to walk and prattle. I knew it was Mr. Stirling, although I could not see his face; and when I reiterated to papa my entreaty that he would write to him, he wiped a tear from his eye:

" You are right, dearie. Heaven help me! you do need a friend, I know how much; give me the paper and ink—I will write."

" I am not thinking of myself, father," I exclaimed, eagerly; " I want no one but you and Jeannie; oh, I do not want friends, but——"

" I am a poor friend, an enemy rather—— "

I put the paper before papa, and motioned him that I wouldn't hear a word more, and he dipped the pen in ink and began :

"I can't write, Chatty—I'm not well." He threw down the pen and burst into tears :

"I can't write, my dearie. I can't do anything to be of use to you—not even of procuring you a friend, and God knows when you will want one! I never can be any use to you. I can burden your life with sorrow, and bitterness, and wretchedness—that's all. All the rest I could bear with patience, but it seems so hard to bring all this upon you —and so young too. My God, forgive me! I don't deserve to have any one left to me, I'm so ungrateful. Poor Chatty!"

Then he clasped me tight in his arms, and sobbed like a heart-broken child.

"Dear, dear father, don't cry; don't grieve for me; I am happy, indeed I am."

And I could say no more for the quick rising tears. It was a long time before he grew calm. I carefully avoided the mention of Mr. Stirling's name. Papa looked dreamily out of the window.

"Why, papa," I exclaimed, cheerfully, and seating myself on a stool at his feet, "you have not heard Jeannie's letter yet; it is such a nice long one." And I drew it out of my pocket and began to read; anything to draw him from that state of dreaming torpor; tears were even better than that.

The evening passed off as usual; I took down the Bible and read a psalm or two to him, as was my wont; then he gave me his good-night kiss and went to bed.

I sit thinking over many things to-night. My poor father! How strange it was that he should long so passionately for his manhood's friend, and yet that he should be so unwilling to seek him. Ah, I could almost understand the feeling; the

radiant vision of Arrowmere, the palmy days of his lordly
house and lordly wealth, the form of his Helen Charlton as
the beautiful bride of his youth, and the mistress and glory of
his splendid home—all, all came back to him then, and he
was crushed with the weight of so much happiness and so
much sorrow. By-and-by, I think of Lindsay. He still loved
me. How could I doubt it? We should meet again. I
should see his face and hear his voice, and he would be
unchanged. My heart was a glad prophet.

Jeannie would be with me too; and she loved me so
fondly. I took out her dear letter, and read it over and
over again.

"It is all quite settled now, and we are coming to Ingham
on the fourteenth of October, and mamma has written about
the house, and Lindsay has promised to run down and see
that everything is comfortable and in order a week before.
Of course he will call upon you. How angry Angelica will
be! Somehow, she never seems in a good temper when
Lindsay says anything about you; I rather think she fancies
he likes her, but it can't be; they are so totally different
and ——"

Suddenly I hear the sound of a heavy fall, and start up,
pale and trembling with a terrible dread and fear; for it is
a sound that from a sorrowful experience I know well. I
rush up-stairs with a swiftness that affright alone can give,
and on the threshold of my father's bed room I pause for
one minute, utterly powerless and speechless.

My worst apprehensions are verified. It is another stroke
of paralysis, and he lies on the floor, prostrate, convulsed,
helpless.

There was no time for grief or reflection. With the best
care we raised him up, and then Ellice ran off for Mr. Bean,
whilst I remained watching at the bedside. Those weary,
weary minutes, they seemed as if they would not pass!

Ever and anon I kept turning my eyes from the bed to the
clock, and when half an hour was gone I felt as if I must
have waited a whole day.   But when Mr. Bean had come
and gone I almost envied my former state of incertitude—
the suspense which was nearly hopefulness.   Not that the
good kind doctor told me there was no chance of recovery,
he merely shook hands with me very gravely and quietly,
and said—

" There are many chances for and against—only keep
up your spirits, and hope for the best."

But I knew well that if there had been room for hope he
would have told me.

Ellice and I both sat up with papa that night, but Mr.
Bean promised to send a nurse in the morning ; her wages
would make a sad hole in our weekly income, but there was
no help for it.   I could not let Ellice do the duty of servant
and help me to nurse too, and I must take care of my own
health, it was invaluable to me now.   How seldom is real
unselfishness seen, and how beautiful it is, and angelic !
Papa and I were nothing to Ellice but as employers who
paid her moderately, and yet, because the girl's affectionate
heart had been touched by our poverty and isolation, and
because we had repaid her faithfulness by confidence and
esteem, she was willing to do anything for our sakes.
Ignorant, untutored, true-hearted Ellice, thou hast taught
me a parable that hath a Bible-simplicity and sublimity.
May I ever remember it !

In about a fortnight we were able to dismiss the nurse,
which was a great saving and satisfaction; for papa slept
very well at nights, and there would no longer be the strong
tea to make, and the brandy to buy.   And I was sorely
hard up for money.   There was no more due to papa till
after Michaelmas, and I had only a few pounds to carry me
through till then, and lots of extra expenses.   I tried my

best to be cheerful, and banish anxiety, but the spectre of
Poverty was never entirely driven from my mind. But
there was nothing I could do, save trust in God. Everything was put away now—Fenimore Cooper, Tacitus, and
long dreaming strolls by the beach ; all the day, and all the
day's business and care, was engrossed by the invalid. I
could hardly think of Lindsay even, for the grief and fore-
boding of my heart. I still took a snatch of air and sea
breeze at eventide, to keep myself in health, but nothing
more : from morning to night, and sometimes from night
till morning again, I sat at his bedside, hoping and praying
for a sign of returning strength and consciousness. At last
it came ; after four weeks had passed, my father spoke
again, and was enabled to sit up in his arm-chair.

"Courage, courage, little girl!" said good Mr. Bean,
joyfully ; "didn't I say the chances were equal. He'll do,
I tell you ; he'll do ! God bless you, Chatty, you're a good
child ; he'll get better, depend on it."

My eyes filled with tears.

"You have been so kind to us, sir."

"Kind !"

It was too much for the doctor, and he bolted off. I
took courage, indeed, when I heard my father begin to find
fault with the weather, and the Ingham grocers ; still there
was a child-like helplessness and dependency about him
which was new, and made me very uneasy. He seemed to
have lost all memory, and called Mr. Bean by the name of
his physician at Arrowmere, as if his illness had somewhat
affected his senses. I spoke my fears to the doctor, and
he said—

"I think it will pass in time ; at least I have a great
hope that, with the weakness, this confusion and indistinctness will in a great degree go, but it will take time " then,
after some moments' thoughtful silence, he continued :

"Excuse the question which I am about to ask. I do it from no curiosity. I think that your father will get over this; he may never, perhaps, be so strong as he was before, but he may survive it for many—for a long time. Be assured that I speak conscientiously when I say so, for it would be wrong to raise false hopes; but in any case, it is probable that you will survive him;—would—that is— would his death affect—would you be left with an ample provision?"

"I am afraid not; at least I am sure not."

Mr. Bean considered a little, and then suddenly changed the subject.

"A little cheerful society would work wonders on your father, I do believe. You have no friends here?"

"No one."

"Mr. Stirling knew your father once, some years ago, I remember he told me."

"Yes, in papa's better days."

"Why not make known to him that Mr. Warne is residing here?"

"Papa will not consent; I have asked him often."

"Ah, well, I'll see what he says to it."

And when Mr. Bean came down-stairs again, he rubbed his hands gleefully, and exclaimed, "It's settled! I knew it would be; put on your bonnet directly, Chatty, and take the place of your papa's visiting card at Mr. Stirling's."

## CHAPTER XV.

I FELT a strange shyness and trepidation as I was ushered into Mr. Stirling's house. It was a large and elegant mansion, furnished inside with a simplicity and elegance which struck me far more than the untasteful smartness and gaudiness of Mrs. Dunstan's villa. Beautiful statues, such as I had never before seen, were arranged in the spacious hall, and the ceiling was arched and carved all over with a fineness and symmetry that created in my mind quite a sensation of wonder. Here and there were stands of lovely flowers in bloom, and from a wide glass door, that was half open, I caught a glimpse of smooth shaven grass, with flower-beds intermixed, and a fountain playing in the midst. Pictures that I longed to stand still and look at hung on the walls, and one of the numerous doors, standing ajar, disclosed to my view the well-filled shelves of a library. Never before had I been where so much loveliness of art and nature had been combined. I should have enjoyed the sight far more, had I not been perplexing myself, over and over again, as to what I should say to Mr. Stirling.

At last he came. I just ventured to look up for one minute, and that was all; but even that momentary glance sufficed to give me an ease and assurance that just before I had been longing to possess. Somehow I had felt a sort of awe of Mr. Stirling's presence, as if he had been a modern Plato or Aristotle, and now I smiled to see how very little awfulness there was about him. He was an aristocratic looking man, about eight-and-thirty—perhaps a year or two more—with a face that had a wondrously sweet expression in it, and a speaking of much intellect and character; he was tall, but stooped slightly; and that, added to a touch of grey in his hair, and a look of habitual thoughtfulness and melancholy, made him doubtless appear older than he really was. I was quite taken aback when I saw him, he was so totally different to what I had expected, but I was certainly not disappointed. There was none of the magnificent contemplativeness that I had looked for, none of the philosophic and heroic sternness and grandeur that I had imaginatively pictured. In Mr. Stirling's countenance, I read simplicity, elevation, and strong determination of character—nothing more; and there was an open straight-forwardness in his eyes that made me feel sure I should never have cause to alter my opinion. I cannot remember what I said first, but I blushed very much, and hastened to get to papa's name.

He looked extremely puzzled.

"Mr. Inglis Warne, did I understand aright? Mr. Warne, of Arrowmere?"

"Yes; I have brought a message from him, sir."

"And you are—you are——"

"I am his daughter," I said, quickly.

For a minute he fixed his eyes upon me, with a whimsical expression of astonishment and perplexity.

"Inglis Warne's daughter—I'm very glad to see you."

He shook hands cordially, and then sat down, looking more puzzled than before.

"Papa is living here—has been living here for some time."

"At Ingham? how sorry I am that I did not know it before. Ah, we were such good friends! How glad I am! Did he come this spring?"

"Papa has been living here for many years," I continued, whilst my eyes filled; "he has had some sad reverses since you knew him, sir, and his health is shattered, too."

For a minute I hesitated from emotion, and then added—

"Arrowmere does not belong to him now, and he is very poor, and infirm, and has no friends; will you come and see him, sir?"

He did not answer for a minute, but regarded me with an expression of great sorrow and interest; then he jumped up hastily, and said—

"I will call on your father at once, Miss Warne. Oh, I am so sorry to hear of this."

I rose, and we both returned together. For the first quarter of a mile our conversation was only of the weather and of those commonplaces with which English people not well acquainted invariably entertain each other. He informed me that it was a lovely day; and I enlightened him by the amusing intelligence that we had been three weeks without rain. Chance at length put us in the way of a more enlarged topic; for, when we had emerged from Ingham, my companion, naturally enough, asked me how far we had to go.

I indicated the direction of our house.

"It's a dreary place in winter," I said, "and in any weather has a dismal out-of-the-way look about it, which more particularly strikes strangers; I am used to it."

"Then you have always resided with your father?"

"Yes, my mother died before—just before papa's troubles, and he has no one left to him but me. We came to Ingham when I was but seven years old, and I can remember no other place."

"And perhaps it was better for you—you did not experience the painfulness of the loss of such a fortune at such an age."

"I think it was happier—at least I should have been perfectly happy to be poor with papa, if he were happy too."

"Ay, I do not wonder that he repines. He was such a liberal, jolly country-gentleman, and full of generosity and spirits—poor fellow!"

"His health is broken, too," I continued, sadly, "as much as his spirits; he is an old man now."

Mr. Stirling quickened his pace, as if impatient to arrive.

"How I wish I had known sooner," he said, as if to himself, and then turning to me—

"Poor child!" he exclaimed, with a look full of benevolence and compassion, "you are very young to have had so much sadness. It must be lonely for you at Ingham. Have you no friends here?"

"None, excepting Mr. Bean; he has been very kind to papa; I have no other friend but one."

"And who is that?" asked Mr. Stirling, simply, as if he were speaking to a child.

"Jeannie Dunstan."

"Ah, the Dunstans come here sometimes. I remember Jeannie as a nice little girl: are they very old friends of yours?"

Then I told him the accident which had brought us together. There was some hesitation in my manner, and a flush upon my cheek, for I had to mention Lindsay's name, and it was awkward for me to speak of the time *when* Mrs. Dunstan had visited Mr. Stirling's house; but I told him the whole history, and he only smiled quietly and said—

"If Mrs. Dunstan leaves Jeannie to herself, she will grow up a very amiable and estimable woman."

"I believe she will."

"And so you know Mr. Bean," he continued, "and speak warmly of him of course. What a virtuous and charitable man he is! A little too speculative and visionary, perhaps; but no matter, his alms find their way as easily from his purse as the philosophical theories from his brain. I don't believe the world holds a better being. It's quite a treat, Miss Warne, to find a little pure gold in the world— there is so much copper and counterfeit coin; and the worst of it is, all circulates well. We shall certainly have a moral bankruptcy one day."

"I shall not lose much by it," I said, confidently; "where I have hazarded most, I am surest."

Mr. Stirling smiled.

"Take care," he answered : "those only are safe who hazard nothing."

And I replied, almost gaily—

"I have no fear."

Then we walked on in silence, my companion plucking handfuls of heath and wild-flowers as he went along, and pulling them to pieces in an abstracted mood. Now and then he stopped, and seemed to take a mental sketch of every feature of the scene ; and a deep, thoughtful sadness seemed to have fallen over him. His face grew paler and paler as we went on, and he walked in a quick, nervous way; perhaps he was thinking of all that had passed since he and my father had last met.

"There is the house !" I exclaimed, as it came in sight.

He looked up eagerly.

The small white tenement, with its bleak exterior and surroundings, standing as it did in its solitariness, far from all habitation of human kind, the little humble garden and patch of flowers and vegetables around it : the undefined sketch was easily filled up ; and I saw from Mr. Stirling's countenance that the suggestions had revealed to him the whole sad story. However he turned cheerfully to me, and said—

"I cannot yet imagine, Miss Warne, how your father came to fix his residence at Ingham: he had so many friends in Essex."

"That was the principal reason—they were only acquaintances; if they had been friends I think he would have remained there."

"Ah, I understand you perfectly; the Charlton family were always noted for their pride, and I suppose your father had imbibed it. How time passes! the last time I saw him, he had just bought a coral and bells for his little heir, Charlton he called it; he was then full of life and spirits. And so the poor child died?"

"Oh, no! I am his heir," I said, sadly; "he never had a son."

Then we reached the house; and Mr. Stirling followed me straight into papa's room. My father sat in his arm-chair, by the window, looking out in a sort of dreamy abstraction; his eyes wore a wistful, perplexed expression, as if he were striving vainly to clear his thoughts, and his lips had a troubled look of restlessness and indecision. How wasted and sorrowful and care-worn he was! I dared not so much as glance at Mr. Stirling; I dreaded to see how much he would be surprised and grieved.

"Father dear," I said, stepping forward, "here is Mr. Stirling—he returned——"

I could say no more, for the tears that stayed my utter-ance, but no more was needed, and papa's face was tearful and glad, like a little child's, as he held out both his trem-bling hands to the friend of a happy, happy time—a time past which was to him as a buried world.

---

## CHAPTER XVI.

"Eighteen years; it's a long time!"

My father rested his eyes on Mr. Stirling, speculatively; Mr. Stirling's rested on me.

"It is a long time, sir: that little girl of yours is nearly a woman now—she was a baby then; I was a boy—I shall soon be an old man; eighteen years is a long time."

" You an old man ? " said my father, doubtfully ; " you
will not be an old man for years to come."

The other smiled.

" My dear sir, one may be old in feelings, and yet not in
age, you know.  I do not reckon by the common calendar
of years, and months, and days—circumstances, and accidents, and habits, effect in a short time the average wear
and tear of years.  For my part, the date of an individual's
birthday gives me no idea whatever of his age : this sounds
paradoxical, but is it not so ? "

My father assented, and added, wistfully—

" But you have been prosperous, very prosperous."

He was thinking doubtless of rent-rolls, and estates that
had been handed down from countless generations ; Mr.
Stirling was thinking of other things, and smiled a sad
smile.                              .

I sat in a shaded corner, and studied his features with
earnestness.  This was the man who, for conscience-sake,
had braved the scorn and contumely of the world.  Truly
he was greater than the greatest of kingdom-conquerors.
Was he thinking of the sacrifice which had so shadowed his
life, so that sadness passed over his features ? or was he
rather thinking of the littleness and poverty of that sacrifice, compared with his large sin, and the suffering it had
brought.  Oh yes! it was of this last ; he was not a man
to judge vainly of himself, or to look back with a regret
upon a past resolution ; sensitiveness and refinement were
traced in delicate lines upon his face, but the power of an
imperial goodness and of an imperial will were written there
also, and in characters of stern, majestic strength.  The
simplicity of a child was written on that countenance, and
the courage of a lion—a wicked man must quail in fear
before it.

" Chatty, child," said my father, " draw back the window
7

curtain; Mr. Stirling can't see out: isn't it a dreary prospect?"

"The sky is very blue, and you have a glorious view of the sea. I can imagine it looking dreary, but to my eyes it is not so now; lonely it may be, but the pleasure-boats suggest the idea of many dwelling-places near. No, Mr. Warne, I have seen many a drearier place than this; and," he added, placing a fatherly hand upon my shoulder, "you are not alone."

"No, but it is wretched for the poor child, so dull and bleak!"

Mr. Stirling put back the hair from my face, and looked from me to my father, with a smile:

"She dull—dull with such a bright face as that! Why, she looks as if she never knew that there was such a word as *ennui*."

"Yes, she is high-spirited, thank God, or she would have died long ago," pursued papa, persistently; "and the place is dreadfully cold and perishing in winter, I wonder she hasn't gone into consumption; besides, it s the education I regret more than anything; she has had no advantages, poor thing. Her mother used to draw and play so prettily!"

"But I am not so very ignorant, papa," I said, deprecatingly, and cast my eyes on the ground with a blush.

"Bravo!" exclaimed Mr. Stirling, looking amused, and drawing his chair opposite to mine. "Bravo, my child, and now let's hear what you do know."

"She knows how to be as good as an angel to me," interposed papa, but I held up my finger to motion his silence.

"Ay, I could guess that, and that alone is worth all the learning in the world; but come, little one, tell me what is your favourite reading, or rather who are your favourite authors?"

I reflected for a few minutes, and answered—" Shakes-peare, Addison, Goldsmith, Burns, and Thackeray."

" A goodly galaxy, truly, and you have a fine taste—a sound, good English taste of your own; and now tell me why you have chosen these particular five."

" I can hardly tell; I think because I can turn to their books with the same pleasure and never tire."

" Well done, you have defined your reason accurately and justly. Why, Mr. Warne, she can like a good book and tell you why; this is better than all the piano-rattlings and water-colour abortions in the world, and the music and drawing that young ladies learn is, in nine cases out of ten, little better than this. My dear friend, don't wish your Chatty to be any other than she is."

Then he turned to me, and entered so kindly and inte-restedly into my pursuits and thoughts, that I felt at once how dear and valuable a friend I had found.

When we rose to go, my father held out both his thin hands with a wistful expression.

" You will come again soon," he said; " do come when you can; I haven't seen the face of a friend for years, and I like—I like to talk over the old days."

" Oh, I will come often, depend on it; and we will have another argument about Lord John Russell, and Palmerston, and the peace question; perhaps I shall be able to beat you then, only your little Chatty, there, keeps you so well up in all the public news, that my chance is lessened considerably."

My father looked at me fondly and proudly.

" Yes, she's a good girl; she always reads me the *Times* from beginning to end. There have been no less than thirty gold watches lost this month. How careless people are! I have had mine this five-and-twenty years."

He pulled it out, and was much pleased at Mr. Stirling's praise of it. Somehow, one's own watch is always the best

goer in the world. Papa's was, though to my perfect knowledge there never was a week when it did not either lose
or gain.

Mr. Bean had said rightly. Mr. Stirling's society *did*
work wonders on papa ; it was always something to look
forward to with pleasure, then arose again the old, warm
cordiality and a real and lasting interest. Mr. Stirling had
a wonderful tact in conversation ; an art I should rather call
it, though he was so simple and unaffected in everything
that even that word is not properly applicable. He did not
console papa when he gave him a long dissertation on his
manifold grievances and injustices, knowing very well how
useless consolation would be, but listened in silence and led
him on gradually and easily to other topics, and he always
contrived that the topics should be interesting to him.
The more I saw of him the more I found how far from
reality my preconceived opinions of him had been. Because
he was a wise and a good man, I had fancied he must
be quite different in every respect to the common herd
of mortals; I had looked for philosophical reflections
and moral axioms to fall from his lips continually, and
that he was superior to all the trifling enjoyments and
vexations which so much engross the mind of most people.
Never had I been more mistaken ; a wise and a good man
he certainly was, but he was by no means a philosopher,
still less a moralist; his conversation was essentially playful
and varied, at the same time ; without being grave, it was
always earnest and always original. And I believe that his
conversation was eminently characteristic, although there
were some under-currents and depths in his nature to which
he seldom, if ever, gave utterance.

My father was still unable to come downstairs, but even
to see him sit in his arm-chair and look out of the window
and scold at the gulls as in the " old, old fashion," was a

very grateful sight to me; but he did not scold at them so
much as he used to do, his thoughts were more occupied in
counting the chances of a visit from Mr. Stirling; and if
there was the least probability of it, he was content to do
nothing all day but watch for him.

"Chatty," he said one day to me, "how long did you
say it was now till Mrs. Dunstan's visit?"

"Six weeks, papa."

"Oh, six weeks; I hope the time will pass slowly till
then."

"Why so, father?"

"I shan't know how to miss you, Chatty, I should be so
miserable alone."

"I won't go often; I would rather stay at home with you."

"Yes, I know you would; but it will be so wretched
for me to think that I am keeping you from the only society
and the only pleasure you can have, and yet I can't bear to
have you out of my sight.  Oh, my child, better for you if
I had died that night!"

At this moment Ellice appeared with a basketful of fruit
which Mr. Bean had just sent to me, and for the next half-
hour papa's attention was wholly taken up in helping me to
peel apples for a pie. A little while after Mr. Stirling came.

"Ah, here you are," he said, as he entered; "it's just
as I expected—Chatty reading the news, and Mr. Warne
scolding at Lord John Russell with all his might.  Always
at the post of duty, Chatty, like a true soldier."

"Yes, she's a great deal too good to me; you do not
half know how good she is," said my father, tenderly.
"Poor Chatty, it's a poor service that you're in."

"An honourable one, however," Mr. Stirling added,
with a smile; "you have just decorated her with a bright
star, I'm sure."

"And a very hard service," my father continued.

"But scars are honourable as well as stars, you know," and then he turned to me—"Have you been out for a walk to-day?"

"No," I answered, blushing guiltily.

"Then put on your bonnet and go directly."

I hesitated; it was a kind thought of Mr. Stirling's, but not a welcome one. I would much rather have given up the walk than the pleasure of his society, but it was very difficult for me to tell him so; he might have guessed it.

"She will get ill, I am sure," said my father, "by staying within doors so much. Chatty, you must take more care of yourself; your health is of more consequence than mine."

There was no help for it; so, unwillingly enough, I left the room to prepare for my ramble. As I returned Mr. Stirling came out of the gate.

"Is it not a pleasant evening?" he said; "come now, Chatty, you have not had half fresh air enough yet: turn back a little way with me; that's right, I thought you would. I want to have a little talk with you very much; well, to begin—in the first place, I think I see a sensible improvement in your father's spirits."

"I am very, very glad. I have thought so too at times."

"You say at times; then the improvement is variable?"

"Yes, at least I fear so; he is always so much better after one of your visits."

Mr. Stirling's face brightened, and I continued—

"I cannot express to you how grateful I am for your——"

"Don't say a word more. I can assure you that the consciousness of being in the smallest degree serviceable to my old friend, brings me more happiness than I can anyhow confer. He was doing the very worst thing for himself when he resolved upon this Ingham seclusion, for solitude is a medicine that very few constitutions can stand.

London would have been better, or any other large town ;
for in a large community it is possible to live quite quietly,
and observe the crowd and stir of activity going on around."

"I have often thought so; poor papa has been very
solitary."

"And it must be lonely for you too."

"Yes, I have felt inclined to be discontented with the
sameness and dulness of my life, at times ; but not lately—
not since——"

"Since that adventure that brought you and Jeannie
Dunstan together, I presume," Mr. Stirling said, with a
smile : "and how long ago is that ? "

"Two years this autumn."

"Ah, they were staying in my house at the time then.
I remember something about it ; and that Lindsay Jocelyn
came in, covered with rain and mud, but I was occupied at
the time, and made very few inquiries. How little did I
dream that Inglis Warne was living in the lonely place he
described to me ! "

I turned to go now, for it was drawing time for papa's
supper.

"Good evening, Chatty. Never pass a day without a
good run, there's a good child, it is so necessary to you.
I shall bring up my little Ned next Sunday afternoon, and
then you will be obliged to keep out with him, to see that
he doesn't tumble in the water, or fall from the rocks. But
will you be at home ? "

"Yes, I am sure of it."

"Then you have not imbibed Mr. Vasey's idea, that
without a treble church service attendance, a Sunday is
very badly and irreligiously spent ? "

"Oh no, I believe I can see my duty pretty clearly. I
hope I can."

"I am sure you do, but Mr. Vasey has no theory of

duty—only as connected with the observances and regula-
tions of the Church! the more's the pity—and error."

"And a good many others agree with him."

"Yes, it is very sad! there is no longer a spirit, but a
Church worship. It is astonishing to see how little humility,
and how little real love and vitality exists in the human
mind universally. It is only by the occasional breath of a
mighty spirit that the spark is kept alive—but good night,
my dear child; little Ned never likes to go to bed till he
has said good night and his prayers to me, and I am sure
Mr. Warne will be wanting you."

Mr. Stirling came on Sunday, as he had promised, and
brought his little Ned with him—a merry, rosy child, with
something of his father's openness and nobility of character
written on his infantine features. We were the best of friends,
Ned and I, for I always loved children; and when it was
time to go, he put his little arms around my neck, and
lisped forth—

"Me come again soon, Tatty."

And after that Sunday, Mr. Stirling seldom came alone.

---

## CHAPTER XVII.

THE summer was passing now, and no one can tell how
I longed for the autumn, when I should see him once again.
Every morning I awoke with the glad thought, "Another
day nearer to Lindsay;" every night I went to bed, thankful that the day was gone. My father grew much better; I
had no present cause for anxiety, and my spirits arose with
the elasticity of youthfulness and hope. I did not distract

myself with the thought that my love was in vain ; I did not question the truthfulness and goodness of the one I loved ; I believed him to be brave, and gallant, and noble ; and for the time I was very happy. It was quite a holiday of peace and joyousness, after the long watchings and anxiety ; and I basked in to-day's sun, and never thought of to-morrow.

Mr. Stirling's goodness no words of mine can express ; his name ought to be written in letters of gold all through this book. His generosity was as profuse and unlimited as the bountiful rains from Heaven, but with the generosity was mingled a delicacy of mind incredible ; he would rather have cut off his right hand than hurt the feelings of the poorest of mankind. And he would often eschew the pleasure of giving, from an over-scrupulous fear that his gifts might wound. Never had I seen so much refinement and so much uprightness combined. Heaven bless him !

He would bring, day after day, little baskets of rare fruit, or delicacies, in his own hands, and set them down in the hall, that they should not be discovered till he was gone— so much did he abhor an ostentation of liberality ; and if I attempted to thank him, he would raise his hand, in an attitude of such imploring, deprecative, and positive distress, that I was forced to desist.

One day the weather had been sultry and oppressive, but Mr. Stirling never stood for the weather ; he came later than usual, however, and when he rose to go, the sun had dropped below the horizon. As I opened the door for him, a groom, riding a splendid chestnut horse, dashed up to the little gate ; he alighted at once, and drew it near to Mr. Stirling.

" Oh, what a noble animal ! " I exclaimed, in a rapture of admiration. " Sir, do wait a moment, and let me tell papa to come and look at him, he used to be so fond of horses.'

" Hush ! ' said Mr. Stirling, whilst a shade of annoyance
came over his features, " stay a moment, child. Jones, I
gave no orders——"

" Beg pardon, sir," interrupted the man, respectfully,
" but it was my mistress ; she said you had had so much
walking to-day, sir."

" Oh, very well, that will do."

The man touched his cap, and turned homeward ; and
Mr. Stirling led the horse gently on to the strip of turf out-
side the garden, and sprang lightly into the saddle. He
held out his hand to me :

" You can guess why I did not wish your father to see
the horse, can you not, Chatty ? Your very argument for,
was mine against it. He used to be a glorious rider, and
kept a magnificent stud. It would wake up a thousand sorrowful thoughts. Oh, I wouldn't have such a thing happen
for the world !"

And this was but one instance of a consideration and
rare perception of the feelings of others, which we witnessed
daily.

There was still one thing which now and then sent a
sharp pain through my heart. Since papa's last illness, he
seemed to be more childlessly helpless than he formerly was,
and his memory was strangely gone. His spirits were better
than I had ever seen them ; his health and appetite were
better also, but ever and anon he would wake up from a
reverie as if from a sleep, and ask a question about things
which had passed and gone years ago ; sometimes he would
call me Helen, and then he would correct himself hastily
with a melancholy smile. Yet I hardly knew whether I had
any right to be alarmed ; never had he been as calm, and
unrepining, and placid as he was now. Never had my
home-life been so tranquil.

Tho golden August sunlight flecks the hushed waves of
the sea, and floods our little room with a glory; a broken
ray falls on my father's head, like a halo. Ah, how much
there yet remains to tell of former strength and former dignity in that pale face and wasted form! I am kneeling by
his side, and read from a favourite and old volume which
lies upon his knees, with his arm drawn fondly around me.

"What interest hath this empty world in me; and what
is there in it that may seem so lovely as to entice my desires
from my God, or make me loth to come away? Methinks
when I look upon it with a deliberate eye, it is a howling
wilderness, and too many of its inhabitants are untamed
monsters. I can view all its beauty as deformity, and drown
all its pleasures ·in a few penitent tears; or the wind of a
sigh will scatter them away. Oh, let not this flesh so seduce
my soul as to prefer this weary life before the joys that are
about Thy throne! And though death itself be unwelcome
to Nature, yet let Thy grace make Thy glory appear to me
so desirable that the King of Terrors may be the messenger
of my joy!"

Papa drew me suddenly closer to him, and kissed my
forehead. "Dearie," he said, tenderly, "if it were not for
you, death would indeed be the messenger of my joy. I am so
tired, oh, so tired! yet I would fain stay a little longer with
my Chatty. Heaven forgive me, if I love you too much, my
child."

At this moment a long shadow fell across the room; I
looked up and saw Mr. Stirling; he had got a heap of books
and periodicals under his arm, and laid them on the table
with a pleased look at my sparkling eyes.

"Ah! I knew you would be glad to get them; there's
meat and drink for you for weeks to come; only don't over-
dose yourself with one commodity; divide your intellectual
dinner between meat and apple-pie. Do you understand?

'Ne quid nimis,' you know, and read sometimes for amusement as well as instruction." Then he seated himself by papa.

"Do you know what I was thinking of when you came in?" asked papa, gravely. "I was thinking that if it were not for her, I should be glad to die. I have lived long enough. I am weary of everything."

"Don't say that. What a happiness it must be for you to see your child growing up as she is, to be so good, clever, and graceful."

My father's eyes rested affectionately on me.

"Yes, I could not wish her to be better than she is, and of late she has grown to be the image of Helen, only Helen was taller. But the eyes, and mouth, and forehead! They are Helen's own, and so pretty too."

"And you have a great many things to enjoy besides."

"But consider how much I have lost!" my father answered gloomily. "I have been most unfortunate."

"My dear friend, I think that very few can say they have been most unfortunate."

"Why so?"

"Unfortunate is such a comprehensive term; and I am one of those who believe that there is hardly such a word at all. The only black misery in the world is the shadow of a past sin; temporary sorrows and troubles, of course, fall to the lot of each, but after a time the clouds which have obscured our sight fall away, and we see in them the Mighty Hand of a Providence only."

"I wish I could see things so."

"It is difficult to you doubtless to look upon your losses, and afflictions, and trials, and say—'These are all good!' for few, perhaps, have been as much tried as yourself, but you can believe it, can you not? I think that no one can look for one minute abroad, either in the material or moral world, without believing it."

"You are right; you are right!" exclaimed papa, with emotion. "I have no right to complain; it's worse for Chatty than for me, just in the best days of her youth as she is!"

"And Chatty has taken no harm," Mr. Stirling continued, with a smile; "she is good, and intelligent, and happy. Look at her now, how bright she looks over those books. Would a stranger say she had the appearance of one whose life had been so dreary and nun-like as you have pictured it? Oh, no, Chatty has much to be thankful for also, and she thinks so, I am sure."

Papa was very grave and tranquil that night after Mr. Stirling was gone. I felt almost inclined to be alarmed at his abstracted, musing manner; but the abstractedness was no new thing of late, and the thoughtfulness perhaps only arose from the evening's conversation. I went to bed thankful.

---

## CHAPTER XVIII.

To-morrow Lindsay and I shall meet again. Autumn has come at last, and with it the golden harvest of hopes long sown. To-morrow will bring back the old happiness; Jeannie has written to ask me to spend the first evening with them, and the first would be to-morrow.

It was very difficult for me to realize the full extent of the happiness that was so near. I had longed for it so passionately that I could hardly believe in a few hours only it would all be poured into my heart. To-morrow I should meet him again! I did not wonder or question whether he, too, anticipated the meeting; I did not trouble myself with the thought that perhaps I was flinging to the winds and waves all the deep love and tenderness of my nature. I did not fear for the future. I gave way to intense hopefulness and blissfulness only, and said over and over in my mind—

"To-morrow I shall see him again."

At length I took up my candle to say good-night to papa. The "honey heavy dew of slumber" seemed far from my eye-lids yet, and of late it had been my habit, before retiring to rest, to visit his room. If he were wakeful or restless I read him to sleep, and if his lips were parched I mixed him a draught of lemonade, so he always looked for me before settling for the night.

"Is that you, Chatty?" he said, as I entered; "I don't believe I shall ever go to sleep to-night, it is so hot and oppressive; come and sit by me, my dearie, for a little while."

I seated myself by the bedside, and took both his hands between my own; they were cold and trembling.

"What a good child you have been to me, Chatty. Oh, how often I've wished that I might get well, and be of some comfort to you; but I never shall now! I don't think I shall live long, I feel so old and worn out; and to-night, somehow, I feel a sort of thickness and darkness come over me, as if I could neither see nor remember anything."

"Let Ellice go for Mr. Bean!" I said, terribly alarmed at the strangeness of his look and manner.

"No; I dare say it's nothing—nothing that his medicines can restore; but I have felt this coming on for some days, —a sort of weariness and weakness. Oh, Chatty, my dear, patient, angel-child, forgive me!—forgive me all the sadness and heaviness I have brought upon you."

I could not speak for the tears which streamed down my cheeks; but I kissed him, over and over again.

"You will be left all alone, dearie; it's a hard lot, for one so young to be in the world without father, mother, or sister; but you will be happy? promise me that you will try and be happy, dear, for my sake."

"You will not leave me yet!—father, you must not leave me yet!" I exclaimed, in an agony of passionate grief.

"No, I would not leave you if I could stay; I am tired of living, but I would fain stay with you, my poor Chatty. I pray God for life, for your sake, but I do not think it can last long now. Oh, you have been so good to me! all these long years of poverty, and all my gloominess and fretfulness, you have borne like an angel. I should be glad to go, if it were not that I left you behind! I am so tired of everything, and I feel as if I were going back to Arrowmere. Poor Helen! how she cried to part from me; for our life was all sunshine and prosperity then. I shall soon meet her again now."

"Oh, papa, papa!" I said piteously, and threw my arms around him. "What can I do without you? You will not leave me yet?"

He wept bitterly now, and clasped me to his bosom as if he would not let me go:

"It will be lonely for you, and you will be so poor too. Oh, my darling, my darling!"

After a few minutes, he grew calmer, and said, in an unnatural voice of composure—

"Mr. Stirling will always be kind to you, and so will Mr. Bean; in any trouble you have some one to go to, thank God: and Mr. Stirling has promised to try and get a higher interest for the money, and you will then be able to manage; and he told me, that if you wouldn't mind, he would send his little boy, by-and-by, for you to teach. I've thought it would be an amusement to you." For a short time he paused, and then said:

"I know I have often complained against God's providence; but He will forgive it. He will forgive it all, for the sake of my good, uncomplaining, dutiful Chatty! God bless you, my child! and He will. You will always be happy, dearie, because you have been so good to me."

Then his head sank back on the pillow, and he seemed to sleep.

Yet there was no breathing!

I uttered a loud cry, a call upon his name—a call of love, and anguish, and despair, but it had no power to disturb that awful sleep. Oh! was this some hideous nightmare, from which I was wakening; and only a dream that I was left all alone?

---

## CHAPTER XIX.

It is a terrible thing to awake to the consciousness of having lost a friend whose place none other can fill; to feel that the beloved being to whom your love and presence was necessary, no longer needs that love—no longer is sensible of that presence; that the face that gladdened at your coming, and the weary form which leant upon you for support, are alike gone "to house with darkness," and with death, to silence, to——we know not what.

At such a time, when the first awe and the first wondering at the mysterious change has passed away, it is an especial comfort to think that we have done our duty—a heavy grief to remember an unkind or a careless word; and it seems to us if, could the opportunity return again, we would be doubly watchful, doubly loving, doubly tender. But it is too late now; the dear object of our love and of our sorrow is gone down to the grave, and alike his cares, his affections, his injuries with him. No kindness can reach him, and no sorrow: in this last I take comfort.

I had very kind friends in my heavy affliction; and their consolations were of that quiet, unobtrusive nature, which were best calculated to soften the bitterness of my heart. Mr. Bean, with a delicacy of feeling which was peculiarly characteristic, took upon himself at once all the ordering and arranging of the last sad office to the dead, and nega- tived any interposition of mine, with an authoritative—

"Yes, we'll make it right between us, by-and-by."

Mrs. Bean, in a more ostentatious and business-like way, but with as much real kindness, directed the making of my mourning, and did a dozen little services for me, for which she would take no thanks. Even poor old Mr. Binnie could not hear of my loss without coming all the way from the library, after his day's work was done, to sympathise with me. But to Mr. Stirling I owed most of all. He under- stood my loneliness and my grief without the medium of words; and, knowing all my past history, did not strive to console me; for there is no consolation for such sorrow as mine, but the thought that the beloved one was beyond the reach of all change and trouble. And withal he was so gentle, so kind, and so father-like; that I could feel how much he entered into the solitude and sadness of my inner- life; he used to enter the house, unannounced, as though he considered himself at home, and greeted me with a few quiet words, that implied a deeper kindness and interest than they expressed; and without harping too much on the melancholy chords, he did not, as every one else did, draw an impenetrable barrier between the time that was gone and the present. After a day or two, he brought little Ned with him; the sight of the child's healthful, beautiful face, sub-

8

dued and serious, filled my eyes with tears; and they fell faster and faster, when he jumped on my knees, and throwing his little arms around me lisped forth—

" Don't cry—don't cry, Tatty dear."

One day, the first after the dreary week of seclusion and stillness, Jeannie came to see me.

I had been sitting by the sea-side alone, watching the blue waves, and trying to clear the mists and indistinctness which enveloped my future, when before I could perceive the sound of a footstep, a shadow flecked the sand, and a warm tear-wet face was pressed to mine.  Ah, how happy I was to meet her! but for the first few moments, neither of us could speak for our sorrow and our joy.

" It seemed as if the time would never come," Jeannie said, holding my hand, and looking into my eyes with a glad smile; "oh, I have so longed to see you, Chatty; and all last week I kept thinking of you, and would have come, only mamma would not let me; she said I did not know etiquette at all—but you would have forgiven all the errors of etiquette for the sake of my love, would you not? "

" Oh, yes! "

" I said so.  Dear, dear Chatty, how glad I am to see you; don't look quite so sorrowful—oh, I am so sorry you have lost your dear father, you must be very lonely; I wish I could help to make you happy; I'm not much use to you."

How pretty Jeannie looked then! a shadow of sadness overspread her graceful and delicate features, but it only seemed to heighten the expression and character of the face, and it was a face that always took the hue of her passing thoughts and emotions.  This was its chief attractiveness, though there was a great deal of loveliness, independently of expression, in the brightness and glossiness of her well-arranged hair, in the clearness and sparkle of her eyes, in the rosiness and beauty of her complexion, and in the deep red and beautiful archness of her lips.

I took her hands in mine, and pressed them affectionately.

"You are of use to me, Jeannie—of more use than I can tell you; whom have I to love me but yourself?"

"You must come and see us very often, Chatty; a little society will drive away your sad thoughts, and you must come and stay with us by-and-by. We have no one with us yet, but we shall soon have a housefull, and you will come then, I know, to oblige me. Lindsay can't stay with us, but he has promised to run down often on the Saturday evening to spend Sunday with us—won't it be nice? How delightful it is to be at Ingham again! What would I not give to make you happy, Chatty!"

"You do a great deal towards it," I said, fondly stroking her hair.

Jeannie shook her head sadly.

"Not much—not much," she said, in a mournful voice; "I cannot bring back to you what you have lost."

After a few minutes' silence, she brightened up again.

"When will you begin French and German? I can speak French very well, but I am afraid you will soon be before me with the other."

"How kind you are, Jeannie! but I don't think I can tell you yet: not till I shall have made the arrangements."

"Arrangements?"

"Yes; my father has not left me sufficient to live upon; I must do something to earn some money—or give up my home and—get a situation as a governess—or anything."

Jeannie covered her face with her hands and sobbed bitterly.

When Jeannie was gone, I had a long reflection with regard to my future life. One thing was certain—if I failed in my endeavour to obtain employment and remuneration in

the town or neighbourhood of Ingham, I must seek it elsewhere, and give up my home.  For a long time I resolved
in my mind the advantages and disadvantages of either
alternative.  The excitement and enterprise of boldly seeking my way in the world would have had much allurement
for my adventuresome spirit, only of late years Ingham had
become dear to my heart.  Memory and hope shed a halo over
it—imagination and reality endeared it.  Oh no! however
hard or humble my lot might be in the lone White House
by the Sea, I would never, never leave it—unless, indeed,
a hard necessity should compel me.  The remembrances of
the friend who was gone, the charm which Lindsay's presence had thrown round it, Jeannie's love, and Mr. Stirling's
friendship—I resolved to try very earnestly for success,
rather than lose all these.

But I could not go to Mrs. Dunstan's yet.  I was so
utterly stunned and stricken by my sudden loss, that for a
while all other feelings and thoughts were merged in the
one great sorrow.  At night I went to sleep weeping, and
in the morning I awoke from sad dreams to a sadder reality;
sometimes, whilst musing alone, I fancied I heard the sound
of his voice and step, and started with a vague joy, as if I
must be dreaming still; then the truth would dawn upon
me—he is dead; and my tears would fall again.

He was gone then!  I was an orphan now; with not one
being in the world bound to my heart by the strong, sweet
claims of relationship.  Mother, father, brother, sister—oh,
how I envied the grateful names!  It was hard to be left
alone in the world, young as I was; to feel that I must rely
on myself henceforth, in trouble and in suffering; that I
had no one whose whole life in joy and sadness was alike
linked to my own.  True I had friends—kind, true loving
friends—but in their world of home and heart I was second

only, and I could not reasonably expect it to be otherwise. Jeannie loved me faithfully and fondly, but Jeannie was growing to be a woman; she would soon enter deeply into a large and wide circle of enticing society; she would doubtless marry—fair and gentle and winning as she was: then I should not be second in her heart, even. And Mr. Stirling: dear kind friend, am I ungrateful for your friendship and benevolence? I trust not; yet, alas! how can I show my gratitude and love? Your heart is filled with the tender and endearing attachment of wife and child; your cup runneth over with blessings, and I cannot add one crystal drop to its fulness. Thus, even in my friendships I am unhappy, for I can repay them only with prayers to God.

And the one to whom my voice was music, and my face sunshine; to whom I was more than all the world beside, and dearer than life itself—and yet even whose deep love mine could repay: he was gone. I should never see him again; never hear the tones of his voice, or the sound of his step—never, never more, and my life might extend to long years.

When the evenings were fair, I gathered the choicest flowers from our little garden, and laid them on the new-made grave. The churchyard was lonely and remote, the blue sky was above me, and the dark sea rolled around; but in the vastness and grandeur of the scene there was no one to see my grief. Looking upon his grave made me feel how divided I was from him who had so loved me; my heart seemed breaking with its weight of grief, and I buried my face in my hands and cried—

"Papa, papa! oh, why did you leave me?"

I sat down on the grass, and covered the flowers with tears and kisses. Meet sacrifices were they to place upon the altar of human love; beautiful as they are, like mortal affections over which death hath power for a time, and which yet are imperishable and will live again, still more beautiful and purified.

"Father, has the grave so much divided us then? have you no part in the life of your child? Do I weep bitterly for you, and yet you know it not? and is there for ever, and for evermore, in this state of existence, a Lethe between us two? Oh no, no! I cannot—I will not believe it! Thy spirit speaks to me in the singing of the silver waves, in the breeze that comes in at my window, in the glimmer of the stars, and the breath of flowers. What thou art now, and through what hidden phases of being thou hast moved, I know not; but this I feel, that there is a link joining us, which even death could not break asunder."

The thought gave me a calm serenity, yet as I turned to go home, to the home where he was not, again arose to my lips—

"I am all alone. Oh, why did you leave me? Why did you leave me?"

## CHAPTER XX.

It is a cold evening in November. Very dreary blows the wind round the casement, but it is cheerful and bright enough in Mrs. Dunstan's dining-room. When I say cheerful, I only speak with regard to the aspect of the drawn crimson curtains and the bright fire, for there was rather a look of restraint and unsociableness in the party assembled in it. Angelica sits beside me; strange that two people who have no one taste in common, who feel no pleasure but rather stiffness and constraint in each other's presence, it was very strange that whenever I was at Mrs. Dunstan's chance placed me in her near neighbourhood. I never sought her society, I rather avoided it, and I am sure she did not seek mine; still, so it was, by some curious accident, that my chair happened invariably to be the one next hers. We did not say much to each other; I tried to talk several times, wishing to shake off the reserve which amounted to prejudice between us, but it was of no use. Yet why should it be so? The dinner-cloth is laid; it has been already laid a long time, but Lindsay is coming to-night and we are waiting for him; he is expected every minute, and there is a look of impatience and an expectation expressed upon each face: but differently—very differently.

Angelica is evidently anticipating the impression she shall make; one can read that plainly enough in the restlessness of her features and in the coquettish glances she gives on the mirror opposite; but the confident smile on her lips looks as if she felt little fear of success.

Perhaps she has reason. Certainly she looks very handsome to-night in her gorgeous pink silk dress, and with sparkling jewels and gold chains glittering on her, as though she were some Indian princess. There is no softness about her; no gentleness speaking from her looks, and no intellect; character there is, but not a loveable one. Still I must allow that she has beauty and a good deal of it, although it is a haughty, imperious, wilful beauty that has no charms for me—but I must turn my eyes and observations elsewhere now, for her dark eyes flash upon me as if she were reading my inmost thoughts.

How different are the two cousins! Jeannie is as simple, and unpretending, and natural as a child; and her character shows itself in every action and look. Lindsay is evidently in her thoughts as much as in Angelica's, but there is no ostentation and no effort at display in her white dress and blue ribbons, and there is no triumphant expression of vanity and coquetry on her face. Angelica never speaks of Lindsay, but Jeannie has talked of him all day long; and flits ever and anon to the window, and stands listening for the sound of wheels with her head peering between the curtains.

The Rev. Decimus is not here to-night, but his chair is not unfilled, and Mrs. Dunstan's smiles and graces are by no means sparingly bestowed upon his successor. Poor Mr. Dowley! All hope is over for you, at least I fear so— for the supplanter is dignified with a moustache, and a title! Count Civray de Perpini! How elegantly the name glides off Mrs. Dunstan's tongue! He is a distinguished foreigner whom she met in Paris, and who was so enchanted with her society that he has followed her to Ingham, and established himself in the Marine Hotel. Angelica is equally enchanted with him; but it is curious that Jeannie and I should both participate from the first in an indifference, I should rather say an antipathy, to the smooth blandness and excessive politeness which to them is so delightful.

But the Count is rather taciturn now; and takes out his watch every now and then, with a look as much as to say, "I certainly do not approve of waiting dinner for any one." And as time wore on, by slow and steady minutes, the look grew more and more to a—"Who is this individual, that we are kept starving so long? It's a great deal too bad." Opposite to the fire, with his head and apparently his whole mind buried in the day's paper, sat another cousin of Jeannie's, Ross Dunstan. I do not know yet whether I quite like him, but I think I shall in time; at least Jeannie says—

"I don't think many people do like my cousin Ross;

I never knew any one that did yet at first, but every one
has a great respect for him, and a sort of fear; you know
what I mean, Chatty. He is not very sociable, or amiable,
or pleasant, like Lindsay, but he is as honourable and
upright as any one can be, and very clever too—when I
say clever I don't mean that he has any particular talent,
as for writing, or music, or anything of that sort, but I
mean clever and sharp at everything, and business-like."

This is his character as Jeannie draws it to me, and at
present I have had no opportunity of judging further. His
look is not very prepossessing; but, though his features are
irregular and ungraceful, there is an expression of power
and originality about them which is as uncommon as it is
striking, and I long to know more of him.

"There he is; there's Lindsay at last!" exclaimed
Jeannie, excitedly, clapping her hands for joy, and bound-
ing out of the room to meet him at the door.

She was not mistaken; the wheels drew nearer, and
stopped.

Mrs. Dunstan touched the bell.

"Now we'll have dinner," she said, turning consolingly
to the afflicted Count, whose face all at once beamed with
satisfaction.

Angelica reared herself up, and gave a final smooth to
her hair and shake to her skirt; Ross dropped the paper,
and stood up before the fire reflectively; I sat quite motionless and still, and my colour went and came.

It was only two minutes that we waited; whilst Lindsay
took off his wrappers in the hall, and cordially greeted
Jeannie; but in that two minutes a whole harvest of golden
memories and hopes flooded my heart. It was long since
we had met; and, though the hand of sorrow had been laid
somewhat heavily on me since, the depth and the earnestness of my love was in no degree lessened or abated.

Would he, like me, remember the quiet happy evenings in the White House by the Sea? Ah! even if he did remember them, how unlike his recollections would be to mine!

I bent my head over my book, and tried to still the trembling of my heart, but the next minute he entered, his handsome face lighted up with a smile with the warm reception, and very gravely submitting to Mrs. Dunstan's long introduction to the Count; then she turned to me with a formal "Miss Warne—"

But Jeannie interrupted, eagerly—

"Oh, mamma, Lindsay knows Chatty very well; don't you, Lindsay?"

At which he came up to me, and offered his hand with the thoughtful look that was so natural to him.

"Yes, Chatty and I are old friends; I am very glad to find myself at Ingham again."

Then he added, in a lower key—

"The sight of your black dress recalls to my mind a very sad change that has taken place since I was here last. I cannot tell you how sorry I am."

My eyes filled with tears, as I thanked him; then, after a few minutes more, we sat down to dinner. The Count was very hungry, Mrs. Dunstan and Angelica very gracious, and Jeannie too much engrossed in the pleasure of seeing Lindsay again, to think of anything else; her face was turned up to his, radiant in its happiness, whilst he asked her all about the school in Paris, and her pursuits at Ingham. As to Ross and myself, we were both somewhat silent.

"Now, don't you think, from my description, that Chatty and I are going to lead a very happy time of it all the winter; and it won't be wasted time either, will it, cousin Ross?"

" First tell me what you are going to do, Jeannie."

Here Angelica interposed with an energetic and satirical
laugh :—

" Oh, Mr. Dunstan, pray don't ask.  I advise you, from
real kindness—"

Jeannie coloured with vexation, but Angelica never succeeded in putting her down.

" And why ?  Be more explicit, Angelica, please : you
wish to hear, do you not, Ross ? "

" Of course."

" So go on, Angelica ; you just said cousin Ross will be
frightened—I don't think he will."

Angelica's eyes flashed angrily.

" He cannot help admiring your scientific and philosophical pursuits," she said, ironically : " only fancy, Mr.
Dunstan ; Latin, astronomy——"

" And who is the Latin student ? " asked Ross, quietly.

" Oh, Chatty of course ; pray be careful how you address
yourself to Miss Charleton Warne ; there is nothing, accord
ing to Jeannie's account, that she doesn't know."

" Angelica, how absurd you are !" exclaimed Jeannie,
with sparkling eyes, for she never lacked spirit where she
was brought to an encounter with Angelica, more particu·
larly if it regarded myself.  " Ross, it's all nonsense, and
don't you think that it is better spent time, to try and gather
knowledge, than to——"

" Read novels all day long ? " Ross added, with a smile.

" Oh, certainly."

" And Chatty is learning French and German," Jeannie
continued, warmly ; " and I am sure I would rather spend
a morning in helping her than I would over the cleverest
novel that ever was written."

Lindsay and Ross both smiled at Jeannie's enthusiasm,
Then Ross turned to me :—

" What is your motive for being so studious ? " he said, with a scrutinizing look.  Lindsay looked too, and I felt the ancestral pride rising within, but I mastered it, and said very composedly—

" Necessity.  I hope to turn them to a profitable account."

At this moment every one moved from the table.  Lindsay drew me to the window.

" Dear Miss Warne—Chatty, if you will still allow me to call you so.  Oh, I am so very sorry—you cannot, cannot mean what you were saying just now ? "

I shook my head gravely.

" There is no help for it ; I must do something to get some money ; I have not sufficient to live upon."

He looked very grave ; then, darting a glance round the room, rejoined in a gay tone :—

" Well, we won't talk about it now ; let us enjoy the present, and hope for everything.  Come, smile on me, Chatty : I want to bring back something of the former wild-rose to your cheek, and sunshine to your eyes ; and I have looked forward, I cannot tell you how much, to this meeting."

I bent my head down, to hide the rising blushes.  He stooped also.

" Will you not say one word of welcome ; will you not tell me that you reciprocate this feeling," he said, in a low voice, " if even in a small degree only ?"

" I am very glad to see you, Lindsay."

" Thank you, thank you a thousand times ; to hear you call me by my name, as in by-gone days, is indeed a pleasure.  Ah, that was such a pleasant summer, Chatty ! "

" And you have been very busy since then," I said, timidly.

" Dreadfully ; I have been working night and day."

I looked up at him. Certainly there were no traces of hard work or midnight study on his handsome animated face, but then he had already had a few days' holiday, and, to the young and robust, a short time suffices to make up for lost vigour. How tall, and strong, and handsome, he was!

"We barristers," he continued, "are not our own property, but other people's, you see, and are therefore supposed to have no wants and necessities in common with other men; but a little resting-time is before me now, thank Heaven! and I mean to enjoy it to the utmost; and there is one thing which will add, more than all others, to my enjoyment."

He looked at me earnestly, and added in an under tone—

"Can you not guess what?"

I shook my head doubtfully.

"The presence of one person. Oh, Chatty, you can guess now, can you not?"

---

## CHAPTER XXI.

"Sunday again!" Angelica said, with a yawn; "what long dull days Sundays are!"

Mrs. Dunstan sighed sympathetically.

"Yes, and longer here than anywhere; in London, one never need go to church unless one likes."

"And I suppose we must, that's the worst of country places; one gets so overlooked and noticed."

"It's pleasant to be conspicuous too," Mrs. Dunstan observed.

"Yes, but you pay dearly for it."

"But going to church is a duty we owe to society, my love; and I am sure no one can grow tired of Mr. Dowley's sermons."

Ross looked at me; an involuntary smile had risen to my lips; he saw it, and his glance had a meaning in it that I could read thoroughly; we both understood each other's thoughts.

"And," Mrs. Dunstan continued, quite unconsciously, "at Mr. Stirling's nothing grieved me so much as his total indifference to religion. How horrid for a man of his standing to be an atheist!"

"What did you say Mr. Stirling was, mamma?" Jeannie asked, in a voice of bewilderment.

"An atheist, a deist, or something; I don't know exactly what!" Mrs. Dunstan exclaimed, impatiently. "I only know that he never goes to church, and that he never put down his name when the subscriptions were raised for tract distribution, and district visiting. How can people be so uncharitable, who have hearts at all!"

"I don't think Mr. Stirling is uncharitable," I said, decisively.

"Very likely not, Miss Warne; people's ideas differ so much about such things—"

"And Miss Warne has such extraordinary notions," Angelica joined in, maliciously. "You think Mr. Stirling a saint, don't you, Chatty?"

"I think him a good man, and a wise one," I said, firmly.

"Bravo, bravo!" Jeannie said gleefully. "I should never wish for a better champion than Chatty. If all the world ran Chatty's friend down, she would not be a bit afraid. Would you?"

Lindsay's eyes were on me; Ross looked also.

"I hope not," I answered blushing.

"And you would not," Ross said, impressively.

When the breakfast party broke up, I withdrew to one of the windows, and began to read. The rest of the party were going to church, but Jeannie had a headache, and entreated me to stay with her, so there was a long morning before me; I took up an interesting work, resolving to make it a pleasant one.

In a few minutes, I felt conscious of being alone in the room with Lindsay. I could read no longer, although my face was bent low over the pages, and my frame trembled violently. He had changed his resolution, then? He rose and approached me; I dared not look up, but I heard the movement, and in another second he was standing in the same window embrasure, leaning on the panels, and looking down upon my face.

Did he guess that I loved him? Had he read the meaning of my troubled look and agitated manner when he approached me? I knew not; but I almost hoped that he returned my love, even with a hope that was akin to believing. And oh, what a blissfulness to be beloved by him! It seemed to me then, that if I possessed his love I should be too happy—life would be a Paradise.

"Studious Chatty, industrious Chatty," he said, smilingly.

I put the book into his hands.

"Longfellow's 'Hyperion:' what a sweet book it is! I have read it over and over again, and am not tired of it yet."

"And I have never seen it till now, therefore my treat is hardly begun. It is a sweet book; and the reflections are so simple, and yet so true."

"Yes, they always seem like your own thoughts put into shape. Do you dream much?"

"I am afraid I do."

"Afraid! but do you not think dreaming is pleasant?"

"Oh yes, but——"

"Waking must come, of course; but for myself, I like to enjoy the dream while it lasts, and never think of what's coming."

"But very few have that faculty."

"I believe it to be an uncommon one; do you not think with me, that such a temperament is the most likely of any other to be happy?"

"There is no doubt of it."

"Then be my disciple."

"I have been so a long time, at least to a great degree."

"I am rejoiced to hear it; I feel assurep you will never find a better master." And I thought, as he said this smilingly, that I should always believe so too.

Then Jeannie entered.

Quickly, very quickly the minutes passed. I had not a sad thought then, so strongly and so entirely did my love for him usurp the sovereignty of my heart. And he seemed pleased to be near me, too; every now and then, in the earnestness or interest of his conversation, he bent his head down till the waving locks of his dark hair touched my forehead. Oh, how strangely and rapturously my heart beat then! And when he talked to me of his thoughts, ambitions, and endeavours—when he opened to me the world of his inner-life, as if I had been the friend of long and tried years—all my reserve, and timidity, and embarrassment wore off, and I was animated, frank, and natural as a child.

A few minutes after one, the door burst open, and Mrs. Dunstan and Angelica entered.

Angelica smiled with a contemptuous and angry expression.

"Ah, Miss Warne," she said, ironically, "how profitably and becomingly you spend your Sunday morning! I suppose you have got to the end of your book?"

Jeannie came up to me and took the book as it lay open on my knees.

"Why, Chatty," she said, laughing merrily, "what a tête-à-tête you and Lindsay have had ; you have not turned a leaf since we left you ! Lindsay, it's very naughty of you to come and prevent Chatty from being industrious."

"Of course, Chatty was very unwilling to be prevented," Angelica exclaimed, sarcastically, and then went out of the room with a peculiar swing which always indicated an unpleasant mood; and the swing was by no means a rare thing.

"How sweetly amiable my cousin looks !" Jeannie said, after watching her out with an amused look; "really it's too bad—one never can please Angelica. Try and get her into a good temper, Lindsay, do."

"You seem to have a great opinion of my powers of conciliation, little Jeannie," he answered, with a smile ; "how am I to set to work ? "

"I don't know, but I am sure you can please her when no one else can." Jeannie spoke with childish artlessness," but the speech was an awkward one ; Lindsay turned away, and only remarking that he had promised to call on a friend, left the room.

"Oh, Chatty," Jeannie said, with a comical piteousness, "I am so glad I stayed with you. I never could like Mr. Dowley's sermons, and never shall ; all the time he is giving out a string of elegant words and flowery metaphors, I cannot tell what he is driving at. Mamma says he spiritualizes religion, but I don't see it ; he wordifies it. I would at any time rather have a talk with you, ten times, than I would listen to the finest sermon he ever wrote."

She paused a moment, and then continued, in a serious tone:

"You are so different to me, Chatty — so good and

9

thoughtful, I never thought seriously about anything till I
knew you; and I owe you so much—I shall owe it you as
long as I live."

My darling's face was wet with tears as she embraced me.

"You have taught me what I should never have learned
if it had not been for you; such a lesson of patience, and
goodness, and charitableness: and not only by your conver-
sations with me, but by your life. Oh, Chatty, what would
I give, to be like you? Till now I have never had any
troubles or sorrows, but whenever they do come I will try
and bear them as you have done yours. I have often
thought about this, and have felt so grateful that I have
known you before the time of my trials has come, but not
half grateful enough."

"You think better of me than I deserve, Jeannie," I
answered, for her words humbled me; "your affection for
me hides my faults."

"No, no," said the warm-hearted girl, kissing me. "Oh
no, Chatty, no such thing, I assure you; I'm not a bit
partial, and I'm right-seeing where my own heart is concerned. Lindsay says so, and therefore it must be right."

Jeannie and I with the same opinion again! for we both
believe and trust Lindsay's word as "Holy Writ." It is
curious enough that our ideas coincide so often and so
nearly.

---

## CHAPTER XXII.

I PROMISED to stay a month with Jeannie before entering
upon any definite arrangements for my future life. And I
needed the rest sorely; for the watching and the anxieties,

the hope and the fear, and the sorrow of the last few months
had made a fearful inroad on my health ; and I wanted to
recruit it ere I began the work which was henceforth to be for
my daily bread.   Such a holiday, therefore—society, change,
and a total diversity of occupation—was just the medicine
I needed ; and, though Mrs. Dunstan was a weak-minded
woman, as well as a frivolous and a worldly one, there was
a spice of real good nature in her disposition, however indolent it might be.   Besides, I was Jeannie's friend, and that
was a passport to her hospitality and kindness ; albeit, the
kindness was at times tempered with inconsiderateness, and
the hospitality with a tone of patronage.   Still she was
really kind to me, and meant to be so; an orphaned—lowly
—poor as I was, I felt that for that kindness I ought to be
grateful indeed.

Although there was a great deal of visiting, Jeannie and
I never let a day pass in idleness ; all the mornings, whilst
Mrs. Dunstan and Angelica were employed in making calls
or receiving them, we shut ourselves up in the breakfast-
room over our books; no one was admitted into our studious
retirement but Ross, for with him we were sure of meeting
encouragement rather than raillery.   He was an uncommon
character—Ross Dunstan—a constant enigma and perplexity to me.   Had he a heart like other men ? had he a
susceptibility of love—admiration—or for the esteem of
others ?  Sometimes I doubted it, as day after day I studied
the iron inflexibility of his features ; and the more I found
how difficult a study it was, so the more my curiosity and
interest increased.   I am one of those who place a great
confidence in the human countenance—who look ever on it
for a shadowing and hieroglyphic of the immortal mind ;
but it was very difficult to read a face like Ross Dunstan's.
Power, and force and firmness of character were stamped
there plainly enough, but there was nothing more.   Whether

the strength was modified by gentleness, and the power by softness, I could not tell, though day after day I watched unweariedly. One thing I observed, but I should never have disclosed my discovery, for it was not an agreeable one, had not Jeannie said one day to me:

"I do not know why, but somehow I can see that Ross doesn't like Lindsay at all; I can't make it out—every one else does."

After that I felt that the thought was not a mere fancy, but a truth, and I observed his conduct narrowly.

He was perfectly gentlemanlike and polite to Lindsay—courteous even, in so far as the rules of society have defined the meaning of the word—but the politeness and the courteousness were so entirely distant and wanting in cordiality, that they were more frigid even than marked coldness. In conversation he never cut short Lindsay's arguments by the curt and pointed expressions with which he otherwise invariably beat his adversary; and he might have done so easily, for he and Lindsay never held the same opinion about an important question; and Lindsay always seemed to choose debateable and uncertain ground, whether from a playful antagonism to Ross or from principle I know not; besides Ross was infinitely the cleverer.

But he never did so; he never said the smart, and witty, and cutting things to Lindsay which he did to any one else; somehow I could not help thinking that he deprecated the idea of his dislike to him being seen—that he constantly and tacitly made an effort to conceal it. But he did not conceal it; I read it in the cynical smile upon his lips whenever Lindsay was talking earnestly to Jeannie, and her fair face was raised to his with only trustfulness and admiration written on it. I read it in the sharp glance half-pitying half-contemptuous which met me whenever I spoke of

him I loved; and I never did it but with the greatest
reverence and respect.

If it had not been for this thing, I think Ross and I
should have been the best of friends. He was so entirely
free from affectation and prejudice, so strong-minded and
self-reliant, and so utterly superior to all frivolity, meanness,
and worldliness, that I could but feel a regard and esteem
for him. And there was a kind of sympathy between us
from the first; I was interested in everything he said, and
took a delight in his clever satire and criticism; now no
one else did at Helmsley-End Hall, and consequently, whenever he said anything witty or sarcastic, he always looked at
me with the consciousness of my enjoyment. He had taken
an interest in me too; my isolated and independent position
were not unknown to him, and I believe he spoke with more
openness and frankness to me than he did to any one: but
from the first moment that I discovered his aversion to
Lindsay, and that he was conscious of my discovery, a chill
and a restraint were upon us.

So the days went on till Christmas. Every Saturday
evening Lindsay came down to Helmsley-End Hall as usual,
and his visit worked its accustomed excitement. Angelica's
eyes flashed with a darker and more unreadable expression
now than formerly, as she used to enter the dining-room
after her toilet, shining in silks, and decked with jewels till

> " The rings that were on her fingers
> Cast light throughout the hall."

Jeannie's cheeks were flushed with the impatience of
pleasure as she sat on the window-seat listening for the
sound of wheels, which announced his coming, and the
count's with the impatience of dinner. Upon Mrs. Dunstan
it had no other effect than an extra sweetness and blandness
towards the count.

And I, sitting apart, with my black dress and down-looking eyes, which lighted up at his footstep, as the enthusiastic votary at a revelation from his saint—I——But oh, kind reader, surely I am not so poor a daguerreotypist of human hearts and histories that thou canst not see all this, without the tedious telling!

My life at Mrs. Dunstan's was one entire dream of love, and hope, and joy. His coming and going shed a halo and lustre over the common things of life which never faded, and it was only at night, when quiet came over the house, that the full recollection of my orphaned loneliness came across my mind. Then I shed floods of passionate tears, and implored God to guide me in the ways of innocence, and peace, and virtue, since I was left without a protector; and sometimes after my evening's prayer, a calm would come, sweeter even than the delirium of the day's happiness had been.

## CHAPTER XXIII.

AH, how dreary a home looks which death has made desolate! The day before Christmas day I returned home; I was still literally a visitor at Mrs. Dunstan's, but I felt that it was time now for me to fix upon my plans: my principal stay and help was Mr. Stirling; he had promised to assist me in my endeavours, and I felt sure that he would keep his word. He had written to me asking me to be at home, as he wished to talk over my affairs, and promising to spend Christmas day with Jeannie, I set off at once to the White House. As I returned homewards I could think of nothing else but of my father, and of the sad summer

watchings; lately the sorrowful memories had been somewhat subdued by the excitement and vivid variety of my life
at the Hall, but now they returned upon me with all the
fulness of reality. My heart seemed as if it would burst
with grief as I wandered over the dismal untenanted rooms.
I sat down on the chair, where I had received the last
blessing of the friend who was dead, and wept bitterly;
I thanked God again and again that I had tried to the
utmost to do my duty to him, and the reflection of an eternal
and untiring Goodness watching over me from above, filled
me with peace and patience. I resolved that whatever trials
might be in store for me I would do my duty, and trust in
God.

Mr. Stirling came alone, and his face had a troubled
expression on it which I had never seen before. After the
first words of greeting, he took my hands in his, and said,
gravely,

"My dear child, I am afraid that what I have to say will
disappoint you."

I looked up wonderingly.

"You promised me, Chatty, when your father died, that
you would be guided by me in the choice and direction of
your life."

"And I will, always, always!" I said, gratefully.

"Even if my counsel is unwelcome?" he said, smiling.

"Oh yes, yes!" I answered, tearfully, and raised his
hand to my lips. "You are so kind to me, Mr. Stirling, I
can never repay you."

"You can indeed, and you will do so amply, if you will
implicitly follow my advice. You are not a child, and
though your experiences are narrow, you have an infinite
perception and intelligence, and I think you will see at once
the judiciousness of my plan; dear child, you must give up
your home."

I answered only by a blank look of dismay.

"I know that this step will grieve you, but at the same time it is unavoidable. Chatty, listen to me. Consider it in what light you may, your position, if you remained here, would be a painful and a hard one. You would be very lonely, and at the same time have to work very hard, and the mere burden and weight of your responsibility would be a trial of which you do not dream. Besides, even if you obtained your wishes, and a sufficient employment to make up your income what it formerly was; it would be unsafe and quite unpracticable for a young girl to live in this remote and lonely place, as you first thought of doing. Do you not agree with me?"

"Yes—certainly," I said, sadly.

"I think my plan is far better," Mr. Stirling continued, with a benevolent bright smile. "Now Chatty, as I have read perfectly well the sparkle of those Charlton eyes——"

"I am afraid I am proud," I replied humbly.

Mr. Stirling smiled again.

"Never mind. I think your pride is of a sort that will be your friend rather than your enemy. Well then, I will speak to you in quite a business-like way: my little Ned will soon be arrived at alphabet estate; now, I know no one whom I should like to teach him so well as my good little friend Chatty, and the boy dotes upon you. Will you accept my offer and be his governess? I will do my utmost to render you happy."

"I am sure of it," I said, whilst the grateful tears filled my eyes. "Oh, Mr. Stirling, I do not deserve such kindness."

"Indeed you do, and the kindness on my part is not so magnificent as you may suppose. Put it to yourself now, and you will see if I am quite disinterested. Shall I not secure to my child a teacher, and a friend who will think

all day long of his happiness and improvement ; who will
lie down to rest with a prayer that he may grow up virtuous
and strong-minded, and who will set him, every day of her
own life, a right good example of what his ought to be ? "

There was a very earnest, glad expression on Mr. Stirling's face as he spoke ; my heart was too full for words ;
and he added, in a lower voice—

" And do you not think, Chatty, that it will always be
a great pleasure and satisfaction to me to have under my
roof, as a child of my own, the daughter of so old a
friend ? "

I could speak now ; not that his last words had stilled
the gratitude, the love, and the thankfulness which swelled
within my bosom, but they were all too powerful to let me
keep silent; and though I spoke hurriedly and hesitatingly,
I managed to express somewhat of my thoughts.

Then all the definite arrangements were made. I was
to go to Mr. Stirling's as soon as my stay at Mrs. Dunstan's
should be over; meanwhile, he promised to take all the
dreary business off my hands, with regard to selling the
furniture ; a few things, dear and valuable to me from
association, were to be set aside for my room in his house,
and a broker would soon clear off the rest.

" I dare say you will be sorry to have every link broken
which connects you to your past life," Mr. Stirling said,
as he noticed the sadness of my countenance ; " but this
feeling will wear off; it is a natural one."

" Oh, yes ! I never knew any other home but that, and
papa and I seemed to be all the world to each other ; I
cannot help looking back to the old time. Poor papa ! "

" And you will always look back to it, whatever happiness the future has in store for you ; now most of all.
All the ancient landmarks are removed, and you feel as if
in a strange country, but the solitariness will go when new

ones are set up. And you will be happy, Chatty, I am sure of it, because you have done your duty."

When Mr. Stirling was gone, Ellice came to me. She had evidently been crying, but still there was no look of unhappiness in her face.

"Oh, Miss Chatty!" she exclaimed, "I know that you will be happy; and so shall I, but I can't bear to leave the house; somehow, though it is so out-of-the-way, and so dismal, I have felt quite an affection for it. It seems only yesterday since you were a little girl, and used to say your prayers to me, night and morning; and whenever your poor papa was fretful and sorrowful, you came into the kitchen, and cried yourself to sleep on my lap. And often and often, master has called me into the parlour and told me what a dear, good child you were, and begged me to be kind to you, if you were left. And so I would, dear, and would have worked night and day, rather than you should have wanted anything. Bless you, Miss Chatty!"

The affectionate girl kissed me heartily.

"And I never would have married—no, not if James Stirn had vowed not to wait for me. I wouldn't have married to leave you, but you have got better friends now, thank God for it."

I thanked Ellice, and asked her, as a poor but useful way of showing my appreciation of her faithful services, to choose from the furniture whatever might be any worth, before the broker came; for which she kissed me again, with a reiteration of blessings.

We retired to rest early. Ellice was soon fast asleep, doubtless dreaming of fitting up her best kitchen with our parlour sideboard and faded carpet; but I could not help thinking of the yesterday of my life, and of the to-morrow.

So it was the last night I should ever spend in the White House by the Sea. Memory might hallow the place—

imagination might recall the time—but the memories and picture-visions would be shadows—shadows only.   For

> "Where Time and Death have passed
> Love can do nought but weep."

———◦○◦———

## CHAPTER XXIV.

WHY does Ross come here so often?

The thought has perplexed me many times; he is so unlike every one else, so wrapt up in the reserve of his own speculative mind, so widely apart in his views, opinions, and interests, that it seems impossible to imagine him taking a positive pleasure in anything else.   But it is not business or advancement that brings him down to Ingham-Helmsley; if it is not pleasure, what is it then?   The very name of pleasure makes me smile, when I recall his hard, dry manner, his grave inflexibility of countenance, and the half abstract, half reflective tone when he speaks—and yet why does he come so often?

Ingham is fifty miles from London; and he always takes the latest train on Saturday evening and the earliest on Monday morning—either from press of business, or, more probably, to avoid the company of Lindsay.   Now I cannot conceive any motive but a very strong one that would urge him when worn-out and fagged with the week's work (he is a lawyer), to prefer a tedious railway journey to a comfortable lounge in his chambers.

Sometimes I fancy he is in love with Jeannie; evidently the easy gracefulness and childish confidence of her invariable manner to him, pleases him inexpressibly. I can see it in the brightening of his eyes, whenever she turns to him in any difficulty, and Ross is the highest authority to both Jeannie and me ; I can see it in the gentleness, almost tenderness, with which he addresses her. Besides, is there anything wonderful that he should love Jeannie ? so fair, so loveable, so loving as she is. Could any one help loving her ?

As this thought flashes across my mind, a sharp un-utterable pain shoots through my heart—a wild unnatural fire burns within my bosom. Heaven help me ! of what do I dream ?

Oh, Jeannie, Jeannie !

But I will not harbour the thought ; I strive to forget its existence even, and meet Jeannie and Lindsay with my accustomed look and greeting. Jeannie flies to me and kisses me, again and again ; Lindsay takes both my hands in his, and wishes me a merry Christmas and a happy New Year.

Then he draws my hand under his arm, and we all three walk over the crisp, frosty ground towards Mrs. Dunstan's house.

" I am so glad there is another week yet of the old year ! " Jeannie exclaimed : " it has been such a happy one to me ; I don't want it to go yet."

" Pleasant things are always gone the quickest," Lindsay answered ; " are they not, Chatty ? "

" It's too bad of you," Jeannie interrupted, " to damp me in this way ; but there is another month then, you know, before I shall have to leave Chatty. Mamma won't go to London till February."

" And then how I can triumph over you ! " Lindsay added, laughing. " How I can triumph over little Jeannie ! Whilst you are shut up *nolens volens*, I, like all other lords of the creation, can go where I like, and can come down and see Chatty when you are obliged to content yourself with a letter ! "

" Oh, I'm so glad ! you will come down and see Chatty sometimes, won't you ? " Jeannie said, with ineffable simplicity and sweetness. I looked up into his face, too, for an answer.

" Can you doubt it ? " he said, in a low voice.

I do not know whether the words were addressed either to Jeannie or myself ; but his eyes were on me, and his voice had an undertone of meaning in it that I took trustfully and hopefully into the deep secrecies of my heart. As we approached the house, the figure of a gentleman advanced from the portico to meet us.

" Ross ! " Jeannie cried, in an animated voice, and disengaged her hand from Lindsay's arm, as if to rush and meet him.

" Ay ! how the most stoical monsieur will add to our Christmas festivity ! " Lindsay exclaimed, laughing.

" You don't like Ross," Jeannie said, quickly, with the least shade of a blush on her cheek.

" I never said so."

Lindsay's voice was almost cold, and Jeannie blushed deeper still with vexation ; but she never quitted his side to meet Ross, and her greeting had a touch of embarrassment.

They walked on in advance, and Ross came beside me ; I think Jeannie was asking pardon for her words, or that Lindsay was excusing his own, for the fair young face was raised to his anxiously, and then turned away with a bright smile.

" Poor Jeannie ! "

I looked up with surprise ; they were the first words my companion had uttered, and I could not catch at even their vaguest meaning.

" Why do you say so ? " I asked.

Ross turned round with a sudden start ; first he bit his lips with an expression of annoyance, then said with a curious smile :—

" You have a good deal of common sense, Miss Charlton Warne, but though it is a very simple thing, you wouldn't understand it."

" Thank you, sir," I answered merrily, "for your contradictory opinion of me, which strikes me as not being very easy to understand. If the reason of your pitying Jeannie was so simple, *why* cannot I comprehend it ; I am really anxious to know."

" You are fond of her ?

" Oh yes ! she is my sister—my only friend."

I spoke warmly, and for a minute or two Ross gazed at me with great earnestness, then he broke off abruptly with—

" How long is Mr. Jocelyn going to stay here ? "

I forgot my curiosity at once, and answered with a slight blush :

" Till the end of the week, I believe, at least he has half promised Jeannie to do so."

Ross bit his lip again.

" It is astonishing to me how that Mr. Jocelyn contrives to wind every one's affections round his fingers."

" I don't think it is very astonishing," I said, resolutely, and with sparkling eyes.

" Oh, no Miss Warne, I beg your pardon."

There was a touch of sarcasm in his voice, and I answered coldly—

" There is no occasion."

We walked on in awkward silence for some minutes. I tried to think of some little common-place phrase to break it, but rejected every one either as inappropriate or formal. We were now within a few hundred yards of the house, and

I longed to reach the door eagerly. I was so sorry that any shadow had come between the intercourse formerly existing between Ross and myself, and I could not help acknowledging that I felt less cordial in my heart to him. All of a sudden he turned to me very quickly, and said—

"Don't be angry with me, Miss Warne. You and I have been hitherto such good friends that I would rather do anything than displease you—except be a hypocrite."

"Oh, Mr. Dunstan!" I exclaimed, smiling, what do you mean?—you speak such riddles to-day. I had no right to be displeased with you, although I am afraid I was inclined to be so."

"Bravo! nothing pleases me so much as candour. I like you very much, Miss Warne."

"And what did you mean just now?"

The same expression, half of annoyance half contempt, came over his countenance.

"I know you will be angry, and that you will never like me again——"

He broke off suddenly and smiled, such a genuine pleasant smile! I hardly thought it possible for him to smile so, and continued:

"Don't accuse me of self-esteem; I did not mean to be so egotistical and vain, but there has been a friendliness and mutual cordiality between us, has there not, till now?"

"Yes."

"And why should it not be so still, you will say? It all depends upon yourself, Chatty; I appeal to your intelligence, and understanding—if I see only a horrible superstition and deceit, a trickery of painted images, false jewellery, and unholy imitations of holy pictures—if I, with my older experience and better knowledge of the world, can see this, where you by the torchlight of young imagination, and undeceived love, and goodness, see only a beautiful temple

with God's truth shining within it, and wherein you can say
your prayers safely at the altar———"

He stopped suddenly, as he met my look of wonder; and
added, in his usual quiet manner:

"I suppose, Miss Warne, if I further add my conviction,
that one day sooner or later, you will think as I do—that—
that I am understood."

"I am no Romanist!" I answered, more puzzled than
ever.

At this moment, Jeannie, hanging on Lindsay's arm, and
looking up to him with eyes full of trustfulness and joy,
passed into the portico.

Ross raised his hand to where their faces had just been
turned to us, and looked significantly at me.

"No, no, Miss Warne, I know you are not; but which is
the greater number, think you?   Hearts that are brought
to woe in this world by being sacrificed to false gods—or
souls to damnation in the next, from the same cause?"

Then, without a word more, we entered the house.

---

## CHAPTER XXV

THE day after Christmas-day Mrs. Dunstan gave a ball.   I
think that a great many motives actuated her to do this.
First of all, to dazzle the Count; for that the suave flatteries
and moustachioed charms of the noble Civray Emanuel
Louis Philippe de Perpini, of Château Pons in Normandy,
and Hotel de Perpini, Paris, had greatly warmed the heart
and imagination of Mrs. Dunstan, there required no ghost
to tell me.   It was but natural that her vanity and pride of

wealth should lead her to make a still more splendid show
than she had hitherto done ; and she wished to dazzle and
astonish all Ingham as well : she wished to make a brilliant
display of her riches, her jewellery, her plate, and in fine, of
her extravagance.

So the preparations were set on foot. Carpenters and
joiners were employed by dozens to erect a temporary
dancing-room, on the lawn, as none of the smart drawing-
rooms were considered spacious enough ; orders were sent
up to some of the fitting-up warehouses in Oxford-street,
for velvet and moreen hangings, glass chandeliers, coloured
lamps, gilt and gold vases, frosted silver ornaments—for
anything, in fact, which was glittering, gorgeous, and expensive. From eight in the morning till ten at night Mrs.
Dunstan's bell had a restless time of it. Fruit, wine, con-
fectionery, furniture, millinery, every possible *et cetera* which
rich people can get for money, and everyone else can do
without, was brought in, in mysterious packages, through
the back-door. At first I resolutely turned a deaf ear to
all Jeannie's entreaties that I would be there. I was not
used to anything of the kind ; I was a stranger to all the
gaieties which are so delightful, more or less, to the tastes
of the young ; and I felt no desire to pass the charmed
circle. Besides, the shadows of grief were as sombre
round my heart as the black crape on my dress ; I should
be far happier listening to Mr. Stirling, and with little Ned
for a playfellow.

"I shan't enjoy the ball half so much without you,
Chatty," said Jeannie, yielding reluctantly to my arguments. "Ross, do you not think she might come ? "

It was the evening of Christmas-day, and our conversation had naturally turned upon to-morrow's grand event.
Ross was sitting a little apart, and, as Jeannie appealed to
him, looked up. For the first time since morning our eyes

met, and I coloured involuntarily. I felt a sort of dread
and reluctance in looking at Ross now. Perhaps he saw
it, for he answered in a measured distant voice :

" Really, Jeannie, I think Chatty is far more able to tell
than I."

" Why do you teaze Chatty so ? " pettishly rejoined
Angelica. " I think she is quite right, not to be at the
ball ; anyhow, Jeannie, if she don't wish to come, why, let
the matter rest."

Jeannie smiled saucily.

" I don't do things in the way you do, Angelica."

Lindsay smiled too, and Jeannie wrote, childishly, on
the edge of the book I was reading—

" Angelica, for some reason or other, does not wish you
to be here to-morrow, and that's all the more reason I wish
you should."

By-and-by the fireside party broke up; Mrs. Dunstan
and the Count sat down to a game of chess; Ross drew
forth a note-case and pored over it intently with a contracted brow ; Angelica leaned back in her wicker chair, in
a silent, sullen mood ; Jeannie—simple, infantine, artless
Jeannie—brought out a heap of coloured tissue-paper, over
which she bent her fair head, with all its shining tresses,
wholly engrossed in making flowers and decorations for the
evergreen festoons of the dancing-room ; Lindsay looked
into the fire with a characteristic and by no means unusual
melancholy expression on his features, and I stole up-stairs
into my room.

I could not help thinking of Ross's words ; they had
haunted me the whole day, with a painful disagreeable impression from which I could not free myself, and I wanted
to get rid of it if I could. But how could I ? To speak
of the subject again to Ross, I felt was utterly impossible.
Oh ! what terrible delusion had so blinded him ? I would

have given worlds to justify Lindsay in his eyes, to take away the dark shadow which so deceived him, and to set his character, nobly, manly, and truthful as it was, in clearness before his eyes. That Ross was grossly, cruelly in error I felt assured ; that I could not alter his manner of thinking, I was surer still.

Yet I would try. Alas, that I was so weak! I, who would have staked all my future happiness and hope on his honour and goodness ; I, who would even have laid down my life for him joyfully. It was hard to love him so, and yet have no power to serve him!

I leaned on the landing window in a fit of dreamy thought. It was a splendid winter's night, starlight and clear and still ; the faint light shed by the lamp in the ceiling gave a dusky and dim appearance to the pictured walls and oak carvings, and there was an unwonted hush all over the house. It was very pleasant to stand there and think of Lindsay ; and it was so seldom I had a quiet time for reflection now. Presently I heard a clear and deep voice humming a pensive melody in the hall ; it came nearer, and the next moment he was standing by my side.

"Day-dreaming?" he said, in a low tone ; "Chatty, may I disturb you?"

"Oh, yes."

"I want to say something to you—a favour to ask of you?"

"Me? what can it be?"

"I am afraid you will not grant it, and yet it is a small one, Chatty—a very small one."

"Go on," I said, smiling ; "if it is a small one, why need you fear I shall not grant it?"

"I need not fear, then? Oh, Chatty, how glad I am! Will you, after having refused every one's entreaties to

remain here to-morrow, do so when I ask you—entreat you
even ? "

I looked up in much surprise.

" You wonder at the singularity of my request ; and it
does seem singular, but I do want you very, very much to
be at this ball.  It is not such a great thing to ask, after
all, is it, Chatty ? "

" No, a small one, but——"

I hesitated, and he bent his head lower down, and said
softly, the action and the words causing my heart to beat
with a wild joy—

" Oh, do not refuse ; you must not: I would grant you
any favour you might ask me."

His hair touched my forehead as he spoke ; and the
touch burned me like a lightning stroke.  My frame trembled, and my voice shook as I answered—

" I will grant it."

He repeated a hundred thanks ; he sang playfully, and
whistled as if from very gleefulness : he shook both my
hands ; he stroked my hair ; and used a dozen expressions
of pleasure and praise, as if to a good child.

At the drawing-room door I stopped suddenly, in dismay.

" How inconsistent and childish they will all think me !"

" Never mind.  'Inconsistency is the sign of a great
mind,' you know, so says a philosopher of the present day.
Why, surely, Chatty, you are not afraid, so brave and
resolute as you are.  Would you shrink from serving a
friend because the service incurs an unpleasantness ?  You
shake your head.  I thought so."

" But I am doing you no service," I said, demurely.

" A favour is always a service."

He smiled his old accustomed, half grave, half playful
smile, and opened the door, still retaining my hand on his
arm.

The party were all just as we had left them, but all looked up as we entered the room. And somehow every one looked astonished.

" A triumph ! a triumph ! " Lindsay exclaimed, glancing round with an exultant expression.

The astonishment increased trebly.

" A triumph !  Mrs. Dunstan, Jeannie, Angelica, all listen, Mr. Ross Dunstan, Count de Perpini ; listen ! "

" What is the matter ? " cried Jeannie, jumping up hastily, and letting fall her whole treasure of mock flowers and coloured snips.  " What is the matter, Lindsay ? how pleased you look ! "

" Good news, Jeannie, and what will please you, too, and Angelica too."

Angelica looked up, and something of the cloudiness on her brow passed off.

"How can you be so tantalizing ? " she said, in a pleased-annoyed tone.

" Well then," Lindsay exclaimed, with hilarity unaccountable in his voice and manner, " I have persuaded Chatty at last to—to remain for the ball ! "

Mrs. Dunstan and the Count resumed their game with a mutual shrug of the shoulders ; Jeannie jumped up and kissed me in the exuberance of her joy ; Angelica curled her lip with unwonted disdain and contemptuousness ; Ross glanced at me sharply for an instant, and then resumed his book.

Jeannie's work was over for to-night ; so, happy as a young bird, she placed three chairs by the fire, and she and Lindsay and I sat there together, in quiet, happy conversation, all the rest of the evening.

Only one thing disturbed us : the angry fiery flash of Angelica's eyes, as she glanced at us ever and anon.  But we were all getting used to her wayward moods now, and I was too joyful and too excited to bestow much thought upon anything.

And Lindsay—never had I seen him so humorous, so light-hearted, so animated as that night. How glad I was that I had pleased him !

---

## CHAPTER XXVI.

Ross is gone ! On the morning of the ball he took his leave. Business, he said, called him immediately to London, and his manner was distant and ceremonious to the utmost. I was too happy in my own thoughts to occupy myself with his departure, and, speaking candidly, I felt relieved that he was gone ; every one else was too busy to think of him, and his name was not mentioned all day. Poor Ross !—and yet he was more clever and better than any of us !

When he had turned away from me with a quiet and formal—" Good-by, Chatty," though I spoke formally too, my heart smote me, for Ross had been very kind to me. And yet, why so ? I recalled Lindsay, and my cheek burned proudly. I could not have said a gentler word to Ross for the world.

I was to wear one of Jeannie's dresses, a simple white muslin, and with only white roses for trimming. It was Lindsay's taste, Jeannie said, and whose taste was so good as his ? But, though Jeannie and I were much of the same stature and form, there were several little alterations to make ; here was a strip of ribbon hanging down, or a jagged hem, there a rose torn from its leaves, or the leaves without the rose, but all these could be soon set right, and the dress

well contented me; it was so summer-like, so light and
youthful; and with a good heart I sat down to my task.

Whilst so employed, Lindsay entered; he did not speak,
but had a pleased smile on his face, and placed in my hands
a small bunch of rare hot-house flowers.

"For you to wear this evening, Chatty. I got them on
purpose."

I could not thank him at first, but my blushing cheeks
and glistening eyes told him more than words could have
done.

"I am so glad they have pleased you," he said, and then
went away as silently as he came.

In that hour I was weak, I was vain, I was childish,
I confess it all; I could think no more of the ball, no more
of my employment, but kissed the charmed flowers again
and again, and watered them with plenteous happy tears.
They were to me a key to Paradise—the ' Open sesame' to
a mystical and a delicious realm. How radiant, far-soaring,
and heavenly my thoughts were, no words can express. And
if amongst my readers there be any that have dreamed this
dream with me, that have like me passed from a dark
Egypt to a fair and rich Goshen, who have passed many
years in loneliness, one in the blissfulness of young love—
for them no words will be needed.

I felt assured that he returned my love. How could I
doubt it? He had shown pleasure in my presence, and had
not forgotten me when away; he had spoken to me of his
inmost thoughts and feelings; he had always appealed to
my opinions—and he had given me flowers.

No wonder that this conviction so enraptured me. I had
never seen any one like him before; so cavalierly, so noble
both in look and bearing, so manly and yet gentle, so self-
reliant and yet generous. Oh, it was a very fair picture
that I cherished at heart!

I was just carrying off my precious flowers when Angelica entered. Her sharp glance fastened on them instantaneously.

"Ha! where did you get them from? what are they for?"

"To wear this evening."

"Who gave them to you?"

She darted an ungentle hand at them, but I drew back.

"Take care," I said, quietly, "I value them."

"Then he gave them to you?"

"He? how strange you are, Angelica! whom do you mean?"

"Let me look at them," she said, unheeding my question.

An odd mixture of assumed annoyance and playfulness was in her manner; I could see that Lindsay's gift aroused still more the latent antipathy she conceived for me.

"Do not let me touch them. Oh no, let no one for the world breathe on them! Chatty, you are a baby, worse than a baby—a fool. You think that Lindsay Jocelyn cares for you—not he. I wouldn't touch the flowers for the world, I should poison them. Ah, take the precious things upstairs, put them in a glass case—keep them till they are dead, dead, dead! Think that he loves you—think that he will marry you—treasure what thoughts you please. It will be the same in the end. If nothing else teaches you, time will. Love him, win his affections and his promises; think that he will never fail in either——"

I would hear no more. I knew what an ungovernable fiery temperament, and what a treacherous, passionate leaven, was mixed in her Indian nature, and the words were all blunted arrows. But I would not hear more: pride revolted, and pride made me resolute; and without bestowing on her a word or look I quitted the room. But my persecutor was not easily daunted. Closely on my heels she followed me upstairs.

"Ah! you look haughty; you borrow Ross Dunstan's contemptuous smile. Do you think I fear you? no—not I. Touch the flowers I *will*: Miss Charlton Warne, do you hear? you are not Ross, remember; or if you were, what do I care for him? You think Lindsay loves you—you expect he will marry you, and hold his flowers as dear as if they had fallen from heaven. But the god is not for *you.* How you admire him; how you listen to his words, and look up to him when he vouchsafes a smile, and tremble when he speaks your name! But know, Chatty Warne, this is not the way to win his love. Oh no, no, you do not understand Lindsay Jocelyn."

She looked at me fixedly for a moment, her dark wild eyes dilating with a fire of ungoverned passion and vehemence, then exclaimed—

"You love him! Do you think you can deceive *me?* And you think to win him—you think that your weak woman's adoration, and meek following his shadow, will win the lofty star to your feet. Ha! you have prepared yourself a pleasing delusion for the future. Not so—not in worshipping and spirit-submitting veneration is Lindsay Jocelyn to be won! Poor simple fool that you are! of just such ones as you are the whole class of man's dupes. Do you not see that what is farthest removed, most difficult of access, most hard to attain, is always most sought after? And do you not know that what is to be had for nothing is never prized. Pshaw! the game is lost, utterly lost, to you, Chatty Warne, long ago."

"Then why do you hate me, Angelica?" I said, quietly.

"That has nothing to do with it. The game has been in my own hands all along."

"I do not think so."

"Because you are jealous."

"Oh, by no means, you have no right to affirm that I love Lindsay."

"Pshaw! what a child you are! Then why were you so afraid that I should touch the flowers?"

"The reason is obvious enough; you would pull them to pieces."

I fixed my eyes on her sharply, and for a moment she averted her own, but it was only for a moment; then her lips curled, and she answered—

"But if you do not value them, what would it matter if I did?"

"Angelica, you are as much of a child as myself," I answered smiling: "why, do you not know that I want them for the ball this evening—every one wears flowers, and if it were not for these, I should have none."

I think she hardly knew whether I was in jest or earnest, for she looked at me curiously, as if she would fain read my inmost thoughts; but I bent my head down low, till my face was almost hidden from her; so low even that my lips touched the treasured gift. I confess that there was a sensation of pride mixed with the pleasure and hopes which his gift brought me; there they lay, the white wax-like blossoms surrounded with their dark green shining leaves, beautiful in every part, but beautiful most of all because they were linked with association to him. Ah, how sweet to me were alike the flowers and thoughts which hung round them! Yet perhaps Angelica had said aright: was I not a child, a fool?—might not the blossoms and the hopes alike wither?

"Come, Angelica," I said, frankly, for I was willing to forgive her much, knowing, as I did, what an irregular and reckless teaching her wayward youth had received. "Come, Angelica, let us be friends, why should we not be so, since we are not rivals?"

I made a desperate effort to conquer the distrust and uncharitableness I felt within me, and placed the flowers on the table.

It was a tacit appeal to her generosity, as well as a conquest over self; I moved about the room with an affected carelessness, but keeping a watchful look on her all the time. I think a struggle was going on in her mind too; she stood quite still, and with her face turned directly from me, but I could catch a glimpse now and then of a quivering lip and a working brow; presently her eyes turned on me, with an almost tiger glance, so fiery, so eager. Then—then she moves forward—she stretches out her hand; in another moment the ground is covered with rich white blossoms!

## CHAPTER XXVII.

I DID not speak; I could not trust myself to speak, while such a tumult of hasty impetuous thoughts swelled within my heart; but I opened the door wide, I commanded her, half by a gesture, half by a look that implied an abhorrence of her presence, to leave me. And she went. Then I knelt on the ground, and carefully, very carefully picked up all the scattered petals; not one I allowed to escape me.

Whilst thus employed, Jeannie entered.

"Oh, Chatty, how came this? the lovely flowers Lindsay just bought for you! What a pity!"

"It is indeed."

"But how could it happen, Chatty? they couldn't *fall* to pieces."

"But flowers go, to pull to pieces—"

"Pull? why, Chatty, do tell me how this came about?"

"Angelica!"

I said no more; and there was no need. Jeannie's eyes met mine, with a mutual expression of distrust and presentiment.

"She is jealous—she loves him!" were her first words.

Then she looked at me again; but this time I turned away my face; there was something in the half-curious, half-inquiring way in which she seemed to ask my very thoughts that well nigh abashed me. I had thoughts even that were too precious and recessed for Jeannie's eyes.

"It was very nice of Lindsay to get them for you," she began, in a half-hesitating manner that was foreign to her; "but why should Angelica be so jealous? Lindsay has never —do you think—I mean, have you any idea——?"

"My dear Jeannie," I said, smiling, "what *do* you mean?"

She put her arm around me, and whispered, as if the thought were too sacred for utterance—"Does he love you?"

I drew the fair ingenuous face towards me, and gazed earnestly on it: there was an expression of perplexity in her eyes, of trouble almost, which I had never read there before; and the eyes were averted quickly, as if she were unwilling to be so scrutinized.

"What is it, dear?"

"That isn't fair," she answered, blushing; "answer me first."

"Will you then tell me what made my little Jeannie so grave just now?"

"I was not exactly grave," she said, with perfect simplicity, and blushing still deeper; "but the idea was so strange and so sudden! It never entered my head before that Lindsay should fall in love with *you;* and yet I do not see why I should be surprised : there is nothing extraordinary in it, is there ? "

" I think so : but he has *not* fallen in love with me, that I know of, Jeannie."

For some minutes, her head was bent over the heap of scattered petals I held on my lap ; and she kept gathering little bunches of them together, and then dividing them again, as if unconsciously. At length I broke silence :

" Well, Jeannie, are you pleased, or sorry ? "

" I should like to have you always happy——"

" And do you think his love would make me so ? "

" Oh yes ! how can you ask ? could any one help being happy with him ? "

" You would like me to marry Lindsay, then ? "

" If he loved you as much as I do."

I embraced her warmly ; but we neither of us recurred to the subject ; somehow, without a word being said, we both of us felt that it was not a grateful one.

" But, about the flowers ; how could Angelica do so ? "

" I cannot imagine ; without the slightest cause she is so very jealous."

" How she loves him, Chatty ! I could almost pity her. I am sure he does not care for her."

" I can hardly call Angelica's feeling for Lindsay, love," I said, decisively.

" No ?—why not ? "

" She has not soul enough. Love is tender and trusting, and unselfish : love is content to *serve*, it does not seek to *reign*. Do you think Angelica is capable of anything like this ? Oh no, hers is but a wild passion—an ambition to possess what all the world would admire. It would be a triumph for her to see Lindsay at her feet—nothing more. I don't call this love, Jeannie."

" I understand. Ah, Chatty, you know how to love ! "

Just then, there was a sound of quick footsteps on the stairs, and of a manly but sweet voice humming an old Scotch air. Jeannie started up hastily, and ran to the door.

"Lindsay, come here one minute; do, dear Lindsay!"

"And what does little Jeannie want now, eh?"

And then he murmured something about Jeannie never letting him be at peace one minute, but the words were belied by the readiness with which he obeyed her, and the pleasant smile on his handsome mouth.

"Whew! what now?" he said, with a comical whistle and puzzled face: "upon my word, Chatty, this is very complimentary to my poor flowers; but now, Jeannie, didn't you do it?"

"Now, Lindsay, that's very unkind," said Jeannie, half smiling, half crying, "what do you mean? I was just as sorry about it as Chatty."

He drew her towards him, and kissed her cheek, penitently, for Lindsay, even now, forgot at times that Jeannie was no longer a child.

"But tell me about it, Jeannie, do."

So Jeannie told him. At the first mention of Angelica's name, I saw that he coloured slightly, and a curious expression passed over his features; it might be pain or vanity gratified, or mere annoyance, and it might also be a compound of all three; I cannot tell; but I was inclined to think that the former feeling predominated, for he merely said:—

"Caprice, that's all; there's no accounting for those hot Indian tempers, but you shall not be the loser, Chatty. I will procure you some more flowers—only," and he smiled meaningly—"only as your forces are so inefficient to protect them, I will keep them myself till we meet in the ball-room."

## CHAPTER XXVIII.

A STRANGE, incomprehensible being was Angelica; there was no shame written on her face when I encountered her again; no down-looking of the eyes which could be understood as a token of inward humiliation at the passionate and infantine malice which she had just shown. I met her gaze earnestly, fixedly, and with as much of—"Are you not ashamed of yourself?" as I could anyhow put on, but to no purpose. I suppose some people are born without a conscience; certainly she had none. She opened her eyes wide when she saw me, with a most unmistakeable don't-care-for-you look, and with a defiant curl, or rather sneer, on her under lip which told me, as plainly as the plainest words could have done, that it was of no use for me to carry it with a high hand, for that by so doing I could neither frown her down into anything like self-abasement or into a shadow of fear for myself; so I felt that the best course to pursue (best, as being the only practicable one) was to be good-tempered about it, and show her that if she was not afraid of me, I was not afraid of her; and that I was by no means of too angelic a frame of mind, to enjoy a laugh at her expense in my own heart.

"What are you going to wear to-night, Chatty?" she said to me, with the greatest *sang-froid*, as we rose from the dinner-table.

"A white muslin."

As Jeannie spoke for me she blushed deeply.

"It is one that Jeannie has been kind enough to lend me," I answered; "I have no ball dresses of my own."

She looked at me hardly.

"I am not ashamed to confess my poverty," I continued,

with a smile. " Perhaps if I had made the confession soonei you would have spared my poor flowers; I have no other ornaments."

" Pshaw! I will lend you a dozen gold bracelets—will that satisfy you?"

I recoiled.

" I would not wear one of your bracelets for the world."

" Then why harp on the wretched flowers; what would you have? If I were in your place, and were too poverty-stricken to buy jewellery, I should be only too glad to borrow some of somebody else."

" I had rather go without them."

" Yes; you are so absurdly proud."

" But even if I were rich, I should not wear much jewellery; I don't care for it. Now a simple bunch of flowers that a friend has given me is very different; I should have more pleasure in wearing it than I should have in all the precious stones and gold that are in your possession."

She made no answer, but fixed her dark lustrous eyes upon me searchingly.

" You don't believe me," I said.

" Yes, I do; whatever you are, I don't think you are a hypocrite."

" Oh, thank you," I exclaimed, with a mock politeness; " you are too gracious really! but don't you agree with me?"

" About what?"

" The flowers."

" Ah, you were saying some sentimental thing about the gift of a friend being more gratifying to wear than——

I put my hand on her arm.

" Angelica, whatever you are, don't be a hypocrite. I know that in your secret heart you agree with me, or——"

" Or what?"

" I am not quite such a fool as you imagine me!" I

answered quickly; "besides, the deduction is simple enough—or you would not have pulled Lindsay's gift to pieces."

I think she was rather taken aback at my plainness; at any rate she moved from my side without giving me another word or look, and she seldom did so when she had an expressive word or look to give.

Angelica was in love with Lindsay, then! Well, I had seen it long ago; there was no occasion for me to feel annoyed or disquieted now, for was not my love returned?

Yes, I believed that he loved me. How could I help believing so? And yet—and yet a cold chill came over me. Out of the intensity of my love for Lindsay, arose a fear of Angelica. I quailed in my spirit as I thought of the terrible power she held over my fate. Still, I feared less for myself than for him. I could endure the thought of my own unhappiness, but I could not endure the thought of his misery; and misery a union with Angelica must entail upon him.

She was not intellectual; she had no heart: unable as she was to be the joy and solace of a domestic hearth, still less was she capable of entering into the pursuits and tone of a mind so cultivated and refined as his. I could bear the idea of Lindsay's loving another, but that that one should be incapable of rendering him happy was insupportable.

And she was clever: clever, cunning, far-sighted, unprincipled, and selfish. I trembled with apprehension, and grew sick at heart. Ah, how little he knew of my fears and prayers for his happiness!

## CHAPTER XXIX.

" Nearly nine o'clock ?  Oh, I'm so glad !  we can go down now ;  Chatty, are you ready ? "

" Yes, quite."

" How nice you look !  you haven't half looked at yourself yet ;  come to the large mirror in the ante-room ;  it's quite empty—you must."

So, half dragging, half pushing, Jeannie led me to the mirror.  For a minute I stood before it, and the burden of my reverie was this :—

" So, Chatty Warne, you have metamorphosed yourself from the little quiet nun of the lonely White House by the Sea into a ball-room lady, and have entered energetically and rapturously into the ' giddy round of vain delight ' which hitherto you have so much despised.  But you don't care for it : you would rather be away ?  Ah, this sophistry is all very well now that you are bedecked in white muslin and roses, and on the point of setting your foot in the ball-room.  It's an easy thing to despise what you are sure not to lose.  You *do* care for it, Chatty Warne ; you are dying with anxiety to see if Lindsay Jocelyn remembers his promise ; you are fevered with suspense to know if among the eighty-three Ingham-Helmsley belles he will show you the slightest mark of preference.  You fear, you tremble, you look hesitatingly and diffidently on your unpretending appearance : well, is the conviction new to you that you are not pretty ?  Did you never notice before that your features are not classic ?  Did you ever arrogate to yourself a queenly bearing ? if so, you are much deceived.  You are a simple-hearted sensible-looking country girl, that is all, with a quiet, gentlewomanly manner, that is neither majestic nor com-

manding, and with features not quite regular enough to be
handsome, but too regular to be called plain. Why, are
you not content now? Do you not know, Chatty Warne,
that if Lindsay Jocelyn loved you, you would be entirely
beautiful in his eyes? Do you think every one else admires
and reverences him as you do? What did Ross say? You
think he hates him? of course, *de facto*, because Ross does
not hero-worship Lindsay as you do, you think he hates
him. Ah! there is nothing so foolish as to reason with any
one in love——"

How long this debate between reason and feeling would
have gone on, I cannot say, but at that moment a shining,
radiant figure was reflected in the glass before me. It was
Angelica, and I started violently.

Never had I seen her so gorgeous and striking as she
appeared before us now; "she shimmered like the sun" in
a perfect galaxy of jewels and gold; her skirt, of the richest
white brocade, embroidered with gilt stars and flowers,
swept like a train upon the ground, and the diamond tiara
which sparkled on her shining black hair might have graced
the head of majesty. Indeed, she was the very personification of an eastern queen; her dusky features were perfectly
formed and delicate; her eyes had that indolent, swimming
look under which you can see a world of fire and passion,
and her figure was slight, yet rounded and graceful.

We stood side by side.

In height we were much alike, but in every other respect
how different! Angelica thought so too, for her eyes flashed
triumphantly as she turned to me and said—

"If you're satisfied, Miss Charlton Warne, we'll go
down."

In a few minutes the ball-room began to fill; Mrs. Dunstan's pale, indolent features flushed with excitement and
hostess-responsibility, although she was energetically backed

by the smooth-spoken and shining Count Civray, who looked
in his scrupulous and affected dress the ideal of a French
beau passé.    And oh, what a mixed and motley assemblage
were there !  First of all were the Vellacotts : Mr. Vellacott
is a clergyman ;  he gets three hundred a year, and on this
he supports a wife who must have a sea-coast cottage every
autumn, and cannot dine at any other hour but aristocratic
seven ;  five daughters who ride single, who are too well
bred to learn anything of household duties but to order the
servants and the fashionable but most uncomfortable meals,
and whose duty and delight it is to excommunicate all the
Sunday school children who give way to the vanity of curls
or parasols ; seven sons, who, of course, " being nephews to
the Bishop of N——," must be brought up to professions ;
and two servants!    On my word, in spite of the seven
o'clock dinners and the mutton hashes, I pity the servants
least of all.    They, at least, if they share the burden, have
not the ambition and humiliation of gentility.    The Misses
Vellacott are tall girls who might be more prepossessing if
their carriage was not so ungraceful, and their dress a little
more neat, but I must confess their conversation does not
please me ; they are continually dilating on the elegancies
and luxuries of their home, the strawberry parties, the
musical soirées, the green-house beauties, the plentiful
supply of new and expensive books, the multifarious masters,
and the forty guinea ponies.    Now it is a particular and
obstinate idiosyncrasy of mine to be somewhat incredulous
of what is insisted upon with so much pains.    I have always
observed that with a certain class of vain and aspiring
people it is a rule to be continually asserting their right to
something to which they have not the least pretensions.
Now this is a great folly, and the more to be wondered at
since it is so easily seen through.    But *revenons à nos
danseurs :* then there were all the richest and smartest of

the Ingham-Helmsley shipowners, for the most part individuals of one stamp and set; good-natured, doubtless, and kind-hearted, but whose character, both in the abstract and concrete, you could read at once; for, backwards or forwards, spelled which way you will, there was but one signature—love and admiration of money. You could see it in the comprehensive glance with which the heads of the families took in an average estimate, rating all conclusive signs and evidences, the annual amount of Mrs. Dunstan's income; you could see it in the way in which the younger members looked superciliously from your unadorned white muslin to their stiff satins and blazing jewellery. And the aristocracy of Ingham-Helmsley were there also; Sir Bingham Lloyd and his vulgar wife; Sir John Markham, M.P.; and Lord K——'s daughters (the paterfamilias is unfortunately confined by gout upstairs every Christmas, just when the tradesmen most want him below), the Honourable Cirencester Pyne, who ran off with another man's wife because he couldn't afford to keep his own; and a multitude of others—young, old, middle-aged—all smiling, all bland, all apparently delighted with each other. Ah, how little does the surface resemble that which lies underneath!

It was past ten o'clock, and as yet Lindsay had not appeared. "It's a little vanity of dear Lindsay's," Jeannie whispered to me, "to be late; do you understand? he likes to create a sensation, it amuses him. How Angelica is watching for him! see, how she plumes herself whenever the door is opened; she anticipates a triumph to-night, but she doesn't know Lindsay. Well, we'll see; I hope she won't get one."

Then Jeannie looked in Angelica's direction again, and added—

"She will get attention, of course; all handsome co-quettes do."

Presently, a tall and striking-looking man entered the room; there was an involuntary hush, for all eyes were turned on the new-comer. It was Lindsay. He advanced slowly up the room, with an easy gracefulness and nonchalance of carriage that was very foreign to the would-be prepossession, and affected man-of-the-world-ism of the fashionable young men of Ingham-Helmsley: a quiet, almost thoughtful smile played on his lips, as he returned the gracious salutations which were given him, and he was just known enough to be interesting to such stranger-seeking, stranger-loving people as Mrs. Dunstan's guests. A vacant chair was by Angelica; he passed it, and I saw her eyes flash with rising anger as he did so. My heart beat quickly with an indefinite sensation of joy. In another moment he was by my side.

" You see," he said, softly, "that I have not forgotten my promise."

Then bending down, he fastened a small cluster of roses to my brooch, and added—" You deserve double and treble such a service as this, for I owe you so much."

" Me! what have I done for you ? " I asked tremblingly, for his presence always unnerved me.

" Much ; to you I owe the chief pleasure of this evening —your presence."

Then he exclaimed in a different voice—

" You have never been in a ball-room before ; what do you think of it all ? "

" The question is a difficult one. I hardly know yet what my ideas are."

" Analyze them : do you like it ? "

" I do not know ; I feel very happy——"

" As happy as ever you felt in your life before ? "

" Yes; I have not often been very happy."

For a minute he looked at me searchingly.

"And yet," he continued, musingly, "it would be difficult for you to name one individual cause for this feeling; is it not so? It does not arise from finding yourself in such society, refined of mind, and faultless of manners, though it be!"

This was said with irony, and I smiled.

"Oh no, no!"

"And it does not arise from the mere love of gaiety; your taste does not lie that way. Right again, Chatty?"

"Yes."

"Ah!" he said, gaily, "had I the wisdom of forty Solomons, I can see by your face, Chatty, that you are determined my wisdom shall not prevail against you. You will not tell me?"

"Not for the world."

"Then I shall imagine it to be just what I please. They are forming for a quadrille. Give me your hand."

After the quadrille, came a Lancer's. Lindsay danced with Jeannie this time, but they were *vis-à-vis* to me, and as my companion only addressed me once, and then to ask if I did not think the room growing excessively warm, looking excessively sheepish whilst he did so, I could hear all the witty and pleasant things Lindsay was saying, and for which he invariably looked to me for an answer. And so the hours wore on; and he was never long from my side, and I was very happy, except now and then, when amidst the white drapery and festoons a pair of black shining eyes flashed on me with a jealous and passionate look.

Only once I saw him with her; her head was raised to his, and she was speaking to him with a variable and hurried manner,—now pleadingly, reproachfully—now vehemently, energetically—her eyes changing their expression as she spoke, from softness to eagerness, and from eagerness to softness again, as her voice altered. Twice Lindsay bent his head low, and answered her. He did not say much, two or three words only, but Angelica laid her hand on his arm significantly, and looked up into his face with a grateful look; then they were both silent.

Strange, but at that moment I remembered Ross's words, and the remembrance sent a pang through my heart.

"Pshaw! 'tis nothing. Angelica has been scolding him because he hasn't danced with her; that's all: and he has promised to be more attentive in future. He told me a little while ago that he expected a regular storm."

It was Jeannie who spoke; she had suddenly broken in on my reverie, and divined with uncommon tact the subject of my thoughts. I blushed at my own self-deception, and took care not to welcome the terrible thought again.

By-and-by the dancing-room cleared: parties of two and four strolled up and down the music gallery, through the refreshment-rooms and conservatory, and groups were knotted at every entrance; there was a warm perfume of flowers and wine, and a low indistinct murmur of much conversation. Lindsay was again with us; he had not mentioned Angelica's name, but when she passed us he averted his face and smiled sarcastically. The smile was directed to me, and I read in it a deep meaning.

"Come into the hall," said Jeannie, rising; "I think it will be cool there, for no one seems to know where to find it, and I want to have you see how pretty the flower-stands and statues and Chinese lamps look, Lindsay; you know it was fitted up entirely according to *my* direction."

Lindsay rose, for he was always pleased to praise Jeannie, and we went.

It was charming; the entrance-ways, all excepting one, were hidden by rows of winter shrubs and flowers, in huge pots of fantastic shape, and among which were placed vases and statuary, shining out from the dark green leaves. The

place was only partially lighted—here Jeannie's taste had
done her good stead—by brightly coloured Chinese lamps ;
and though we could hear the surrounding hum of conversation, it was very quiet and refreshing.

Lindsay was very silent ; his face resting on his hand,
and his eyes fixed on the ground, abstractedly, and we were
quiet also.  Once he said—

" Do not let us go back again yet ; " and there was
almost a sadness in his voice ; but that was all.

At last, when the music began, Jeannie jumped up,
saying she had forgotten an engagement with Mr. Erasmus
Vellacott for the next waltz.   When she was gone, Lindsay
turned to me and began—

" What a dear child Jeannie is ?"

" Yes ; who could help loving her ? "

" No one ; I am not sure that she has a fault.   Do you
think she likes me, Chatty ? "

" I am sure of it."

" I am rejoiced to hear you say so.   I am very fond of
her ; she is like a little sister to me.  How she loves you ! "

" I have no other friend."

Then I corrected myself, and added—

" At least, I have only one other."

I blushed, and Lindsay knit his brows :

" Then you do not consider me a friend ? " he said, in a
half-offended tone.

" I said one other."

" And that one is Mr. Stirling : it is not so ? "

I hesitated.

" Chatty," he continued, in a reproachful voice, " I am
disappointed.   I had hoped that you would at least bestow
on me the name of friend."

He drew back, with contracted brow and compressed lips.

" Forgive me," I said, mustering courage, " I did not

mean that—I should be glad and proud—oh, Lindsay, I have so few friends; you will forgive my words, and let me look up to you as a friend, will you not?"

He held out his hand to me, with his old playful, kindly smile, and clasped mine with a friendly touch.

"A contract," he said, smiling, "never to be broken."

At that moment; when the words were hardly out of his lips, and his hand still held mine, there was a rustle in the green leaves behind me; and before I could turn my head to look, the string which had confined the marble Diana to its place gave way: the statue reeled—it fell—fell with a heavy and sharp blow on my forehead. My eyes swam; a feeling of sickness and giddiness came over me, and the blood streamed down from the wound on to the ground. Then Lindsay bore me, strongly and tenderly, as if I were a child, to my own room; and though I was stunned and faint and speechless, I forgot half the pain in the pleasure of listening to the solicitude of the beloved voice.

---

## CHAPTER XXX.

AFTER my wound had been dressed, and the physician was gone, Lindsay rose to go; only Jeannie would be left in the room, and a vague sense of fear overpowered me. I held out my hand as if to detain him, and whispered—

"Oh, do not go yet—please do not, till Susan comes."

He smiled a kind assent, and seated himself on a chair, beside the sofa, on which I lay. Jeannie sat on a little stool by the fire opposite, regarding me with anxious and affectionate looks.

When I spoke, she bent her head forward and said, in a low voice, to Lindsay—

"She seems to be under a fear of something. How strange it is! so courageous as Chatty is in ordinary, too.'

She regarded him questioningly, but ho only shook his head, and raised his finger to his lips, as if to enjoin silence.

How heavy and complete that silence was! I lay perfectly motionless, and without the power of stirring, gazing with fixed, strained, fearful eyes on the half-opened door. I could not see anything else. I tried to see anything, think of anything, but that dreadful door; it was no use, and the fascination was agony. By-and-by, I saw a tall figure move softly, very softly across the room, shut the door and bolt it. Then I looked in that direction no more, and felt as if I could rest. It was not so. Once or twice, indeed, I closed my eyes and slept. But oh, what a dreadful sleep was that! the nightmare visions were even worse than the day hallucinations. A horrible numbness and powerlessness seemed to paralyze me like a spell; and a fiendlike shape, omnipresent and revengeful, hovered near, intent to take away my life. I tried to break away from the charm—to rise—to flee away, but I could not, and awoke, crying—

"She is coming, she is coming! Lindsay, save me!"

They both rose in alarm, and stood beside me. Jeannie pressed her cool palm on my burning forehead, and Lindsay took my trembling hands in his.

"It was a dream," I said, in a faint voice; "oh, do not let me go to sleep again."

"You shall not," he said, gently; "and we are both with you—Jeannie and I."

By-and-by, there was a tap at the door. I started convulsively.

"It's only Susan!" Jeannie exclaimed; "shall I let her in, Chatty dear?"

Susan was a privileged "old servant" of Mrs. Dunstan's, of strong nerves, good heart and sound principles; consequently she was trustworthy and trusted: nothing could be done without her, and nothing was kept from her.

"Oh yes; I shall be quite contented with her; and do you both go to rest, you need it."

"I do not: and if I were, I could sleep in the arm-chair here, by the fire," answered Jeannie, decisively. "I would not leave you for the world."

"You are quite right, Jeannie; good night, then." He bent over me, and added, in a lower key, "Be composed, I entreat you, and try and rest tranquilly; when the excitement of the first shock is over, you will feel much better; believe me, there is nothing to fear now; and even if there were, shall not I watch over you?"

I tried to smile my thanks, and then he went. Jeannie shut the door, barred it, and, having assisted Susan in undressing me, ensconced herself on the sofa I had quitted; Susan took the arm-chair, and Lindsay's words acting like a charm upon me, I fell into a sweet and soothing sleep. It did not last long, however; I awoke with a nervous, throbbing pain at my temples, and an overworn, listless sensation that I had never experienced before. By daylight the physician was at my bedside again.

"You have had a restless night?" he said, abruptly.

"Yes."

"And yet I administered a sedative, and you are unused to them, are you not; you have never been very ill before?"

"No."

"Strange."

He scrutinized me minutely for a few minutes, and then continued—

" And you are not constitutionally nervous ? "

"Not in the least."

Again he mused.

" It was not the accident alone that can have so affected
you.　There was some other cause associated with it; am
I not right ? "

I assented, and he motioned Susan to leave the room ;
Jeannie had left it an hour since at my entreaty to take
some real rest in her own room, and the physician and I
were alone.　He was a tall, uncommon looking man, with
quiet down-looking eyes that to some observers might seem
to denote an indolent and careless temperament, but which I
have always found, on further study, characterize a type of
men (and those down-looking, unrevealing eyes are rare)
who read others well, but are never read; who see farthest
but are never supposed to see anything at all.　And such individuals are close students of the philosophy of human nature.

" There is some one in this house," I said, in a lowered
but distinct voice, " who hates me."

" Go on, you have something else to say ? "

" And the cause of her hate is—jealousy."

" Is there any ground for it ? "

"Perhaps so ! " I answered, flushing slightly.

The face opposite mine assumed a very grave look.　I
could see that Dr. Lambert's shrewd surmises had filled up
my suggestions accurately.

" You cannot advise me, sir ? " I said, despondingly.

"I am afraid not; your case is a very peculiar and
difficult one; the only safe course would be to——"

" Go away ?　That would imply cowardice."

" Yes, I am aware of it; but consider—only to one
person that cowardice would be apparent, and that one—
knowing what she is, what matters it what her opinion of
you may be ? "

"You guess, then ?"

He smiled.

"Of course; do you think I have attended this house so long and not formed an estimate of the members? But, my dear young lady, *some* course must be taken. Are you aware that there is Spanish as well as Indian blood in her veins?"

Involuntarily I shuddered.

"Do not distress yourself now," said Dr. Lambert, kindly; "a few days hence will do; keep to your room, and try to be as composed as you can: as long as you are a prisoner here, *I* can answer for your safety."

Then he rang for Susan, spoke a few words to her in an undertone, shook hands cordially with me, and went.

———◆———

## CHAPTER XXXI.

DR. LAMBERT and I became good friends. He was interested in me, and I knew it; besides, though there was so much necessary difference between myself and the clever experienced doctor, and though in character there could be hardly a point of resemblance, there was a tone and idiosyncrasy of his mind into which I could enter at once, and comprehend perfectly. This he saw, and it pleased him.

Almost a week passed; my wound was healing fast, and with returning strength returned something of my old courage also; but I still kept to my own room, and Dr. Lambert, although his visits could hardly be termed professional ones now, still continued them daily.

"Miss Warne," he said to me one day, after we had had

a long conversation, " I wish you had not been a lady—I mean that you had been of the other sex."

" Why so, sir ? " I asked smiling, at his earnestness.

" Why ? because you have the stuff in you to make a MAN! and very rare material that is now-a-days ; well, in the first place you have got brains—your perceptive powers are quick, active, and correct ; in the next place, you have got a mind—all the experiences, reflections, and conclusions that you have harvested up are of use to you.  You can *perceive*, but, what is a far rarer faculty, you can *reason*. On my word, Miss Warne, you surprise me—your educa-tion——"

" I have had none, sir."

" Pardon me," resumed the physician, tartly, " you have had the very best education, for you have been *self-taught ;* but you do surprise me, I assure you.   Your life has been uni-formly spent at Ingham, I believe, you have informed me ? "

" Entirely so."

" And I have not known one woman in fifty—not one in a hundred—under twenty, who has shown, even in a long acquaintance, the acuteness of observation, and the just and clear discrimination that you have shown me during our short intercourse.   Yet I have known women of all ages, spheres, and characters, women who have travelled half their lives, women who have lived in large circles of society, both in London and Paris—and you have never been beyond a little out-of-the-way old-fashioned town on the coast.  But what matters it ?    Human nature is the same everywhere. 'Tis but the same word spelled differently.   You would like to travel, I dare say ? "

" Very much."

" Of course ; and if you went up the Rhine and came home by Paris you would think you had seen the world. Some American writer calls travelling a ' fool's paradise ; '

I don't quite think so. There is much to be learned in foreign travel, doubtless ; but on an average, take a man who has spent half his life in wandering up and down the world—who has seen Athens, Jerusalem, and Rome ; take another who has reached the same term of life, but which he has passed in some active calling in a great city or community ; let them both be of mediocre abilities, neither quite sages nor fools, and ten to one if the latter be not the wiser of the two, and the most useful member of society as well. You agree with me ? "

"As far as my knowledge of the subject guides me, quite."

" Of course ; so you would if your knowledge of the thing were a half-century's experience. You're no fool, Miss Warne, I assure you."

" I am glad you think so, sir."

" Ah," said the doctor, contemplatively drawing on his glove, " a strange patchwork is society, and the human character in general ! and we country practitioners, though some might not think so, get a good many insights and gleanings thereof. By-the-by, you needn't wear that bandage again ; never mind the look of the scar, it will soon go. Well, and what determination have you come to ? —to face the enemy like a true-born Briton ? "

" Oh yes, there is nothing else to be done."

" I thought so ; though if I were in your place, I must say I do not think I should be so brave about it. Open warfare I don't mind, but Spanish jealousy and Indian stealth, where a cavalier is concerned, is quite another thing. Poisons, stilettos, sharp marble vases hurled at one unawares ; really," he added, with a shrug of the shoulders, but smiling nevertheless, " these are not at all to my taste. Good-by. Keep up here till I come again."

The doctor's retreating steps had hardly died away when Jeannie opened the door on tip-toe.

"Are you alone, Chatty ? " she almost whispered.

"Quite. But why, Jeannie, what's the matter ? "

She had flung herself into my arms, and was weeping violently.

" What can it be ? Do tell me ; you do not know how distressed I am."

" The count—the count ! " sobbed Jeannie, more bitterly than ever.

" Count—Civray; what of him ? He isn't going to marry you, nolens volens, is he ? "

The sobs continued. "My dear Jeannie," I said, tenderly, " I ought not to have jested with you at such a time. Look up, say that you forgive me, and tell me what this grief is."

My quiet, earnest words were not without effect; she dried her eyes, and said—

" Oh, Chatty, mamma has just told me she is going to marry the count ! "

" Marry him ? "

I did not wonder at Jeannie's tears now; and my heart was very sad for her.

" Yes," continued the poor child, stopping in her sentences to give way to a fresh burst of tears, " and she says that she will for the future live mostly in Paris, and I hate Paris so, and that very likely she will never come to Ingham again, and oh, Chatty, I detest him so much ! How can I be happy, having to live in his house always, and to pay him respect as if he were my father : and to think that I shall have to live in Paris, and never see you——"

"Do not say never, Jeannie."

" It will almost be never, for the Count hates watering-places, and mamma says it is high time for me to be polished up by society. Oh dear, Chatty, I am so unhappy ; and I made mamma angry too."

" How was that ? "

12

" She called me into the drawing-room, to tell me of this, and the count was there too, and when she told me to rush into the arms of my new father, I stood still, looking downcast enough, and feeling ready to cry. Then the count said, ' Mees is vare ashamed,' meaning shy, but I exclaimed, ' Oh no, monsieur, I am not shy at all," and ran out of the room. Of course mamma was very angry, and when he was gone called me to her, and told me how very unbecoming my conduct was, and I really was sorry. But that horrid count !—I felt so mortified and vexed. How can mamma like him ! "

" Beauty is in the eyes of a gazer; your mamma often wonders why you like me so much."

" But she likes you too, in her way, and so does every one—except Angelica. This is the last day of Lindsay's stay; can't you come downstairs ? " she asked, her thoughts suddenly turned into another channel.

" Dr. Lambert ordered me not, but I should very much like to do so. When is he coming again ? "

" Lindsay ? oh, it will not be long, but he will only be able to stay a day or two. What a pleasant Christmas I thought this was to be ! "

" So it has been in some respects."

" It would have been all along, but for Angelica and the count," murmured poor Jeannie, dolefully.

" But I try to be happy in spite of Angelica, and you must do the same, in spite of the count."

" I will try," she said, gravely, " but I cannot be like you, Chatty."

" And what time is Lindsay going ? "

" By the nine o'clock train, I think. Ah, now I remember, I am sure of it, for mamma has asked some people to dinner, and he said he would stay as late as he could. He will come and say good-by to you, of course : I will arrange the room, and make it look pretty; Lindsay notices these things so."

So, forgetful of the terrible count, she busied about, with a glad and childish gracefulness which warmed my heart to see; and marvellous was the effect of her touching-up—the room looked quite bright and elegant; then, promising me that she would return when her toilette was over, she left me to dress for the dinner party.

At six o'clock, the guests arrived, and I was left again alone. Susan offered me her companionship, but I liked best to be alone, and my nervousness had quite worn off, although I still felt a dread of Angelica's society. So, stirring up my little fire to a bright blaze, I leant back in the arm-chair, and fell into a reverie.

By-and-by, I heard the sound of music. The dinner was over then, and the guests were in the drawing-room. Would he not seize the opportunity now?

The moments passed slowly. I sat in still sorrowful loneliness, and quivered and grew pale at every sound.

The clock struck eight. Only one hour more!

Oh, how tumultuously and expectantly my heart beat! He had called himself my friend: was I so valued, that only the frivolities of a dinner-party were sufficient to banish me from his thoughts?

At length the stillness and solitude became insupportable to me. I could bear the suspense of my prison no longer; and, opening the door gently, paced up and down the corridor.

I could hear no sound, save now and then a door was opened in the servants' hall, and the faint murmurs of conversation came to me from the drawing-room below. It was a bright clear night; a night reminding me of that one on which I had stood there, when he had come to my side to ask me to be at the ball—his hair had touched my forehead as he bent over me, and his voice had murmured, in low earnest tones: "Do not refuse—I would grant you any favour you might ask me." And all that he required of me had been my presence.

I leaned upon the balustrade, and looked out of the same window where we had stood together. As I gazed on the beautiful stars in their calm grandeur, my eyes filled with tears. I felt that I wronged him by this mistrustfulness; the doubt and bitterness of my heart passed away, and it expanded and overflowed with happiness.

Suddenly I heard the sound of voices and footsteps on the gravel path beneath. Involuntarily I held my breath and leaned forward. I could see nothing clearly, but so silent and hushed was the night, that every word and expression of these two voices reached my ears with perfect distinctness. One was Angelica's and the other—the other was his!

And he was saying :

"*Love her? oh no. But is there not a triumph in winning love, even when you have none to give in return?*"

I did not faint—I did not utter a sound—but silently, very silently, I drew back from the window, and closing the door of my little room, sat down tearless, marble-like and subdued. For the iron had entered into my soul, and the gate of my Paradise was shut for ever.

---

## CHAPTER XXXII.

I HEARD his step on the oaken staircase. Another time the sound of that light springing tread, that my heart could tell from a hundred, would have made it dance and beat high with joy; but now——

I sent back the tide of overwhelming emotions with a strong agonised effort, and rose to meet him with a stony look, and a voice from which life and hope had died away, but it was *calm*.   That was all I wanted.

" So I am come to say good-by, little prisoner," he exclaimed, in the same unchanged musical tones ; " but I hope you will be free from your chains when I come again."

" I shake them off to-day," I answered, studiously keeping my back to the light.

" I am delighted to hear it ; still, I do not think your ' Prison Hours ' have been unhappy ones ; the fetters hung lightly on you ? "

" Very lightly."

We had been unconsciously following up an allegory, and my last words were spoken with sadness.

" But," I exclaimed, feigning gaiety and breaking from the constraint, " chains are chains nevertheless, and I am glad to be free again.   And you are returning to London ?"

" Yes.   The duties of my life compel me to forego its pleasures ; a professional man's time is no longer his own ; he gives it to society, and society is ungrateful ; I am tired of it.   Our rewards are unworthy our services."

" But then there is——" I hesitated.

" What ? pray finish your sentence."

" The ambition of rising.   Is not that something ? "

" That is a true woman's speech.   Chatty, Chatty, ambition in books and ambition in practice are different things. But I know what you mean, and I have *felt* the meaning of the word once.   Ambition in its noblest and purest sense— it was a long time ago."

The uncertain blaze of the fire shone on his face as he spoke, and there was a light in his eyes and a quiver in his lips.

" Ah," he exclaimed, changing his tone and turning

away, "that was a long time ago; in my romantic days, Chatty, when my cheek was smooth, and my heart simple, I fell in love. Voilà tout! Well, I suppose I must soon say good-by—but I hate the word so."

I averted my face, and did not speak.

"I have no bright hours in my existence," he continued, "save those which are spent here; and your presence has contributed so much to make them so."

I still looked towards the fire. I felt that I was turning death-pale. A cold dew gathered on my forehead. I trembled from head to foot. Oh, had he known how I loved him, would he—could he have been so cruel? Just then the door was opened suddenly by one of Mrs. Dunstan's servants:

"It you please, sir, the horse is ready; and it wants only a quarter to nine, sir."

"Coming directly: tell Thompson, he can ride on and get my ticket."

The servant retired.

"Then I suppose I must go."

He approached me, and held out his hand; as I stepped forward, the light of the fire flickered on my troubled, tear-wet face: I saw the colour heighten on his cheek; and, as if moved by some sudden impulse, it might be by compassion, he stooped hastily, and pressed his lips upon my brow.

In less than a minute more, he had mounted his horse and galloped off. I listened till the sound of the horse's feet had died away in the distance. Then I buried my face in my hands and wept.

## CHAPTER XXXIII.

THERE are some circumstances in life that bring upon our hearts, in the space of one hour, the shadows and heaviness of many years. We awake with the sun and are glad ; the birds sing, the air is perfumed with the breath of manifold sweet flowers ; the cool untroubled waters reflect the sky-blue of the heavens, where the lark carols joyfully. Then in a moment all is changed; the earth is as fair as it ever was ; no change has come to the skies, and woods, and streams; all is smiling, serene and beautiful—but the unseen serpent has entered into our Eden, and it is Eden no longer. And I think that to the young there is no sorrow so killing, so utterly hopeless and deep-sinking as to find that the friend we loved and trusted, and prayed for—the one of all others in the wide world to whom we have given the wealth of our inner-world of affections—is careless of our love—contemptuous of our trustfulness, and unworthy of our friendship.

A beloved one goes down into the grave, and the place he has filled is empty, and the hearth which knew him is desolate. We pour out our sorrow in tears, but not as those who have no hope ; for his heart was loyal till the end, and there is no cloud on the memory which is dearer to us than any living thing. But when our rich and unlimited affections are played with, mocked at, and trod under foot, by one whom we felt that we could not love too well, for this there is no cure but repentance and the slow consolation of time !

And oh ! if they to whom the winning of youthful and unsuspecting hearts is merely a sport and an amusement—if, I say, they could but know to the full extent the pain and the wrong they inflict—could they but know how often their lightness and fickleness are the seeds of a whole life's unhappiness and evil, is it possible they would not relent and forbear ?

Call it fickleness—call it amusement, who will, but it is something more. Effects are difficult to be estimated in their multitude and variety, but causes once clearly arrived at are easily weighed ; and if he is called a murderer who takes away the life of his fellow, what shall he be called who robs an existence of much happiness, often of much good, sometimes of both, till all that was fair and holy is warped by an infinitude of evil ?

---

## CHAPTER XXXIV.

But I was not crushed. After the first outburst of grief had passed away, indignation and pride took its place. The old Charlton spirit rose within me. I had loved him, but I would love him no longer ; I could love the Lindsay of my imagination, the brave, noble-hearted, generous Lindsay of former days ; the other—the one who had been so heartless and so cruel—henceforth I must despise. I would try to forget him. Alas, it was very hard to forget what had a day before been the sunshine and glory of my life.

So, it had come to this. Lindsay was cowardly, false, mean. He had stooped to deceit, he had stooped to base-ness, he had stooped to treachery. Who then was to be trusted ? Since my temple had fallen to the ground, the whole earth seemed to crumble from my feet. I tried to be calm, resigned, but I never knew till now what resignation meant.

The whole house was hushed, but I could not sleep. I

fell into a retrospect of other days. I recalled the night I had first met him; every feature and occurrence of that evening's adventure rose before me in minute distinctness. I remembered quite well papa's bewilderment, and the scene in the kitchen of the lonely White House by the Sea. Lindsay leaning against the wall, his arms folded, and the bright locks hanging over his brow. How I had trembled when he spoke to me, and when I encountered the gaze of those fine thoughtful eyes, Mrs. Dunstan's affectation and Angelica's rudeness. Ah, she hated me from the first! well, she had no cause to hate me now. Somehow, I looked back very regretfully to the White House now. My life there was troubled and sad, every day brought forth trials and difficulties—poverty, despondency and loneliness: all these I had to contend with, and yet I looked back to them. Is this difficult to understand? There I was unenvied and peaceful; there I had loved Lindsay Jocelyn, and *had not known him.*

Poor, poor papa! could he have seen me then, he would not have thought I was obeying his last command.

When I awoke the next morning, having fallen into an uncomfortable sleep at daybreak, Jeannie was standing by my bedside with a letter in her hand.

"Why, Chatty dear," she exclaimed, "how uneasily you have been sleeping! you were dreaming some horrible thing I am sure, for you have been saying such strange, wild things. Well, I have got a letter for you."

"For me?"

"Yes; read it."

Instantly the thought flashed across my brain that it must be from Lindsay, for I was but half awake, and all sorts of impossible contingencies flew over my mind in the space of a second; I took it from her with trembling hands. But it ran as follows:—

" MY DEAR CHILD,—Come to me *at once*. I know that I am demanding a sacrifice of you, but I also know well that it will be made. My carriage can wait any length of time it will require you to make your preparations for departure.

" Your affectionate friend,

" EDWARD STIRLING."

Mr. Stirling little thought how pleasant obedience was. To be free from Angelica's hateful society—from the painfulness and misery of Lindsay's presence—to go away—anywhere, so as it were but away—oh, it seemed to me that this letter was a mercy from Heaven !

" I will go at once," I said.

" Go ? go where ? what *do* you mean ? " asked poor Jeannie, in extreme bewilderment.

I put the letter in her hand.

" Send me up a cup of coffee, Jeannie, will you, and a morsel of toast. I can be ready in half-an-hour with your help. Don't cry, dear ; I must go, you know, since he wishes it ; and I shall see you often."

" That horrid count and Angelica,"—sobbed Jeannie, " and you away ! What shall I do without you ? "

" My dear Jeannie," I said, gravely, " you do not wish to grieve me, I know, and you do grieve me very much by these tears. I too shall be very, very sorry to leave you ; but is not any sorrow made lighter by bearing it patiently ? and everything, even these little occurrences, Jeannie, are ordered by One who knows what is best for us. So dry your eyes, and help me, like my own brave resolute little Jeannie."

My words were not without effect ; she brushed away her tears, set to work on my packing up ; and, by a strong effort, mastered her emotion, even when she bade me farewell.

Angelica and Mrs. Dunstan stood in the hall.

Angelica was quite cordial; she congratulated me on my convalescence, shook hands warmly, and held my reticule and books for five minutes, whilst I was submitting to Mrs. Dunstan's very pompous embraces—but the good lady meant kindly, and I ought not to satirize her.

In a quarter of an hour I was set down at the portico of Mr. Stirling's house. He was standing at the door waiting for me, and pressed a kind kiss of welcome on my brow.

"I knew you would come, my child," he said, with a touch of sadness in his voice, " and would to Heaven that I could have welcomed you to your new home under happier circumstances."

He opened the library door, and drew me in. Then, motioning me to sit down, he placed himself opposite, and for the first time I noticed that his face was pale and careworn.

"I have another daughter now," he said, letting his hand rest on my shoulder.

I looked up wonderingly.

"Yes," he continued, smiling faintly, "I have two daughters now—but one is weak, and helpless, and dependent, and the other is neither of these three things, and I look to her for help, and consolation, and support. Am I to be disappointed?"

"I will do my best," I answered, with heart-felt gratitude.

"I know it; and I know that my expectations will be amply fulfilled; but now you will wonder why I have sent for you. Chatty, my poor wife is dying."

I started and turned pale.

"Yes," he added in the same quiet, measured tones, " at least Dr. Lambert gives me but a faint shadow of hope; and, strange to say, there seems no real disease—only a gradual wasting and wearing away of strength, and an unaccountable depression of spirits.  It has seemed coming on a long time, even before the birth of this poor little girl.  You wonder why I say so, but will she not be motherless—has she not come into a life of many sorrows ?  But to return ; the physicians met yesterday, and they met unanimonsly agreed that nothing would be more beneficial than the cheerful society of one of her own sex. Besides," a slight flush passed over his features, and he continued, "besides, no one is with her but strangers and selfish hirelings—you will be a sister to her, Chatty, and watch over her, will you not ? "

" I will, indeed I will," I answered fervently.

" Heaven bless you, my child, both for the words and the truthfulness with which they were uttered.  Ah, Chatty, what should I do without you ?"

---

## CHAPTER XXXV

THE poor pale face that flushed up as I entered was still very lovely.  It was a face that bespoke uncommon gentleness and patience of character, and there was no visible trace of low birth either in the delicate features, or in the slender and drooping figure which reminded you of a broken flower.  She was lying on a couch; her head drooping wearily on the pillow in a desponding, listless attitude, that grieved my heart to witness. Little Ned, who was a great help to the embarrassment of our first meeting, soon decoyed me into a game of ninepins on the hearth-rug, but I could not help turning from the happy child to the young mother.  Lovely as she was now, she must have been lovelier still in the days of early girl-

hood.   My imagination went back to the time when the
sunken cheek was rosy and rounded with health and hope,
and the soft dark eyes sparkled with young happiness.   I
conjectured the deep brown hair gathered in thick braids
over the clear forehead, and smiles dancing round the
corners of the bright lips.   Ah, well might she have been a
mother's joy, and a father's pride !   Then I thought of the
heavy sorrows which had taken the bloom from the early
rose-bud, and which had bowed the spirits of the poor
parents in the dust of humiliation.   It was a problem.   She
had been deeply wronged, and she had deeply erred ; but
for her wrong she had received a noble atonement, and for
her error she had fulfilled years of penitence, suffering, and
patient endurance.   The world might sneer at the one and
scoff at the other, but before the Great White Throne in
Heaven, and before all the wise and good on earth, they
shall both be acquitted.

" Hush, darling, mamma is ill, and Ned mustn't make a
noise, because it hurts mamma."

The child opened his large blue eyes as I spoke, and
rising, tottered in little hushed steps to the poor invalid's
side, then he stood on tip-toe, and kissed her cheek.   It
was a tacit appeal to forgiveness, and the tears rose to
my eyes.

" Me be so quiet, Tatty," he whispered, putting his arms
around my neck ;  " me be so quiet, poor mamma ! "

By-and-by, a stout, consequential nurse appeared, bearing
a jelly on a silver tray.   The tray was of the richest and
heaviest pattern ; the jelly looked colourless and insipid.

"Mrs. Burroughs," said the invalid, speaking in nervous
timid tones, "I wish you would be so kind as to put more
wine in the jelly next time.   I cannot eat this, it is so
tasteless."

" Oh, as you like of course, ma'am," was the officious

unpleasant answer, "I been't agoin to dictate to you, but your hand is as hot as fire, ma'am, and wine is a sure thing to bring on fever. I did take such pains a making this here jelly that I thought it would suit."

The spoon was raised to the lips once again, but as quickly laid down.

"I dare say it's my taste; I'm sadly dainty, I know. Never mind, Mrs. Burroughs. Don't make any more."

"I beg your pardon," I said quickly, for the woman's cool rudeness had quite conquered my averseness to interference: "I beg your pardon, but I really think in Mrs. Stirling's weak state the more strengthening things she takes the better, and a little wine could do no possible harm. Let me make you one? I am a very good hand, and know what an invalid's taste is."

"Don't leave me," she answered in a pleading voice, laying her hand on my arm.

"Oh no, there is no occasion. I will make it here"

"It isn't exactly the place, miss," sulkily urged the domestic, thinking, I suppose, of the numerous steps.

"Never mind; bring up the things directly, please."

Mrs. Burroughs was conquered; she felt that my will was as strong as her own and therefore submitted, though with a great air of offended dignity, to which, however, I paid no regard; consequently she treated me with the greatest respect ever after. But this was not the only instance of the way in which Mrs. Stirling's servants tyrannized over her, that I observed that day. Towards noontime a smart girl, with her cap flying off her head, and a face as scarlet as indignation and warm temper could make it, burst into the room.

"If you please, ma'am, if this is the way in which Hannah is to put upon me just as she likes, I won't stand it. It was only yesterday she declared I had a right

to help in the library as much as she, and to-day she
says that the ante-room is all my work, and please, ma'am,
if she is to order and do just as she likes I won't stand it
no longer."

" Make it up between you as you can," began poor Mrs.
Stirling faintly.

The girl was preparing for a fresh burst, but I drew her
gently out of the room :

" You must not come up to your mistress with complaints
now," I said gravely. "Do you not see how ill she is ?
If you want anything come to me."

The girl looked puzzled, and bit her nails :

" Hannah is so———"

She stammered and held down her head. I could see
that her temper was cooling.

" Let it be settled in this way. You do the ante-room
one day and Hannah another ; that will do."

" Yes, miss, I don't mind what I do, only I won't be hard
done by, by Hannah."

" You need not ; but if any differences arise come to
me."

When I returned, the poor invalid's eyes rested on me
with a grateful look of relief.

" I am so much obliged to you. Somehow, I never have
been able to manage the servants comfortably ; yet I have
let them have their own way a good deal."

" Perhaps that was the reason why they have given you
so much trouble."

" I don't know ; but you cannot imagine what a trial it
has been. Sometimes they have gone to my husband, and
nothing grieves me so much as that. I know how much he
dislikes being worried about such things ; and he is so
good too."

A large tear stole down her cheek.

"And ever since I married him I tried so hard to have everything smooth and pleasant, but I have not succeeded very well. There was always some contention being raised in the kitchen, and when I could not pacify them, they went straight to him. You see, I was almost afraid of them, and they took advantage of it from the first. If anything went wrong it was always contrived to have been in consequence of my orders, and a good many things have gone wrong. My husband has some little fancies about his meals being at particular times, and other things, which are trifles in themselves, but which I know are necessary to him ; and though I have wished it so much, I have never been able to get the servants accustomed to his ways. Yet he has never complained."

More she said to the same effect, and I listened and sympathized and consoled her, till the grateful tears ran down her cheeks. All the constraint was worn off now; we called each other by our Christian names, and she confided in me as if I were a sister. By little and little, I learned how deeply the poor wife had suffered from conscious inferiority to a gifted and imperial nature, and how great must have been the husband's solitude !

"I have tried hard to be a companion to him," said Ellen, humbly and sorrowfully, "but how could I ? I have loved him very, very dearly, and all my thought and care has been to do a wife's duty ; but oh, I was so unfit to be his wife ! I thought when I first married him that my love would make up for all ; and he has always said that it did, but all along I have felt (how could I help it ?) what a difference there was between us, and how lonely he has been."

So passed my first day at Mr. Stirling's ; and in the evening my jelly was tasted and liked, and duly praised, which occasioned Mrs. Burroughs to bounce out of the

room, declaring she never knew a lady as understood such
a vulgar thing as cookery afore, and Ellen to turn timidly
from me to her husband and say :

" Chatty has almost made me feel well again, and has
taken such a load off my shoulders, for she says she will
take the keys and order Mrs. Burroughs, and scold the
servants and all."

Mr. Stirling smiled, and passed his hand caressingly over
my head.

" Good little housekeeper," he said, " well done ! Ah,
Chatty, I see that you have learned the chief and noblest
aim of life ! "

I looked up with a puzzled face.

" I. dare say you can hardly reconcile the two ideas,—
making jellies for a poor invalid to relish, and ordering the
comfort of a household, with a noble and chief aim of life,
but it is so. My child, study it and search into it as they will,
from the host of philosophers and scholars, a few monarchs
of thought will now and then arise to declare the truth, and
the truth is enough for us. The whole scheme of all religions
and philosophies, and wise men's theories,—the whole moral
of all science and physics, and sociology may be summed up
in three words, which were spoken by ONE eighteen hundred
years ago,—" Love one another."

His whole face was lighted up with the excellence of
virtue and with the enthusiasm of wisdom as he spoke ; and
Ellen lifted her hands, as if an angel were praying in the
room. I was silent, from humility, for the words that arose
to my lips were not worthy the thoughts which were in my
mind.

## CHAPTER XXXVI.

So then, my dream at last was over! Alas! woman's pride had a strong battle to fight with love; but it was conqueror at last, and the eagle fluttered its wings victoriously over the poor vexed heart.

I did not know before how strong my love had been; I could not know all the beauty and brightness of my star till it had fallen from the sky for ever. Then I felt the darkness, and it hung heavily around my heart.

Ah! he knew but little of the suffering he caused me; I trusted in charity towards him that he knew it not; I tried hard to forgive him, I tried hard to think gentler of the wrong he had caused me, but I could not help contrasting what in his selfishness had been amusement only, to what in my heart had been so pure and exalted a passion.

Nothing, however, could have served so effectually to drive away all morbid and painful remembrances, as the new phase of life on which I now entered. I had no leisure for sadness, hardly leisure for thinking even; and it was well for me that it was so. Ellen never liked me to be out of her sight, and I seldom left her for an hour. She seemed to regard my presence, not only as being protective, but as tranquillizing and necessary; she felt calmer, better, happier when I was by, and she was so young, so lovely, and so fragile, that my interest and tenderness increased daily. I read to her from the few books that she loved and understood—from Burns' sweet and melancholy poems, from Jeremy Taylor's Life of Christ, the Pilgrim's Progress, or some of the simple and beautiful allegories of the Christian Religion. At such times she would listen with intense interest, and ask explanations with the ingenuousness of a child. There was not the least attempt

to conceal ignorance, and none of that narrowness and con-
traction of ideas which is usually seen in uncultivated minds.

But nothing pleased her so much as to converse with me
about the old days in the White House by the Sea.    She
was never tired of hearing the story over and over again,
nor was I unwilling to recount it.    It is always a pleasure
to talk to an eager listener, and besides, there was an inexpressible though mournful charm in recalling " those other
times."    Sometimes I read passages from those books which
had given a particular bent to my mind, or had awakened a
deep echo in my heart.    These served to illustrate my story,
and she always comprehended them ; and, indeed, strong
individualities can be made plain even to the understanding
of a child.    She was dying.    Every day the cheeks and
temples grew more hollow ; every day the weak frame grew
weaker still.    It was a sort of consumption ; there was no
actual pain, but the disease made slow and steady progress,
and the progress was visible to all eyes.

And the shadow was visible to herself.    She did not say
so—she did not talk of death ; but as days wore on, her
eyes would fill with wistful tears as they dwelt on her husband's form, and every night, when her little ones were
brought for her good-night kiss, she would cling to them
with a passionate embrace, as if she felt it might be her
last.    Ah, poor, poor Ellen ! who but a mother can know
the depth of thy love, and of thy sorrow ?

" Chatty," she said to me, one evening, " do you remember the poem you read to me the other day ? you said
it had given you such comfort when you were left alone in
the White House.    Repeat a verse or two."

" —— Since death is but a bridge 'twixt earth and heaven,
A link between two worlds, and both are fair ;
But heaven is fairest, for we gather there
A harvest of repose after much sin forgiven.

" And on that bridge stand angels waiting for me
With looks of love and smiles of welcome sweet,
   To guide my trembling feet
     Into the presence of my Master's glory."

" Ah, they were the lines I most liked ! how kind of you to remember them ! Dear, dear Chatty, what can I ever do to repay your love and kindness ! You always seem to know my wishes before I speak them, and even what you read to me always seems to suit my feelings. When you first read that little poem to me the other day, I was think-ing how dreadful it must be to die and leave behind all one's dearest friends, but before you left off reading the darkness passed away. Some of the lines appear written on purpose for me, *they speak to my heart;* do you understand me, Chatty; I cannot exactly say what I mean ?"

" Oh yes : and poetry that speaks to the heart always pleases me, however simple it may be."

" And you found out, somehow, my taste too. Kiss me, dear. Ah, come closer, for it is growing dark, and I cannot see you there. Come closer, Chatty, and let me hold your hand in mine, for I cannot tell you how I love you ! "

## CHAPTER XXXVII.

" AND this system, Miss Charlton Warne, this system of maintaining too great distinctions has the worst effects. Upon my word, the world is getting very bad—very bad indeed !"

" Is it worse than it ever was, sir ?" I observed, with a smile.

"Nonsense; you keep running from the point, and pretending not to understand me, but you do understand me, and I mean that you *shall* understand me. This distinction ought to be put down. *Vice* ought to be punished as well as *Crime*," and having said this, Dr. Lambert folded his arms, and looked into my face for a reply.

"It would be a difficult thing to do."

"Ah, you've hit it. I fancy it *would* be difficult, and it will never be done in this world."

"But," I continued, timidly, "do you not think even in this life, to a great measure, that which we sow we reap—I mean, that all actions, whether morally or legally evil, bring their consequences upon the one who has caused them? I cannot help thinking so."

The doctor mused.

"To a great measure—you do well to qualify your sentence. To a measure—yes. But consider: the evil that is done is by no means single; one bad action is a seed dropped in a fruitful soil (for all soils are fruitful for weeds, you know); it brings forth a plentiful crop, and the seed of that second planting is carried hither and thither by the birds and winds, and so the fruits of that one seed increase and spread wide to an incalculable degree. It is a fearful thought, but am I not right, nevertheless?"

"I must certainly admit it."

"Well; and do you think that an entire compensation is rendered in this life? The figures stand as one to a thousand; is the man who is guilty of one sin punished for a number indefinite? Ah, Chatty! if before committing an act against our conscience and the Law that God has written in our hearts, if we would but consider the awful responsibility we incur, it would be better for us and for all the rest of our fellow-creatures—but I must not stand here gossiping any longer; so, my little friend, good-by. Stay, how pale

you look! come now, I have a little errand of mercy for you,
will you do it?"

"With pleasure, but——"

"You think you ought not to leave our poor invalid. I
promise you you shall not be gone more than an hour, and
you really require a breath of air. You're a dear, good
little girl, and must be taken care of. So put on your
bonnet and off, off and away!"

He then put a piece of money in my hand, and added:

"Take this to the first cottage in that little old row which
leads off from the Quay. You will find there a fitting object
for charity and reflection. Adieu. You will be orthodox in
my opinion when you return."

As I walked along, the doctor's words rang in my ears.
Was it really so? I shuddered as I thought of the terrible
consequences of human actions; it seemed to me at that
moment, as if I would rather die than live to feel the
agony of remorse—as if I, having once contemplated the
direfulness of error, would be firm, and true, and just for
evermore. Then a voice said within me: "Trust not
thyself; have forgiveness for others: thou knowest not yet
how they have suffered, nor how thou mayest be led into
temptation." I felt rebuked and humbled. So, O God,
may I ever be rebuked when I build upon my own strength
and not upon Thee!

Upon reaching my destination I found that my charitable
mission had been anticipated. The door of the cottage stood
open, and a young woman, apparently about twenty, was
curtesying to four tall and cadaverous-looking, middle-aged
ladies who were gathered round her. At a first glance I
recognised them as the Misses Keen, the district visitors,
the terror of all small children, the fearless guardians of the
Ingham morality, and the prop of the Ingham Church.
They were all much alike, wiry in stature, and withered in

face, with long worked bags, out of which poked rolls of
terrible tracts ; what else the bags contained I know not,
but I never heard of any contents but the tracts. Now the
Misses Keen were not very welcome visitors at the cottages
of the poor, nor do I wonder at it. They looked upon
all the lower classes as beings of an inferior kind, totally
devoid of all feeling and sensibility, and they were im-
moderately curious. They recommended all sorts of
barbarous proceedings with refractory little boys or girls ;
they preached long sermons on the foolishness of grown-up
daughters, pink bonnets, and lovers ; they cut off the pet
child's curls in the Sunday-school ; they popped into the
kitchen when the family were at dinner, to see how well
they lived; and they peered into the cupboard to discover
the feast which they were going to have on Sunday. But
to return. Having each of them given me a sharp glance,
they proceeded with their admonitory prologue, the girl
listening with blushing downcast face.

It was very characteristic. Little energetic, hard bits of
morality flew alternately from their lips, in sharp snappish
sentences, which, to use an old Suffolk expression, seemed
as though they would bite your head off. In the midst of
one of these, which came to its end explosively, the speaker
darted a few steps forward, and pointing a screwy umbrella
to a cradle which she had not perceived before, exclaimed
in a panic-stricken voice—" Whose baby is that ? "

The poor girl seemed ready to faint ; her lips quivered as
she articulated almost inaudibly,

" Mine."

" Yours ? " The keen phalanx drew back in alarm.

" I have been unfortunate ! " murmured the unhappy
mother, but she could say no more, and burst into a flood
of tears.

I should be sorry to repeat what these Englishwomen said

to their fallen and wretched sister. It did not last long, however—such a torrent of high words in the highest key could not last long ; and in a few seconds, gathering up their dresses, as if the very hem of their robes would be tainted by touching the floor she trod, they swept out of the house.

I soon learned the outline of the girl's history. It was an old story; youthful innocence, poverty, the poison of a factory-room, bad company, temptation, betrayal. The factory had been opposite to a barrack, and her beauty (she was still pretty) had attracted the fancy of an officer, who used to watch for her when, late at night, she returned to her humble lodgings.

"And oh," she said to me between the bursts of tears—" Oh, may God pardon him as I do ! At first, I wished I were dead, it seemed so hard to live and be looked down upon, and despised by every one ; but then I thought of my poor little baby—who would take care of it, and love it, if I were gone ? and it cannot help its shame. Besides, God will not despise me, and will hear my prayers for you, and the kind doctor who sent you to me. If it had not been for him, I should have had no heart to pray."

Thinking of many things, I returned homewards. As I raised my eyes to see what o'clock it was by a neighbouring church, I caught sight of a carriage driven furiously forward, from which peeped two plumed bonnets, and a fierce moustache. It was Mrs. Dunstan, Angelica, and the count. They had passed me in a minute, for Angelica never tolerated slow driving, but the glimpse sufficed to turn the scale of my thoughts. I could think of nothing, but the scene from the balustrade, the starlight night, the dusky figures, and the voice which had said—"Love her? oh no! But is there not a triumph in winning love, even where you have none to give in return ?"

Then I realized the full weight of my disappointment and anguish. I shuddered as I recalled the sickened, aching sense of loneliness which filled my heart, when his step had died away, and that night of wakefulness and woe. Alas, I did not know till then how I had loved him!

Just at that moment, a hand was laid on my arm. I looked up and beheld him standing before me, with the wonted glow of health and vigour on his cheek, and the serene light shining in his eyes.

"Why, Chatty, how intently you are thinking! You walk with your eyes looking on the ground, like one of the heathen philosophers. Take my arm. You must let me accompany you a little way."

For a little time we were silent. I could not talk common-places to him, or assume a gaiety I did not feel.

At length he looked down upon my face, and said in a low voice—

"Oh, Chatty, why did you go away? For me all the sunshine and joy of the house is gone, now."

Formerly the sweetness of his voice would have thrilled me with a deep joy; I trembled still, but with a different feeling. Releasing my hold from his arm, I said, in a calm controlled voice—

"Why do you seek to deceive me thus? Have I wronged you, or offended you, that you treat me as if I were a child —or a fool?"

I saw a slight paleness come over his face as he tried to take my hand, and would have spoken. But I held aloof, and motioned him to be silent.

"Lindsay Jocelyn, listen to me. I will be heard, and then I will listen also."

I overcame by a vigorous effort the tremor of my voice, and continued earnestly:

"Perhaps my conduct may be unmaidenly and bold—I

cannot help it. By my own conscience I am fully acquitted. Lindsay, you do *not* love me; why do you seek to make me believe that my presence is necessary to your happiness? why have you said so much that might have led me to believe that you loved me? From our first meeting under Mrs. Dunstan's roof, answer me—have you not sought my society from that of all others?—have you not said that, and inferred that it was that which brought you so often to Helmsley-End?—have you not, in various instances, given me good reason to think that it might be so—answer me?"

"But hear me, Chatty——"

"First answer me this one question. Have you not tried to win my affections? Whatever your opinion of me may be, at least respect me enough to be truthful with me. You have tried to win my love from mere vanity, is it not so?"

He turned his face away and made no answer.

"You do not seek to deny it. I knew that you could not do so. But all the time that you were doing this—all the time that you were gratifying this vain love of testing your power, I ask you, did it never occur to you that you were doing a heartless and cowardly thing?—did it never occur to you that what was sport to you might be a sorrow of many years to me? I am young; I was younger still when I first saw you. I have never been beyond Ingham—I do not know what the world is—I believed you to be brave, and good, and honourable—how could I think otherwise?"

Tears rose to my eyes as the recollection of our first meeting came to my mind, but I dashed them proudly away, and continued, not heeding the hand that was laid on my arm reproachfully:

"Why, then, should I doubt your words and the evidence of your daily conduct towards me when belief might be so welcome? Oh, Lindsay, it was unworthy of you: you have been unjust to yourself, most unjust to me."

He covered his face with his hands, and I saw that he was very pale.

"Supposing I had yielded to the impressions you studied to make upon me—supposing (and was it not probable?) that I had loved you with the whole depth of which I am capable, when once I had made the discovery of the cruel deceitfulness you had played upon me, I should have been most unhappy; unhappy for months—for years;. for who knows how long? Woman's life is different to man's; she is removed from the turmoil and ambition of public life, and consequently her sorrows and joys dropping into a smoother current make a wider circle. But one thing more—Lindsay, grant me one favour. Promise me that you will never act towards another as you have done to me."

I looked up to him for an answer, but none came.

"Forgive me," I said softly. "If I have said too much, I am sorry for it. Lindsay, forgive me."

"No, you have said nothing but what I have deserved," at length he answered. "Oh, Chatty, I never knew before what a wretch I am! But your request is granted—I will do my best to fulfil it." I held out my hand.

"You forgive me, then, Chatty?"

"Fully and freely. Let us be friends. Say that I am forgiven also."

"I have nothing to forgive. You have been kind to me —very kind."

He spoke sternly and bitterly.

"You have told me candidly and plainly what I really am. I never thought I should see myself in such a light, much less through the eyes of another. But you have spoken truly, and I thank you. You cannot think more meanly of me than I do of myself at this moment; and I believe that you have done me a service which no one else in the world would do."

He turned as if to go, with curled lips and contracted brow; then, as if influenced by some new and sudden thought, he drew near to me again; and said, in a softened voice—

" But let us be friends. I have need of a friend like you, Chatty. I will endeavour to keep my promise—I will indeed; and if in the future you see me led away from promptings of my better nature, think that at least it was not without an effort that I surrendered; the rest is in the hands of Fate. We cannot alter our destiny."

" It is in our own hands," I answered, gravely.

" Yes; so does the sailor know his way across the sea, but the night is dark, and his boat is tossed like a feather on the waves."

He wrung my hand in his own; and, without a word more, left me.

Half-an-hour after that, as I stood holding a long dialogue with my old friend, Mr. Bean, in the shaded neighbourhood of a narrow row, the same carriage dashed past us, glittering in the broad sunlight of the street; but, in spite of the speed and the glare, I caught sight of another face bending over Angelica's. It was Lindsay; and he was smiling, and speaking with his accustomed look—apparently happy, natural, animated: I returned home with a very heavy heart.

---

## CHAPTER XXXVIII.

The darkness of night was gathering around the little town by the coast, and the darkness of death was gathering on the mortal vision of Ellen Stirling.

Fainter and fainter came the heavily drawn breath; faster

and faster faded the outward sense of all things from the
glassy eyes.

" Come nearer—nearer—I cannot see you."

We all surrounded her. She smiled faintly and said with
a great effort, " Kiss me ! "

Then we each bent down and kissed her cheek. All were
weeping ; she alone was calm.

" Good-by—good-by—dear, dear Edward ! "

Her head sank on my shoulder. The stillness of the
room was very solemn ; for some minutes it lasted unbroken,
then I touched the sunken cheek, and cried aloud. It was
all over. One spirit more had passed away from a world of
mingled happiness and woe,—

> " Through shades and silent rest to endless joy."

It was a mournful week that followed ; but it was happy
for me that my thoughts and hands were not unoccupied for
a moment ; otherwise I should never have been able to
maintain that outward tranquillity and composure which is
so difficult to assume when the heart is full of sorrow, and
which is so eminently the duty of those who are around the
bereaved.

All day long Mr. Stirling kept in his study : once or twice
he sent for me to write letters for him, and gave me the
directions in a collected voice, but his face looked pale and
overworn ; I could see how much the effort cost him. He
spoke kindly to me, and bade me take care of myself, but
that was all ; I felt that he wished to be alone, and went to
my own room to write the letters. In the evening I knocked
gently at the door again.

He opened it, and motioned me to come in.

" It is dinner-time, sir ; you must come and have some
dinner with me. I cannot eat alone."

" Poor Chatty ! you have been alone all day too ! "

He stroked my hair, and smiled kindly on me.

"No, I will not be so selfish. And, Chatty, I forgot to ask you before—the children and servants have——"

"I did not forget; it is all arranged."

"And you will go with me—you understand me—she wished it."

I assented, and he seemed pleased to think that I had made the arrangements for the funeral without troubling him. The dinner passed off heavily, and so did the four days following. He joined me in the evening, and took his place at the table, but we were both silent and constrained. I fetched little Ned from the nursery, and took him on my knee.

"Ned has been a good child to-day hasn't he?"

"Yes—yes," he lisped, clasping his little arms around my neck.

"Kiss papa. Go to papa, and tell him how good Ned has been."

The child slipped from my knees, and raised his head to receive the cheek that was held down to him, then he suddenly ran back, and hid his face in my lap.

"Mamma—mamma?" he whispered.

Mr. Stirling passed his hand over his eyes and left the room.

At last the mournful day came. I had a difficult matter in keeping a calm exterior; I was reminded so forcibly of the last time that I had paid the same duty to my poor father, and Mr. Stirling had come to comfort me. Ah, if I could be to him what he had been to me! It was a lovely day in February; the birds were singing, the sky was clear, the air was mild and balmy; it seemed so sad to consign her, on such a day—she who was young and fair—to the silence of the tomb, and the slumbers—

"Deep—deep
Never to waken more."

When we returned, Mr. Stirling shut himself up in his study ; I could not speak to him, when I had once glanced at his face ; there was a look of inner sorrow and controlled feeling on it that forbade sympathy ; I went straight to my own room.   How the long hours passed I know not.   I fell into a long train of reflection.   I thought of what had passed before my eyes within the last few days : Youth —Life—Death—the Grave.   I shut out all circumstances and accidents of present existence.   To pass away from the fair earth and the friends of one's heart, and from the hope and the disappointment, the endeavour and victory of life— to be as one has been, no more—to glide from the tangible living world to a future of which the mysteries are hidden from us : the thought seemed incomprehensible.   Then I thought of the words of those whose souls have seemed to hold communion with the dead, and who have so written that we can fear the Messenger no longer, but obey its voice, trustingly and serenely, like little children.

Towards evening I descended to the dining-room.   It was empty and the dinner was brought on and taken away untasted.   I wished to go to Mr. Stirling, but I dared not.   It grew dark ; the lamps were lighted, and I tried to read, but my efforts were unavailing.   At length I could bear the suspense and irresolution no longer.   I shut my book and went straight to the library-door ; the fire had gone out, and the room was cold and cheerless ; Mr. Stirling sat by the fire-place, his head resting on his hand, and his whole attitude implied sadness and abstraction.   He did not speak, or seem to notice my entrance ; but, having made the first step, I drew courage, and sitting down at his feet put my hand in his.

Then he drew me to his breast, and said softly :

" My child—my comforter ! "

## CHAPTER XXXIX.

A week passed, and the usual order of things was restored in Mr. Stirling's house. Mrs. Burroughs was still retained as being indispensable to the poor little motherless child ; besides, she had really a kind heart ; and, by dint of carrying the reins of government with a very high hand, I found that I could not only keep her in proper submission to my authority, but the entire body of the other servants also. There was simply one thing to do., viz., to let them see that you were resolved to have your own way, and your point was gained at once. Meantime the course of life I marked out for myself was a uniform but peaceful—and might it not ultimately be an entirely happy one ?  I could look forward now to a period when the dream and the waking alike might be remembered without regret, and when even I should think of *him* I had loved without trembling. A phase of my life was passing away ; Mrs. Dunstan was going abroad—was it likely that she would ever again return to Ingham ?  It was most unlikely. Jeannie— Angelica—Ross—who could tell when we should meet again ?  The White House by the Sea was desolate— Helmsley-End Hall would soon be desolate also. To me they would both speak of a former time, and a former hope.  Both had faded—utterly faded.

> " Save some remembrances of dreamlike joys
>     That scarcely seem to have belonged to me."

The last link that bound me to that memory would soon be snapt now.  It was inevitable—and then Lindsay and I should be as if we had never met.

Jeannie would always love me.  Thank Heaven, I should

find no change in her, but the link would be broken never-theless.

So I set to work resolutely to look cheerfully upon the future. I busied myself in a hundred plans and prospects for the long summer days. There would be some months yet, before little Ned was old enough to begin his studies with me. I procured a heap of German books, and bent my whole mind to the mastery of Goethe's magnificent language—then I was deficient in a great many points of necessary knowledge, besides being a total stranger to many interesting branches of our national literature. Mr. Stirling filled my little book-case with easy works of astronomy and physics, and we had daily readings in the English dramatists and essayists. His taste was unique and characteristic. Affectation and obscurity he abhorred; a beautiful thought expressed in simple words never failed to draw from him a warm enthusiasm. One day he found me reading Carlyle's History of the Revolution; he took the book from my hands, and locked it up. I have never seen it since. At another time he caught me translating Fichte on the Divine Idea; it shared the same merciless fate. I begged hard to finish them.

"Pshaw!" he exclaimed, impatiently, "child, child, you will be as mad as the rest of them, 'Facilis est descensus Averni,' you know. You have got a little sound common sense in your head. For Heaven's sake keep it there. Go and read Professor Johnstone or the Vicar of Wakefield, and never let me hear a word more about the Divine Idea!"

"You will not deny that the books are very clever and original, sir?" I asked, wickedly.

"Go and read Dr. Goldsmith like a good girl. Original? Why, yes; but an originality that's far beyond my capacity to appreciate or understand. No doubt it's all very fine,

14

and very clever, but for my part, Chatty, I must own, such talent is lost upon me."

I had got to the door, when he called me back.

"Chatty, I read the other day a line which I intended to repeat to you, but forgot—' There are many more ready to say a wise thing than to do a good one;' isn't that true?"

"Very," I answered, smiling.

"Now," he continued, "after that appeal to your good feelings, I have no hesitation in making this request to you—will you go now and then to see that poor girl Dr. Lambert told you of, and see that she wants for nothing?"

"Oh, I shall be very glad! I had almost forgotten her; I will go to-day."

"That's right; you're a good child, God bless you!"

On returning from my errand, I was greatly surprised to see Mrs. Dunstan's carriage at the door, and as I passed the hall she was coming out of his study; her head erect, her cheek flushed, and her whole demeanour bearing evidence of a perturbed state of mind. Apparently she did not perceive me, or did not wish to do so, for she brushed haughtily past, and, with only a slight inclination of the head to Mr. Stirling, entered the carriage. What motive could have induced her to call? I could think of no plausible one, but the circumstance excited my curiosity greatly; nevertheless a multitude of trifling occurrences concurred to drive away both the curiosity and the incident that had occasioned it. Ned had got a new toy—a humming-top—and couldn't set it off. Tatty darling would come and show Ned how, wouldn't she, just for a little minute? So of course Tatty darling went, and the minute extended to half an hour. Then this exciting amusement was interrupted by the gardener. It was the time to move the standard roses from the nursery garden—would Miss

Chatty be so kind as to tell him where they were to go?
Soon after Dr. Lambert called; we fell into a long discussion, which took various turnings and windings till it
arrived at the wonderful process of daguerreotyping, and
was immersed deep in collodion, when he jumped up, and
having ejaculated some hopeless expression of despair about
having forgotten an engagement, made a frantic dash at
his hat and disappeared. So when at dinner-time Mr.
Stirling turned to me with a smile, and asked me if I
were not surprised at the visit he had received in the
morning, I looked up with astonishment.

"Well, Chatty, and Mrs. Dunstan had some news to
tell me."

I suddenly recollected.

"Her approching marriage, perhaps?"

"Exactly so; it is not news to you, then; and what do
you think of the romantic lover?"

"I do not like him at all."

"I thought so. Poor Jeannie! But Mrs. Dunstan may
storm as she pleases; the child's interests shall not be
sacrificed."

"Jeannie's interests? I do not understand you."

"I was left executor by the late Mr. Dunstan, and guardian to Jeannie—did you not know it before? and the said
Mr. Dunstan (who was an old friend of mine) left a very
just and discreet will; but Mrs. Dunstan does not think so.
The will is this:—The property, which is considerable, is
left in two shares, one to the wife and one to the child, the
interest of which, however, the former was to enjoy so long
as Jeannie remained unmarried—with this clause, however,
that if Mrs. Dunstan should see fit to marry again, I was to
hold Jeannie's entire property—interest, capital, and all—for
her during her minority, and have care of it after, whilst she
is single. Some one, perhaps the amiable husband-elect him-

self, who I have no doubt is a very good spender of other
people's money, has been telling Mrs. Dunstan that that
clause in the will is not correct, and that if Jeannie gave
consent, she could receive her usual income ; and I offended
her very much by saying that twenty lawyers could not
prove the clause contrary to my words, and that I shall hold
to it, to a letter. How the matter will end I know not ; I
suppose by Mrs. Dunstan marrying the amorous count : if
so, Jeannie will live here."

" Here ?—in this house ? " I exclaimed, brightening.

" Yes. How pleased you look ; ah, she will be like a
sister to you ; I never thought of that."

If it could but be so ! Jeannie and I together always—
under the same roof. The very idea gave a new lightness
to my heart and an unwonted buoyancy to my smile. But
it was for a minute only. Tears came into my eyes, and
suddenly came across my recollection the words that Mr.
Stirling had spoken to me on the evening of our first meeting : " Take care ; those only are safe who have hazarded
nothing." And I had answered (thinking of him I loved),
" I have no fear."

" Why so sad, my child ? " asked Mr. Stirling, kindly.
" You looked happy a minute ago."

But I could only answer him with an assumed gaiety, and
wear a joyousness that was surface deep !

---

## CHAPTER XL.

IT was a great and unexpected happiness, however, this
prospect of Jeannie and I sharing the same home together,
and I thanked God for it. I resolved to go the next day to
Helmsley-End. I could not rest in uncertainty, and it was

not one of Lindsay's leisure days; I should not therefore
have the painfulness of a rencontre with him. It happened, however, that the next day proved drizzling and
clouded; my walk must be deferred. Perhaps Jeannie
would write to me. I watched for the postman anxiously.
At last he came; but there was only one letter, and it was
for Mr. Stirling: as he glanced over its contents, I saw an
expression of surprise pass over his face, not unmixed with
pleasure.

" I shall not ride this morning, Thompson," he said to
the servant; " I expect a visitor."

Then, looking to me, he added, smiling—

" An old acquaintance of yours, Chatty."

When the breakfast was over he went into his study. By-
and-by, I heard a sharp ring at the door, followed by a step
upon the hall. I started and turned pale, for I should have
known that light buoyant step among a thousand others.
Half-an-hour passed, then the study door was opened, and I
heard Mr. Stirling say—

" Stay, you must come and see my little adopted daughter, Chatty Warne; she tells me you have known each other
a long time; here is her sanctum. She should hear this
pleasant news from your own lips."

" Nothing would give me more pleasure, but I have not
really two minutes to spare this morning; I return to town
at midday."

" Very well; you will soon be here again, I suppose ? "

" Oh, yes; I shall take the last train on Saturday night,
and will call on you—but I suppose—that is, I may consider the arrangement as definite, may I not ? " Lindsay's
voice was strangely hurried and excited.

" Certainly. I assure you nothing could have given me
greater satisfaction; and Chatty will be delighted, I know."

" Good-by. I am so sorry I have no more time. Tell

Chatty—that is—Jeannie wished me to say that she wants her to spend a day or two with her; and give her—give her my—I mean our kind regards. Good-by, my dear sir. Au revoir."

"Well, Chatty," said Mr. Stirling, entering a few minutes after. "I have some more news to tell you. Lindsay Jocelyn has just been here—can you guess his errand?"

"I am a very bad guesser," I answered, striving for composure.

"Then I suppose I must tell you. Well then, he is going to be married!"

Instantly Angelica flashed before my mind.

"Oh, not to her—not to her!" I exclaimed, hastily.

"You seem quite frightened. Why, you silly child, what are you thinking of? The bride elect is amiable, innocent, and lovely. Do you not know such a one?" I shook my head with a look of blank surprise, and Mr. Stirling continued, "One, moreover, whom I believe you dearly love."

"Jeannie?"

"Right. The bride he has chosen is Jeannie Dunstan. Is it not good news? She will be very happy; what woman would not be happy with one like Lindsay Jocelyn? So refined, so manly, so generous, and handsome as he is! Dear little Jeannie! I am very, very glad."

It was fortunate for me that I had learned to control my emotions. I therefore could say with tolerable firmness—

"I hope he will make her happy."

"And the money difficulty is happily got over," my companion continued, reflectively; "for he tells me that Mrs. Dunstan is very willing to receive him as a son-in-law, and that he has quite talked over her scepticism regarding the will. He has a marvellous influence over peoples' minds, you know; and it is settled that when Mrs. Dunstan leaves

Ingham, Jeannie is to have her own choice, go abroad or remain here. By-the-by, she wants you to go there for a day or two, but I wish she didn't. I don't know how to spare my Chatty for a minute."

He laid his hand affectionately on my shoulder.

"I shall not go," I said quietly: "I would rather not."

"But I had rather you should, my child: the change will do you good, and you require it more than ever. Even now you are quite pale, and your hand trembles. Yes, Jeannie will be so glad to have you. Do go, to please me."

Left alone, I found it difficult to realize the new truth which had been forced on my mind. Lindsay married— and to whom? Would he be happy?—was he worthy of her? Both these considerations awoke a doubt. If he loved her, her happiness was at once secured; but then was it so? Jeannie was utterly unsuited to him; their characters were widely different, and different in a way that could not commingle harmoniously. She was childlike—simple— yielding; ever ready to be guided by others, and ever ready to take the colour of her own thoughts from those who were around her. This temperament would require one stronger than its own. Jeannie must have some one to follow and reverence and look up to in everything. I could not but feel that Lindsay was not such a one. I could see from my observance of his character that he was the creature of impulse. These impulses varied—they were alternately generous, noble, vain, self-reliant, egotistical. Influence went a great way with him; the influence of one he loved would be great indeed.

Ah, what a fair picture I drew to myself of that generous but faulty nature, guided and subdued, and spurred on to energy and lofty purpose by a loving and high-souled wife! Jeannie was loving, Jeannie was frank, artless, pure minded, but she was meek, subdued, timid: she was not fit to be his wife.

And did he love her as I felt that he could love ?   Oh no, no, it could not be ; yet why did he take this step ? Jeannie was an heiress—he was indolent and without fortune. Might not pecuniary interests have urged him ?

No, I would not think so meanly of him ; I had no right to do so.   I will act the part of a friend always, and pray for the blessings of heaven to fall upon him.   I still held firm to my resolution of not going to Mrs. Dunstan's : but my resolutions and efforts to get off the dreaded visit were unavailing, for on Saturday morning a carriage drove up, and between Jeannie's affectionate note to Mr. Stirling, and the reiterated commands and entreaties of the latter, I was literally forced to yield ; but they little thought in their love and kindness of the mental suffering which compliance entailed upon me.

---

## CHAPTER XLI.

She was watching for me, with such a radiant face.

" Oh, Chatty," she exclaimed, drawing me in and embracing me ; " Oh, Chatty, I am so happy ! "

"I know it," I said, kissing the fair young innocent forehead ; " your looks tell me more than any words.   You would be a bad hand at keeping a secret, Jeannie, with such a tell-tale countenance."

" And who could help being happy ? " she continued : " who could help being happy, Chatty, when he is so brave, and noble, and handsome ? Who could help loving him ? and oh, I hope that I may be able to make him happy !   I pray to Heaven that I may : I know that I am unworthy of him ;

but I love him more than I can tell, and I will try very, very hard to do so."

Her eyes were bright with love, and hope, and tenderness, and my own filled, half from the sight of her joy, half from my own sorrow; but I brushed them away hastily, and she was too engrossed to remark either the tears or the gesture.

"And Angelica?" I asked.

"Oh, I think Angelica, having discovered that Lindsay did not love her, cares little about it; but her conduct is so strange that I hardly know what to think. She is wonderfully gracious to me—quite affectionate, in fact; gives me hosts of presents, and calls me all sorts of endearing epithets: now this is all the more strange as she has never before seemed to think me worth the trouble of caring for. Yesterday I said to her :—

"'How odd you are, Angelica! Since my engagement to Lindsay you have behaved quite differently to me.'

"'Differently, how?' she exclaimed, almost angrily.

"'You must know without my telling you,' I answered. She made no reply, and I do not think has been quite so cordial and caressing since; but now, Chatty, is it not extraordinary of her to act so? I can account for it in no other way, except that she does not care much whom he marries so long as she could not get him herself."

"Possibly, and do not let us talk of her again."

"Oh, no," Jeannie said, quickly, "anything but of her. Chatty, how happy we shall be together!"

"You will live at Mr. Stirling's then?"

"Till—till we are married, yes," she replied, with a blush; "but let us dress now, and go into the dining-room. It is so delightful to sit there and watch for him."

In half-an-hour we descended; the dinner-table was already set, and Mrs. Dunstan, the count, and Angelica lounged before the fire expectantly, with uncut newspapers

in their hands ; but it was still light, and Lindsay would
not be here yet.  Jeannie and I drew to the embrasured
window, and watched for him ; she bright, hopeful, flushed
with eager joy—I, pale, subdued, and sorrowful.  At length
it grew dusk—

> "And the little wee bit starn
> Rises high in the east ;
> And the little wee bit heart
> Rises high in the breast."

"He will be here in a few minutes," she whispered to
me ; and, before she had done speaking, the distant sound
of wheels was heard.  Jeannie fluttered, breathless and
sparkling, to the hall-door ; a little space elapsed, and then
she entered leaning on his arm : he, handsome, kingly,
erect ; she, so downcast, so shy, so happy.

When the dinner was over he requested her to play for
him, and she sat down to the piano and accompanied his
rich, sweet voice whilst he sang some simple and plaintive
Scotch ballads.  Then he asked for a favourite set of waltzes,
which she played with much grace and lightness ; when they
were nearly ended, he approached me and whispered, looking
at her whilst he spoke :

"She is young, innocent, and loves me ; Chatty, do you
think I shall be able to make her happy ?"

"Yes," I answered, resolutely.  "I am sure you will,
if——"

"You hesitate ; your voice is stern ; 'if I try to do so'—
is not that what is in your thoughts ? and you doubt it ?
Chatty, you are hard upon me.  I *will* try.  Do you believe
me ?"

I looked upon him earnestly ; the expression of his eyes
was grave, kindly, and frank.  I felt as if I had been too
hard upon him.

"I do believe you," I answered, more softly.

"Thank you.   And you will not forget your promise;
you will be a friend to me always, will you not? If you see
me henceforth forgetting my high duties and self-respect,
you will reprove me, and lead me back to honour and to
unselfishness, will you not?"

I promised, and he continued:

"Do not judge me by other men: you may see some
leading an easy and safe course; men whose blood runs
lukewarm in their veins, whose passions are still waters—
such men are never tempted, and the world calls them virtuous: and there are some who are born with fiery tempera-
ments and strong impulses; sometimes such men become
great, sometimes the turning of a feather may bring on their
ruin, and then the finger of all is raised in mockery over
their fall!"

His voice quivered with excitement, and in a hurried
undertone he added—

"Dear Chatty, to you alone I have revealed something of
my impulsive and dangerous nature. To what it has led me
you have been a witness. I have injured you, you reproved
me courageously; you forgave me nobly. So, if I sin
seventy times seven, you will also forgive me, will you not?"

I gave my word of promise, and then he re-seated himself
by Jeannie's side.  As he did so, there was suddenly heard
the sound of a carriage driving quickly up the avenue, followed instantly by a violent ring of the bell.

Every one looked up in surprise.  Mrs. Dunstan took out
her watch: "Twenty minutes to ten, and the train comes
in at half-past nine; it must be Ross——"

"But Ross has not been here for so long, mamma,"
Jeannie interrupted, deprecatingly. "He would scarcely
come ——"

"Quand on parle du diable on en voit la queue!" said
Mrs. Dunstan, as the door opened and the subject of their

conversation entered. "My dear Ross, I am so glad to see you."

She shook her visitor's hand with much warmth, and when he had greeted the rest of the party, motioned him to take the chair next to her own. Lindsay had fallen into his old attitude, with his head bending over Jeannie, and his hand playing caressingly with her shining chestnut hair. I saw Mrs. Dunstan glance cursorily at them, and then lay her hand on Ross's arm, and speak to him with a smiling affectation. At the first sentence, he lifted his eyes to the count, said a few congratulatory words, with an odd smile which he tried to suppress, and again relapsed into his cold indifference. Mrs. Dunstan's hand touched his arm a second time; in this instance she said but three words, and spoke without coquetry or meaning.

Ross's brow grew dark.

He darted a sharp short glance in the direction of the lovers; his lips were compressed as with an expression of sudden pain; his pale face flushed slightly for an instant, and then was paler than before. No one observed this but myself; Angelica's head was turned another way, Mrs. Dunstan had begun an interesting dialogue with the count, and Lindsay and Jeannie were occupied with each other; but that strong and uncommon emotion, such as I should never have supposed it possible for Ross Dunstan to feel, he whose constitution and temperament seemed to be of iron, that momentary ruffling of the smooth surface, brought with it an incontestible conviction. He loved Jeannie.

And with that conviction, came a hundred other thoughts, which though till now forgotten only added burden to the proof. Why had he come down so often to Helmsley-End? Why had he testified so much pleasure at her naïve welcomes? Why had he taken such trouble in gratifying her wishes? Why had he softened down, as it were, to suit her gentleness ? And might not jealousy have added somewhat to his preconceived aversion to Lindsay ?

Any how, I could forgive him freely, since I saw he suffered ; and when he came up to me, I held out my hand frankly to him, and said—

" I am glad you are here ; I wanted to see you so much."

" You ? " he exclaimed, in a voice of surprise, and at the same time drawing a chair beside me. " I should have thought I was the last person you would have wished to see."

" Yes," I answered, blushing, " I did want to see you, and I am sorry that I ever gave you reason to infer the contrary. Mr. Dunstan, you told me in kindness what you believed to be true, and I was childish enough to be angry : will you forgive me ? "

" Oh, I have forgiven you long ago, so let us be good friends. And I have now something else to talk to you about."

He drew his chair closer, and added, in a low voice—

" It has come to this, then."

His eye was fixed on the lovers, and I understood what he meant.

" Will she be happy ? " he continued, moodily.

" He seems very fond of her."

" And she loves him ? "

" I think so," I replied, " indeed I am assured of it. I have heard it from her own lips."

He turned round quickly, and laid his hand on my arm ; with a convulsive movement.

" Chatty," he whispered, in a terrible voice of energy and despair, " it must not be ! Save her, save her ! You are her friend—you love her ? "

" Truly, most truly."

"As you value the happiness of her whole life, save her from this step. Entreat her on your knees with tears; oh, she must not, shall not marry him."

His vehemence startled me, and I was silent.

"You will do this, will you not?" he added, in a calmer tone: "remember how much may depend upon the course she takes."

"But," I asked, urged by a desire to do Lindsay justice, "why do you speak thus—what is he, what has he done, that you should have so much fear for Jeannie? Oh, I do think he will strive to render her happy—I do indeed! I know that he is faulty, I know that his principles yield to impulse and the passing excitement of the minute, but his heart is generous."

"Listen to me," Ross continued, impressively and coldly. "You do me injustice, but I forgive you. You have been reasoning like a true woman, from your feelings—do not seek to interrupt me—nor can I wonder at it. Lindsay Jocelyn has created in your mind an interest that I could not possibly have done, and when I speak against him, I can but expect that you will be ready to defend him. Chatty, I am not one who would willingly do injury to any man. I would not injure Lindsay Jocelyn to the value of a hair, and I should be the last to impute to him any unrighteous thing, to sully his fair name in the eyes of those who love him—but he is not TRUE! You would know more; that, however, is not in my power to tell you. I should not think it consistent with my honour to make known to any one a personal secret, which has come to my knowledge by chance. He is not true—he is not to be trusted. Handsome he is —handsome, winning, and I believe in the main possessed of a kind heart—but he is false, selfish, unstable, unprincipled. Do you still think that I see with a jaundiced eye? I would stake my existence on what I have told you. I know him well. Now," he added, fixing his penetrating glance upon me, "now, is it not incumbent on you to do your utmost to prevent this marriage ? "

"She would not listen to me," I said, sorrowfully.

"You believe that she loves him, then ? " he asked, in an eager voice.

"I believe that she loves him with all her heart."

"I cannot speak to her myself," he said, musingly.

"Indeed I will do all you wish me," I exclaimed ; "but I know, I am quite certain, it would be of no avail. Oh, what can be done ! "

"I will speak to her myself, in spite of everything," Ross answered, in a hurried whisper, for the party was breaking up ; "one effort shall be made, and God speed it."

## CHAPTER XLII.

AND the effort was made. How much it cost Ross's chivalrous and noble nature, I little then knew, but all his words were vain—vain. She wept ; she implored him to think more generously of Lindsay, but she never gave way for one instant. Brave, faithful, true-hearted little Jeannie ! Nothing that Ross could say had power to shake her decision, even though at all other times, his slighest word had carried with it "confirmation strong as Holy Writ ; " Lindsay might have many, many faults—he might occasion her sorrow, but she loved him, and she would be true to him whatever might happen.

"I have done a friend's part," said Ross to me, in a voice of bitter gloominess, "a part, moreover, which I

believe no one in my situation would have done, but I can
do no more—I can only leave the rest in the hands of God,
and go, since now my very presence must be hateful to her.
And oh, Chatty, who can help loving her the better for her
steadfastness! Yet I can do no good ; she will be happier
when I am away."

Sunday dragged itself out wearily ; there seemed to be a
constraint on every one, and I could not but look back to
the quiet happy Sundays I was wont to spent at Mr.
Stirling's ; Sundays that were holy days, in the spirit,
and not in the letter, and which were never spent without
profit. Monday was hardly better ; but on Monday night
Lindsay was to go. The next morning Ross would leave
also, and I reckoned upon some quiet days with Jeannie.

Both these days Angelica had never addressed to me a
single word ; indeed she had hardly spoken to any one, her
eyes wore an unnatural look of restlessness and unquiet
thought ; an unwonted colour had flushed her dark complexion, and her whole aspect was that of an individual
whose mind was under the influence of some extraordinary
and strong excitement. She never stayed in the same
place for five consecutive minutes ; she took up a book, a
leaf was turned, and then the book was flung down, and
she flitted away. At dinner-time her conduct was still
more singular ; I kept a constant watch on her, and I
observed that since I had entered the house she had never
eaten a morsel.

And yet, I do not believe that this was observed by any
one but myself. Mrs. Dunstan was too much interested by
her duties as host, the count was too much of a gourmand,
Jeannie too much occupied in talking to Lindsay, and Ross
too full of his own thoughts. Besides, one's eyes must
have been very quick to see through it. The plate was put
before her ; she tasted her wine, handled her knife and

fork, made a gesture of impatience ; and seemed delighted
when the next course was brought to the table ; this was
repeated several times during the course of the dinner. I
also noticed that her presence seemed to make Lindsay
nervous and excitable ; he would carefully evade encounter-
ing her glance, and seize every opportunity to be alone
with Jeannie. Once, in the early part of the evening on
which he was to leave, he was standing in a thoughtful
attitude by the window ; it was nearly twilight, and Jeannie
was playing some of his favourite Scotch airs. Suddenly
Angelica glided softly to his side ; the light was obscure,
but I could see that she laid her hand on his arm, and
looked up into his face as if imploringly : he bent very low
and whispered a few words, then she reared her head, looked
up in his face for a minute, and, with a haughty and erect
carriage, left the room.

Ross drew me significantly into the niche of a bay window.

"Are you convinced at last ? " he asked in almost an
ironical voice.

"To what do you allude ?"

"There is *understanding* between them. This is but a
drop in the ocean of proofs, but it is a drop clear enough.
You saw it?"

"Yes."

"And you still doubt ? Chatty, Chatty, you blind yourself to reason. Confess, is this the first time you have
had such a suspicion ? "

The remembrance of the evening on which I had leaned
on the balustrade came to me forcibly.

"No," I answered, with firmness, "I will speak the truth.
It is not."

He leaned his head on his hand in gloomy meditation.

"But," I continued, struck with a new thought, "he
does not love her; he avoids her; he tries to shake off

15

her influence. I have seen instances of it twenty times to-day."

"I wish I could think of it in any other light than that which I now do. He may try to shake off her influence—what then? Think you his will is as strong as hers? A woman in love—and a Spaniard! Good Heaven, I cannot think of her without a shudder!"

I said no more, and indeed I had no heart to talk, for I felt so much confidence in Ross, and so little in myself, that I could not help yielding to his uncheering mood.

Nine o'clock came, and Lindsay went; the rest of the evening passed heavily enough, and never before had I welcomed Mrs. Dunstan's prayer-bell with so much thankfulness. At eleven it rang, and then all the household, including butler, ladies'-maids, cooks, footmen, and page, were marshalled into the lower part of the room; no absenting was allowed, for in this Mrs. Dunstan was as strict as a Puritan, and even Angelica had reappeared. The chapter was read as usual, and the prayer begun, when all on a sudden, a wild, ringing scream was heard, and Angelica, holding her hands tight across her forehead, rushed out of the room, like one bereft of reason. Instantly every one rose from their knees, pale with terror. Mrs. Dunstan sank, half fainting, into a chair, and Jeannie looked alternately from Ross to me, unable to speak from surprise and affright.

"My engagement——" she murmured at last.

"Oh, it is that at the bottom of it," exclaimed poor Mrs. Dunstan almost hysterically, "it is all that; ever since she heard of it, she has not been like herself, and now it has turned her brain. Oh, Ross, what is to be done? Chatty, send for Dr. Lambert. Stevens, go to her!"

But Stevens looked at Thompson, and Thompson looked at Denny; no one stirred.

"Go to her, I say!" reiterated Mrs. Dunstan, in a voice

of agonized distress. "Oh, what shall we do? We might have thought it would end so."

"Calm yourself, my dear aunt," Ross said, composedly; "I do not think you have any great cause of alarm. I believe that her brain is no more affected than mine is. It is but an ebullition of passion, and a crisis of uncontrollable feeling, which is constitutional, and I have no doubt will pass over. Still it is highly advisable that some steps should be taken."

His keen collected glance passed over the file of servants; they quailed under it. "Chatty," he continued, "you are strong-minded and self-controlled. You are the only fit person. Go!"

Mrs. Dunstan and Jeannie each took hold of my hands.

"Oh, no, no!" they said. "Why should she endanger herself?" but I released myself from their grasp, and took up a night-candle.

Ross's eye fell on me approvingly, and I went.

I do not seek to say that it was without a slight tremor and nervousness, but it was momentary, for time and circumstance had habituated me to self-restraint and composure. The door stood open, and the light of my candle revealed to me the figure of Angelica walking to and fro in the room, her long black hair hanging over her shoulders, her small hands clasped over her temples, and her dark eyes shining with a wild lustre. She no longer hated me; why should I fear? I crossed the threshold boldly.

"Angelica," I said softly; "Angelica."

She started as she heard my voice, and motioned me angrily away, but I put down the candle, and touched her hand; it was burning hot.

"No," I said calmly, "I will not go; you may command me, but it is of no avail; I will stay till you are more composed."

"Go, go!" she exclaimed in a voice of impatience.

"Go! why will you irritate me thus? Have I not enough
to bear already? Go!" She seized my wrist with a
vice-like grasp, but I sat quite still, and met her sharp
gaze unmovedly; at this time I was pale, and carried the
trace of much mental suffering in my eyes.

"You above all others," she added, in a quieter voice,
"you who should have pity in your heart for me, for you
loved. Ah! none others read your secret. You kept it
very, very close, but I saw it—I saw it from the first. I
saw it from that autumn evening when we met—do you
remember?—in that lonely house by the sea. And you
thought that no one saw how your eyes followed him when
he spoke, and how the colour quivered on your cheek, and
the words trembled on your lips when you felt that he was
looking at you—and I hated you—I hated you, but I do
not hate you now, for you loved him in vain—all in vain!"

The burning hand was taken from my wrist, and she
raised her head, exclaiming with a triumphant, unnatural
laugh: "All in vain! and since that I never hated you,
Chatty Warne. I never hated you when I found that he
made a mockery of your love. Oh, no! I never liked any
one better than I liked you then. At least you have got that
to thank him for, Chatty—for my affection!—my affection—
and I can like as well as I can hate, I assure you. Oh, I
can like very well indeed!"

Then she sat down on a low seat, and gave way to a
terrible burst of hysterical crying and laughing.

---

## CHAPTER XLIII.

Two or three wretched and uncomfortable days passed.
Mrs. Dunstan never, but once, dared to enter Angelica's
room; I believe she thought her mad, and indeed her

hollow, glaring eyes, and extravagant behaviour, might
have induced others, wiser than Mrs. Dunstan, to form the
same opinion. She never rested night nor day—she took
neither sleep, food, nor aliment of any kind. Sometimes
she would sit for some minutes with her head resting on
her hand, gazing at the fire with an expression of listless
indifference, and now and then speaking to herself in low,
unintelligible accents ; then she would rise suddenly, pace
the room up and down with unquiet, hasty steps, her hands
clasped over her brow, her lips shut, as if keeping down
some strong inner suffering. How beautiful she was ! Yet
that beauty had something fearful in it now. Dr. Lambert
was called in ; but what could he do ? It was a case of
pure mental excitement—excitement of the strongest kind,
and which affected the system, but which the system in no
wise affected. Her mind was drowned with the vehemence
of disappointment and despair ; in such a personal case no
science could avail. He recommended me to be constantly
with her, to humour her as far as possible, and, above all
things, not to urge her to take nourishment ; she would be
much more likely to do anything which was strenuously
opposed, and *vice versâ*. He then shook his head very
gravely, and took his leave.

Ross did not go ; I entreated him to stay a few days
longer, and Mrs. Dunstan joined in my petitions with tears
in her eyes. She was so upset—so nervous, she was
assured she should not be able to sleep a wink if he went,
for he seemed to be a protection to the house. Poor Mrs.
Dunstan was really to be pitied ; she had taken Angelica
beneath her roof, from her school-girl days, and had put up
with all her wayward humours with a patience and good-
nature that was almost a virtue. Of later years she had
allowed her to have her own way, merely from fear of con-
tradiction, and all the little household bubbles of contention
had been of Angelica's making. And I really believe that

partly from the ties of relationship, and partly from long intercourse, Mrs. Dunstan almost loved her. Certainly no one else could rule her as the young Indian girl did.

I never left her for one moment, and I solemnly believe that, through the mercy of God, I was thereby the means of saving a human life. I shudder even now as I recall this dark and terrible epoch of my life. It was on a stormy night: the March winds howled and raged like agonized spirits; the hail and rain beat with a wailing sobbing sound against the casements. The fierceness of the tempest seemed to impart a new vehemence to her grief. She rose from her bed, and paced the corridor, robed in white, and with dishevelled hair, like an unhappy ghost. Then she covered her face in her hands, and moaned aloud. I was lying very still and quiet; she thought I slept; suddenly she murmured words of fearful import, and going to her escritoire, passed her hand over a secret drawer, and drew out a small round case. An expression of awful resolution and despair came over her face; she uttered his name, then— oh, fearful, fearful thought!—I saw it raised to her lips!

A horrible spell of nightmare seemed to bind me, but I made a desperate effort and screamed aloud. With the speed of lightning the case was replaced, the secret drawer closed, and the escritoire moved away.

"Pardon me," I said, with as much calmness as I could, "it was only a spasm which awoke me; I am subject to it, but—but if you would do me a small service I think I could sleep again. In my valise in Jeannie's room, is a little bottle of smelling salts which always relieve me on such occasions. Would you fetch it for me?"

She acquiesced, and with trembling haste I took down the escritoire; it was not locked, and the spring of the drawer yielded easily to my touch; to pour out the contents of the fatal phial was the work of a moment, to fill it again with water, was done in another. Before she returned, I was in my old position. The night passed, I know not how; towards morning I fell into a short sleep; when I awoke a change had come.

Angelica was sitting on a wicker chair by the fire, in her old attitude of dreaming carelessness, but one glance sufficed to tell me that some mysterious power had influenced her. She was dressed in her usual way, and with her usual magnificence and care. The smooth black hair was gathered up in loose, but elegant fashion around her slender throat and olive cheek; diamonds and sapphires glittered on her fingers and arms; the becoming and customary morning dress of white muslin contrasted with her dusky loveliness. Her cheeks were sunken, but burned with a glow of rose, her eyes sparkled with a strange expression of triumph, and seemed to look into the book of Fate, whilst she ever and anon muttered mysterious words about Victory or Death.

When she saw me awake, she ran eagerly up to my bedside.

"See!" she exclaimed, "you have now no cause to remain here; I shall wander about like a ghost, and terrify my aunt no more. The storm last night seemed to take all the fever from me. Look at me. Is not my brow clear, and my eye steady? Feel my pulse; does it not beat as regularly as your own? Won't my good aunt be glad to hear it? Come, you must make haste and go to her. But I forgot, why should not I go with you?"

She assisted me to dress with her own hands, and taking my arm descended to the breakfast-room. Poor Mrs. Dunstan seemed ready to sink with terror. Jeannie, more brave, rose and shook hands with her, in her usual way. It was a curious breakfast. Every one kept talking, from the consciousness of every one's disinclination to talk. When it was over, Ross drew me aside.

"So, Chatty," he said, with a smile, "your mad Richard is herself again! I can't help fancying that none of us can see through the whole affair, but skin-deep. Why should she have affected such fondness to Jeannie of late? There was evidently deception in that; it was a blind, no doubt, to hide some revengeful design. I wish we could get Jeannie away from the place. I am quite uneasy with regard to her. I shall get Mrs. Dunstan's consent to letting her return with me to London, to stay with my married brother. You will help to persuade her, will you not?"

"Oh, most gladly."

"And, Chatty," Ross continued, in a tone of sarcastic contempt, "my aunt has been letting a little light upon my mind with regard to Lindsay Jocelyn. That amiable young gentleman, I believe, never testified any particular affection for my cousin till a few days ago?"

I made no answer, and he went on.

"And he first testified that particular attention just after Mrs. Dunstan's approaching marriage to the count was announced? Mark his proceedings: Mrs. Dunstan was greatly indignant because her late husband left Jeannie an equal fortune with herself, and to devolve entirely upon her, in case of the former marrying again. All this my aunt pours into Lindsay Jocelyn's ears; for she, like every one else, might say with Noricus in the old play:

"Tout en lui nous parut être au-dessus de l'homme :
Ce n'est point un mortel, un héros ; c'est un dieu :"

so entirely and unscrupulously does she ascribe to him all that is good and beautiful in human kind. Well, she tells him how determined she is to marry, and how certain it is that half the late Mr. Dunstan's tens of thousands will fall into the executor's hands for Jeannie. He is indolent, he is fond of ease, he has little or no property. Jeannie's fortune will render him wealthy, independent of labour —— But I will say no more. God knows I have faults enough of my own ; only I cannot help trembling for Jeannie—poor child!"

Early in the afternoon Lindsay came; he was looking very bright and joyous, and, with only a word of greeting, went to the stables to order horses for a ride with Jeannie. They did not return till nearly dinner-time: Jeannie ran up-stairs with a face flushed with health and happiness to dress; the groom led away the horses, and Lindsay strolled into the gardens. For a long time he wandered about, till it grew dusk, and I could hardly distinguish his tall figure from the winter shrubberies. At length I saw something white fluttering beside him. Half-an-hour passed, it grew dusker still, but when I could no longer distinguish the tall figure towering in the distance, the fluttering of the white robe indicated his presence.

At seven the dinner-bell rang. Oh, I shall never forget that dinner, as long as I live! A shadow seemed to have fallen upon all, but darkest, heaviest upon Lindsay; for he sat by my side, fearfully pale and silent, as if his spirit had no power to break from a terrible spell that bound it.

---

## CHAPTER XLIV.

It is past midnight, and yet I cannot sleep. A strange unaccountable oppression weighs upon my heart, as of a foreshadowing of evil—yet why so? Child, weak, foolish that I am—has not life sorrows and dark realities enough without an imagining and seeking after them?

I try hard to shake off this morbid mood. It was an old habit of mine, during the last two years of my father's life, to make up for the little leisure I had in the day-time, by an hour or two's study at night, when the rest were asleep; sometimes, if the book were interesting, it would be almost midnight ere I closed it. Those quiet readings were very delightful to me, and even now, when I had no longer occasion for doing      had never given up the habit

So taking up a volume of Macaulay's glorious essays, I draw an easy chair to the fire, and begin to read. I choose the book from many others, as one that cannot fail to engage my mind, and yet, after the first few lines, the letters seem to turn themselves upside down, and spell imaginary words ; all the meaning is lost upon me, and I lay aside the book in despair. Surely I am not growing nervous ? Heaven forbid—no, it must be that the gas-lights affect my eyes. Well, I will just wait till the fire is out, then I will go to bed.

I sleep in Jeannie's room to-night. She entreated me so earnestly that I could not refuse ; but I do not think there is any fear of hearing Angelica's ghost-like step, and weird soliloquies. She begged Mrs. Dunstan, almost on her knees, to let her be alone that night : she promised, with a thousand protestations, that she would sleep serenely, and composedly; the house should be undisturbed ; not a sound should be heard, and Mrs. Dunstan was only too glad to consent.

Angelica had kept her word. The house was very, very silent, not a sound was heard.

Yet I cannot sleep. Once I fell into a long train of thought ; it was almost like sleep, so tranquil, and full of dreams, but in the midst I was awakened by a sound as of footsteps. It was a very slight sound. Had the stillness been less complete I should not have heard it, yet I could not be deceived. Some one was walking along the corridor, very stealthily, very cautiously, very noiselessly. My heart beat quickly as I listened. For a few minutes I heard no more, then came the sound again, only it seemed to be echoed, as if two persons were walking instead of one. The footsteps passed my door, crossed the corridor, then died away in the distance, and the stillness was as unbroken as before.

I trembled violently ; yet why this fear and apprehension?

Pshaw! it is only Angelica; the feverish restlessness has
not quite left her yet, and she is trying to cool her burning
brain by the night air; she has done it many times before,
why should she not do it again?  It was my diseased fancy
that magnified the single footsteps; night-watching and
overworked anxiety made me fearful, childish and melancholy, I resolved to go to bed, and sleep soundly.  As I
crossed the room to kiss Jeannie's fair young face, which
smiled so peacefully in her slumbers, I passed the window,
and unconsciously looked out.  It was a clear starlight
night, and I could see nothing, but suddenly my heart
stood still with a sickening feeling of terror.  There is a
sound without of horses' feet and carriage-wheels; first the
sound is subdued but near, as if a vehicle were starting
slowly, then there is a slight click, as if the back gate was
shut carefully, and then the carriage drives off at a furious
pace, and the pace grows quicker and quicker, till it is no
more heard.

For a few minutes I stand at the window, breathless and
powerless, with a dread sense of fear.  And yet it cannot,
cannot be! the mere suspicion of the thought is too dreadful to bear.  Anything, the worst even, is preferable to this
harrowing suspense.  I lighted a night-candle, and sought
with faltering steps Angelica's room.  It was empty—
empty, dark, and disordered.  The bed had not been slept
upon, the floor was strewed with dresses and shawls, loose
money was scattered upon the table, the drawers and ward-
robes stood wide open, the escritoire and jewel-box are
gone.  Oh, Heavens, I cannot doubt it now!

They have fled—fled together!

My first impulse was to go to Mrs. Dunstan.  Then I
recoiled.  No, it would be imprudent to take such a step at
this hour; it might bring on illness, so unexpected a shock
as it would be to her, and so nervously irritable as she was.
And poor, poor Jeannie! what should I do?  A bright

thought flashed across my mind. I would wake up Ross at once. He could advise me.

Shivering in every limb, and blanched with the horror of the conviction which had just dawned upon me, I stood at his door.

"Ross," I said in the most collected tone I was capable of, and tapping on the panel gently, "Ross, I have something to say to you; rise, rise quickly!"

"Who wants me? is any one speaking?"

"It is I, Chatty Warne. Dear Ross, get up, I entreat you; something has happened." In two or three minutes he was dressed and opened the door.

"Good Heavens! why, Chatty, child, what is the matter? My dear girl, do speak—what is it? you are as white as a ghost and tremble from head to foot."

"Angelica——" I faltered—"Angelica and Lindsay, oh Ross! they have gone!"

"Gone?"

He repeated the word twice, and then my meaning seemed to come home to him. A cold sweat rose to his brow.

"Traitor—coward—villain!" he exclaimed, with flashing eyes and set teeth; "but are you sure?—oh, he would not be so cruel to Jeannie!"

I repeated to him what I had heard and seen. I saw a dark tempest of indignation gather on my companion's brow as I proceeded, but he was perfectly calm and self-possessed.

"Wait here!" he said to me, when I had finished. "There is only one more proof needed. I will go at once to his room. Sit down; you are quite faint. I will not be a minute." Soon he returned, holding in his hand a folded paper. "Chatty," he exclaimed, in a hollow voice, "it is *true!* The worst that I ever feared, from his untruthful and fickle heart, has come. His vanity led him to yield to that woman's influence, and now it has brought his ruin. I

found this paper on his dressing-table addressed to you—
read it."

And with aching eyes, and heart-broken thoughts, I read
the following :—" *Love her—comfort her—teach her to forget
me—forget me yourself also, since I am no longer worthy of
your friendship.*" It was written in pencil, and with evidence of great haste and excitement.

"Oh, Ross!" I exclaimed, with clasped hands and
streaming tears, "who will have courage to tell her this?"

He leaned his face upon his hand, in an attitude of deep
grief and meditation.

" So happy, so confiding as she is too," he said at last ;
"it breaks my heart to think of the misery which the
morning will bring to her. But it must be done : it must
be broken to her, gently and carefully."

I looked up wistfully to him.

" I cannot—I cannot !" he exclaimed, with emotion; "I
could look without a tremor upon the rack, but I could not
bear to witness her sorrow. Chatty," he added, in a subdued voice, "dear Chatty, it is a hard task, but you will do
it—will you not ? "

I covered my face in my hands, and burst into an agony
of tears.

Ross wept also.

Oh, it moved my heart to witness the tears of that
strong, brave man! Then it was, that I first felt the
nobleness, and depth, and tenderness of that sterling
nature. I felt how much I had underrated the stern goodness and uprightness which was hidden beneath such an
unwinning exterior, and how far more rare and valuable was
that very sternness and hard demeanour, to the polished
and brilliant bearing that so charmed my fancy.

I touched his arm lightly.

"I will tell her," I said gently. "I will do my best to
comfort her, indeed I will."

"God in heaven bless you, for your good, courageous heart, and reward you!" he murmured fervently. "I cannot."

"But when—when must it be?"

He took out his watch.

"Four o'clock, and she will not rise till seven. If she sleeps, do not wake her; let her be happy whilst she can, and you need rest——"

I shook my head sadly.

"You will not try to sleep? Ah, you are so thoroughly overwrought, you had better then——"

Here his voice quivered.

"When she wakes—when she wakes!" he exclaimed hurriedly, and turning his face away. "Oh, would to God, that it were over!"

———

## CHAPTER XLV.

SHE was just ready to descend to the breakfast room; looking so pretty, and bright, and joyous, with the rose of health and happiness glowing on her cheek, and a light of hopefulness and love shining in her innocent eye—oh, it was hard to tell her then! Yet it must be done, and I had promised.

"Jeannie," I said, striving hard to be calm, "you must not go down yet; I have something to say to you."

She darted a quick, eager glance at my pale features.

"Oh, some dreadful thing has happened! Chatty, do tell me!" I drew her into the room, and seating myself by her side took both her hands in mine.

"Yes, a dreadful thing has happened."

"They have quarrelled—Ross has fought a duel with him—he is killed!" she exclaimed, in a voice broken by an agony of suspense.

"No," I continued; "there has been no quarrel. Ross has had nothing to do with it. Jeannie, you can never marry Lindsay Jocelyn; he is unworthy of your love—you must forget him; forget him entirely."

I put my arm around the poor trembling form, and drew her to my bosom.

"Jeannie, my poor Jeannie! he has gone; gone in the night with——"

She made no answer; she lay utterly still in my arms—still, marble-like, and despairing.

"With Angelica. Jeannie, you know all; he is heartless and ignoble; be brave; despise, forget him."

"Forget him!"

Her voice quivered with the intensity of her mental anguish; she released her hold from my neck, and sinking down on the ground, buried her face in the folds of my dress and wept as if her heart would break. At first I attempted no comfort, for I felt that tears would be a relief; but when hours passed, and though the passionate weeping had ceased, still came at regular intervals the low, choking sob which speaks the deepest suffering, I grew frightened.

"Jeannie," I said, tenderly, "Jeannie, do you love me?"

She pressed my hand in reply.

"And you do not wish me to be unhappy?"

"No; oh no!"

"How can I help being unhappy whilst I see you in this grief? Dear, dear Jeannie, try to be brave, to overcome it. For my sake, for Mrs. Dunstan's, make one effort. He is not worthy of such regret."

"Chatty, forgive me, oh forgive me!" she murmured, "but I loved him so—I loved no one else in the world like him, and I thought he was so good and true; and to find that he never loved me; to know that I shall never, never see him again!"

She drew a long, deep-drawn sigh, and then burst into

tears afresh.  The sobs shook her slight frame, and witnessed the terrible vehemence of her sorrow.  Oh, Jeannie,
Jeannie, none knew the depth and earnestness that were
hidden in thy gentle, silent heart!

Night came.  Her cheeks were hollow as if worn by the
tears of a whole year's sorrow; but she had grown calm,
terribly calm; her lips were shut with a look of despondency;
her eyes had a stony look; she hardly seemed like our
bright, childlike Jeannie of yesterday.

"Tell me all—all!" she whispered.

And I told her.  She did not start, or utter a word, or shed
a tear, but listened to the end in statue-like immovable-
ness.  When I had done, her head sank on my shoulder in
an attitude of hopeless sorrow that was terrible to witness.

I shed tears; I implored her to speak to me, and to try
to look like the Jeannie of old.  I used all the eloquence
of which I was capable, but to no purpose.  Her only
answer was—"Chatty, I loved him, I loved him!"

She had tasted no food all day; at seven the dinner-bell
rang; Mrs. Dunstan came up and entreated her with tears
in her eyes to go down and partake of it.  She consented,
and rose up for the purpose; at first her step tottered, but
I saw that she was struggling hard for composure, and was
resolved to conquer. She dressed herself as usual, arranged
her hair, and adjusted her robe; then she put her arm in
mine, and went downstairs.  Dinner was gone through as
usual, but it was a sad task.  Lindsay's place at the head of
the table was empty, and a thousand minute occurrences
brought vividly to our minds the event of the previous night.
I do not think the presence of death in the house would
have been more solemn than this weight, and icy restraint.
Now and then I looked at Jeannie; she ate, she drank, and
was calm; yes, she was indeed making an effort. But to
me every moment that calmness grew more fearful.

Once Ross bent down to me, and said, in a low voice—

"Speak to her. For Heaven's sake break that awful spell that seems around her; she looks like a marble image of despair; she cannot live if this goes on."

I tried to draw her into conversation, but to no purpose; she uttered a monosyllable or two; the tone of her voice made me shudder, it was so unnatural and forced.

So the day dragged itself out; but when another and another passed, and still she continued the same—tearless, silent, and deathlike—I grew terrified. I feared not only for her health, but her reason also. Every night I went to bed saying, "It cannot last long; there will be a change to-morrow; a crisis must come:" but to-morrow came, and brought no change or hope. She obeyed us in all respects literally; she walked out, she joined us at meals, she went through her ordinary occupations: but as each day passed on she wasted and waned more and more. The long walks by the sea-side, in the beautiful spring days, brought no colour to her cheek, or sparkle to her eye; her favourite books dropped on her knees, and her hands closed over them, in an attitude of listless indifference; she would sit for hours unemployed whilst—

> "Evermore her eye
> Was busy in the distance, shaping things
> That made her heart beat quick."

Mrs. Dunstan talked of change, travel, the gaieties of the London season, but she deprecated the idea of leaving me; still more so the idea of pleasure.

"Dear mamma," she would say, "you are very, very kind, and I know that I am ungrateful; but I do not wish to go away yet. I will try to be happy with Chatty, indeed I will."

And though she never said that I was a comfort to her, I saw it, in the wistful look of welcome with which she greeted me after only an hour's absence, and in the way she clung to me always. I saw it and took hope.

16

## CHAPTER XLVI.

" Going?"

" Yes, I must go, Chatty; I can be of no use here, and I have already somewhat neglected my professional duties. I seem to have entirely forgotten business since the last two weeks."

He was leaning on the wall, and looking out of the window, in an attitude of dreary meditation.

" I am sorry that you must go," I said. " We shall all miss you ; when will you come again ? "

" Never," he answered sorrowfully, " never more till she is happy again. It breaks my heart to see her thus, and all the while to know how she loved him, whilst I——"

He broke off suddenly, and a faint blush overspread his thoughtful and refined features.

" You loved her," I added timidly, "is it not so? Oh, would to Heaven——" But I could not finish my sentence, and blushed also.

" Yes," he continued, in the same mournful tones, " would to Heaven that my love had been returned ! I would have striven to the utmost to render her happy ; and God knows, that no selfish or worldly motive influenced me, when I first hoped to make her my wife. But the hope is taken from me, quite taken from me now, and to think that it was *he* whose work it is, *he* who won her innocent affections only to trample them under foot ; oh, that is the bitterest thought of all ! Had she been beloved worthily, wisely, and tenderly, I could have borne it with patience ; my poor, poor Jeannie ! " For a minute his voice broke down with emotion ; then he continued : " I loved her so well. Chatty, my dear, kind little friend, you have been the only person to read this secret ; tell me, do you not think that despite the roughness and hardness of my outward appearance, I have a heart? do you not think that, despite my seeming coldness of manner, I could have made her happy ? "

" I believe so most truly."

" Bless you for saying so. Ah, Chatty, very, very few of my acquaintances would have answered me so warmly. I pass off as a sort of Timon amongst most of them. I cannot flatter; they call me cold and self-contained : I cannot fritter away my time in senseless frivolities, and this they call being unsociable and uncultivated. But no matter; one or two in the world at least respect and esteem me, and I am not entirely useless. Well," he added in an altered tone," you will not quite forget me, will you ? and you will take care of *her?*"

" Oh ! " I exclaimed sadly, " if I could but devise some method of bringing her to a different state of mind ! That terrible, terrible composure is more grievous to see than the most violent outbursts of grief. Ross, what *shall* I do ? She wastes every day more and more, and the sorrow seems to sink deeper and deeper into her heart. It cannot go on long like this."

" I know it ; I watch her every hour, and every minute, and see the change that comes——" He stopped suddenly, and his eyes lighted up with a flash of anger : " Nothing for years has affected me so much as this man's falseness and treachery ; such things seem to shake one's faith in humanity. And strange," he continued, musingly ; " strange it is, that I should have had so long a sort of doubt and mistrust of him—a presentiment, I might almost call it. Once or twice I observed trifling instances which convinced me of his want of straightforwardness and integrity, and I have had no confidence in him since. Indeed, I have sometimes taxed myself with prejudice and uncharitableness on that account. I will frankly say, however (though nothing could in the least extenuate his conduct), that it would be a difficult task for a stronger and firmer man than he to break off from that woman's influence when he had once submitted to it. There was a kind of fascination in her

glittering black eyes that I believe few could escape. It
seems almost incredible that he could leave Jeannie's sweet
disposition, and quiet loveable nature, for such a one! Oh
that Jeannie ever loved him! But *allons*, let us not speak of
them; the very mention of their names makes the blood
boil in my veins. Is there nothing we can devise—foreign
travel—London society—a long sea voyage?"

I shook my head hopelessly.

"She will not leave me."

"And you are looking pale and careworn also, why could
you not accompany her? Return with my aunt to Normandy for a few weeks."

"It has been already proposed, but she seems to deprecate the idea of leaving Ingham."

"That is the very point to gain. I mean to rouse her
faculties from their morbid state; the idea of any action
whatever is repugnant to her, but that is the only remedy.
I have a sister-in-law residing in London, a fashionable,
wealthy, and really kind-hearted woman—a woman, moreover, whose face and manner are wonderfully attractive. By
this irresistible sweetness and suavity, and without possessing any remarkable tone or strength of character, she obtains
a great ascendancy over people's minds, more particularly
those of the young. I do believe that she, before all others,
could effect this cure. The circle in which she mixes
and takes the lead, is not of an ordinary kind. I think
that Jeannie's mind could not fail to be interested and
awakened. She would see such a varied society as she has
never seen before—crown ministers, foreign ambassadors,
celebrated authors, painters, and musicians; all the men and
women whose works she has read, and whom the world talks
of; Persian princes, Parisian beaux, English wits and table-
talkers. Now, if she were allowed to sit by in a corner, and
idly look on, all this living panorama would avail nothing;
but my sister-in-law has an uncommon tact of discovering

tastes, and bringing out minds. From the first day of
Jeannie's entering her house, she would bring a constant
succession of influence to bear upon her mind which she
could not withstand. Oh, I am sure my scheme will answer!
I will speak to my aunt at once, and get Cecile to write."

"I feel assured it will," I answered, partaking of his enthusiasm, "but there is one thing which if it were to happen
might spoil all."

"What is that?" he said, in a voice of surprise.

"If by any chance she might see——"

"I understand your meaning. Ah! I never thought of
that. But I do not think it is very probable. Most likely
they would go abroad; still it is a chance: but their whereabouts I think I can arrive at. Anyhow I will do my best,
and with speed. Once get her near Cecile, and she would
be saved; but you—you would come with her? I think
you would like my sister-in-law; she is a woman of the
world, and you are as unworldly as it is possible to be; but
she has infinite goodness of heart and some points which
render it impossible, with all her faults, not to love her.
You will come?"

I hesitated: "I should like very much, but I—I am
afraid I could not."

"Why not?"

"Mr. Stirling was my father's friend, and since he died
has taken the place of father towards me. He loves me as
if I were his own child, and I think he would miss me."

Ross smiled, an odd humorous smile.

"Well," he said, shaking my hand cordially, "you are a
good child, and it would be preposterous for me to tell you
what to do, when you have such a wise little head of your
own. But if you can come, do. I should be so pleased to
show London to you. Meantime, good-by."

The old dark look returned to his brow.

"If I can ascertain that they are abroad, Cecile shall

write—if not, God knows only how it will end. Watch over her—love her. Good-by."

"But you will come sometimes?" I said, timidly.

"I *cannot*," he whispered, in a voice of anguish. "I can commend her to Heaven, and rack my brain night and day to devise a method of bringing her to happiness, but it fills my heart with hate and bitterness to see her suffer, and to know *for whom*."

"I will write to you."

He wrung my hand again. "God bless you a thousand times, dear Chatty. Yes, write to me—write to me often."

"I promise you that I will do so."

"And if—— If it can be done safely, Cecile shall write. Adieu."

---

## CHAPTER XLVII.

Mrs. Dunstan belonged to that class of individuals whose whole life is made up of inconsistencies and contradictions. Yet she was not an original. These very inconsistencies and contradictions arose from an idiosyncrasy which is common enough. She had no real ill-nature, yet she had strong antipathies; and though she had no deep feelings, she allowed herself to lean upon and be governed by those who were stronger willed than herself, till this very dependence and subjection took up the place of affection in her temperament. To say that she loved Angelica would be a gross misrepresentation, for it was impossible for any one, however warm-hearted, to love her, in the true sense of the word; but Angelica's faults and caprices ever leaned towards Mrs. Dunstan's weakest points. She was vain, extravagant, heartless, unreasonable, selfish—but at the same time she was handsome, rich, and self-willed. Mrs. Dunstan could pardon all her vanity of wealth and beauty,

and all her frivolity and coquetry, because she was vain, and
rich, and frivolous, and flirting herself. And she gave way
to her captiousness and wild humours, because Angelica had
strong passions and an unconquerable will, and it was
easier and safer to yield to them. As true it is, that they
who are readiest to form a prejudice are the most unwilling
to part with it, so it is true that indolent dispositions are the
first to fly from one extreme to the other, and the last to
forgive when once they have been wronged. Now, Mrs.
Dunstan during the reign of Angelica might almost have
been considered to slight her own child ; not that I think she
did not love Jeannie as well as she was capable of loving at
all, but Jeannie, quiet, innocent, inoffensive Jeannie, was
not so necessary to her as the wild Indian cousin. Jeannie
entered into none of her gaieties, flirtations, or extravagances,
and had a mind far too pure and sensitive to meet on a level
with her own ; therefore she had been treated more like a
child than a companion, and almost with coldness.

But now came the reaction. Jeannie had never occasioned Mrs. Dunstan an hour's unhappiness or discomfort ;
Jeannie had always yielded to her wishes, and treated her
with affectionate respect—and Jeannie had been neglected.
Angelica had given back ingratitude for kindness, treachery
for openness, perfidy for hospitality ; had broken the sanc-
tity of home and robbed Jeannie of happiness. Angelica
could not be sufficiently hated—Jeannie could not be too
well loved. If I ever felt inclined to find fault with Mrs.
Dunstan's manner to my darling, I could forgive it all now.
Her indignation and fondness knew no bounds. She devised
a hundred little plans every day—some futile, but all well
meant—to divert the poor child's mind from the sorrow which
seemed wasting her life away. She gave up her favourite
card-parties at Lady Bingham Lloyd's that she might entertain a small evening party at home ; she closed the second
**volume of the newest** novel that Jeannie might not lose her

morning drive; she conceded to her wish in everything, even though the wish was only implied, and however much it interfered with her own.

A reaction took place in her mind too, with regard to Mr. Stirling. No one had exclaimed against his marriage more than she had; no one had more vehemently scandalized what she termed his high-flown morality, and no one had been more ready to turn her back upon the poor wife. But now came a change. The difference with regard to the will was quite forgotten. All rancour and all spirit of contest was alike buried; and one morning she ordered her un-pretending pony phaeton, which in Angelica's sovereignty she had never dared to use, drove to his house, and asked him, meekly and simply, to forget all that had passed, and to say that as it was her child's wish, she should be most grateful to him if he would take her to his home till she returned to England.

Even the Count Civray, the smooth-spoken, flattering, coxcombical Count, was awed into compassion and manly tenderness by Jeannie's silent sadness.

It was touching to see how that worldly woman and fri-volous empty-headed man softened and melted to pity, at the sight of her youth and of her sorrow. The Count poured forth no more elegant compliments and sentimenta-lisms about her loveliness and vivacity, which had formerly sent her flying from his side at the first opportunity. But now brought out a heap of anecdotes and witty stories, illustrating them by ludicrous grimaces and gestures, and good-naturedly caring not how great a fool he made himself, if he could but bring a smile on her lips. And though the stories were doubtless second-hand enough, the illustrations were eminently original, and heavy-hearted indeed must he be who could behold them with gravity. Then, when he took his leave, his greeting was made with so little ostentation, and so much real feeling !

" Adieu, adieu, ma fille ! " he would say softly, kissing
her brow; " tache bien de te rendre heureuse ; je te confie
à Dieu.   Ca sera bien."

And Jeannie never fled from his side now, and welcomed
him with a grateful look, which expressed far more than
words could have done, how much she appreciated his
solicitude and gentleness.

Again and again the idea of her accompanying Mrs.
Dunstan to Normandy, after the wedding, was recurred to,
but always with the same results.

" Do you know," Mrs. Dunstan said to me one day, after
the subject had been brought forward, " I am really of
opinion now that the wisest plan will be to let her remain at
Ingham quietly, as she so much wishes.   I know that the
place is dull, but it is very pleasant in summer, and I do
think that she ought to follow her own inclinations ; you
and Mr. Stirling will do your utmost to make her happy,
and no good will come from persuading her into what she
seems to dislike.   We will think it over, but a plan of some
sort ought to be resolved upon, and even if the invitation
comes from Park Lane, I hardly think she would go."

Meantime Ross went, and a week passed.   No letter
from Cecile ; no resolution taken ; and Jeannie was growing
paler and paler.   All the household is sad to see how every
day the once buoyant step grows more and more languid,
the blue eyes more and more listless, the hand thinner and
thinner, and how—

> " Ever she droopeth in her minde,
> As nipt by an ungentle winde
> Doth some faire lilye flower."

She who was so joyous, and trusting and lovely.   Oh,
Lindsay, Lindsay!

## CHAPTER XLVIII.

At length the long-looked-for letter from Cecile came. It was written with admirable cleverness, and much delicacy of feeling, showing moreover the versatility, as well as the ready tact, of the writer's mind. I, who knew Jeannie so well, and entered into her inner world of thoughts entirely, could not have sketched and defined the nature of her malady with half so much brevity and completeness. There played over the whole letter, a half-playful, half-sarcastic tone, a tone of lightness and gracefulness combined, which gave me the idea that she was a Frenchwoman, and this hypothesis I afterwards found to be true. None but a Frenchwoman would have followed out, with so much skilfulness and ease, Ross's concise suggestions. "Above all things," she wrote, "do not *urge* any course upon her. I think if you will follow my advice that all will end well. Let the marriage take place as originally intended, and the subject of her visit to Normandy be mentioned no more. Meantime I will quietly write a little note of invitation to her; the note shall seem to come quite *accidentally*, you understand, with not the slightest recurrence to the *affaire de cœur;* it shall be written in a kind of egotistical, off-hand manner, with no reference whatever to her feelings, and with a great deal of reference to my own. My youngest niece is just married—I miss her dreadfully—I am quite miserable—will my kind little cousin be compassionate, and spend a few weeks with me now, when London is getting so gay; and when I have no longer heart to be gay also, since I have now no one on whom I can pour out my ill-humour when I am bored, or my enthusiasm when I am pleased! Oh, we will manage it very nicely, and if the poor child is once here—c'est assez. Leave the rest to me. Je sais bien ménager ces choses-la. Depend on it, when we are young and romantic there is a sort of pleasure to us in giving way to the utmost to our sadness. So dainty sweet is melancholy, and so loth are we to give up even the shattered bits of the idol we have worshipped. One who would persuade us that it is much wiser and much more pleasant to sleep soundly, and enjoy one's breakfast after it, and to take human kind as we find it, laugh at its follies, and get over its indignities and faults as merrily as we can —such a one at the time seems to our morbid disposition to speak heartlessly and coldly, but ten to one if we shan't thank him for it after a time. I dare say poor little sad Jeannie would at this present moment gladly go into a convent if she could, and give up almost a life's happiness because one fickle and handsome young man has deceived her. But present fashion and we who love her are not kind enough to let her bury herself alive; and I have no doubt that you and I shall both live to be thanked for it. For the present, let things go on much the same as if nothing had happened. Make a great fuss at the wedding, the more to distract her thoughts; and try to arrange it so that there is a hurry and bustle at the end; she will then be called upon to write letters, order dress-makers, make pur- chases, &c.; nothing would be more effectual. But my dear Miss Warne, remember that as so dear a friend of Jeannie's, no heartier welcome will be given to her than to yourself. I have heard so much of you from Ross that I am very anxious to make your acquaintance. I will really take no refusal.—CECILE D'AUMALY DUNSTAN."

When I had read the letter, I took it straight to Mrs. Dunstan. She had herself heard from Cecile by the same post, and her face wore a smile of pleasure which for some weeks I had never seen there.

" Is she not good-natured ?" she said, as I entered, "and so clever too ! Do you not think she is right, Chatty ? "

" I have not the least doubt of it. "

"And now we must be very cunning," observed Mrs.

Dunstan, reflectively; "we must not tell her that we have heard from Cecile; that would spoil all at once; and we had better begin the preparations at once. I wish I could make up my mind, Chatty, as to whether white satin would be better than anything else?" I was thinking of Jeannie, and looked up with a vague expression of surprise.

"For the wedding dress," Mrs. Dunstan continued, blushing slightly; "you must really talk these things over with me now, Chatty; I have no one but you to look to for advice, you know!"

"I will do my best," I replied, consolingly, "but I am not much of a connoisseur with regard to such things."

Mrs. Dunstan sighed.

"*She* knew so well," she said, as if to herself, and with something like a regretful voice. At that moment Jeannie entered from the garden with noiseless step; a different expression passed over the mother's face.

"I wish I could forgive her," she exclaimed, in an under tone, "but when I see my child I feel as if I never, never could." Tears filled her eyes, and she left the room.

I fulfilled my promise to Ross, and wrote often. Alas! my letters were sad ones, but he was very grateful for them. At first he answered me in a curt, business-like way, never alluding to his personal feelings, and expressing both his anxiety and his gratitude in a shy, formal manner, which bore no resemblance to the frank openness with which he had of late treated me. But after the few first times this wore off, and he wrote as he spoke—eloquently, earnestly, and with a deep manly feeling. I have those letters now, and I value them as much as I did then. The paper is somewhat yellow and the ink somewhat pale from the effects of time, but the clear, firm characters stand out with the same distinctness, and the grave, vivid sentences speak to my heart the same fervent and tender story. Noble-hearted, generous Ross! And not utterly in vain were opened before me the pages of that revelation.

## CHAPTER XLIX.

CECILE's advice was acted upon to the very letter. The day for the wedding was fixed, and the ultimate arrangements made. Jeannie listened to all with meek acquiescence; she said nothing, but I could see that it was an infinite relief to her to be taken no notice of, and to be allowed to go on in her own quiet way. But she was taken notice of; anxious eyes followed her most trifling movement, and watched every passing expression of her pale face. We could not persuade ourselves that she began to improve; but it was something to have Cecile to rely upon, and faith in her gave Mrs. Dunstan an unwonted cheerfulness to begin preparations for the event of her marriage. And now began a series of excitements and unceasing occupations for a greater part of the inhabitants of our quiet, old-fashioned Ingham. It would be in vain for my poor pen to attempt a description of what was at once so costly, so regal, so gorgeous. I will only say that however bad or good the taste therein displayed might have been, the effect was dazzling, and never before in the recollection of Ingham chroniclers had such a sight been seen before. For forty-eight hours it was one universal gala scene. Bonfires blazed, fireworks glittered, bands played, champagne frothed, children feasted, flags streamed, bells rang. An unaccountable humour came over Mrs. Dunstan, partly of extravagance, partly of vanity, partly of charitableness. The rich revelled, but the poor were not forgotten : old men had dinners, and Sunday-school children frocks: Every one in Ingham-Helmsley seemed to have part and lot in the "great lady's wedding," as it was termed; every eye sparkled, every heart was glad but one—poor Jeannie! Yet she was calm, and assisted me whenever I required her, with a patience and serenity which I tried to believe augured a happier time to come. I could see that she was making

a great effort to be cheerful for Mrs. Dunstan's sake, and
I loved her all the better as I saw how difficult the
task was.

On the morning previous to the marriage Cecile's invitation came. We were all sitting together, Mrs. Dunstan,
Jeannie, and I, and something like a guilty blush mantled
my cheek. I bent my head over my letter-writing and
waited in suspense. Mrs. Dunstan's memorandum-book
was laid down on her knees, and she looked up anxiously;
Jeannie handed her the letter with an imploring look.

"Oh, mamma, I cannot go," she exclaimed; "it is kind
of her to write, but I should be much happier here, indeed
I should."

"She is very amiable, and really wants you, poor thing,"
Mrs. Dunstan urged, hypocritically. "I think she would
be very vexed at a refusal; but do as you like, dear, I wish
you to do exactly as you like."

Jeannie burst into tears, and threw her arms around her
mother's neck:

"Dear mamma, how good and kind you are! I will try
to be happy; I shall be happy, after a time; I feel assured
I shall with Chatty. But to go there—to be obliged to
talk, and laugh, and go out, and be always putting on an
appearance of cheerfulness—oh, mamma, I cannot. I will
try to forget everything, and to be your little Jeannie again,
only let me remain here."

Mrs. Dunstan was sorely perplexed.

"But, dear," she continued, hesitatingly, "Chatty is
asked too, you know; that would make it far more
pleasant."

"Forgive me, forgive me, mamma! I know that I am
ungrateful and self-willed, but I promise, oh, mamma, I
promise, that if you let me remain here I will do my utmost
to be as I used to be, and forget——"

Her voice broke down as she tried to say his name; but

though the tears still stood on her cheeks, she was composed outwardly.

"I will forget all! I will not cause you grief again; don't cry, mamma, and when you come back to England you won't know me, I shall be so happy."

She half-smiled as she said the last words, and kissed Mrs. Dunstan's cheek. It was a seal of the compact; and that day Cecile was written to. Park Lane was no more mentioned, and we took hope. The eventful morning dawned brightly and cloudlessly; and smart carriages full of gay ladies thronged the avenues of Helmsley-End Hall; and Mrs. Dunstan waxed nervous, and the Count smiled elaborate smiles with his false teeth, and looked a model of Parisian perfection—from his curled moustache to his patent boots; and young ladies envied Mrs. Dunstan, and middle-aged ladies found fault with her, and all worshipped the Count; and a multitude of witty things, and of things that passed off for being witty, were said at the breakfast-table; and old gentlemen grew silent over the pasties, and young ones talkative over the champagne; and every one's voice was hearty as he filled his glass to the toast—

"Long life and blessings! Health, wealth, and happiness to the Count and Countess de Perpini!"

---

## CHAPTER L.

Jeannie and I are standing, hand in hand, on the terrace of our new home. Fair is the April sky above; very fair the violet-scented earth around. For the first time since we have ever shared one dwelling, we are at peace; the atmosphere of the house even is a holiday to our over-wrought spirits. We ought to be very happy. I looked up at Jeannie, but I had no need to express the thought which arose within me.

"I am indeed ungrateful," she said softly, her eyes filling.

"Yes, you are ungrateful. The least you could do to thank a kind Providence for all the blessings he showers upon you would be to enjoy them."

I gainsaid my hard words by a kiss on her pale cheek.

"I know that I ought to do so. I know how greatly I sin, but I cannot conquer memory."

"You could not conquer it all at once, but you can by degrees. Listen, Jeannie, dear! I know how painful the subject is to you, but I must speak out this once, and then you shall hear me mention his name no more. If Lindsay Jocelyn had died—died whilst yet he only proved such as you believed him to be, I should not then have condemned your grief—I should not have wondered at it ; but the case is so different. He wronged you—wronged you shamefully, heartlessly, bitterly ; he showed himself to be alike unworthy of your love and respect, much more unworthy of your regret." She started convulsively, and covered her face with her hands, in an agony of grief, but I had set myself to the task, and did not flinch.

"Is it not a great injustice to yourself to waste away your youth and health like this ? It is not only an injustice, Jeannie, this is a solemn consideration, but nevertheless a true one—it is a *sin;* a sin to Heaven, to those who love you, and to yourself."

"I know it—I know it!" she murmured, brokenly.

"Oh, Jeannie," I exclaimed, with earnestness, "I believe no one in the world loves you better than myself; hear me, be guided by me—be happy. I know how great a sorrow this is to you—I know well ; but it is a sorrow that others have suffered ; and are there not many sorrows heavier than this to be borne in life ? Is not remorse greater ? Is not an unloving child a greater ? and do you not think that all these afflictions are daily being suffered.

and many in patience ?   Would it not be a miserable world
indeed if every trial brought a broken heart ?   Ah, Jeannie !
there is no happier time in an existence than that when we
have overcome a sorrow bravely : the sunshine of Heaven
seems to fill our hearts ; we feel a gentle pity and love to
others, and take up, with real thankfulness, each blessing
that drops at our feet.   And think how brave—how good it
is to do this, to lift your eyes to God and say, ' Thy will be
done ! ' "

" I will try—I will indeed try."

" If you try, you will succeed ; and when a few years
have elapsed, and you can look back calmly on what has
passed, you will be heartily thankful that you have done so.
God bless you, Jeannie, for that resolution ! God ever bless
you, dear !" I said with emotion, and embracing her, " You
have made me so happy ! "

For a few moments we were both silent, for our hearts
were too full for words.

And Jeannie did try.   From that day I saw how earnest
and great was her effort to shake off the shackles which so
bound her ; and her daily conduct was a tacit submission to
my word, and fulfilment of her promise.

I was very glad to be in my home once more ; oh, very,
very glad ! and when Mr. Stirling opened his arms wide to
receive me, and said how much he had wanted me whilst I
was away, and when little Ned bounded to receive my embrace, and danced for joy, I felt how much I had to be
thankful for, and how great had been the goodness which
had led me to say always, even from the time when I was
a lonely little child in the White House by the Sea—

" Thou hast taken much, but thou hast given far more
than I deserve ; let my heart ever overflow with love to my
fellow-creatures and to Thee ! "

So the spring waned and summer came ; it was a quiet
and uniform existence. but saving for one thing I should

17

have been entirely happy. I used to weary my romantic girlhood of my solitude and seclusion ; I fancied that could I once go out into the Great Beyond, could I once move in great cities and see strange countries and experience new excitements, my blissfulness would be complete. I never drew visions of such a lot as was now mine, uneventful, monotonous, and quiet; but I was no longer a day-dreamer. I still felt an interest and curiosity in the wide and varied world of which, save from books, I knew nothing, but I also felt that, despite the ardour and enthusiasm of my temperament, I could be content with the goodly heritage God had given me, albeit that heritage was one of entire repose and uniformity.

I said that but for one thing I should have been entirely happy. It was so. I could not shut my eyes to a truth of which I had daily evidence. Jeannie had not learned to forget. It was beautiful to see her gentle steadfastness in the path I had pointed out to her ; the Delectable Mountains were before her eyes, but a Giant Despair held her heart in bondage. She saw that she had much worth living for ; she knew that could she overcome her sadness, she could give infinitesimal joy to those who were most dear to her, and she tried hard. But alas ! no bloom returned to the cheek that had once been so rounded, no sparkle to the eye, no lightness to the step. She moves about like a shadow of her former self, and though she joins us in conversation with apparent cheerfulness I can see that it is only by a great effort. What could I say to Ross ? What could I say to the Countess ? Those letters were the hardest task of the whole week.

Ross grew terribly anxious ; his quick mind at once took in all the meaning of my suggestions and half-expressed fears. But the literal sense of my words seemed to satisfy Mrs. Dunstan's unpenetrating mind (I can never accustom myself to her real title)—Jeannie walked out—she read—

she was cheerful—she wrote to her hopefully, too ; well might the poor Countess believe when she was so anxious to do so.    One day, when I was writing to Normandy, Mr. Stirling said gravely—

"My dear child, I do not like that Mrs. Dunstan should be longer undeceived."

His serious voice and manner frightened me ; I looked up in alarm.

"I do not think," he continued, in the same tones, "that we can help seeing what must come.    Dr. Lambert is of the same opinion."

My heart seemed bursting, but I did not speak.

"It is indeed hard to think that one so young should die."

"Oh no!" I exclaimed with clasped hands and streaming eyes, "oh no, you do not mean that—you cannot—she will not die!"

But my companion did not speak, and I felt that it was because he could give no comfort.

---

## CHAPTER LI.

BUT Jeannie did not die ; the grave was not yet to close over one so young and so beloved ; and with unfeigned gratitude of heart do I record the events of the six months which followed on the date of my last chapter.

By the mercy of God I fell ill ; I may truly say by the mercy of God, for I believe that my illness was the means of saving Jeannie.    The summer was a very hot and dry one ; in the month of August I was attacked by fever, and for many days my life was in danger.    Then, as it were, Jeannie was taken out of herself ; action called forth dormant faculties ; present anxiety and responsibility weighed down the heavy sorrow of her heart till it was felt no more. Night after night she watched by my bedside, and forgot every care for herself so that she could but wait on me ;

and it was this very losing sight of her own individuality
that worked the cure. She might pass nights without
sleep, and days in unceasing activity and wearying services
—such nights and such days as she had never spent in her
life before; but only the more effectually did this anxious
watchfulness and wakefulness serve to drive away the
shadow which hitherto had stood between her and all the
panorama of life that was passing round.

Nothing could equal her fond tenderness and unselfish
care for others. Mr. Stirling's comforts and little Ned and
his sister were not forgotten; all that I had been in the
house since poor Ellen's death, now she tried to be. My
wishes even were anticipated before I had to express them;
and feeling as she did how necessary she was to me, and in
fact to all, she went through the day's duties with an air of
cheerfulness that from first being assumed became habitual.
Nor when I at length gradually began to recover, did her
devotion and self-abnegation in the least slacken. Release
from over anxiety, and weariness from an actively employed
day, procured her tranquil sleep, and freshened her for the
next morning's occupations. She was content to read to
me from my favourite authors for hours : and when I grew
tired of listening would seat herself by my side and gently
place her hand in mine, as if to tell me how she loved me.
Those days of convalescence were very happy ones. It was
pleasant after so many weeks' burning fever to be able to
sit by the window and look down into the dark shades of
the shrubberies, and watch little Ned at play amongst the
green leaves. Then to rest half in sleep, half in wakefulness, and hear the child's merry voice mingle with the sound
of the winds and my dreams : and it was pleasant to dream
peacefully and quietly, after the fearful nightmares of the
fever, and pleasanter still to wake and find Jeannie's eyes
looking up to mine with a serene light, and Mr. Stirling
smiling kindly and joyfully to see me recover.

The first time that I was able to hold my pen I wrote to
Ross, and oh with what thankfulness and gladness of heart
I could write to him now!

I also wrote to the Countess, but a line or two only; there
was no occasion for more; and Jeannie's long, affectionate
letters were now continued.   That same morning little Ned
was brought to me; and I was allowed to have the window
opened, and feel the fresh air once more.

The child clung to me, and cried for joy.

"Oh Tatty, darlin' darlin' Tatty, me so glad; me thought
you were gone to mamma, and would never come again."

My tears wetted the rosy little face pressed to mine.

"And you didn't like to think so then; you are pleased
to see me?"

"Yes—yes; and you mustn't go away, ever—ever!" he
exclaimed, energetically.

At this moment Mr. Stirling entered; he heard the last
words, and coming up to me, said in a low voice—

"No, you must not.   Chatty, I cannot tell you how
lonely I felt, when I feared that my little girl might be
taken from me."

He stooped, and pressed a kiss on my brow, and added
softly—"Nor how I thank God for her recovery.   Chatty,
you have become necessary to me: you must never, never
leave me now."

There was a strange tenderness in his voice, and an emotion in his manner, that startled me; I tried to answer
in my accustomed tone, but the words trembled on my
lips.

"You do not understand me, my child.   Chatty, listen.
I have been a solitary man for years—for many, many
years; I have been loved, loved fondly, but by one who
could not fill up that blank in my existence which only a
spiritualized friendship and free interchange of thought
could have done; you know this already, and you also know

that I have not only been solitary at home but always; I have had no friends, and no society. For this I have had nothing to blame but my own heart: I sinned, and in my very endeavour to atone for my fault, I incurred the contempt of others. A fatal circle was drawn around me, and I was entirely divided from society: this did not hurt my feelings, it only roused my scorn, and it drove me more into the world of my own home and inner resources; but in both these I have been in a great measure alone."

He drew his arm around me and continued—

"At last I am alone no longer. I have found what I have needed so much, and God has sent to me that for which I might have sought over the whole world in vain—a mind alike pure and strong—a heart that is worth all the gold that was found in the New World—one on whom I can lean, but who will also look up to me in all things—one whom my deep love shall render happy, and one to whom my love shall not be given in vain."

Tears of grateful joy and tenderness ran down my cheeks, and I could not speak; but I kissed the hand which held my own, and the action was understood. Then he drew me to his breast, and said in a voice which shook with emotion—

"And henceforth what has hitherto been rendered to God as Duty, shall be rendered in Joy only; and whatever comes of sorrow, will be borne in gratitude, since you will be at my side to share all."

I tasted a fresh happiness in this feeling of love and fellowship. Oh, how blessed to go through life with his strong and pure love shielding me as a consecrated banner from all evil! How delightful to sit, weak and faint as I was, supported by his strong arm, and resting my head on his loyal bosom! Ah, I had need to be thankful to God. And then to feel that I was enabled to minister to his hap-

THE WHITE HOUSE BY THE SEA.

piness, ay, to feel that I was necessary to it ; for had he not
said so, and was not his word to be credited as the Bible?

Those golden, golden autumn days!   They are pencilled
on my heart in a thousand glowing colours ; for inner peace
and happiness lent a glory to each thing, and I moved on
like a saint in the old pictures, with my feet on earth but
my head touched by the light of Heaven.   Hours and hours
were spent in listening to Mr. Stirling's voice as he read
from some of the grand old authors, or as he spoke to me
from the depth and richness of his heart and intellect.   And
what a speaking that was !   I had not known till now but
half of the gold which lay in that deep mine; now it was
brought up and poured luxuriously into my thirsty eager
mind.   But sweeter than all to my ears—sweeter even than
his exalted words of goodness and wisdom—it was to me to
hear him ever and ever call on my name, and ever with an
increasing fondness and gratitude.

One day Jeannie came into my room with a bright sparkle
lighting up her eyes ; she took her old favourite seat by my
side, and laid her head on my knees.

"Chatty," she said, with an effort, "I have come to tell
you something; I have come to say how grateful I am to
you for ——"

"For being ill," I added, playfully.

"No," she continued, gravely, "I mean for all the good
you have effected for me ; do you remember the conversation
we had the day after mamma's wedding?   It was on the
terrace below, and the violets and the daffodils were out—
you must remember, Chatty ? "

"I do, dear ; I remember it quite well."

"And you told me how foolish and wicked it was for me
to be so unhappy, and give way to recollections of *him ;*"
here her voice quivered, and her cheek flushed faintly,
"and it was all your doing that I ever tried to be happy—

all, all," she added with great earnestness, " and I want to thank you."

" But," I said smiling, " I don't think that you are in-debted to me so much as you suppose. Tell me, dear Jean-nie, were you happy before my illness ? You hesitate ; I am sure you were not. Now listen : when I was ill you had no leisure to think over your trouble ; your hands and mind were occupied from morning to night ; a good many nights you had no sleep at all (I know how much I am indebted to you, so it is useless for you to shake your head), and when you did go to rest, your faculties and frame were so overwrought that you slept soundly, and woke up invi-gorated. Your whole thoughts were filled up by your care for me, and do you not see that I said rightly, the fever has to be thanked for all——"

Jeannie looked up with a puzzled face. I encircled her in my arms.

" Let us not thank the means, but the cause," I added, solemnly. " God has been very merciful, Jeannie, thank Him—Him above all ; and not in joy alone, but also in sorrow, since both are sent in Infinite Wisdom, and in Infinite Love."

I think we owed the first idea to Mr. Longfellow, or to Thomas Hood, for at any rate I do not remember anything that called it forth, unless it were the Hyperion, or " Up the Rhine," which Jeannie read to us on the sea-shore. It was the lovely season of autumn, and the hazy stillness of the calm sea and of the scene around, seemed to have fallen over our spirits ; at length Jeannie suddenly exclaimed—

" Oh, I should so like to see the Rhine !" and closed her book with a half sigh.

" I think it would be a splendid idea——"

Mr. Stirling seemed to be talking to himself, and Jeannie and I looked up in surprise.

" Chatty is somewhat pale yet," he continued, smiling at our perplexity, " and Jeannie would be freshened up ; yes, it's a settled thing. Little one, get all things ready, and next week we start for the Rhine."

Jeannie clapped her hands in ecstasy, and my cheek glowed with pleasure.

" You both like the proposition ? "

" Oh yes, oh yes," we echoed in reply.

" And so do I. Then we will go. And Chatty will see London, and I shall see my old college friends, and Jeannie will see Stolzenfels and the Liebenstein, and 'peasant girls with deep blue eyes,' and we shall all be pleased, and like our little quiet Ingham better than ever on our return."

So we went ; and the clouds having rolled off our horizon, we were all ready to enjoy what was novel and striking with hearts of childlike eagerness and gratification. But the Rhine having become so familiar to every one I will only say with regard to it, and what I have never heard said before, that I was in nowise disappointed in the expecta- tions I had conceived of the " exulting and abounding river," neither on the contrary will I seek to deny that I did not find my anticipations more than realized.

At the end of November we returned to Ingham-Hemsley, and then things went on in their smooth and customary course. Every day Jeannie regained healthfulness and spirits ; she never mentioned the name of him who had so cruelly wronged her, and neither did that of Angelica ever escape her lips. A stone and a seal are set over the tomb of buried love and buried despair, and she goes on in her daily life with a calm happiness.

But she is not the same Jeannie as of old ; this sorrow and suffering has wrought a change in her, but such a change as those who love her cannot see with regret. They may think perhaps with a pang of all that has passed, to take away the youthful buoyancy and trusting joyousness of her

nature, but they must also think, with a grave gladness, of
how much more is gained than is lost: how much more
beautiful is the depth and earnestness which grief has im-
parted to her character, than the vivacity and brightness
which it has taken away.

She was a child then, she is a woman now—a thinking,
tender, patient woman.  If we once loved her truly, now we
love her even better, and worthier; for we look on her as a
friend, and as such a friend of whom we have not many.

Snowdrops and aconites are again springing forth.  Little
Ned has gathered a bunch and placed in my vase, for he
knows that I expect a visitor; a bright fire burns in my
little sitting room, and a chair is placed in readiness by it;
I have been teaching Ned his letters, but somehow my
thoughts wander from the page to the window ever and
anon; Jeannie looks expectant also, and has risen
frequently to look out; at length the sound of wheels is
heard.  A slight blush passes over Jeannie's features as
she turns to me and says—

"He is come!"

She draws back to her seat.  I descend to meet my
visitor.

"Dear Ross, you are welcome, most welcome!  We have
been looking for you."

And Ross, for he it is, shakes me warmly by the hand,
his eyes kindling at my hearty words.  He is almost unchanged since last we saw him, only there is an expression
of repose in the dark quick eyes which is foreign, and
though the intellectual brow is pale, over which the black
hair hangs so luxuriantly, the paleness is not as painful as
it formerly was.  It looks less like the paleness of an
habitually excited, restless mind, than the indication of a
thoughtful and grave temperament.

After taking off his wrappers, he follows me upstairs.

"She is changed?" he said hesitatingly, as we reached the door.

"You shall judge for yourself. I promised you that I would not ask you to come till the visit would awaken no old animosities; you shall see how I have kept it."

"And she never knew; you never told her of——"

"Your love? Oh no. She may be nervous at first meeting you, for your presence must recall many unhappy things, but that is all. I believe she will be pleased to see you after that is over. Enter."

We go in. Jeannie rises to greet him with a quiet womanly grace, and though her colour heightens at first, she is perfectly composed. The evening passes pleasantly and without constraint. Little Ned sits quite silent on my knee, awed into an unusual quietness by Ross's impressive and eloquent speaking. And he is wonderfully eloquent to-night. A great parliamentary question at this period agitated the nation—a question involving much English honour, and affecting the opinions of every class and every individual. On the side of true uprightness and patriotism stood Ross, and his eye glowed with an energy and enthusiasm of truth, and his words burned and sparkled with the soul of a true English gentleman, as he spoke. Every now and then I saw him gaze earnestly at Jeannie. She sat in a shaded corner, bending over her work, and apparently an uninterested listener; but at times I saw her eyes were raised from her employment and followed Ross with an unwonted brightness, and once, when he was most eloquent, they were filled with tears; the light fell partially over her fair face, but enough to demonstrate the sweetness and earnestness which characterized it. When the evening was nearly over, I touched Ross's arm lightly and whispered—

"You confess that she is changed?"

"Oh yes. Greatly."

"And the change?"

" Has left nothing to desire.   The marble is finished to
a perfect statue."

His eyes rested on her softly and reflectively.

" She is worthy of you," I said in a low voice, and looked
up into his face.

It was turned away.

" Perhaps you have changed also ? "

"Do you think I am one to change often ? " he asked,
with his old sarcastic smile.

" Pardon me.   I only jested.   No,  you will be very
happy."

"My dear kind friend, bless you for saying so.   But——"

" But what ? you put me out of patience."

"Perhaps she will never love me."

"There—there again ; I have a good mind to banish you
from the house at once.   One thing, do you not believe a
woman more capable to read another's heart than one of
the other sex ? "

" Why, I think so."

"And I am sure of it.   I do not believe Jeannie could
help loving you.   What do you say to that, sir ? "

" You are the kindest, and wisest, and dearest little
woman in the world ! "

" I thought so," I answered, smiling saucily; " and I
believe you are the most misanthropical and cynical Timon
that a woman ever scolded.   Well, *allons :* it is all settled
and now everything is to go on smoothly."


" Why so happy, my darling ? you are quite radiant.
Has Mrs. Burroughs abjured the black bottle, or have you
beaten Dr. Lambert in an argument ? "

" No, but I am very happy, and with cause.   Come and
see."

So saying, I drew him to the window and pointed out
significantly.   There were two figures on the smooth green

lawn; one manly and strong, and bending over the other, which was slender and graceful. The man was talking earnestly, and the girl was listening with a downcast but happy face.

"Well, and what of that?"

"My dear stupid husband, does that suggest *nothing?*"

I looked up archly in his face, and he stooped down and kissed me lovingly.

"Why, I think it does suggest something after all," said the hypocritical dissembler, smiling. "Why, I think it does suggest SOMETHING after all."

And one day—one laughing, sparkling June day—we stood on the terrace together, my husband and I, and both felt that for a time somewhat from the brightness of home had been taken away. We were very sad that day, and yet our sadness was mixed with deep joy. At length Ross's brave, constant heart had received its fitting reward; at length a gentle nature had found its proper resting-place. God's blessing fall on both! And then the usual routine of our quiet life went on again; quiet but with a quiet that varied, even as the sea around us, which is the same always, but reflects myriads of shadows; and though some of these may be of humble fishing boats, and children's forms, yet at times it is moved to awful grandeur and magnificence.

Little Ned and his sister grow daily in grace and stature; Mr. Bean often loses himself in grand philosophical speculations at our fireside: Dr. Lambert and I have many a long dialogue upon human nature and sociology in general; the Countess Perpini is gay, and rich, and happy; old Mr. Binnie may still be seen in the streets of Ingham wending his way to the Library which was the Paradise of my childhood—patience, oh, kind reader, for one more fytte of this story of my life; and then, farewell!

## CHAPTER LII.

"After long years."—BYRON.

THE White House by the Sea is no longer haunted by living form, or human voice. The shutters are closed; the little garden choked with weeds, and the wooden palings broken down with age and neglect. Since my father died, no one ventured to brave the sharp winds, and barren isolated situ·ation, and the sea-gulls are free to screech over its chimneys at will: over the garden path, where his step trod heavily, and his eye wandered in later times watching for his friend, now the brown grass grows, and around all there was an air of loneliness and ruin, an air as of—

> " A dwelling-place, and yet no habitation;
> A house, but under some prodigious ban
> Of excommunication."

And this sense of home where home was no more; of a story told, and of a scroll folded by the hands of Time, weighed upon the spirit with a heavy sadness.

Sitting on a stone bench, among the scenes where I dreamed the sweet dream of my youth, I recited to two earnest listeners, the story of my childhood; and the boy nestled closer to me, and little Ellen's large blue eyes filled with tears as I proceeded.

It was a changeful, capricious day in autumn; just such a day as that on which this history begins. The sky is alternately overcast and glowing; the waves moan, with a restive suspicious sound, and ever and anon the wind rises forbodingly. Only one boat is seen, and the fishing-smacks lie idly on the beach. Strangely and strongly, recalled by the associations of time and place, my memory pictured a day's occurrence of "many and many a year ago," but which had never been wholly forgotten. From the circum-stance of that day had arisen I knew not how, much of suc-

oooding happiness and succeeding sorrow, and each had
taught me their grave lesson: the blissfulness and the grief
were alike faded now, but the lesson remained. And then
came back a host of long hushed recollections, and as my
little companions prattled gaily on, in the walk home, I fell
into a reverie.

"It is very fine, and the sun isn't down yet. Just one
little hide-and-seek, mamma dear. before we go in?"

"Do, do, mamma darling! and I promise not to catch
cold—I won't, I won't!" echoed little Nelly, pleadingly.
"And papa will hide—won't papa?" added Nelly, making
a violent attack upon papa's coat, as he came to meet us.

"And mamma will help to find!" continued Ned.

"No, mamma is tired; but off with you, and don't quite
tear papa to pieces. A kiss? well, one then—there's a
good child. Good-by."

They bounded off, and I entered the house. A golden
flood of sunset filled my little room; and taking off my
bonnet and shawl, I paused to look upon the effulgent
reflections upon the sea in the distance.

As I did so I felt a hand laid on my arm, and starting
violently I looked round.

A tall, dark figure stands before me; a figure that seemed
like a shadow from a buried world, a figure that recalls
mixed feelings of contempt, and disgust, and pity. Yet no,
it cannot be. I am dreaming, dreaming only.

The man that I remember was vigorous, and young, and
handsome, in the prime of early manhood, and in the
strength and robustness of health, and hopefulness. The
man that I see before me is of tall stature, but of a stature
from whence the gracefulness and ease is gone; he stoops
in his carriage, and his cheek is pale and sunken: the
bright locks which waved with so much beauty over the
white forehead are now long and neglected; and the handsome lip is shaded with a dark and careless moustache.

Yet I do not dream.  In spite of the work of time and change, in spite of the wreck which I see, and of the glorious form which I remember ; in spite of the hollow cheeks, and loose slovenliness of the habiliments, I cannot be mistaken.  Involuntarily my lips move, and I utter a familiar but long unspoken name.

"Lindsay, Lindsay Jocelyn!"

I shudder as the words escape me, and draw back.

"Chatty," said the voice, whose sweetness had been the music of my youth, "Chatty, stay ; I entreat you, stay, and listen for one moment.  You loathe me, you hate my presence ?  Ah, you have cause to do so, but in pity speak to me."

The voice was broken with emotion, and I relented.

"You have been forgiven long since," I said, calmly, but coldly, "why have you come here ?  All, all the wrong you inflicted, and the sorrow you occasioned, is alike—a thing past and forgiven.  Let it be forgotten also."  I would have gone, but he clasped his hands in an act of supplication, and exclaimed—

"Oh, do not go, do not send me away thus!  Chatty, hear me.  For Heaven's sake—for the sake of the promise you once made me, hear me!"

I retraced my steps, and stood before him.  Then, retreating a few paces, he folded his arms and said humbly—

"Chatty, hear me!  Had I listened to you years ago, when you bravely and generously stood between me and my evil passions, I should have now been an innocent and a happy man.  But I did not ; and for the fair portion of God's giving which I threw away, I have sowed in sin, and reaped in sorrow illimitable.  You wonder why I am come here to disturb your peace by recalling that which is better to be entirely forgotten ; but, Chatty, hear me.  You promised me that you would be a friend always ; and unworthy, treacherous, cowardly as I have been, I still ask you to keep

your promise. By my belief in the existence of an all-wise
God, by all that I hold sacred in this world, by my assurance of a future state after death, I solemnly swear to you
that I repent!"

His head drooped in an attitude of contrition and humility
on his breast, and his voice shook with emotion.

"I repent of all the evil that I have done; not only have
I repented in the solitude of my heart, but also at the foot
of God. I have knelt in sadness, and loneliness, and in
tears, like a little child, and prayed for pardon and for
strength."

I was softened now, and touching his arm, said gently—

"It will be given you, and you may yet be honoured and
happy."

"Oh," he continued, "I have come many, many miles to
tell you this, and to hear you call me *friend* once more.
Heaven bless you! and if in the future there are any peaceful days for me, to you I shall owe them all; it was the
remembrance of your generous friendship which first led
me to despise myself, and then to long for better things.
My heart returned to you, as if to a sister, and I said
to myself,—If no one else in England will welcome the
return of a sinful but penitent man, she will! Chatty,
do not let me be deceived; if I have sinned it was not
without a great temptation, and my sin has been followed
with its punishment."

I held out both hands to him, but could not speak for the
tears which rushed to my eyes. He did not retreat now,
and stood erect before me.

"You told me once that our fate is in our own hands, and
now I thank you for your words and believe them. You
have done me incalculable benefit, and I can only invoke
the blessings of Heaven to fall upon you. Dear, dear friend,
farewell!"

He leaned forward, and pressed his lips upon my brow.
18

"And your future?" I asked, as he turned to go.

"For me? I have come back to find myself a stranger among those who knew me; and in my calling, they that I left boys have become men, and are far, far before me. I cannot put my hand again to the plough from which I looked back. No! England's children are now called to arms, in defence of her rights, and in that cause I may yet win honour." He paused, and then added, "I go to the East. If I live, I may still prove worthy of your friendship; if I fall, I shall at least die gloriously. Teach your innocent little children to pray for me. Farewell, farewell!"

His step died away in the distance. From the open window came the sound of joyous voices among the shrubberies, around me were a thousand signs of the love and happiness of home. Tears of thankfulness streamed down my cheeks, and I thanked God that I had not been utterly useless to those I loved.

**THE END.**

W. WILFRED HEAD & MARK, Printers, Fleet Lane, Old Bailey, E.C.

1½ 9.1002—5-82.

*Warwick House, Dorset Buildings,*
*Salisbury Square, E.C.*

# WARD, LOCK & CO.'S

## LIST OF

# STANDARD REFERENCE VOLUMES,

### AND

# Popular Useful Books.

---

*Of all Works of Reference published of late years, not one has gained such general approbation as* BEETON'S ILLUSTRATED ENCYCLOPÆDIA. *The importance of this valuable compilation in the cause of mental culture has long been acknowledged, and of its real usefulness to the public the most gratifying proofs have been received. It is undoubtedly one of the Most Comprehensive Works in existence, and is*

## THE CHEAPEST ENCYCLOPÆDIA EVER PUBLISHED.

---

Complete in Four Volumes, royal 8vo, half-roan, price 42s. ; half-calf, 63s.

## BEETON'S

# ILLUSTRATED - ENCYCLOPÆDIA

## OF UNIVERSAL INFORMATION.

### COMPRISING

## GEOGRAPHY, HISTORY, BIOGRAPHY, ART, SCIENCE, AND LITERATURE,

### AND CONTAINING

*4,000 Pages, 50,000 Articles, and 2,000 Engravings*
*and Coloured Maps.*

---

In BEETON'S ILLUSTRATED ENCYCLOPÆDIA will be found complete and authentic information respecting the **Physical and Political Geography, Situation, Population, Commerce and Productions,** as well as the principal **Public Buildings** of every **Country** and important or interesting **Town in the World,** and the leading **Historical Events** with which they have been connected ; concise Biographies of **Eminent Persons,** from the most remote times to the present day ; brief Sketches of the leading features of **Egyptian, Greek, Roman, Oriental, and Scandinavian Mythology** ; a Complete Summary of the **Moral, Mathematical, Physical and Natural Sciences** ; a plain description of the **Arts** ; and an interesting **Synopsis of Literary Knowledge.** The Pronunciation and Etymology of every leading term introduced throughout the Encyclopædia are also given.

☞ "WE KNOW OF NO BOOK which in such small compass gives SO MUCH INFORMATION."—*The Scotsman.*

---

*London: WARD, LOCK & CO., Salisbury Square, E.C.*

## *MRS. BEETON'S HOUSEHOLD MANAGEMENT.*

*Messrs.* WARD, LOCK *&* CO. *have the pleasure to announce that the New, Enlarged, and Improved Edition of Mrs.* BEETON'S BOOK OF HOUSE-HOLD MANAGEMENT, *of world-wide renown, is now ready, containing* 150 *pages of New Information on all matters of Cookery and Domestic Management. Entirely New Coloured Cookery Plates, and numerous new full-page Wood Engravings have likewise been added, thus further improving a work already acknowledged to be*

### THE BEST COOKERY BOOK IN THE WORLD.

*Of this Book over* 300 000 *Copies have been sold; this is the best test of its great utility over every other Cookery Book in the English market.*

Now ready, IMPROVED AND ENLARGED EDITION (337th Thousand), strongly bound, price 7s. 6d.; cloth gilt, gilt edges, 8s. 6d.; half-calf, 10s. 6d.

## MRS. BEETON'S BOOK OF
# HOUSEHOLD MANAGEMENT.

*Comprising every kind of Information on Domestic Economy and Cookery,*

AND CONTAINING

### 1,350 Pages, 4,000 Recipes and Instructions, 1,000 Engravings, and New Coloured Cookery Plates.

Mrs. BEETON'S BOOK OF HOUSEHOLD MANAGEMENT has long been acknowledged *the best of its kind*, and is now in daily use in hundreds of thousands of homes, receiving thereby the greatest honour which in this country has ever been paid to a Cookery Book. The APPENDIX which is now added gives several Hundreds of New Recipes, and Hints without number in all departments of Cookery and the Service of the Table.

Mrs. BEETON'S BOOK OF HOUSEHOLD MANAGEMENT is a Complete Cyclopædia for the Home, including, as it does, information for the *Mistress, Housekeeper, Cook, Kitchen Maid, Butler, Footman, Coachman, Valet, Housemaid, Lady's Maid, Maid-of-all-Work, Laundry Maid, Nursemaid, Nurses, &c., &c.*

Rules for the Management of Servants. Rules for the Rearing and Management of Children. The Doctor. Legal Memoranda.

250 Bills of Fare for Dinners for 6 to 18 Persons; also for Ball Suppers, Breakfasts, Luncheons, and Suppers, as well as for Plain Family Dinners, all arranged to suit the Seasons from January to December.

*⁎⁎⁎ As a Wedding Gift, Birthday Book, or Presentation Volume at any Period of the Year, or upon any Anniversary whatever, Mrs. Beeton's "Household Management" is entitled to the very first place. In half-calf binding, price Half-a-Guinea, the book will last a life-time, and save money every day.*

"Other household books may be regarded as treatises on special departments of the *menage*: this is a Cyclopædia of all things connected with home."—*Daily News.*

"A volume which will be, for many years to come, a TREASURE TO BE MADE MUCH OF IN EVERY ENGLISH HOUSEHOLD. It is an Encyclopædia of family matters, which will not often be referred to in vain, and the easy arrangement of which will at once win the hearts of all its female consulters. Mrs. Beeton has earned for herself, by this volume, a household reputation and a name."—*Standard.*

*London:* WARD, LOCK *&* CO., *Salisbury Square,* E.C.

## THE STANDARD COOKERY BOOKS.

| s. | d. | |
|---|---|---|
| 3 | 6 | **MRS. BEETON'S EVERY-DAY COOKERY AND** HOUSEKEEPING BOOK. Comprising Instructions for Mistresses and Servants, and a Collection of over 1,650 Practical Recipes. With Hundreds of Engravings in the Text, and 142 Coloured Figures showing the Modern Mode of sending Dishes to Table. Cloth gilt, price 3s. 6d. |
| 2 | 6 | **MRS. BEETON'S ALL ABOUT COOKERY.** A Collection of Practical Recipes, arranged in Alphabetical Order, and fully Illustrated. Crown 8vo, cloth gilt, price 2s. 6d. |
| 2 | 6 | **WARD & LOCK'S COOKERY INSTRUCTOR.** An entirely new work on the Practice and Science of Cookery. Illustrated. The reasons for Recipes, which are almost entirely omitted in all Modern Cookery Books, are here clearly given. The work will prove invaluable to Mistresses, Teachers of Cookery, and intelligent Cooks. Crown 8vo, cloth gilt, 2s. 6d. |
| 1 | 6 | **MRS. BEETON'S ENGLISHWOMAN'S COOKERY** BOOK. An Entirely New Edition, Revised and Enlarged. Containing upwards of 600 Recipes, 100 Engravings and Four Coloured Plates. With Directions for Marketing, Diagrams of Joints, Instructions for Carving, the Method of Folding Table Napkins, &c., and Descriptions of Quantities, Times, Costs, Seasons, for the various Dishes. Post 8vo, cloth, price 1s.; cloth gilt, price 1s. 6d. |
| 1 | 0 | |
| 1 | 0 | **THE PEOPLE'S HOUSEKEEPER.** A Complete Guide to Comfort, Economy, and Health. Comprising Cookery, Household Economy, the Family Health, Furnishing, Housework, Clothes, Marketing, Food, &c., &c. Post 8vo, cloth, price 1s. |
| 1 | 0 | **THE ECONOMICAL COOKERY BOOK,** for Housewives, Cooks, and Maids-of-all-Work; with Advice to Mistress and Servant. By Mrs. WARREN. NEW EDITION, with additional pages on Australian Tinned Meats, Soups, and Fish, and numerous Illustrations. Post 8vo, cloth, price 1s. |
| 0 | 6 | **THE SIXPENNY PRACTICAL COOKERY AND** ECONOMICAL RECIPES. Comprising Marketing, Relishes, Boiled Dishes, Vegetables, Soups, Side Dishes, Salads, Stews, Fish, Joints, Sauces, Cheap Dishes, Invalid Cookery, &c. Price 6d. |
| 0 | 6 | **THE COTTAGE COOKERY BOOK.** Containing Simple Lessons in Cookery and Economical Home Management. An Easy and Complete Guide to Economy in the Kitchen, and a most valuable Handbook for Young Housewives. Price 6d. |
| 0 | 1 | **BEETON'S PENNY COOKERY BOOK.** Entirely New Edition, with New Recipes throughout. Three Hundred and Thirtieth Thousand. Containing more than Two Hundred Recipes and Instructions. Price 1d.; post free, 1½d. |
| 0 | 1 | **WARD AND LOCK'S PENNY HOUSEKEEPER** AND GUIDE TO COOKERY. Containing Plain and Reliable Instructions in Cleaning and all Domestic Duties, the Preparation of Soups, Vegetables, Meats of all kinds, Pastry, Jellies, Bread, Home Beverages, &c., and everything necessary for securing a well-ordered Home. Price 1d.; post free, 1½d. |
| 0 | 1 | **BEETON'S PENNY DOMESTIC RECIPE BOOK:** Containing Simple and Practical Information upon things in general use and necessary for every Household. Price 1d.; post free, 1½d. |

*London: WARD, LOCK & CO., Salisbury Square, E.C.*

## HIGH CLASS BOOKS OF REFERENCE.

## THE HAYDN SERIES OF MANUALS.

"THE MOST UNIVERSAL BOOK OF REFERENCE IN A MODERATE COMPASS THAT WE KNOW OF IN THE ENGLISH LANGUAGE."—*The Times.*

**HAYDN'S DICTIONARY OF DATES.** Relating to all Ages and Nations ; for Universal Reference. Containing about 10,000 distinct Articles, and 80,000 Dates and Facts. Sixteenth Edition, Enlarged Corrected and Revised by BENJAMIN VINCENT, Librarian of the Royal Institution of Great Britain. In One thick Vol., medium 8vo, cloth, price 18s. ; half-calf, 24s. ; full or tree-calf, 31s. 6d.

"It is certainly no longer now a mere Dictionary of Dates, but A COMPREHENSIVE DICTIONARY OR ENCYCLOPÆDIA OF GENERAL INFORMATION."—*The Times.*

"It is BY FAR THE READIEST AND MOST RELIABLE WORK OF THE KIND."—*The Standard.*

**VINCENT'S DICTIONARY OF BIOGRAPHY,** Past and Present. Containing the Chief Events in the Lives of Eminent Persons of all Ages and Nations. By BENJAMIN VINCENT, Librarian of the Royal Institution of Great Britain, and Editor of "Haydn's Dictionary of Dates." In One thick Vol., medium 8vo, cloth, 7s. 6d. ; half-calf, 12s. ; full or tree-calf, 18s.

"It has the merit of condensing into the smallest possible compass the leading events in the career of every man and woman of eminence. . It is very carefully edited, and must evidently be the result of constant industry, combined with good judgment and taste."—*The Times.*

*The CHEAPEST BOOK PUBLISHED on DOMESTIC MEDICINE, &c.*

**HAYDN'S DOMESTIC MEDICINE.** By the late EDWIN LANKESTER, M.D., F.R.S., assisted by Distinguished Physicians and Surgeons. New Edition, including an Appendix on Sick Nursing and Mothers' Management. With 32 full pages of Engravings. In One Vol., medium 8vo, cloth gilt, 7s. 6d.; half-calf, 12s.

"Very exhaustive, and embodies an enormous amount of medical information in an intelligible shape."—*The Scotsman.*

"THE FULLEST AND MOST RELIABLE WORK OF ITS KIND."—*Liverpool Albion.*

**HAYDN'S BIBLE DICTIONARY.** For the use of all Readers and Students of the Old and New Testaments, and of the Apocrypha. Edited by the late Rev. CHARLES BOUTELL, M.A. New Edition, brought down to the latest date. With 100 pages of Engravings, separately printed on tinted paper. In One Vol., medium 8vo, cloth gilt, 7s. 6d. ; half-calf, 12s.

"No better one than this is in the market. . . Every local preacher should place this dictionary in his study, and every Sunday-school teacher should have it for reference."—*The Fountain.*

*UNIFORM WITH "HAYDN'S BIBLE DICTIONARY"*

**WHISTON'S JOSEPHUS.** An entirely New Library Edition of WILLIAM WHISTON'S translation of the Works of FLAVIUS JOSEPHUS. Comprising "The Antiquities of the Jews," and "The Wars of the Jews." With Memoir of the Author, Marginal Notes giving the Essence of the Narrative, and 100 pages of Engravings, separately printed on tinted paper. In One Vol., medium 8vo, cloth gilt, 7s. 6d. ; half-calf, 12s.

"The present edition is cheap and good, being clearly printed, and, as already remarked, serviceably embellished with views and object drawings, not one of which is irrelevant to the matter."—*The Daily Telegraph.*

*London:* WARD, LOCK & CO., *Salisbury Square, E.C.*

**EVERYBODY'S LAWYER (Beeton's Law Book).** Entirely New Edition, Revised by a BARRISTER. A Practical Compendium of the General Principles of English Jurisprudence: comprising upwards of 14,600 Statements of the Law. With a full Index, 27,000 References, every numbered paragraph in its particular place, and under its general head. Crown 8vo, 1,680 pp., cloth gilt, 7s. 6d.

*\*\* The sound practical information contained in this voluminous work is equal to that in a whole library of ordinary legal books, costing many guineas. Not only for every non-professional man in a difficulty are its contents valuable, but also for the ordinary reader, to whom a knowledge of the law is more important and interesting than is generally supposed.*

**BEETON'S DICTIONARY OF GEOGRAPHY:** A Universal Gazetteer. Illustrated by Maps—Ancient, Modern, and Biblical, and several Hundred Engravings in separate Plates on toned paper. Containing upwards of 12,000 distinct and complete Articles. Post 8vo, cloth gilt, 7s. 6d.; half-calf, 10s. 6d.

**BEETON'S DICTIONARY OF BIOGRAPHY :** Being the Lives of Eminent Persons of All Times. Containing upwards of 10,000 distinct and complete Articles, profusely Illustrated by Portraits. With the Pronunciation of Every Name. Post 8vo, cloth gilt, 7s. 6d.; half-calf, 10s. 6d.

**BEETON'S DICTIONARY OF NATURAL HISTORY:** A Popular and Scientific Account of Animated Creation. Containing upwards of 2,000 distinct and complete Articles, and more than 400 Engravings. With the Pronunciation of Every Name. Crown 8vo, cloth gilt, 7s. 6d.; half-calf, 10s. 6d.

**BEETON'S BOOK OF HOME PETS:** How to Rear and Manage in Sickness and in Health. With many Coloured Plates, and upwards of 200 Woodcuts from designs principally by HARRISON WEIR. With a Chapter on Ferns. Post 8vo, half-roan, 7s. 6d.; half-calf, 10s. 6d.

**THE TREASURY OF SCIENCE, Natural and Physical.** Comprising Natural Philosophy, Astronomy, Chemistry, Geology, Mineralogy, Botany, Zoology and Physiology. By F. SCHOEDLER, Ph.D. Translated and Edited by HENRY MEDLOCK, Ph.D., &c. With more than 500 Illustrations. Crown 8vo, cloth gilt, 7s. 6d.; half-calf, 10s. 6d.

**A MILLION OF FACTS** of Correct Data and Elementary Information concerning the entire Circle of the Sciences, and on all subjects of Speculation and Practice. By Sir RICHARD PHILLIPS. Carefully Revised and Improved. Crown 8vo, cloth gilt, 7s. 6d.; half-calf, 10s. 6d.

**THE TEACHER'S PICTORIAL BIBLE AND BIBLE DICTIONARY.** With the most approved Marginal References, and Explanatory Oriental and Scriptural Notes, Original Comments, and Selections from the most esteemed Writers. Illustrated with numerous Engravings and Coloured Maps. Crown 8vo, cloth gilt, red edges, 8s. 6d.; French morocco, 10s. 6d.; half-calf, 10s. 6d. ; Turkey morocco, 15s.

**THE SELF-AID CYCLOPÆDIA, for Self-Taught Students.** Comprising General Drawing ; Architectural, Mechanical, and Engineering Drawing ; Ornamental Drawing and Design ; Mechanics and Mechanism ; the Steam Engine. By ROBERT SCOTT BURN, F.S.A.E., &c. With upwards of 1,000 Engravings. Demy 8vo, half-bound, price 10s. 6d.

## ⁖ NEW EDUCATIONAL WORK OF GREAT VALUE.⁖

Just ready, folio, boards, price 5s., with 500 Original Wood Engravings.

WARD AND LOCK'S

# PICTORIAL ATLAS OF NATURE.

## MEN, ANIMALS, AND PLANTS OF ALL QUARTERS OF THE GLOBE.

### FOR HOME AND SCHOOL USE.

IN no department of popular education has the progress that characterises our time been more distinctly marked than in the study of Geography ; and nowhere have the enlarged views of the present day produced a more complete change in the method of tuition and in the scope of the subject. Geography must no longer be taught as a mere study of names, intermingled with certain statistical details of population, distances, measurements of altitudes, &c. A good geographical knowledge of any given quarter of the globe, or of a separate country, must now include a certain familiarity with the characteristic productions of the quarter or country in question, the types it presents in nations, animals, and plants. Thus, ETHNOGRAPHY, the study of races ; ZOOLOGY, the study of animals ; and BOTANY, the study of plants, are all to some extent associated with Geography.

In the improved state of the science of Geography, additional appliances have become necessary for its practical study. The atlas of maps, however complete it may be, only presents one aspect of the subject. The student now requires not only to understand the map that teaches him the topography of a country :— when he has made himself familiar with the surface of a part of the globe, *he requires to be taught what that region has to show as regards inhabitants and animal and vegetable productions.*

WARD AND LOCK'S PICTORIAL ATLAS OF NATURE has been prepared with a view of meeting this want. In a series of FIFTEEN LARGE PLATES it places before the eyes of the student the typical forms of the nations, animals, and plants of the various parts of the world. Each plate contains a map, around which the types are grouped ; and numbers inserted in this map, and corresponding with others in the pictorial illustrations, show the learner where the races of men, and the plants and animals depicted, have their homes.

The greatest care has been taken to render the atlas strictly educational by the utmost accuracy and truth to nature in the pictures. *The plants have been drawn by botanical artists, the animals are not imaginative or fancy sketches, but zoologically correct, and the great majority of heads of men and women are from photographs taken from life, or else sketches from the note books of travellers, to whom the originals have sat.* In many cases the scale of proportion in which an animal or plant has been drawn is given. The animals are represented, where practicable, surrounded by the scenery of their native homes ; besides the plants, the most important parts, such as flowers, fruit, leaves, &c., are separately given to draw the attention of the student especially for his curious or useful points.

Thus the ATLAS OF NATURE becomes a very necessary companion volume to the usual atlas of political geography.

*In the schoolroom and the family circle* alike it will be found most useful and welcome. A teacher, with one of these plates before him, has only to enlarge upon the notes which have been added in the form of suggestive information, to produce a lecture-lesson that can hardly fail to interest his class. Those engaged in tuition will readily see how much time and labour are saved, in the way of explanation, and how much more vivid an impression is produced than by words alone, when a picture of the object itself is placed before the learner, and his faculty of comparison and analysis is brought into action.

*For self-tuition,* those learners, now so numerous, who are educating themselves by means of manuals, will find WARD & LOCK'S ATLAS OF NATURE an ever present help, that will lighten their labours by conveying to the eye, in its clearly and correctly drawn pictures, the explanation of much they will find difficult in their books.

*The utility of the* ATLAS OF NATURE *is not confined to the study of geography even in its widest sense. The Student of Natural History, and of Botany, will find in it an equally useful and suggestive companion.*

London: *WARD, LOCK & CO., Salisbury Square, E.C.*

## A NEW DOMESTIC CYCLOPÆDIA.

IMPORTANT NOTICE.—Now ready, at all Booksellers' and Railway Bookstalls,

### A NEW DOMESTIC CYCLOPÆDIA,

*FORMING A COMPANION VOLUME TO*

### "Mrs. BEETON'S BOOK of HOUSEHOLD MANAGEMENT"

*(of which the 337th Thousand is now on sale),*

ENTITLED

### WARD AND LOCK'S

# HOME BOOK.

With numerous full-page Coloured and other Plates, and about 600 Illustrations in the Text.

Crown 8vo, half-roan, 7s. 6d. ; half-calf, 10s. 6d.

*The enormous popularity of* "MRS. BEETON'S BOOK OF HOUSEHOLD MANAGE-MENT" *has induced the Publishers to prepare, under the above title, a Companion Work, which they hope will be received with an equal amount of favour. The aim of the* HOME BOOK *is to make Home the abode of Comfort, Elegance, and Happiness. Among the subjects treated of will be found:—*

| | |
|---|---|
| The Way to Build, Buy, Rent, and Furnish a House. | Home Dressmaking and Millinery. |
| Taste in the House. | Fancy and Art Needlework. |
| Economical Housekeeping. | Talks on the Toilet. |
| The Management of Children. | Modern Etiquette. |
| Home Needlework. | Employment of Leisure Hours. |

MRS. BEETON'S BOOK OF HOUSEHOLD MANAGEMENT, *as all are aware, deals principally with food and the various modes of its preparation. There are many other matters in connection with the Household, in which inexperienced and even experienced housekeepers need instruction and guidance. These are fully discussed in* WARD AND LOCK'S HOME BOOK. *The work contains countless directions on matters about which everyone is eager to know something, but which are usually left to the expensive teaching of individual experience.*

*The various departments of the* HOME BOOK *have been arranged with clearness and method, and every care has been taken to render the information accurate and trustworthy. The instructions given are the result of personal knowledge and actual discovery and handiwork.*

*The* HOME BOOK *is fully Illustrated, and the illustrations will be found to add greatly, not only to the attractiveness of the work, but to the clearness of its information.*

\*\*\* *Every person possessing* "MRS. BEETON'S BOOK OF HOUSEHOLD MANAGE-MENT" *should not fail to secure at once a copy of the valuable Companion Work,* "WARD AND LOCK'S HOME BOOK." *The Housekeeper possessing the two will have a Library by whose aid everything will go well, and family life be happier and more prosperous every day.*

London : *WARD, LOCK & CO., Salisbury Square, E.C.*

## NEW PUBLICATIONS.

*A NEW AND IMPORTANT SERIES OF USEFUL BOOKS,*

WARD AND LOCK'S

# USEFUL HANDBOOKS.

Crown 8vo, cloth gilt, price 2s. 6d. each.

1. **Ward and Lock's Cookery Instructor.** An entirely New Work on the Practice and Science of Cookery. The reasons for Recipes, which are almost entirely omitted in all Modern Cookery Books, are here clearly given. The work will prove invaluable to Mistresses, Teachers of Cookery, and intelligent Cooks. With Illustrations.

2. **The Law of Domestic Economy.** Including the Licensing Laws and the Adulteration of Food. With a very copious Index.

3. **Profitable and Economical Poultry-Keeping.** By Mrs. ELIOT JAMES, Author of "Indian Household Management." With Illustrations.

**THE IRISH PROBLEM, AND HOW TO SOLVE IT.** An Historical and Critical Review of the Legislation and Events that have led to the Present Difficulties, with Suggestions for Practical Remedies. Demy 8vo, cloth gilt, price 6s. Cheap Edition, linen covers, price 2s. 6d.

**HOW TO PASS EXAMINATIONS FOR PROFESSIONS** AND CIVIL SERVICE; or, The Candidate's Guide to the various Professions, Army, Navy, Civil Service, &c. A Handbook for Students, Parents, and Guardians. Crown 8vo, cloth, price 1s.

**COBBETT'S ENGLISH GRAMMAR.** In a Series of Letters; to which are added Six Lessons intended to prevent Statesmen from using False Grammar, and from Writing in an Awkward Manner. New and carefully Annotated Edition. Crown 8vo, cloth, price 1s.

**The LIFE of BENJAMIN DISRAELI, LORD BEACONS-** FIELD, Statesman and Author. A Record of his Literary and Political Career. With Portrait. Crown 8vo, wrapper boards, 1s.

## THE LADIES' BAZAAR AND FANCY-FAIR BOOKS.

PROFUSELY ILLUSTRATED.

Crown 8vo, fancy wrapper, price 1s. each.

1. **Sylvia's Book of Bazaars and Fancy-Fairs.** How to Organise a Bazaar or Fancy-Fair, and arrange for Contributions of Work, Fitting up the Stalls, suitable Dress, Organisation of Lotteries and Raffles.

2. **Sylvia's Book of New Designs in Knitting, Netting, and** Crochet. Arranged with special reference to Articles Saleable at Bazaars and Fancy-Fairs.

3. **Sylvia's Illustrated Embroidery Book.** Arranged with special reference to Bazaars and Fancy-Fairs. Coloured Embroidery, White Embroidery.

4. **Sylvia's Illustrated Book of Artistic Knicknacks.** Articles suitable for Sale at Bazaars and Fancy-Fairs. Every variety of Decoration for the House and the Person, with minute Instructions for Making them.

*London: WARD, LOCK & CO., Salisbury Square, E.C.*

*AN ENTIRELY NEW ETYMOLOGICAL DICTIONARY.*

Just ready, demy 8vo, cloth, 5s.   WARD & LOCK's

### STANDARD

# ETYMOLOGICAL DICTIONARY

## OF THE ENGLISH LANGUAGE.

A POPULAR AND COMPREHENSIVE GUIDE TO THE PRONUNCIATION,
PARTS OF SPEECH, MEANINGS, AND ETYMOLOGY OF ALL
WORDS, ORDINARY, SCIENTIFIC, AND TECHNOLOGICAL
NOW IN GENERAL USE.

### With 40 pages of Engravings and an Appendix,

COMPRISING

1. ABBREVIATIONS USED IN WRITING AND PRINTING.

2. A BRIEF CLASSICAL DICTIONARY, COMPRISING THE PRINCIPAL DEITIES, HEROES, NOTABLE MEN AND WOMEN, &c., OF GREEK AND ROMAN MYTHOLOGY.

3. LETTERS ; HOW TO BEGIN, END, AND ADDRESS THEM.

4. WORDS, PHRASES, AND PROVERBS, FROM THE LATIN, FREQUENTLY USED IN WRITING AND SPEAKING.

5. WORDS, PHRASES, AND PROVERBS, FROM THE FRENCH, WITH ENGLISH TRANSLATIONS.

6. WORDS, PHRASES, AND PROVERBS, FROM THE ITALIAN AND SPANISH WITH ENGLISH TRANSLATIONS.

---

Messrs. WARD, LOCK AND Co., in announcing this ENTIRELY NEW WORK, which has long been in preparation, desire to call special attention to the several points of excellence to be found in it, and feel sure that this valuable work will command the favour of the public.   The following are the principal points to which attention is called :—

*1. Comprehensiveness.*—New words, that the progress of science, art, and philosophy has rendered necessary as additions to the vocabulary, and thousands of compound words have been introduced.

*2. Brevity.*—To ensure this, care has been taken to avoid redundancy of explanation, while every possible meaning of each word has been given.

*3. Pronunciation.*—Those who may use it will not be puzzled and confused with any arbitrary system of phonetic signs, similar to those usually found in Pronouncing Dictionaries.   Every word of two syllables and more is properly divided and accented ; and all *silent* letters are put in italics.

*4. Etymology.*—The words are arranged in groups, each group being placed under the principal word to which its members are closely allied.   Words similarly spelt, but having distinct etymologies, are separated according to their derivation.

*5. Illustrations.*—40 pages of Illustrations of various objects given, to assist students in arriving at a clear perception of that which is indicated by the name.

---

*London:* WARD, LOCK & CO., *Salisbury Square,* E.C. ⸄

*WARD & LOCK'S POPULAR DICTIONARIES.*

# THE STANDARD DICTIONARIES OF LANGUAGE.

## WEBSTER'S UNIVERSAL PRONOUNCING AND DE-
FINING DICTIONARY OF THE ENGLISH LANGUAGE. Condensed
from Noah Webster's Large Work, with numerous Synonyms, carefully dis-
criminated by CHAUNCEY A. GOODRICH, D.D. With Walker's Key to the Pronunciation of Classical and Scriptural Proper Names; a Vocabulary of Modern
Geographical Names; Phrases and Quotations from the Ancient and Modern
Languages; Abbreviations, &c. Royal 8vo, half bound, 5s.; demy 8vo, cloth,
3s. 6d.

"This Dictionary must commend itself to every intelligent reader. .   .
Let us add, it is carefully and well printed, and very cheap; and having said so
much, we feel assured that further recommendation is unnecessary. It is good, useful, and cheap."—*Liverpool Mail.*

## WEBSTER'S IMPROVED PRONOUNCING DICTION-
ARY OF THE ENGLISH LANGUAGE. Condensed and adapted to English
Orthography and Usage, with additions by CHARLES ROBSON. To which are
added, Accentuated Lists of Scriptural, Classical, and Modern Geographical
Proper Names. Cloth, price 2s. 6d.; strongly half-bound, 3s. 6d.

## WEBSTER'S POCKET PRONOUNCING DICTIONARY
OF THE ENGLISH LANGUAGE. Condensed from the Original Dictionary
by NOAH WEBSTER, LL.D.; with Accentuated Vocabularies of Classical,
Scriptural, and Modern Geographical Names. Revised Edition, by WILLIAM
G. WEBSTER, Son of Noah Webster. Containing 10,000 more words than
"Walker's Dictionary." Royal 16mo, cloth, price 1s.

## WARD & LOCK'S POCKET SHILLING DICTIONARY
OF THE ENGLISH LANGUAGE. Condensed by CHARLES ROBSON, from
NOAH WEBSTER'S Original Work. With Accentuated Lists of Scripture and
Modern Geographical Proper Names. Super-royal 32mo, cloth, 768 pp., 1s.

## WARD AND LOCK'S SHILLING DICTIONARY OF
THE GERMAN LANGUAGE. Containing German-English and English-
German, Geographical Dictionary, Table of Coins, &c. Super-royal 32mo,
cloth, 900 pp., 1s.

## WEBSTER'S SIXPENNY POCKET PRONOUNCING
DICTIONARY OF THE ENGLISH LANGUAGE. Condensed from the
Original Dictionary by NOAH WEBSTER, LL.D.; with Accentuated Vocabu-
laries of Classical, Scriptural, and Modern Geographical Names. Revised
Edition, by WILLIAM G. WEBSTER, Son of Noah Webster. Strongly bound in
cloth, price 6d.

## WEBSTER'S PENNY PRONOUNCING DICTIONARY
OF THE ENGLISH LANGUAGE. Exhibiting the Spelling, Pronunciation,
Part of Speech, and Meaning of all Words in General Use among English-speak-
ing Nations. Containing over 10,000 words. Price 1d.; or, linen wrapper, 2d.

*London: WARD, LOCK & CO., Salisbury Square, E.C.*

## THE WORLD LIBRARY OF STANDARD BOOKS.

*A Series of Standard Works, including many of the acknowledged Master-pieces of Historical and Critical Literature, made more accessible than hitherto to the general reader by publication in a cheap form and at a moderate price.*

Crown 8vo, cloth gilt.

1. **Hallam's Constitutional History of England.** From the Accession of Henry VII. to the Death of George II. By HENRY HALLAM, LL.D., F.R.S. With Lord Macaulay's Essay on the same. 970 pp., 5s. Library Edition, demy 8vo, 7s. 6d.; half-calf, 12s.

2. **Hallam's Europe during the Middle Ages.** 720 pp., 3s. 6d. Library Edition, demy 8vo, 894 pp., 6s.; half-calf, 10s. 6d.

3. **Hallam's Church and State.** By the Author of "The Constitutional History of England." 400 pp., 2s. 6d.

5. **The Wealth of Nations (An Inquiry into the Nature and** Causes of). By ADAM SMITH. 782 pp., 3s. 6d.; half-calf, 7s. 6d. Library Edition, demy 8vo, 800 pp., 6s.; half-calf, 10s. 6d.

6. **Adam Smith's Essays**: Moral Sentiments, Astronomy, Physics, &c. By the Author of "The Wealth of Nations." 476 pp., 3s. 6d.

7. **Hume's History of England.** From the Invasion of Julius Cæsar to the Revolution in 1688. By DAVID HUME. In 3 Vols. 2,2.0 pp., 10s. 6d. Library Edition, demy 8vo, 18s.

8. **Hume's Essays**: Literary, Moral, and Political. 558 pp., 3s. 6d.

9. **Montaigne's Essays.** All the Essays of Michael the Seigneur de Montaigne. Translated by CHARLES COTTON. 684 pp., 3s. 6d.; half-calf, 7s. 6d. Library Edition, demy 8vo, 920 pp., 6s.; half-calf, 10s. 6d.

10. **Warton's History of English Poetry.** From the Eleventh to the Seventeenth Century. By THOMAS WARTON, B.D. 1,032 pp., 6s.

11. **The Court and Times of Queen Elizabeth.** By LUCY AIKIN. 530 pp., 3s. 6d.

12. **Edmund Burke's Choice Pieces.** Containing the Speech on the Law of Libel, Reflections on Revolution in France, on the Sublime and Beautiful, Abridgment of English History. 3s. 6d.

13. **Herbert's Autobiography and History of England under** Henry VIII. By EDWARD, Lord HERBERT, of Cherbury. 770 pp., 3s. 6d.

14. **Walpole's Anecdotes of Painting in England.** By HORACE WALPOLE. 538 pp., 3s. 6d.

15. **M'Culloch's Principles of Political Economy.** With Sketch of the Rise and Progress of the Science. By J. R. M'CULLOCH. 360 pp., 3s. 6d.

16. **Locke's Letters on Toleration.** By JOHN LOCKE. 400 pp., 3s. 6d.

20. **Essays on Beauty and Taste**: On Beauty, by FRANCIS, Lord JEFFREY; On Taste, by ARCHIBALD ALISON, LL.D. 324 pp., 3s. 6d.

21. **Milton's Early Britain, under Trojan, Roman, and Saxon** Rule, by JOHN MILTON. With MORE's England under Richard III., and BACON's England under Henry VIII. 430 pp., 3s. 6d.

23. **Macaulay**: Reviews, Essays, and Poems. 650 pp., 3s. 6d. half-calf, 7s. 6d.

*London:* WARD, LOCK & CO., *Salisbury Square, E.C.*

THE WORLD LIBRARY—*continued.*

24. **Sydney Smith's Essays**, Social and Political. 550 pp., 3s. 6d.

25. **Lord Bacon.** Containing the Proficience and Advancement of Learning, the New Atlantis, Historical Sketches and Essays. 530 pp., 3s. 6d.; half-calf, 7s. 6d.

26. **Essays by Thomas de Quincey.** Containing Confessions of an Opium Eater, Bentley, Parr, Goethe, Letters to a Young Man, &c. 500 pp., 3s. 6d.

27. **Josephus (The Complete Works of).** Translated by WILLIAM WHISTON, A.M. With Life of the Author, and Marginal Notes giving the Essence of the Narrative. 810 pp., 3s. 6d. Library Edition, demy 8vo, 6s.

28. **Paley's Works.** Containing "The Evidences of Christianity," "Horæ Paulinæ," and "Natural Theology." By WILLIAM PALEY, D.D. With Life, Introduction, and Notes. 3s. 6d.

29. **Taylor's Holy Living and Dying.** The Rules and Exercises of Holy Living and Dying. By JEREMY TAYLOR, D.D. With Life, Introduction, and Notes. 2s. 6d.

30. **Milman's History of the Jews.** By H. H. MILMAN, D.D., Dean of St. Paul's. 500 pp., 3s. 6d

31. **Macaulay.** Second Series. **Reviews and Essays.** 3s. 6d.

32. **Locke on the Human Understanding.** 3s. 6d.

33. **Plutarch's Lives.** By LANGHORNE. 5s.

Uniform with the LIBRARY EDITION of "Hume's England," "Hallam's England," &c.

**Shakespeare's Complete Works.** With Life and Glossary. Demy 8vo, cloth, 6s.

WARD AND LOCK'S
## *STANDARD POETS.*

*The nominal price at which this Series is offered to the public places the works of our greatest Poets well within the reach of all.*

Crown 8vo, cloth gilt, price 2s. each.

| | |
|---|---|
| 1. Longfellow. | 15. Shelley. |
| 2. Scott. | 16. Hood.   2nd Series |
| 3. Wordsworth. | 17. Thomson. |
| 4. Milton. | 18. Tupper's Proverbial Philo- |
| 5. Cowper. | sophy. |
| 6. Keats. | 19. Humorous Poems. |
| 7. Hood.   1st Series. | 20. American Poems. |
| 8. Byron. | 21. Whittier. |
| 9. Burns. | 22. Lowell. |
| 10. Mrs. Hemans. | 23. Shakespeare. |
| 11. Pope. | 24. Poetic Treasures. |
| 12. Campbell. | 25. Keble's Christian Year. |
| 13. Coleridge. | 26. Young. |
| 14. Moore. | 27. Poe. |

*London:* WARD, LOCK & CO., *Salisbury Square,* E.C.

## THE STANDARD GARDENING BOOKS.

*Gardening, properly managed, is a source of income to thousands, and of healthful recreation to other thousands. Besides the gratification it affords, the inexhaustible field it opens up for observation and experiment commends its i teresting practice to everyone possessed of a real English home.*

**BEETON'S BOOK OF GARDEN MANAGEMENT.** Embracing all kinds of information connected with Fruit, Flower, and Kitchen Garden Cultivation, Orchid Houses, Bees, &c., &c. Illustrated with Coloured Plate- of surpassing beauty, and numerous Engravings. Post 8vo, cloth gilt, price 7s. 6d.; or in half-calf, 10s. 6d.

*The directions in* BEETON'S GARDEN MANAGEMENT *are conceived in a practical m inner, and are, throughout the work, so simply given that none can fail to understand them. The Coloured Plates show more than a hundred different kinds of Plants and Flowers, and assist in the identification of any doubtful specimen.*

**BEETON'S DICTIONARY OF EVERY-DAY GARDEN-**ING. Constituting a Popular Cyclopædia of the Theory and Practice of Horticulture. Illustrated with Coloured Plates, made after Original Water Colour Drawings copied from Nature, and Woodcuts in the Text. Crown 8vo, cloth gilt, price 3s. 6d.

**ALL ABOUT GARDENING.** Being a Popular Dictionary of Gardening, containing full and practical Instructions in the different Branches of Horticultural Science. Specially adapted to the capabilities and requirements of the Kitchen and Flower Garden at the Present Day. With Illustrations. Crown 8vo, cloth gilt, price 2s. 6d.

**BEETON'S GARDENING BOOK.** Containing full and practical Instructions concerning General Gardening Operations, the Flower Garden, the Fruit Garden, the Kitchen Garden, Pests of the Garden, with a Monthly Calendar of Work to be done in the Garden throughout the Year. With Illustrations. Post 8vo, cloth, price 1s.; or with Coloured Plates, price 1s. 6d.

**KITCHEN AND FLOWER GARDENING FOR PLEA-**SURE AND PROFIT. An Entirely New and Practical Guide to the Cultivation of Vegetables, Fruits, and Flowers. With upwards of 100 Engravings. Crown 8vo, boards, 1s.

**BEETON'S PENNY GARDENING BOOK.** Being a Calendar of Work to be done in the Flower, Fruit, and Kitchen Garden, together with Plain Directions for Growing all Useful Vegetables and most Flowers suited to adorn the Gardens and Homes of Cottagers. Price 1d.; post free, 1½d.

**GLENNY'S ILLUSTRATED GARDEN ALMANAC**
AND FLORIST'S DIRECTORY. Being an Every-day Handbook for Gardeners, both Amateur and Professional. Containing Notices of the Floral Novelties of the Current Year, Articles by Eminent Horticultural Authorities, Directions for Amateurs, Lists of London, Provincial, and Continental Nursery-men, Seedsmen, and Florists, &c. With numerous Illustrations. Published Yearly, in coloured wrapper, price 1s.

*London:* WARD, LOCK & CO., *Salisbury Square, E.C.*

## SYLVIA'S HOME HELP SERIES
### *of Useful Handbooks for Ladies.*

Price 1s. each.

1. **HOW TO DRESS WELL ON A SHILLING A-DAY.** A Guide to Home Dressmaking and Millinery. With a large Sheet of Diagrams for Cutting out Dress Bodices in Three Sizes, and Fifty Diagrams of Children's Clothing.

2. **ART NEEDLEWORK**: A Guide to Embroidery in Crewels, Silks, Appliqué, &c., with Instructions as to Stitches, and explanatory Diagrams. With a large and valuable Sheet of Designs in Crewel Work.

3. **HOSTESS AND GUEST.** A Guide to the Etiquette of Dinners, Suppers, Luncheons, the Precedence of Guests, &c. Illustrated.

4. **BABIES, AND HOW TO TAKE CARE OF THEM.** Containing full and practical Information on every subject connected with "Baby." With a large Pattern Sheet of Infants' Clothing.

5. **DRESS, HEALTH, AND BEAUTY.** Containing Practical Suggestions for the Improvement of Modern Costume, regarded from an Artistic and Sanitary point of view. Illustrated.

6. **THE HOUSE AND ITS FURNITURE.** A Common-Sense Guide to House Building and House Furnishing. Containing plain Directions as to Choosing a Site, Buying, Building, Heating, Lighting, Ventilating, and Completely Furnishing. With 170 Illustrations.

7. **INDIAN HOUSEHOLD MANAGEMENT.** Containing Hints on Bungalows, Packing, Domestic Servants, &c. Invaluable for all visiting India.

8. **HOW TO MANAGE HOUSE AND SERVANTS,** and Make the Most of your Means.

9. **THE MANAGEMENT OF CHILDREN,** in Health, Sickness and Disease.

10. **ARTISTIC HOMES**; or, How to Furnish with Taste. A Handbook for all Housewives. Profusely Illustrated.

11. **HOW TO MAKE HOME HAPPY.** A Book of Household Hints and Information, with 500 Odds and Ends worth Remembering.

12. **HINTS AND HELPS FOR EVERY-DAY EMER-GENCIES.** Including Social, Rural, and Domestic Economy, Household Medicine, Casualties, Pecuniary Embarrassments, Legal Difficulties, &c.

13. **THE ECONOMICAL HOUSEWIFE**; or, How to Make the Most of Everything. With about 50 Illustrations.

14. **SYLVIA'S BOOK OF THE TOILET.** A Lady's Guide to Dress and Beauty. With 30 Illustrations.

15. **HOME NEEDLEWORK.** A Trustworthy Guide to the Art of Plain Sewing. With about 80 Diagrams.

16. **CHILDREN, AND WHAT TO DO WITH THEM.** A Guide for Mothers respecting the Management of their Boys and Girls.

17. **OUR LEISURE HOURS.** A Book of Recreation for the Use of Old and Young. Illustrated.

18. **THE FANCY NEEDLEWORK INSTRUCTION BOOK.** Profusely Illustrated.

19. **THE ETIQUETTE OF MODERN SOCIETY.** Illust.

*London:* WARD, LOCK & CO., *Salisbury Square, E.C.*

Most Valuable and Useful HOUSEHOLD MEDICINES.

# WHELPTON'S
# VEGETABLE PURIFYING PILLS

TRADE MARK (REGISTERED)

A RE one of those rare Medicines which, for their extraordinary properties, have gained an almost

## UNIVERSAL REPUTATION.

Recommended for disorders of the HEAD, CHEST, BOWELS, LIVER, and KIDNEYS; also in RHEUMATISM, ULCERS, SORES, and all SKIN DISEASES— these Pills being a DIRECT PURIFIER OF THE BLOOD.

# WHELPTON'S HEALING OINTMENT

Stands unrivalled for the cure of ULCERS, BURNS, SCALDS, SORES, and in fact almost all SKIN DISEASES, including ECZEMA (TETTER), RINGWORM, &c. Ask your Chemist for descriptive circulars. Once tried will be always used.

Pills and Ointment Wholesale and Retail of

**Messrs. G. WHELPTON & SON, 3, Crane Court, Fleet Street, London, E.C.**

In Boxes, price 7½d., 1s. 1½d., and 2s. 9d., post free in the United Kingdom for 8, 14, or 33 Stamps.

**Sold by all Chemists and Medicine Vendors.** [7275.

---

## ⟶·⊱⊰·⟵ TO LADIES. ⟶·⊱⊰·⟵

# MATTHEWS'S
# FULLER'S

| 6d. & 1s. |
| Boxes. |

| Used in the Royal Nurseries, and highly recommended by the Faculty; it protects the Skin from the sun, winds, chaps, &c., and preserves the Complexion. |

# EARTH.

## *SOLD BY ALL CHEMISTS AND PERFUMERS.*

### USED IN THE ROYAL NURSERIES.

By the Authority of Her Majesty  the Queen, Empress of India

# BORAX DRY SOAP

## "IS THE BEST"

### AND MOST CONVENIENT FOR DAILY USE.

The Queen's Patent for Excellence.    Highest Award in the World.

*In Quarter, Half, and Pound Packets.*

QUARTER POUND, 1d. each.   *Full Directions on each.*

# BORAX EXTRACT OF SOAP.

### "THE GREAT DIRT EXTRACTER,"

"Perfection of Packet Soap." Under Her Majesty's Royal Patent for Utility.
In Quarter, Half, and Pound Packets.  Full Directions on each.

KNOWN THROUGHOUT THE CIVILISED WORLD BY THIS REGISTERED AND SPECIAL TRADE MARK ON EVERY PACKET.

IN SMALL PACKETS, READY FOR IMMEDIATE USE IN EVERY HOME VERY VALUABLE ON SHIPBOARD, IN CAMP, AND ON JOURNEY.

# BORAX (The QUEEN'S ROYAL.) STARCH GLAZE

Imparts Enamel-like Gloss to the Starch, and gives Permanent Stiffness and Brilliancy to Muslin, Lace, Linen Collars, Cuffs, &c.

In Packets, Id., 3d., and Boxes 6d. each.  Full Directions on each.

# PREPARED 'CALIFORNIAN' BORAX.

### "The Household Treasure.—Pure Antiseptic."

Specially Prepared for Personal and Domestic Uses.  Marvellous Purifier, Water Softener, Dirt Expeller, Taint Remover, Food Preserver, and Arrester of Decay.

SPECIALTY FOR TOILET, LARDER, LAUNDRY. KITCHEN, BEDROOM, GREENHOUSE, &c.

In Id., 3d., and 6d. Packets.    Directions and Recipes on each.

Sold by Grocers, Oilmen, and Dealers in Soap Everywhere.
Discovery, Uses, Borax Book, with Sample Packet, Two Stamps direct from the Works.

## PATENT BORAX COMPANY Birmingham.

# DR. J. COLLIS BROWNE'S

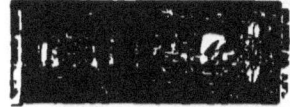

## *ORIGINAL AND ONLY GENUINE*

# CHLORODYNE.

COUGHS, COLDS, ASTHMA, BRONCHITIS.

DR. J. COLLIS BROWNE'S CHLORODYNE. This wonderful remedy was discovered by DR. J. COLLIS BROWNE, and the word CHLORODYNE coined by him expressly to designate it. There never has been a remedy so vastly beneficial to suffering humanity, and it is a subject of deep concern to the public that they should not be imposed upon by having imitations pressed upon them on account of cheapness, and as being the same thing. DR. J. COLLIS BROWNE'S CHLORODYNE is a totally distinct thing from the spurious compounds called Chlorodyne, the use of which only ends in disappointment and failure.

DR. J. COLLIS BROWNE'S CHLORODYNE.—Vice-Chancellor Sir W. PAGE WOOD STATED PUBLICLY in Court that

DR. J. COLLIS BROWNE was UNDOUBTEDLY the INVENTOR of CHLORODYNE, that the whole story of the defendant was deliberately untrue, and he regretted to say it had been sworn to.—See *The Times*, July 13th, 1864.

DR. J. COLLIS BROWNE'S CHLORODYNE is a LIQUID MEDICINE which ASSUAGES PAIN of every kind, affords a calm refreshing sleep WITHOUT HEADACHE, and INVIGORATES the NERVOUS SYSTEM when exhausted.

DR. J. COLLIS BROWNE'S CHLORODYNE is the GREAT SPECIFIC for CHOLERA, DYSENTERY, DIARRHŒA.

The GENERAL BOARD of HEALTH, London, REPORT that it ACTS as a CHARM, one dose generally sufficient,

Dr. GIBBON, Army Medical Staff, Calcutta, says :—"TWO DOSES COMPLETELY CURED ME of DIARRHŒA."

DR. J. COLLIS BROWNE'S CHLORODYNE rapidly cuts short all attacks of EPILEPSY, SPASMS, COLIC, PALPITATION, HYSTERIA.

DR. J. COLLIS BROWNE'S CHLORODYNE is the TRUE PALLIATIVE in NEURALGIA, GOUT, CANCER, TOOTHACHE, RHEUMATISM.

IMPORTANT CAUTION The IMMENSE SALE of this REMEDY has given rise to many UNSCRUPULOUS IMITATIONS.

N.B.—EVERY BOTTLE of GENUINE CHLORODYNE BEARS on the GOVERNMENT STAMP the name of the INVENTOR,

DR. J. COLLIS BROWNE.

SOLD IN BOTTLES, 1s. 1½d., 2s. 9d., 4s. 6d. by all Chemists.

Sole Manufacturer, J. T. DAVENPORT, 33, GREAT RUSSELL STREET, W.C.

---

# ORCHARD'S CURE FOR DEAFNESS.

### Safe and Harmless. Has cured Hundreds.

## "Deaf for Forty Years, and then cured."

SIR,—My sale for your "Cure for Deafness" increases. A man here who has been deaf forty years has had his hearing restored by it.—J. GREEN, Chemist, Christchurch.

*1s. 1½d. per Bottle. Free by post for 14 stamps from*

## EDWIN J ORCHARD, Chemist, SALISBURY.

### Any Chemist can procure it to order.

---

# KEATING'S POWDER

DESTROYS BUGS FLEAS MOTHS BEETLES

Sold in Tins 6d 1/- & 2/6

# KEATING'S LOZENGES

## *THE BEST COUGH REMEDY EVER MADE.*

Sold everywhere in Tins, 1/1½ each.

# GOLD MEDAL, PARIS, 1878.

# FRY'S COCOA EXTRACT.

### GUARANTEED PURE COCOA ONLY.

"Strictly pure, easily assimilated."—
W. W. STODDART, F.I.C., F.C.S., *City and County Analyst, Bristol.*

"Pure Cocoa, a portion of oil extracted."—
CHARLES A. CAMERON, M.D., F.R.C.S.I., *Analyst for Dublin.*

COCOA POD CUT OPEN SHOWING THE NUTS

# FRY'S CARACAS COCOA

Prepared with the celebrated Cocoa of Caracas, combined with other choice descriptions.

"A most delicious and valuable article."—
*Standard.*

15 International Prize Medals awarded to J. S. Fry & Sons.

www.ingramcontent.com/pod-product-compliance
Lightning Source LLC
Chambersburg PA
CBHW031344070726
47496CB00017B/1650